THIS LOVE

Also by Lotte Jeffs

How to Be a Gentlewoman
My Magic Family
The Queer Parent (with Stu Oakley)

THIS LOVE

LOTTE JEFFS

dialogue
books

DIALOGUE BOOKS

First published in Great Britain in 2024 by Dialogue Books

10 9 8 7 6 5 4 3 2 1

A CIP catalogue record for this book
is available from the British Library.

Hardback ISBN 978-0-349-70315-2
Trade paperback ISBN 978-0-349-70316-9

Typeset in Berling by M Rules
Printed and bound in Great Britain by
Clays Ltd, Elcograf S.p.A

Papers used by Dialogue Books are from well-managed forests
and other responsible sources.

FSC
www.fsc.org
MIX
Supporting
responsible forestry
FSC® C104740

Dialogue Books
Carmelite House
50 Victoria Embankment
London EC4Y 0DZ

www.dialoguebooks.co.uk

Dialogue Books, part of Little Brown, Book Group Limited,
an Hachette UK company.

For Will Simpson, Sam Jones
and Joe Marriott – my Aris

Here and there on earth we may encounter a kind of continuation of love in which
this possessive craving of two people for
each other gives way to a new desire and
lust for possession – a shared higher thirst
for an ideal above them. But who knows
such love? Who has experienced it? Its
right name is friendship.

FRIEDRICH NIETZSCHE,
The Gay Science (1882)

We are, I am, you are
by cowardice or courage
the one who find our way
back to this scene
carrying a knife, a camera
a book of myths
in which
our names do not appear.

ADRIENNE RICH,
'Diving into the Wreck'

Poems in this novel were written 'as Ari'
by the poet Thomas Stewart.

PART 1

Chapter 1

Leeds, September 2014

A flash of white light and a hot blast of air, dense with sweat and poppers, spilled out onto the terrace as the door to the club opened, then quickly closed. It was dark again. The Britney remix reduced to a dull thud of bass. A girl – no, a boy approached Mae on the bench where she sat under a string of broken fairy lights, staring into an empty pint glass.

'Are you OK?'

Mae put the back of her hand to her mouth as if to stifle the answer. She tasted salt from tequila shots. She looked up blankly. A few rebellious strands of her white-blonde hair had escaped her otherwise perfect quiff.

'Do you really want to know?' she asked.

The boy nodded and sat down next to her. Mae's black leather trousers squeaked as she shuffled to make space.

'I was queuing at the bar in there, minding my own business, and suddenly I felt someone pressing themselves into the back of me. Clammy hands grasping at my waist.' She shuddered. 'Seemed marginally more likely that this was a come-on than a pickpocket attempt. So I turned around, clocked that it was a girl who makes the most *furious* notes in lectures, and she kissed me. Or I kissed her. Whatever. There was kissing.'

'You move fast.'

'I move drunk.' She coughed, put the pint glass on the floor by her feet and crossed her legs, kicking the glass with the heel of her DMs so it smashed into shards on the flagstones. 'Shit. Sorry. I'm a disaster.'

The boy took a beige leather driving glove from his coat pocket, slipped his hand into it and carefully picked up the pieces. He walked across the terrace, which was really overstating the club's afterthought of outside space, to place them in a chewing-gum-covered bin. It gave Mae a chance to appreciate his long dark hair, which was pulled into a knot on the top of his head. She realised his legs were bare under his coat; he was wearing denim shorts, a white tank top and Chelsea boots. He looked like a wayward gay cowboy, and as he made his way back over, she noticed a long string of pearls wrapped twice around his neck. He took his seat, brushing the motes of shattered glass from his glove.

'Go on . . . ' he said.

Mae took a deep breath; he smelt of old-fashioned eau de cologne. She picked up her story.

'How was I to know that this girl's two – that's right, two – girlfriends were dancing on a podium with an unobstructed view of us at the bar. They marched over and the taller one said to me, "That is a massive disrespect of our boundaries."'

'They're a throuple,' the boy said sagely.

'Sure, but the girl who kissed me certainly didn't mention it. Then *she* shouted, "Open means open, Lisa!" and this Lisa character goes, "We had an agreement. We wrote it down!" And I'm there like, "I did not sign up for this, you lot are messy," so I snuck off, out here, and left them to argue. I don't see why I should be the one whose night is ruined because of their dramas.'

It was cold on the terrace, but the tequila still burned in Mae's chest. She yawned, exhausted by the effort it was to be her sometimes. She unrolled the sleeves of her dark denim shirt and sat on her hands to keep them warm.

'You know I think I'm done with getting tangled up in other people's issues.'

'Word,' the boy said, and nodded. Mae noticed his American accent then. It sounded too glamorous for the back yard of a Leeds gay club, but she didn't want him to notice how intrigued she was just in case it swerved the subject.

'Everything else is OK, but *people*, emotions . . . Why does it always get so complicated?'

'You sound bored.'

'A little, maybe.' She paused. 'Are you a student? I've not seen you around. Wait. Wait, wait.' She was suddenly aware she was slurring. 'I'm so sorry. I haven't asked your name.'

'I'm Ari. A pleasure to meet you.'

'Mae. Third-year English.' They shook hands in an oddly formal gesture.

'Same. As of Monday. I just transferred from New York University.'

'Er, *why*?'

'That's a story for another time,' he said, turning to look as two boys barged out of the club and began passionately kissing directly in front of them.

Ari said he wanted to dance and then asked Mae where all her friends were.

'Good question,' she replied.

The boys stumbled in the violence of their embrace. They crashed into the bin, killing the moment. Mae and Ari laughed. In the no-good cold of two a.m., they faced each other, and as their eyes met, something electric fizzed between them. Ari looked away first. He pulled up the collar of his long faux-fur coat and shivered.

'Well come on then,' said Mae. 'I thought you wanted to dance.'

The following Monday, Ari was already seated at the table in a small seminar room when Mae pushed the door harder than she meant to and practically fell into 'Women Writing the Post-Modern'. It smelt of lapsang souchong and wet coats. There were no shelves, so instead piles of books lined the edge of the room and congregated in a wobbly-looking tower in the unused fireplace. A window looked out onto the lawn in front of the red-brick terraced houses, lashed dark with rain, that comprised the English department. She was happy, if not exactly surprised, to find that Ari was her classmate. He pulled out the black plastic chair next to him for her to take. The other students had kept a polite distance from the new boy, including one third of the throuple, who pretended not to notice Mae as she slipped in next to him.

'Sooo, Saturday night was fun,' Mae said brightly to the girl she'd kissed in Kween. The girl blushed.

Ari smiled like he was in on it and Mae felt, for the first

time since she started university two years ago, what it was to have someone on her team.

Their teacher was a PhD student called Silvia, who wore a gem-encrusted ladybird brooch on the lapel of her blazer and was overly fond of the word 'palimpsest'. Mae found herself saying things like 'to Ari's point . . .' which was strange. She wasn't used to agreeing with someone. After half an hour discussing an Adrienne Rich poem, she and Ari began to finish each other's sentences, one throwing up an idea for the other to catch.

'I think it's kind of about the historical oppression of women,' said Mae of 'Diving into the Wreck'.

'Yes, *and* the fluidity of feminine and masculine,' said Ari. No one else in the class said much at all. Mae peered over his shoulder at the indecipherable notes he'd written in pencil in the margins of his book.

'Hey, no cheating,' Ari whispered playfully when he caught her looking. Mae opened her own copy to the same page, saying nothing but knowing he'd see that the space around her text was even denser with scribbles.

After class, they stood on the stone steps of the library with coffee in tiny beige plastic cups from a vending machine inside. It had stopped raining, and now the sky was back-to-school blue.

'How come you left NYU to come to Leeds then?' asked Mae. 'You must think everything here is deeply uncool. I mean . . .' she looked around, 'this coffee for a start.'

'I don't actually. I like it. Not the coffee. But everything else. You know, the pace and the people here, it's all so much less . . .' Ari shook his head as if it was too much to remember. 'It's just better for me, being somewhere like this.'

'You're avoiding my question, though. *Why* did you end up here?' She noticed his shoulders tense, and he angled away from her. Mae counted to ten in the silence, then panicked. 'I'm sorry. My mum says I'm too blunt. I'm working on it.'

'No, don't apologise. It's just . . . '

'There's no need to explain,' said Mae while thinking the exact opposite. 'I understand.' Ari was *interesting*, and for now that was all that mattered. 'How about I take you on a little tour of the city before your next lecture?' she offered, keen to shake the mood. He said he'd like nothing more.

On the way to the town hall, the one vaguely noteworthy tourist attraction she could think of, Mae asked, 'Do you know what you want to be? When you graduate, I mean.'

'I have zero clue. I find it hard to picture the future, you know, and myself in it. I guess . . . I want to write.'

Mae was a naturally fast walker, and she noted that Ari with his long legs – which were now sensibly attired in army trousers – didn't struggle to keep up.

'But is writing an actual job or more of a pastime?'

'I don't think I'm cut out for much else.'

'What would you do all day? Float through fields with a notebook in your pocket?' This was exactly what her mother would have said, and as the words slipped out of her mouth, she regretted them.

'There would be some floating, I'm sure.' Ari didn't seem offended. 'What about you?'

Mae answered like she'd rehearsed it. 'I need to do something that changes the world. Make a mark.'

'For example?' asked Ari, half laughing at the grandness of her ambition.

'Campaigning, charity work, helping vulnerable kids – it's got to be *active*. Wake up every day, know that there's a point to what I'm doing. Important. I figured if I studied English, I'd have options.'

'How tiring.'

Mae slowed her pace; she bit her lip, and Ari looked at her as if he wanted more.

'OK, fine, there's this other side of me that thinks finding a woman to love, having a house with a garden, a kid or two, a whippet called Willow, that's the real dream. Tragically hetero, I know.'

'Oh, but she *can* have it all!' Ari moved his hands like a dancer. He shifted in and out of camp. 'And you will. I can tell. You don't need to be ashamed about wanting those things. They don't belong to straight people; we are entitled to that kind of happiness too.'

'Ta-da,' said Mae at the foot of the baroque clock tower, letting his comment fall unacknowledged. Ari looked up and whistled as if the building was one of the Seven Wonders of the World.

'This is cool,' he said. 'It's a beautiful city.'

His enthusiasm was unexpected, and she liked it. Most people their age were eye-rolly and cynical, as if the world owed them something. Ari's energy lifted her, she felt an unfamiliar lightness.

'I'd be honoured to read some of your writing,' she said, 'if you'd let me.'

'I'm not convinced I could cope with your rigorous feedback.'

'I am capable of being sensitive,' she said, plunging her hands into her jeans pockets.

'Hey, I've known you for a hot second and I see that.'

'Really?' She was unconvinced.

'Likely, not everyone notices, because, well, look at you!' He pushed Mae so she was at arm's length and he could take in all of her. 'When I first saw you on the terrace at Kween, I thought, Jeez, she's a tough guy – in those leather trousers, those boots, that belt. Then you started talking and I was like, whoa. Okaay.'

'I talk too much.'

'I like it!'

'You're nice.'

'Am I?' Ari smiled as if a photographer had just yelled 'Cheese.'

Mae spontaneously hugged him. 'We should get back,' she said then, suddenly self-conscious about the intensity of the gesture. Ari took her arm and comfortably entwined it with his own. They started walking back up Calverley Street towards the university.

Chapter 2

It was a Wednesday night, but it felt like the weekend. When Mae arrived at Sam's house share in Headingley, early as usual, she watched as her friend pushed the tatty sofa to the edge of the living room to create a dance floor.

'I mean, practically Studio 54, right?' Sam laughed gesturing at the stained peach carpet and the walls, which were covered in Blu Tack stains. 'Someone stole my disco ball at the last party, so I'm afraid this will have to do.'

Sam was impossible not to like. He was a third-year English student too and was friends with the freshers, the second years and even their teachers. While their peers popped pills for depression and read Sartre to feel seen, Sam was refreshingly at peace with himself. Black, gay, public-school educated – he proudly owned each of these identities. And he was happy. That was what made him so different to the other students. And so popular.

His baggy Evisu jeans revealed the waist of his pink cotton boxers and a hairy belly as he reached up to straighten the one framed print hanging on the wall, a pop-art Marilyn Monroe. Mae gave him a peck on his cheek, feeling the unfamiliar brush of stubble on her lips. She hung up her coat in the hallway and turned the overhead lamp off in the living room before lighting some candles with a box of matches she found on a bookshelf. She plugged his iPod into the speaker and searched through the playlists for 'party'.

The house was soon full of students; people she recognised from lectures began lurking in corners. She longed for Ari to arrive, because no one else wanted to talk about anything important, which was all Mae ever wanted to do. Before she'd left home for university, her mother had offered her some advice: 'Darling, just try to ease in a bit more. You don't need to leap on people with your opinions, it makes them very uncomfortable.'

Before long, the kitchen was a mess of opened crisp packets, cheap wine and pots of olives that guests had brought to seem sophisticated. Mae started decanting hummus into bowls.

'You're so extra,' said a good-looking girl wearing a black T-shirt that sported the slogan 'Fuck Me I'm Famous' in diamanté studs. She pulled herself up onto the kitchen counter and sat with her legs dangling like a kid on a swing. Mae moved on to washing up wine glasses in the sink next to her.

'I'll take that as a compliment,' she said, turning to face the girl.

She was a hard femme, with a ring on her thumb to prove a coded allegiance. Mae wiped a glass dry and passed it to her.

'Even crap wine tastes better in one of these than in a chipped coffee mug. Here ...' She picked up the nearest open bottle and poured. The girl took a sip and licked her bottom lip in a way Mae read, correctly, as an invitation.

'Sam's got a waterbed, you know,' she said with an unnecessary wink.

'I know,' Mae replied plainly. 'So retro.' Normally she would have played, but with Ari on his way, she didn't want to start a game she couldn't finish.

'If you wanted to get away from the noise ... talk ... we could go up. I'm sure Sam wouldn't mind.'

'I'm actually waiting for a friend, but thanks.'

'Ari Hines, right? I've heard some crazy rumours about him. Didn't his dad go to prison for a massive financial scandal? Which makes sense, 'cos he told Sam his life in New York was basically *Gossip Girl*. Sooooper rich. Then there's this other theory going round that he was a child star but got caught up in something ... '

Mae rolled her eyes as if she knew the truth. But despite having hung out with her new best friend every day for the past month, she didn't.

'So, what's his deal? Why does anyone leave New York to come to *Leeds*? Like, that literally never happens.'

Mae felt more entitled than anyone else to have the answer. 'I guess it's *literally* no one's business,' she said, trying to sound light-hearted.

Sam came crashing into the kitchen then.

'Jules! I didn't see you arrive! You've met Mae, then.'

'We were just talking.'

'It's a party, not a seminar, losers.'

As a black queer kid at private school, Sam had learnt to master the kind of good-natured banter that could quickly assimilate you. Mae found it impossible to match his energy. He stood with his back to Jules so she could jump on. She squealed as he spun her round, and Mae snuck out of the kitchen with a clean glass that she intended to fill to the brim with red wine from the bottle she'd brought with her.

When she walked purposefully into the living room, she immediately knew that Ari had arrived, because everyone was 'on' suddenly and laughing that little bit louder. She filled her glass and turned around, and there he was. Dancing alone, moving effortlessly. She thought it remarkable how loose he could appear despite not drinking alcohol or touching any kind of drugs. He wore the black silk house coat he'd found in a charity shop in town, with jeans, heeled boots and a shirt barely buttoned at all but framing his long pearl necklace. She knew there was a rose embroidered on the left pocket of his shirt that no one else could see. She felt the deep exhale of his presence.

'Mae,' he called out as the track changed to something slower. She pushed through the boys peacocking in his eyeline, taking his hand and twirling into him.

'Thank God you're here,' she whispered in his ear, feeling glances cling to them as they danced together. 'See that girl over there – diamanté slogan tee?'

'Oh my goodness, Mae, she's *famous*!' Ari sounded languidly American amid guttural Brits. 'And well, according to her T-shirt, she wanted you to fuck her?'

'There was a suggestion.'

Ari fell elegantly onto the sofa and Mae sat down next to him, inadvertently forcing its previous occupants to move out of their way.

'Her name's Jules, right? Sam was telling me about her the other night. Apparently she's good fun. Studying medicine ... Has lots of hot doctor friends she's promised to introduce us to.'

'The other night?'

'You wanted to finish your essay – Sam and I went for a burger in town.'

Ari nodded his head to the music, as if it was no big deal. Mae tried to emulate his nonchalance. She was reluctant to abandon him, but her glass was empty, so was the bottle, and she was scared to sober up, because once she became pain-fully self-aware, she'd want to leave.

'Back in a sec,' she said, levering herself off the sofa.

On her way to get more wine, Sam grabbed her arm and pulled her out into the concrete back yard for a smoke. They stood close together for warmth as he retrieved a spliff from a cigarette packet, lit it and took a long performative toke.

'I'm in love with Ari,' he said, before trying to blow a smoke ring and failing. 'Does he even notice me? Could he, you know, *date* me? What do you think, Mae?'

It was unusual for Sam to seem unsure about anything. His confidence was starting to unravel under their new friend's gaze. But the idea of having to share Ari felt complicated for Mae and she couldn't articulate why. Sam passed her the joint and she held it between her thumb and index finger, because when she was a teenager, someone had told her that was how boys smoked.

'Ari's just not in that place. It's not you, I know he likes you . . .' She took a drag, then a second and a third. She felt her head rush.

Sam smiled and finished her sentence. 'Just not like that.'

She was too high to notice his tone. She squeezed his shoul-der and then stumbled back inside and through the crowd to find Ari. He wasn't on the sofa where she'd left him. She scanned the room, but moving her eyes made her head hurt. She clocked their Queering the Canon lecturer, a man in his early forties who Sam had thought would be a hilarious addition to the party. He was slut-dropping, badly, to 'No Scrubs' and reaching out to catch a first-year boy's waist and pull him closer. Then Mae noticed Ari through the doorway and could see there was a commotion happening in the kitchen. She pushed through the living room full of people and found Jules with her hands on his chest, trying to calm him down.

'What's happening?' Mae was diminished of wits suddenly and felt the words take their slow shape in her mouth.

'He just flipped out,' said Jules. 'He was going to punch that old dude dancing in the living room.'

'OK, thank you, I've got this.' Mae gently pushed Jules out of the way and put her hands on Ari's shoulders, as much to steady herself as to lock eyes with her friend. Ari's jaw was clenched tight and he breathed heavily through his nose.

'Hey,' she said, 'tell me.'

'He's a teacher. We're supposed to *respect* him and he's behaving like a frat boy. And look at all those first years around him – they'd suck him off for a higher mark if he asked. It's not OK.'

Mae laughed nervously. In the six weeks they'd known each other, she'd never seen her friend even close to this level of anger. 'You look like you want to kill him.'

'It's not a joke, Mae. It's fucking gross.'

'I think you're overreacting. French exit?'

Ari nodded, relaxing the tension that gripped his body. Mae squeezed his hand and led him to the front door, where she found her pilot jacket under a pile of coats. Ari, as usual, was sober. Mae, as established, was not. He helped her with the zip on her jacket and they walked quickly to keep warm. It was a clear October night. She hoped the fresh air would sober her up so she was ready on the off-chance Ari might want to talk about what had happened. But Ari never wanted to talk about himself, at least not in any depth. Silence hung over him like a piñata at a kids' party, and despite Mae's heavy-handed bashing, it had yet to split and spill its treats.

Once they fell into a comfortable rhythm heading down Woodhouse Lane, he apologised.

'Sorry about that.' There was a full stop in his voice, and had Mae been feeling sharper of mind, it would have prevented her from asking any follow-up questions.

'Why do you care that some cringey tutor is twerking badly at a stupid student party? I don't get it.'

Gaps had started to show in their nascent friendship. What she knew about his personal life was limited to the basics: he lived with his mother, his aunt Alice and his six-year-old cousin in a cottage in the countryside. His mother drove him into the city every day for his classes. Whenever she asked him more about his private life, he always said the same thing.

'Oh Mae. Let's just be us in this second, OK.' This time he added, 'It was just a moment. It stirred something. It passed.'

'Jules was asking me about you. Saying there are rumours. She doesn't understand why you're here. No one does, Ari.'

'You make it sound like I'm an alien. People are allowed to leave America, you know. What did you say to her?'

'To Jules? Nothing. How could I? I don't know anything.'

'Mae, please. Not now.'

'Fine,' she said as they approached the top of her street. 'At least you're consistent.'

Mae lived above a key-cutting shop in the town centre. She sublet off the door bitch at Kween, who was shacked up with a sugar mummy in Otley for the foreseeable. If the looks she got from fellow students when she told them she didn't live in halls or a house share were anything to go by, she was the only person in the history of university life who had chosen to live alone.

Inside her tiny flat there was a window ledge big enough for a herb garden, which she took almost too good care of, and even though her bedroom, living room and kitchen were all essentially the same room, she divided the space with some screens she'd found in a skip. She was meticulous about washing her two mugs, two forks and two plates every night before bed, and she folded all her clothes into perfect piles, which she kept in a stack of vintage trunks. A futon took up most of the space, and a lamp was perched on top of a highly curated pile of lesbian feminist poetry books.

Mae put the kettle on and threw mint tea bags into her two mugs.

'Sam likes you. You know that, right?' she said.

'Oh, he's like that with everybody. Such a flirt.'

'No, he flat-out told me he's into you.'

Ari looked concerned. 'This is exactly what I didn't want to happen,' he sighed, and went to the bathroom with his head in his hands. He had only recently asked if it was OK for him to keep his own toothbrush and bottle of face cream on the edge of her sink.

Mae stripped to her white boxers and pulled on a vest she kept folded under her pillow. On a whim, she decided she needed a nightcap, so poured an inch of whisky into a water glass while Ari was occupied and knocked it back like medicine. She didn't know why Ari was sober or why he didn't seem to want to have sex with Sam, but she felt the weight of its importance. She sat up on her futon, her back pressed against the cool white wall. She wasn't tired. He came out of the bathroom smelling minty and expensive and lay down next to her. He propped his head on her lap and closed his eyes. Mae looked at him intently. He was beautiful. She was high.

Ari has two eyes, a nose and a mouth, she thought. He has two eyes and a mouth. Oh, and a nose. There is his lovely nose.

'Sweet Jesus, Mae,' he said, opening his eyes and jolting as if defibrillated back to life. He manoeuvred his head from her lap and sat up next to her. Mae just carried on staring at the space where he'd been.

'How high *are* you?' he asked her.

Mae wondered the same thing but was now transfixed by the long dark hair falling over his face.

'You're *elaborately* staring,' he said. 'Actually, don't stop.' He framed his face with his hands and pouted.

Mae felt the room was spinning.

'It's the whisky ... wine. I mean ... what are you, like celibate or something?'

'I made some bad decisions, romantically speaking, back in New York. So I'm taking a break from sex and all associated shenanigans. You'll be the first to know if that changes.'

'But Ari, you're too beautiful. It's a waste!'

'Shh,' he said, now gently placing a finger on her lips. 'Let's both get some sleep, OK? We've got class tomorrow.'

He kicked off his trousers so he could come under the duvet. Mae was very particular about outdoor clothes in the bed.

'Eww, hairy.' She kicked his bare legs away from hers. He laughed and pulled the cover around him with a flourish. Mae turned away and curled up, hugging her pillow for warmth. She fell asleep quickly, knowing he was just close enough.

Chapter 3

The morning after what Sam had aspirationally called a Bonfire Night dinner party but was more of a regular 'hang' with pizza and a bag of fireworks they forgot to set off, Mae woke up early nursing a tangy cheap wine hangover. It was still dark out. She felt the blister on the tip of her finger from an indoor sparkler she'd held for too long.

She envied Ari's ability to sleep in. No amount of loud and deliberate pottering would rouse him, so in the end she moved her portable speaker closer to the bed and played Diana Ross at a moderately unpleasant volume.

She was feeling bad about an essay she hadn't started, and needed to get to the library, but the first thing Ari said when he rolled out of bed and into a downward dog stretch was, 'Morning, handsome. I think we should go to the party at the student union tonight.' He knew Sam would be there. Although Ari told himself he didn't want a relationship, didn't even want sex, he did wonder if there was something at the edges of these possibilities. Something he could entertain without it spilling into the drama he was trying to avoid. Especially with Sam, who was so deliciously uncomplicated.

Mae groaned. 'OK, OK,' she said. 'We shall . . . *participate*.'

As she watched Ari reassemble his outfit from last night on this morning's body, she noted how masterful he was with clothes. He dressed with a textured flamboyance. He could mix a charity shop velvet jacket, moth-eaten at the elbows, with subtle signifiers of his reformed Upper East Side existence, like a Saint Laurent cashmere sweater. The designer labels were never on show but classily concealed at the dark nape of his neck.

He pulled a pair of jeans and a baby-blue shirt from the pile stacked neatly by her bed. She silently took what he'd picked out for her into the bathroom to change.

'Your hair's great, seriously, leave it exactly like that,' he said when she was dressed. He looked at her like an art critic in front of a powerful new piece. 'Perfection!'

Mae blushed as she scooped a pile of library books into her rucksack. 'Oh you charmer,' she laughed. 'We're late.'

On the way to campus, her mother phoned. Janet was also *intrigued* by Ari. But unlike her daughter, she was unafraid to admit it. 'What a fascinating creature!' was how she put it when Mae had first allowed her to say hello to him and it had turned into a long and effusive conversation. Mae normally considered her mother a spectacularly bad judge of character. After all, Janet carried on donating to her yoga/aerobics/dance instructor's crowd-funded 'urban ashram' even after it became patently clear to everyone else that Tyna – *with a Y* – wasn't coming back. She held firm as the weeks Tyna didn't show up for class turned into months: 'She's such a sweet girl, so kind.'

'Darling, is that you? Mae, darling, are you there?'

'Hi, Mum. I can't really chat. I'm with Ari and we've got a seminar.'

Ari snatched the phone from her hand and set it to speaker.

'Janet!' he gushed. 'How are you? You know, it's funny, I was just wondering how your book club went down and if the ladies enjoyed *The Swimming-Pool Library* as much as I hoped?'

Mae scowled at him. She was starting to find these little chats unbearable.

'Well, I must say, it was jolly eye-opening,' replied Janet. 'And we had a rather long discussion about homosexuality and all the ins and outs.'

Mae pretended to vomit and Ari pressed his lips together to hide a smile.

'I'm so glad you enjoyed it,' he said.

'We did! It really was the most fun.'

Mae noticed that her mother's voice dropped into a sigh when Ari passed the phone back. A decade of tension condensed into a tight 'well then'.

It was the *way* she'd found out, Janet always said. The *shock* of it, because it's not what you expect from your daughter, that's all. That's all. She would love Mae, though, *no matter what*. As though being gay was akin to manslaughter or drug addiction or any number of things no parent *wants* for their child but must endure.

Janet had walked in on her daughter kissing Maxine, the girl who made the best flat whites at her health club's café. Mae realised now that she had subconsciously engineered it – choosing someone older who her parents knew and liked, inviting her over on a Tuesday, when Janet got home from work early. It was all a bit dramatic at the time (Mae was sixteen, and Maxine was, as Janet pointed out at the scene, 'a woman!'). But it meant it was done. There was no need to have the coming-out conversation she dreaded.

Her parents had known, really, since she was twelve, when something happened with her best friend that her mother and father spent the entirety of her early teenage years pretending hadn't. But after Maxine, there was no more pretending. Janet wrapped her disappointment in Mae's 'choices' around her like a pashmina, acting as if her daughter should be grateful for her efforts to understand why and how she had 'become' a lesbian. She wasn't cross, she assured her. Just confused. Mae tunnelled deeper into herself. And now, at a time when most of her peers were getting to know their parents as people, she was pulling further and further away. They were strangers.

'OK, Mum. Love to Dad. I'm really busy, got to dash now.'

Before hanging up, Janet emitted a 'hmm' that fell like a missile into the silence.

Mae crossed her arms over her denim jacket and pulled the sheepskin collar up. She began walking at a pace that left Ari behind, and he skipped to catch up.

'You seem mad.'

'I'm not.'

'Okaaay.'

They walked in silence. Mae's hangover needled behind her eyes. What did she really know about the boy by her side? Ari was someone she could listen to without planning what the next thing she was going to say would be. He had a compelling confidence and he made her snort when she laughed. He wrote poetry and watched Spanish soap operas. He could vogue and play bridge, occasionally at the same time. On campus they had quickly earned the status of a power couple. She was vain enough to notice they looked good together – Mae all pretty boi with bleached-blonde hair, Dax-waxed back, dressed like a millennial James Dean. When Ari called her handsome, she felt superhuman. Being a girl who passed as a boy, and he a boy who could pass as a girl, meant power and freedom to her. Gender couldn't hold them. But that was all surface, and a surface so shiny it was reflective.

'Fine. I am pissed off,' she blurted out. 'You're so pally with my mum. She likes you more than me already, and you've never even met! She gave me such a hard time for being queer, but with you it's all a wonderful novelty.' Mae slowed her frantic pace and looked around to check no passing students could hear. She whispered, 'You come to my flat all the time. You're better at being friends with my friends than I ever was. And yet I know next to nothing about your family, or where you live. Let alone your past.'

Ari inhaled and nodded slowly. 'OK,' he said on the out breath. 'That's fair.' They walked in silence for a bit, then he said, 'The first thing to know is that my dad is a . . . He doesn't understand me .'

'Oh totally. I get it. My dad can be so annoying. He asked me if I liked k.d. lang the other day, like cringe – shall we just say the names of famous lesbians and call it father–daughter bonding?'

'No,' Ari said sharply. 'That's him being kind, Mae. Can't you see that?'

Mae felt the hot slap of a scolding. Embarrassed, and unsure how to respond, she settled for a perfunctory 'Right.'

Ari flinched, as if worried he had been too hard on his friend. Such outbursts from Mae in awkward moments were nothing new.

Softer now, he said, 'Hey, why don't you come over? I feel bad I've not asked you sooner. It's just life, you know – it's all happening here in the city. I'm barely there myself. Oh my gosh, you should come next month! Alice puts the Christmas tree up on December first, and you'll *love* the cottage when it's all decorated. We'll make it magical for you. Stay a while, if you want. You'll meet my mom. And my aunt, and little Letty, my cousin. They'd love it; they've heard so much about you.'

Mae's heart leapt, but she answered casually. 'Sounds like the least you can do after I agreed to be your chaperone to the student union tonight.' She gave him a playful push, feeling like she'd finally passed the test.

'You'll make an excellent beard,' he said, taking all weight from the moment and tossing it deftly away.

They arrived on campus, and under the looming concrete lecture theatre, their schedules took them in different directions. Mae felt the tug of Ari's absence until they met back at her flat that evening. It hadn't taken long for their routines to be set like tracks in snow. Within weeks of meeting, it was decided they always got ready together at Mae's before nights out, and that evening was no exception. She watched Ari as he danced about foolishly, trying her clothes on, dedicating himself completely to making her laugh. No one else had spent so much time at her place. She never brought girls back; she preferred to stay at theirs because it was easier to leave in the morning than it was to chuck them out.

Mae didn't like the threat of other people's mess in her space, emotional or physical. But with Ari, it was different. That night they were going to go to the Refectory, which was the student union bar. They went out together six nights a week. If it wasn't the Ref, they'd be at Kween – the queerest and de facto coolest club in town – or someone-they-didn't-hate's house party. Mae would have preferred to always go to Kween, as gay nights occupied a superior place in her hierarchy of nightlife. But Ari thought that student dos were 'cute'.

'Are you ready, handsome?'

'Ready as I'll ever be for the Ref,' Mae called with a sigh from the bathroom, where she was swapping the single gold earring she wore in her left ear for a silver stud. She was moving slowly. She'd changed into a black polo-neck jumper that she felt expressed her lack of enthusiasm for the event. Meanwhile, Ari had managed to turn the same outfit he'd worn for the past two days into something that looked entirely new. Tucked into his trousers, the kimono he'd had on at Sam's dinner party became an artfully oversized shirt, accessorised with one of Mae's silver chains instead of the pearls. He tied the shirt he had been wearing underneath through his belt hooks so it looked like a silk scarf.

'One day we'll be the kind of people who get cars to parties,' said Mae as they made their way to the bus stop in the rain.

'I've been that person. Didn't like him much at the time, but maybe with you it would be better.'

At the Ref, there was a kiosk serving drinks, and eight black leather sofas. Whatever time of day you visited, people were playing cards and eating floppy cheese and ham sandwiches. Mae looked down at her wrist, stamped with the name of the venue as though she belonged to it now, and shuddered. She refused to queue for the cloakroom, so they bundled their winter coats and her wet umbrella into a pile they hid behind a curtain and pushed their way to the bar.

'Honey, this room is filled with all your worst things: the harem of ex-lovers; the too-bright lighting; and let's not mention the music,' Ari observed as they waited in the crush of students trying to order drinks. 'We can go if you like?'

'Thanks for noticing,' Mae laughed, 'but it's cool. I'll survive.'

'I'm glad.' He smiled at her, and then allowed his eyes to flick quickly through the crowds, searching out Sam. He spotted him on a sofa, holding court and gesticulating wildly. Sam caught him looking, jumped up on the sofa and waved him over. Ari pretended not to notice and turned back towards the bar.

'Fuck drinks, let's dance.' He pulled Mae out of the queue and began moving mock-seductively around her, right in Sam's eyeline.

Normally when they went clubbing, Mae left Ari dancing while she cruised for new faces. But she was tired and couldn't be bothered to flirt, so she let herself be part of Ari's show instead. Ari drew people to him. She noticed how he seemed to expand and contract as both the object and the subject of desire, and it wasn't just Sam who blatantly wanted him.

A third-year girl who was president of the Literature Society, and too straight to bother with in Mae's opinion, started grinding up against him to the music. She clawed at his shirt and pressed her cheek to his to shout things in his ear. Ari smiled in a way Mae didn't recognise. She felt her eyes narrowing and started to get annoyed.

'Excuse me,' she said, tapping the girl on the shoulder. She pushed herself into the space where she'd been, and the girl backed away.

'Please can we go now,' Mae said to Ari. 'This place is hetero central.'

'I'm gonna stay,' he said, waving the girl back.

Mae was shocked. It was the first time they'd ever disagreed on when it was time to leave a party. The music changed just as he spoke, and it sounded like he was shouting.

'Also,' he added, 'why did you do that? I liked her.'

'Eww, really? She was awful. She was clinging to your every word, it was embarrassing.'

'I liked her.'

'Liked her how?'

Mae worried then that something precious between them was breaking. He looked at her like it was impossible to explain and shook his head.

'Well, I'm going then,' she said. 'You stay and enjoy yourself. See you tomorrow maybe.'

'OK. Bye, handsome.'

Disappointment lay heavy and familiar on her chest. She disentangled her coat from Ari's elegant khaki trench and pulled it on. She walked home, arms crossed and head down, determined not to open the umbrella in her pocket but to suffer the cold, unrelenting rain. The thought that her invitation to a Christmas weekend at Ari's cottage would be revoked played on repeat. She felt stupid for ruining her one chance to inch closer to him.

Back at the flat, she changed out of her wet clothes, made an espresso in a pot on her camping stove, watered her cheese plant and listened to the radio. She turned on the electric heater and warmed her feet against the blast of hot air. She felt restless, and tears crept close to the surface. She wished she could stop thinking about the weird exchange with Ari and its potential consequences. But she couldn't equate the look he gave her, or the way he let that girl drape herself all over him, with anything she thought she knew about him. She tried reading *Paradise Lost* to distract herself, but the words seemed to tease her with their complexity.

About an hour later, her doorbell rang.

'You should say you're sorry,' a voice crackled through the intercom.

She buzzed him up and left the door to her flat open, then rewashed a clean mug at the sink so she could have her back to him when he walked in. But he stood in the doorway without speaking for so long, she turned to see if he was still there.

'Well?' he said softly.

'I'm sorry! I'm sorry I misread the situation. And you are allowed to have other friends.' Mae sighed; saying it out loud meant she had to believe it.

Ari crossed the threshold and leant casually against the wall opposite her. He was handling this annoyingly well, like he was accustomed to dealing with irrational people and their demands on him. He surveyed her bedsit as though he was looking at it for the first time.

'You know you live like a fifty-year-old lesbian whose part-ner has just left her and who's re-establishing life on her own terms . . . No, wait,' said Ari, his eyes sparkling mischievously. 'Actually, you live like a forty-five-year-old lesbian who spent her young adult life in jail for murdering her, um . . . her ex's new lover. And now you're trying to adjust to life on the outside, dreaming of the places you'll go.' He gestured grandly to the landscapes she'd ripped from travel magazines and stuck to the wall behind her bed. 'In both scenarios I'm wondering why you don't have a cat.'

'Fuck off, please,' Mae said, pretending to be cross. She placed the now exceptionally clean mug on the small draining board and sat down on one of her two chairs.

'Can I take a shower?' Ari asked. 'I'm soaked. *Someone* took the umbrella.'

She nodded.

On the way to the bathroom, he sashayed over to her and kissed her cheek chastely.

'Hey, Ari, wait . . . Are we still on for that Christmas thing? My coming to your house, I mean?'

He was standing so close she could feel his breath. 'Of course.'

Mae began tending to her plants while Ari slid off to complete his ablutions. He never let his hair down in public, but when he came out of her cupboard-of-a-bathroom it was glistening wet. He'd wrapped a towel around his waist and left his hair to drip a trail of water across the floor.

'Why don't you dry that lustrous mane of yours properly. You'll catch a chill.'

'OK, *Mom*.' He whisked the towel from his waist, wrapping it in a turban around his head.

Mae didn't know where to look and Ari seemed to enjoy the awkwardness.

'You read all cool, but girl, you're a bigger prude than my grandma. Look at me!'

She was pruning her basil.

'I don't want to.'

'Why?'

'Because . . . because most of the time I forget you're a boy, but right now . . .' her mouth was dry, and she swallowed, 'I can't.'

He said it again, his tone neutral. 'Look at me.'

Mae put her scissors down and did as Ari asked. She took in all of him. She had never seen a man without his clothes on in real life before. At home, her dad came out of the bathroom in a shirt, jumper and chinos every morning. She just assumed that under every checked shirt was another checked shirt.

Ari was broader than she'd realised and had shiny dark pubic hair that tapered into a thin line up past his navel. His skin was pale but looked like it would go a golden brown in the sun. And his penis, well . . . how had the male appendage got such an impressive reputation? Mae wondered. It really went to show the power of patriarchal PR. He stood completely still and smiled like he was used to being looked at. Then she was laughing, or was she crying; something weird was happening between them that Mae didn't understand. She picked up the towel from the floor and threw it at him.

'OK, seriously, stop it now, I like you better dressed.' She squirmed, trying to regain some composure.

Ari wrapped the towel around him like a lady in a spa, unfazed by her discomfort.

'Can I borrow some clean clothes?'

'Sure.'

And as he dressed in her boxer shorts and one of her black vests, she realised that Ari was hers again. She felt the narcotic rush of relief.

Chapter 4

In bed, Professor John Martin Scott PhD wanted Ari to call him 'Daddy'. He obliged, reluctantly. It was quite a turn-off, as it made him think about all the times he'd shouted, 'Daddy, stop, please,' when his actual father spat words like 'fag' and 'fairy' in his face while he cowered against the glass brick wall dividing the kitchen from the polished oak living room of their penthouse on East 93rd.

Ari's family home had been featured in *Architectural Digest* when they first remodelled, and he liked to imagine how the picture captions should have run: *The living room, which offers panoramic views of Central Park, is furnished with modernist seating upholstered in a fabric that happily conceals the red wine stain made when Randolph Hines, a prominent cosmetic doctor and husband of Connie, an ex-fashion model, knocked a cut-crystal glass out of her hand and declared her a pathetic, lazy bitch.*

Professor Scott knew nothing much about Ari's personal life, except that his daughter, Lilly, had been in the same grade as Ari at high school, but as they weren't friends, it was 'absolutely not an issue at all' to invite the freshman creative writing and English major to the secret walk-up the professor kept in Greenwich Village for a tryst or two. Ari later called the studio the Closet; he had been entertaining boys there for decades.

It all started after Ari's second lecture, in mid-September, when Professor Scott shouted, 'Mr Hines?' as he was leaving the auditorium.

Oh shit, my dad's here was Ari's first thought, and he froze like a frightened animal. He was almost at the door, the other students pushing out past him, when Professor Scott said it again, and after a second, Ari realised that he meant him.

'Ari, I wanted to talk to you about these poems you submitted.' He held a brown envelope evidently containing Ari's assignment tight to his chest. 'You know, these pieces are very . . .' He searched for a word and forgot it when their eyes met. He smiled limply and said, '. . . good.'

Flattered, Ari began staying behind more regularly to discuss his writing. By October, sitting next to Professor Scott on the front row of an empty auditorium to talk felt almost normal.

'Should I read aloud again?' Ari asked, fetching a small black notebook from his satchel.

'I'd like that.' As usual, the professor closed his eyes and clasped his hands in his lap. He tipped his head so it rested against the back of the plastic chair. Ari knew his words off by heart, so watched his teacher's pleasure build as he delivered them. Professor Scott's eyelids twitched, his breathing became deep and slow, and he unclasped his hands to dig his fingers into the soft corduroy that bunched around his thighs. Ari sensed what he wanted as if it was a storm brewing on a hot day. The thought both disgusted and excited him.

I often think about the mermaid carving out her voice

from the back of her throat,
sharp, like the edge of a shell

the first step she takes on the beach
is one of pain –
sharp edges in her feet
like broken glass,
ankle-bite, a cutting –

if this is what it means to be
a human, if love is hacking up
my words into seaweed
my identity into foam

then all the amulets I've collected
dream-jars and dust-shine
are as humiliating as the way the wind
flaps your smile like a flag, those eyes see

what they want to see, always will,
as predictable as the waves
lapping on your forsaken land.

'Exquisite,' said Professor Scott, still lost in it.

'Thanks. I mean, it needs work. I think I could strip it back even more in places, you know.'

'Would you like to join me in my studio this afternoon, Ari? I have a spot in the village. Perhaps we could work on it together there?'

It was then that Ari knew for sure: this guy talks a lot of Keats, but he really just wants to bone. And there simply wasn't a compelling enough reason to stop him from agreeing.

They walked up the seventy-three creaky stairs to a grotty room above a deli that smelt of meat. Professor Scott read John Donne aloud while Ari drank champagne from a bottle he'd taken from a tired-looking mini fridge.

'Why don't you get more comfortable?' said the professor, helping Ari out of his denim jacket and then his white T-shirt. Ari was beginning to feel a familiar anaesthetic wash over him.

'This . . .' he said, slowly removing the rest of his clothes while Professor Scott watched, 'this is what you want.'

'Oh my America!' he exclaimed in response, and Ari almost laughed out loud. The champagne was kicking in.

He lay on a sofa bed that had an anaemic yellow sheet half-heartedly draped over it. His teacher clambered on top of him. Now, the same big hands that had changed two daughters' diapers, that had undone the zipper on his wife's dress for over thirty years and marked countless student papers so kindly he was everyone's favourite tutor greedily left no part of Ari's naked body un-pawed.

Afterwards, Ari fell asleep, or more accurately passed out, until the professor gently whispered that it was time to go and ushered him out into the dark fall night. It was coming up to Halloween, and he watched as groups of people already dressed as Catwoman and Captain America barrelled arm in arm and happily boisterous along Bleecker Street heading to a party.

He felt spent and alone. He phoned his semi-boyfriend, Elliot, as he began walking towards the twenty-four-hour diner that they hung out in sometimes.

'Hey, I'm coming to find you.' He realised he was slurring his words.

'You sound out of it, baby,' said Elliot. 'Are you OK?'

Ari's artsy, ethical college buddies were so different to the bratty mean girls he'd hung around with in high school. They disapproved of drugs, for a start, and at his elite private school on the Upper East Side, cocaine had been the epitome of cool. His new friends drank biodynamic wine at house parties and took sex extremely seriously.

'I'm just tired. I'll see you soon.'

He was used to lying. Used to asking the questions to deflect from ever having to answer anything real about himself. Keeping what had happened with Professor Scott secret wouldn't be hard.

Ari was pleased that his social scene was taking a new shape now he was what his father called 'a walking fucking cliché of a liberal arts student'. But his college friends, who sat around in basement cafés drinking espressos, and water from French tumblers, earnestly quoting Audre Lorde, weren't without their own challenges. Ari looked and behaved like the kind of person they always *hoped* they'd be friends with at college in New York. He ticked lots of boxes for other people. But those boxes boxed him in.

Nevertheless, he was grateful for the company and distraction. He stood outside the diner, taking deep, sobering
breaths. He watched Elliot through the window, hunched
over a storyboard for his short film. He was talking con-
spiratorially with their friends Jaz and Mitchell, who were
vigorous high-fivers. Ari stepped inside.

'Gentlemen!'

'Whoa, Ari – what happened, man?' said Jaz, swapping the
usual cheery hand-slap for a concerned hug.

Ari wondered if his sordid afternoon with Professor Scott
had somehow rubbed off on his dishevelled outfit. He was
exhausted. His limbs heavy and his eyes half closed. He felt
like Pinocchio hanging limp from his strings, waiting for
someone to pick him up and make him dance. He sat down
next to Elliot.

'I'm fine. I've just been writing. I was in the zone – you guys
know what it's like – *transported*. No biggie.'

''Kay, cool. Well, you can help us convince Elliot here that
there is such a thing as *too* meta. This scene is not working, dude.'

Ari pretended to look at the storyboard. He felt Elliot press
his leg against his, then his hand reached under the table and
he pushed his fingers into the gaps between Ari's. The way
Elliot looked at him was a burden. Elliot was cute, but there
was zero spark and Ari just didn't have the heart to tell him.
He had accidentally let him believe there was a dimension
to their friendship that didn't really exist. Smothered by
Elliot's longing and desire, he suddenly couldn't shake the
feeling of Professor Scott's wispy white beard brushing
against his back.

'You know what,' he said, 'you guys are right. I'm not feel-ing too good. I think I'm done. I'll catch you all tomorrow.'

Elliot looked wounded. Ari stood up and gripped a chair for balance; the champagne had left a stale taste in his mouth and his head was throbbing. He bowed to hug his friends, hoping he smelt less rank than he felt. He noted their subtly raised eyebrows and Elliot's hangdog expression before walk-ing out of the door.

Hailing a taxi, he headed home. He had sacrificed a fresh-man suite in Brooklyn Heights to live with his parents in their penthouse and commute to campus. He couldn't leave his mother alone with Randolph. Not that he was able to protect her exactly, but he was there, for afterwards.

As the taxi pulled up outside his building on the corner of 93rd and Fifth Avenue, he handed two twenty-dollar bills to the driver and hurried inside, desperate for the sanctuary of his bedroom.

'Good evening, Mr Hines.' The doorman winked, and Ari wondered for a split second how he knew he'd spent the after-noon having sex with a man old enough to be his grandpa. He called the elevator, avoiding eye contact.

When the doors opened like theatre curtains into the apartment, he caught the last of the daily shouting and heard his father's office door slam with a final gasp and a bang. This had been going on so long it was familiar, and, in a fucked-up way, comforting because of that. Ari and Connie understood the nuances of Randolph's moods, the tiny triggers and the wells of his anger. Navigating life together was a game, and when they lost, they wanted to try again, again, again. They never won.

'You shouldn't be here,' Connie said when Ari quietly stepped into the kitchen and wrapped his arms around his mother. She stood at the counter, shakily pouring a glass of wine. 'You don't need to take care of me, sweetie. You should be with your friends. I don't want you to miss out on college life because of this. Because of him.'

It was shocking how small she felt in his arms. Ari still thought of her as the supermodel she once was; but her beauty was fragile now where once it had been famously, traffic-stoppingly powerful. When he was in eighth grade, there had been a full-length vertical billboard of her in a designer brand's winter campaign up in Times Square for the whole of September. He would skip school sometimes just to go look at it and watch other people looking at it. She was wearing a pantsuit and Rockefeller-high shoes. A superhero.

Chapter 5

Ari surveyed his attic bedroom, anticipating what Mae would think when she arrived later that afternoon. There was no getting around the fact that sharing the space with his mom was weird. He had arranged the two single beds to be as far from each other as possible, but every night he could still hear Connie tossing and turning, plagued by her private nightmares. Her side of the room was neat, bed always perfectly made with a silk Versace Medusa blanket on top. It was one of the few luxuries she'd brought from New York, and the gold looked garish under the wooden beams.

Aunt Alice had furnished the room in a rush when Connie told her they were coming to stay just a day before arriving. It looked to Ari as if she'd swept a thrift store for knick-knacks. He'd grown quite attached to the little porcelain Pinocchio on the table by his bed, but Connie had quickly disposed of the family of glass turtles, the Russian doll and the collection of shells that had been scattered across every available surface.

His mother got the wardrobe, but they shared the vanity table. Connie had lined up her potions and perfumes in rows.

There was a skylight, but otherwise no windows, so even on the sunniest of days the attic was barely sepia.

Ari never normally did so, but with Mae coming he untangled his sheets and folded the clothes that were permanently strewn across the bed. He felt nervous about the visit.

'Hoping to impress your girlfriend?' teased Connie when she creaked up the stairs to their room and found him fussing.

'I hope you're not planning to do this embarrassing mom routine when Mae gets here.' Ari playfully threw a bunched-up pair of black jeans at his mother. 'At least help me? She has very high standards. Oh, and for the thousandth time, she's not my *girlfriend*.'

'Like that girl Harper wasn't your girlfriend and then I walked in on you making out in your bedroom that time?' Connie handed Ari back the jeans, still unfolded.

'Mae is a gold-star lesbian. And anyway, I don't have any kinda crush. She's more like my brother. You'll see. And she doesn't know I've been with girls, so please, Mom, seriously. No cute stories.'

He left Connie to beautify herself for his friend's arrival and headed downstairs, where Alice and Letty were dressing the Christmas tree. Like the rest of Alice's home, the concept was eclectic, and all manner of trinkets were hung until the branches seemed to groan under their weight. Ari lifted his young cousin onto his shoulders so she could put the angel on top.

'Do you think Mae will like it?' Letty asked.

'Oh, she'll love it, Letty-loo.' He spun her in the air before carefully placing her down on the sofa.

Alice swept pine needles from under the tree, then stood back to inspect her handiwork. 'I feel like the Queen's coming for tea. The amount of pressure you've put on us to get the Christmas decorations up, Ari love. Oh, bugger it – a bulb's gone in these fairy lights, they won't switch on.'

'I just want you all to like each other, and it's gorgeous, Alice. Thank you. The cottage looks beautiful. Don't worry about the lights. It's so sparkly, she won't notice.'

Alice lit some big Roman candles, then shoved the fresh holly she'd picked from the woods into vases. 'Done. Now, I'm to get her from Guiseley, am I? What time does madam's train get in't station?'

'Shit, we need to leave now. She can't *abide* lateness.'

As they sped along country roads, Christmas songs cutting off abruptly when the radio lost reception then blasting back on again at the top of each hill, Ari felt an uncharted happiness.

Mae was already waiting in the car park at the station. She had on her pilot's jacket, with the sheepskin collar turned up around her neck. She was jogging on the spot to keep warm when Alice pulled up opposite her. The car was still moving as Ari flung the door open.

'Welcome to Manhattan!' he shouted from across the road before running over and scooping her into his arms. He threw her overnight bag into the boot and held the front door open for her. 'May I present my most fabulous Aunt Alice.'

Mae reached out for a handshake, but Alice pulled her in for a bear hug. In a tweed flat cap and Barbour jacket, Ari thought his aunt looked more like a farmer than the school teacher she was.

'Hop in then, Mae, and let's get you lovers home.'

*

The cottage smelt of wood smoke and pine. Mae greeted Connie with two air kisses. Ari watched as her eyes widened, taking in the unusual glamour of his mother. She'd dressed up in high-waisted Armani suit trousers with a white silk blouse tucked in and a Cartier diamond necklace that shimmered at her collarbone. Her feet were bare and she held an unlit cigarette in a vintage cigarette holder. She looked like a grown-up Holly Golightly.

'Charmed, I'm sure,' she said, hamming up the grandeur for Ari's amusement.

Mae beamed. 'You have a beautiful home, Alice,' she said as Ari took her coat and hung it on a hook by the door.

Alice pushed her gently towards the living room. 'I wouldn't go that far, love, but we're cosy enough, aren't we, Letty?'

Ari lifted up his cousin, who had been hiding on the stairs, watching everyone, before tentatively poking her head around the door. He held her at eye level and she stared at Mae intently.

'What's your favourite animal?' she asked with great seriousness.

Mae pretended to think about it for a second, then said, 'Dogs. Specifically, whippets.'

Letty slid down Ari's leg to the floor. 'I knew it,' she said. 'I knew it I knew it I knew it.' She skipped out of the room with Connie and Alice following, leaving Mae and Ari alone.

'Was that the right answer, then?' Mae laughed.

'Oh yes. Letty has this theory that she only likes people who like dogs. She's devastated that Alice is allergic and they can't have their own . . . Take a seat.'

Mae flopped down onto the sofa. 'Shoes off?'

'I honestly don't think Alice cares.'

She unlaced her DMs anyway and placed them out of sight. 'It feels so weird to be here. It's not what I expected.'

'How so?' Ari was intrigued to know how his friend's versions of him were stacking up.

'I feel like I'm in a theatre set. It's so perfect. I mean, it's not perfect but that's what makes it perfect. You all just seem to fit together, like it shouldn't work but it does.'

'High praise indeed,' said Ari. They had a long night ahead with dinner, and Alice would want to play a game after, no doubt. There were still ample opportunities for the fragile equilibrium they'd cultivated in the cottage to come undone with Mae's presence.

He needn't have worried. Mae slotted in as if she was the missing piece all along. He gave her a tour, which ended in the attic.

'It's nice,' she said tactfully. 'I like how you've divided the space. Have you considered some screens? It might give you privacy.'

Ari laughed at his friend's insatiable practicality. Back downstairs, as the initial bubbling excitement of the event turned into more of an easy simmer, Mae helped Letty brush her My Little Ponys' tails while Alice finished making dinner and Ari laid the table. Connie alternated between standing outside the front door smoking and sitting in the armchair by the fire, watching Mae with her niece but saying very little.

'So how does life here compare to back in New York?' Mae asked Connie across the dinner table a few hours later. Ari could tell that after three glasses of wine she was feeling looser. He hoped she'd stop before she reached her limit. Drunk Mae would not be as welcome here, he anticipated.

Connie smiled kindly at her. Alice and Ari looked away, both feeling the uncertainty of her answer.

'It is extraordinarily different, dear. In ways I don't imagine you could ever fathom. We are very lucky to be here.'

Mae nodded encouragingly, evidently hoping for more. But Connie stabbed a roast potato and popped it in her mouth.

'Would you believe your old aunt has a date tonight?' Alice piped up just in time to rescue the happy mood. 'Second date, actually.'

Letty covered her ears dramatically.

'I cannot believe how many dates you go on!' Ari exclaimed. 'You're worse than Mae.'

'I don't do badly for a middle-aged woman in a remote Yorkshire village, do I, love?'

'Who's the lucky lady?' asked Mae.

'Vicar's ex-wife. Later-life lesbian. Making up for lost time, if you know what I mean.' She winked at Mae.

'Careful, Mae will get jealous,' Ari teased.

'I will! Hey, Alice, swing any of your rejects my way. I've always had a thing for older women.' Mae suddenly looked worried that she'd overstepped. Ari reached for her hand under the table and was thankful that his mother and aunt laughed. They were recalculating their friendship in real time. A shift was happening, taking them together somewhere new.

After lunch, they sat around the fire as if this had always been their ritual. Ari went into the kitchen to attempt to make everyone tea. Was it milk or tea bag first? He could never remember. When he came back with a tray of hot drinks, Mae was on all fours at the base of the Christmas tree. She fiddled with the wires, and pressed the switch on the wall. The lights flickered for a second, then emitted a steady glow.

Chapter 6

She finished her essay two days before the deadline. Ari had demanded to know why she was like this. 'It's kinda at odds with the whole *Rebel Without a Cause* thing you've got going on,' he said. 'Like, how can you be this cool *and* this much of a geek? It doesn't compute!' She wasn't sure either, but her parents had never put any pressure on her to succeed at school, and that had somehow made it entirely necessary to do so.

'My gold-star, top-of-the-class best friend. I haven't even started *thinking* about the essay. Sorry to let the side down,' explained Ari when Mae had phoned to ask how he was getting on with the same assignment.

'I just don't need the drama of pulling an all-nighter,' she said, pressing her phone between her cheek and her shoulder as she opened the window of her flat to let the sunshine and cold air exorcise it after an intense bout of studying. 'I've got enough of that with my love life.' She laughed. 'I wish I could be more like you,' she added, sitting at her little kitchen table, but it was clear she didn't mean it. Studying hard, meeting deadlines, getting high marks; the clarity and order of it all made her feel deliciously at peace.

'No, honey, I wish I could be more like you,' said Ari. But he didn't mean it either. There was no need for Ari to work as hard as her because his mind burned brighter. He didn't have to try.

'Anyway, to celebrate finishing *my* essay, I've got us cinema tickets for tonight. We spend too much time in nightclubs and not enough time enriching ourselves culturally, don't you think? It's a French film. Something about tortured lesbians who spend a lot of time in the bath, no doubt.'

'*Oh là là*,' said Ari. 'I wouldn't miss it.'

It was late afternoon and the sky was already a velvety black. Mae shivered as she waited for Ari outside the cinema, blowing on her gloved hands to keep them warm. She watched her friend strut down the high street towards her, gave him a brisk hug, noting the time, then hurried him inside. Just as they were about to walk to their seats, Ari grabbed her arm and pulled her into the adjacent screen, which was playing a rom com called *Big Day*.

'We'll enjoy this way more, trust me,' he whispered.

Mae had packed a few cans of beer for herself and a Fanta for Ari in her rucksack. She waited for the lights to dim before getting them out. 'Cheers,' she said after the momentary annoyance that they weren't going to be intellectually enriched after all had passed.

Ari's stories of drinking back when he was in New York – the few he'd let slip, anyway – always ended badly. It made Mae grateful she had only ever known him sober. Their dynamic meant she could be the one to get casually wasted, and Ari would look after her. It had worked for the past four months, and she enjoyed having an excuse to be vulnerable. His gentleness towards her when she was in a state rubbed away at her hard edges.

Freed by looking at the screen, rather than directly at him, she felt emboldened to broach the subject of his sobriety once more.

'What was it like really, quitting drinking?' she whispered as she passed him the Fanta.

He didn't answer.

'Fuck, sorry I . . . I'm so bad at this. You know what I mean.' She continued to gabble. 'Like if you were partying and shagging around in New York, and if you were addicted, it must have been *hard*, you know, to quit . . . '

On the screen, a white woman brushed her teeth ecstatically. Mae felt like an idiot. Ari took a sip of his drink, then said, in a voice loud enough for the people in the row in front to turn and stare at them, 'I was never an addict. I always knew I could stop, given a reason to. Once we got to Alice's, I found I didn't crave any of that stuff in the same way. I craved *this*. Being all right, happy, having a friend like you. I wanted that more than getting every kind of fucked. So, those first few months before I enrolled in class, I allowed myself to *feel* some stuff I'd been hiding from for the first time in a long time.'

They stood up to let a group of people shimmy past to their seats.

'Such as?' whispered Mae once everyone had sat down and started opening their sweet packets. Ari's past contained more dashes than an Emily Dickinson poem.

He turned to look at her as the screen went black. 'I would go on these long walks on the moors, very Heathcliff of me, I know. I thought about it all. And now I'm done. And I get it, you want the wreck. I'm not even giving you the story of the wreck. But can I just enjoy who we are together, without the shadow? Be us for a little while longer?'

Mae once again felt tricked into her friend's *carpe diem*. It was like watching a magician hide a coin under cups. An infuriatingly good show. The opening credits started rolling then, and a loud 'Shh!' came from behind them.

After the movie, Mae couldn't figure out a way to get back to the conversation she'd hoped to have. She planned to ask Ari more about his dad, but she was worried she would never be able to figure out the right words and that she was too naïve to be his confidante. But she was dying to be the keeper of his secrets. That knowledge would tie him to her, with a knot so tight and intricate it couldn't be undone.

'The acting was terrible,' was what she said instead.

'You are so predictable!' he laughed.

They came out of the cinema into a full-frontal Saturday night in the town centre. Boys dressed in skinny blue jeans and shiny black shoes, girls shivering in spaghetti straps clutching tiny handbags walked raucously past them to join the end of a nightclub queue. Mae often forgot such straight people existed, so infrequently did their paths cross in the cloistered queer world of university. For Ari, they may as well have been alternative life forms from another planet. He was fascinated and amused by the way the boys walked in too-tight smart shirts, shoulders hunched up against the cold, and the girls cantered behind them. One shouted, 'Oi, Calvin, wait!'

Ari smiled at them. 'Yass, ladies, looking fierce. Nails! Hair! Heels! Werk!' He stopped still, put one hand on his hip and pointed at a big group of lads heading their way.

Mae looked at the floor, hoping no one would take offence.

'You boys have a great night, y'hear,' he said in a hammy fake Texas accent, blowing them each a kiss.

'Thanks, mister, you too,' said one.

'Nice jumpsuit, mate,' said another.

'Since when did you know what a fucking jumpsuit is, Steve?' Mae heard the girlfriend trill after him.

One man gave Ari a drunk hug. Another a high-five. Everyone liked him. It was astounding. Mae hung back, impressed and not wanting to spoil his magic.

Walking arm in arm with Ari made Mae feel invincible. They turned off the main drag and into the collection of cobbled alleys and side streets that comprised the city's gay village. In a kitsch ice cream and waffle shop that stayed open all night and attracted an insalubrious post-clubbing crowd, Mae ordered a black coffee from the twink behind the counter, and Ari a cup of tea and a knickerbocker glory as extra as the green silk jumpsuit he'd paired with silver boots for their casual cinema outing. They sat at a large round Formica table at the back of the diner. Ari offered Mae a spoonful of ice cream. She appreciated the gesture but had a thing about sharing food.

'And yet you'd go down on a girl in a club toilet?' Ari laughed. 'You are the ultimate contrarian.'

The café's soundtrack of anthemic gay pop filled the silence. Mae wondered whether giving Ari an offering from her past might mean he'd repay it with a story of his own.

'I had a best friend once before, you know,' she said, gearing up for the tale.

'Right, that's it, I'm leaving.' He made a show of getting up, then fell back into his chair, laughing. 'I'm shocked, how dare you.' He quit teasing her when he noticed Mae wasn't smiling.

'We met in the first year of secondary school. Her name was Freya, and the problem was, I liked her like I wasn't supposed to.' Mae started nervously, stirring her coffee and talking in a low voice so the drunk drama students on a nearby table couldn't hear.

'I was twelve and it definitely was not cool to still be playing imaginary games. But I didn't know what else to do with my break times at school. Everyone else seemed good at standing around eating crisps and shouting about things. I tried to join in, but it felt like no one really knew what the rules were, and I was a lot more comfortable with the stuff going on in my head.'

'Like . . . ?'

'Like incredibly detailed daydreams, make-believe worlds that I lived in completely. Freya asked me what I was thinking about one lunchtime, and when I told her, she said it sounded like a cool story and she wanted to play.

'She would sleep over every couple of weeks and I used to touch my foot to her foot under the covers as if by accident. I'd count how long it would be until she moved and all I felt was the cold duvet again. Sixty-three seconds was the record. But Freya didn't want anyone else to know about our imaginary games, as she said it wasn't very mature.

'I remember how I loved everything about her that was different to me. She had three flavours of lip gloss and I didn't even own a ChapStick. She had breasts and I had a flat chest. She fancied boys and I thought they were all idiots. But it was the sameness that attracted me to her the most: a girl kissing another girl! Soft lips on soft lips. Imagine! I suggested we play "teenagers" one night when she was sleeping over and had let my foot touch hers for a full minute and a half.

'I said, "We could be boyfriend and girlfriend, or whatever," trying to make it sound totally casual. Freya nodded. I'm *sure* she nodded. So I put my hands on her breasts because that's what I'd seen in films. She pushed me off her and sprang out of bed. I'll never forget her reaction. "Eww, Mae, eww," she said. "It's a game, you're not supposed to really do it." She went downstairs in her pyjamas and phoned her mum, who came to pick her up. My dad had a whispered conversation with her at the door. I watched from the top of the stairs. They both shook their heads a lot and I felt disgusting.'

'I guess that was the end of your imaginary games?' Ari left the glacé cherry in a pool of melted ice cream at the bottom of the glass and motioned to the waiter. Then he looked anew at Mae. She felt untethered by the compassion in his eyes.

'Yep. Freya stopped speaking to me and told everyone rather grandly that I had "crossed a line". She didn't specify which line and that made it seem worse. I was a social pariah then, and before either Freya or I could explain what had really happened, the story took on a life of its own. It became legend, etched onto desks, written in permanent marker on loo doors. No one at school wanted to be seen talking to me. I could forget about friends. The next few years were all about survival.'

Ari had listened to this last part without moving a muscle. The whole story had fallen out of Mae like sugar from a sachet. Next to her constant fidgeting and knee shaking and need to twizzle something in her hand at all times, he was always so still and composed, every expression precise. He put his hand on hers and used the other to take a sip of his now cold tea.

At the time, shame had hit Mae like a tidal wave.

'It's probably for the best,' was what her dad said after they had all heard the message Freya's mum left on the answerphone explaining why Freya wouldn't be coming over any more.

'Delete it, Michael. Get rid of it,' Janet had snapped.

Mae's dad had fumbled to press the delete button, and they sat in a silence that Mae felt her parents were still sitting in with her now.

'But you found the queers eventually, right?' asked Ari, shaking her from the memory. 'The people you've told me about from back home when you were a baby dyke heartbreaker?'

Mae shifted uncomfortably in her seat. 'As I got older, I needed to kiss girls who kissed me back. And then when I liked someone, it felt safest to ditch them for someone new, then newer.' She had learnt that desire was dangerous when she stayed still with it. She had to keep her feelings moving so they wouldn't stick. Ari was the first person to understand why.

Chapter 7

New York, a year or so earlier

Ari had been feeling itchy and bored of Elliot and his university friends. They were so *achingly* earnest. His affair with the professor satiated something, but it wasn't enough. He longed for the rampant nihilism that he'd lost himself in at high school. So, one Friday night in the middle of fall semester, he arranged a reunion with some of the girlfriends he'd pretended to like back when they were in senior year together. They were to meet at an expensive Asian restaurant in the Meatpacking District. It was one of the places in Manhattan that didn't ask for ID as long as the nineteen-year-olds kept tipping.

Dr Hines's six o'clock eyebrow lift client had cancelled at the last minute, contributing to his tight mood, and he was pacing the living room with a Scotch, waiting for Ari to get in his way.

'You're seriously going out like that?' he said.

'I am,' Ari replied, bolder than he'd intended, and Randolph smiled unkindly then ripped open Ari's cream silk blouse. Pearl buttons dropped to the floor and scattered in the silence. Father and son made eye contact, by accident, and in that split second saw all the complicated corners of each other's shame.

Ari knew better than to protest. He picked up his purse, flinging the gold chain across his body so that it held the two sides of his shirt together.

'Don't wait up,' he said. He made his way to the elevator that opened into the reception room, pushed the down button, and waited, praying that this was where it ended.

'Is that your mother's purse?'

The doors to the elevator dinged open and he stepped in, willing them to close.

'She gave it to me,' he said, 'for my birthday.' Randolph's spluttering, twisted face was the last thing he saw before the doors slid shut.

Downstairs, he leant against the wall of his building, panic fluttering at the top of his chest. He took a steadying breath and smoothed down his shirt where the buttons should have been, then walked quickly the six blocks to the Mark Hotel and without stopping glided straight through the glass doors and up to the black lacquered bar, where he sat on a red leather stool and ordered two vodka rocks from a server he'd fucked in the alleyway when he was seventeen. Slowly the very specific guilt he felt about leaving his mom alone with his consequences slipped into more of a general malaise.

Later, he was barely present for dinner with his old friends. Not that the harem of mean girls cared. He looked good and that was what mattered. He managed to eat two sushi rolls before a curdling feeling in his stomach stopped him from making any further dent in the feast they'd ordered, more to prove their wealth than to actually eat. The night ended, as nights with his high-school friends often did, in a hotel room with a pack of young Wall Street guys. Ari knew that his serving pretty was something straight men were comfortable taking ownership of. He was 'one of the girls'. How far this went depended usually on how much cocaine he snorted off the corner of someone's black card, and how much *that* made him willing to take off his self, as if it was a tuxedo jacket he could hang on the back of a chair.

Ari could be anyone's fantasy if he felt like it. That night, he couldn't remember exactly what happened in the build-up, but he knew he'd finished off the better-looking banker while Maddox was sick in a champagne bucket. He woke up the next morning on the back seat of Maddox's town car in a garage under her building. His nostrils burned; his mouth felt like cotton wool. He flipped open his phone:

Lmk when ur alive, u looked so peaceful I figured I'd leave you there to sleep. Mx

Maddox had her housekeeper bring him down a toothbrush and toothpaste, which he took as his cue to peel himself from the car and out through the fire exit onto Park Avenue. Grateful that it was the weekend, and he didn't need to run to a lecture, he walked slowly home along the perimeter of the park. He was anxious about the state he'd find his mother in.

Back at the apartment, he was surprised to encounter a scene of domestic peace. Randolph was sitting at the kitchen table reading the *New York Times*, Connie was making coffee. Ari had no time to unpick the atmosphere because Randolph slapped the newspaper on the kitchen table and declared that they were going to brunch, as a family. And could Ari at least try not to look like he'd escaped from the circus, and could Connie just fucking smile once in a while or didn't they teach her that at modelling school?

It was a slate-grey November morning and Ari would rather have been anywhere else than sitting around a restaurant table with his parents. When he caught his mom's eye, they both had to stifle a laugh and hide behind their menus, it felt so ridiculous. The place was sceney and buzzing with off-duty somebodies. It was all red leather and shiny brass fixtures, and Ari found the clatter of crockery coupled with the cacophony of show-offy chatter insufferable.

Randolph sent his eggs back twice. Once because they were undercooked. 'Do you need me to come back there and poach them myself?' he said, looking for a laugh from one of them and not getting it. And then again because they were overdone. 'These are golf balls!'

The server, a guy Ari recognised from the scene, mouthed, 'Wow,' and when he took his plate, Ari whispered, 'Save me.'

The three of them had literally nothing to say to each other, so they sat in uncomfortable silence until two men with gym bodies and faces that looked as if they'd been badly Photoshopped appeared at the table. One was clutching a small French bulldog, and they were both smiling as much as their frozen muscles would allow.

'Jonathan! Peter!' Randolph jack-in-the-boxed from his seat, suddenly dripping in charm. And then, to Ari's horror, leant in to air-kiss them both. 'You're looking well, boys,' he said.

'Oh, and who do we have to thank for that, Doctor?' said

the one not holding the dog. They proceeded to loudly discuss their personal trainers, the closure of their members' club's rooftop pool, and where Randolph had his suits made.

'You know, I said to Jonathan after our last appointment, I *must* get the name of Dr Hines's tailor, he always looks so well *fitted*, didn't I say that, honey?'

The man with the tiny dog cradled in his bulging biceps nodded enthusiastically. 'You did, honey,' he said.

'Oh, you two,' said Randolph. 'Stop it, you're embarrassing me!'

They laughed. Ari and Connie looked on aghast.

'We're seeing Pablo at two, so gotta shoot. Ciao,' said Jonathan.

'Ciao,' said Peter.

'Ciao, boys, bye,' said Randolph.

Of course, he didn't introduce his family, and neither of the men or their dog seemed to notice them. For the duration of the conversation, Connie and Ari had been sitting at the table staring up at them in disbelief. How bizarre it was to catch a glimpse of the man who terrorised them wearing this mask.

'Gotta be one of the best married couples I know,' said Randolph to no one in particular after they left. Dead to the irony, he went on, 'Really great guys.'

This incident compounded Ari's belief that the homophobia his father directed his way was lacking substance. When he called him a pussy and a freak, it was like watching an actor at a table read: he wasn't fully committed. Ari's queerness gave Randolph something convenient to hang his hatred from, but the true source of his anger, the place it started, was something else, Ari was sure of it.

Chapter 8

Otley, February 2015

Connie picked Ari and Mae up from town, as she now did most Saturday evenings so that the pair could spend the weekend in the country. Ari said his mom enjoyed being their designated driver and was happy to fetch them from Mae's place and weave through the country roads, still conspicuously A-list in her sister's VW Golf. She'd deposit them back in the bosom of the small cottage any time they asked. She liked to drive, as it was a chance to talk and smoke.

'Are you attracted to my mother?' Ari whispered to Mae after she'd lingered a beat too long inhaling Connie's hard-to-place perfume when she hugged her hello. Mae laughed and shook her head, settling into her familiar spot in the back seat.

'OK, fine,' he said. 'Just don't get obsessed.'

'You're one to talk – my mum would divorce my dad for you in a heartbeat,' she snapped back, and Ari laughed.

As they drove, Connie regaled them with stories of life before she married. Mae couldn't get enough of the drama backstage at fashion shows, big photo shoots and obscenely decadent parties. Her instinct was to be revolted by the world

Connie described, but something about the mad passion and reckless pursuit of beauty piqued her interest in spite of herself.

Connie was only in her mid-fifties, and as her soon-to-be ex-husband had been named one of *New York Magazine*'s most trusted cosmetic doctors five years in a row, some minor 'tweakments', as she called them, had erased any hint of wrinkles.

'Is he handsome?' asked Mae, fishing for details and hoping Connie might be more forthcoming than her son. 'Does he look like Ari?'

'Oh sweetie. I'll let Ari tell you all about Randolph.'

'I'd rather not,' Ari said from the front seat. He turned his head to look out of the window, signalling the end of the conversation.

'Say what you like about your father,' Connie said as they waited for the lights to change, 'but at least he was generous with his botulinum toxin.' She laughed like a cartoon villain, flicked her cigarette out of the rolled-down window, and sped off on amber.

Aunt Alice answered the door of her cottage.

'Come in, come in.' She gestured at Mae. 'Don't stand on ceremony. I'll get you a tea, what'll you have? I've all the middle-aged lesbian classics. Fennel, liquorice, chamomile?'

Connie headed straight up the narrow wooden staircase to bed, pleading exhaustion and blowing everyone kisses in a way that made Mae blush. Ari unlaced his shiny silver boots and put them carefully next to the mud-covered hiking shoes under the coat rack in a still life that accurately depicted his extravagant presence in Alice's humble abode.

'Mae, you're a stick, look at you,' Aunt Alice continued, fussing Mae and Ari into the kitchen, where the smells of a hearty dinner still lingered. 'Now I know it's late, but you'll have a slice of cake too, won't you? Oh! And tell me about that girl you were seeing, the one with the nose ring. She's still on the scene, is she?'

'Nope,' Mae said.

'Oh no. I liked the sound of her. What about—'

Ari gave his aunt a warning look on Mae's behalf.

'OK, OK, she's over, that's over,' said Alice, reading the room. 'Got it, moving on.'

Mae sat at the table so the heat from the Aga warmed her back. Alice placed a steaming mug of fragrant tea and a slice of Battenberg in front of her. Ari said he'd make up the sofa bed in the living room.

When he'd left the kitchen, his aunt shook her head. 'It'll take him half an hour to figure out how to do it. You'll have to help him, dear, you know he doesn't have a clue about these things. The sheets are in the airing cupboard.'

The way Alice and Connie spoke to Mae felt so easy in comparison to her own parents' over-the-top niceness. Janet and Michael treated her like a Fabergé egg – precious and breakable. She felt it was too late for them to really know her now. Ari's family saw her how she wanted to be seen and it loosened something inside of her. She was happy at the cottage, but with that happiness came a fear that it could all be taken away and then she'd be left with nothing but her parents. No aunts or uncles, cousins or grandparents to speak of; just the sharp triangle she made with Mum and Dad.

'Actually, Alice . . . I was wondering if I could ask you some-thing,' she said, seizing her moment. 'Ari's so secretive about New York. He has hinted that his dad was an asshole . . . '

'Understatement!' Alice interjected.

'But in what way? What did he do? Why did they end up here?'

'When they first moved in, Randolph used to call the house at nine o'clock every night. I'd prop the receiver up against the bananas in the fruit bowl while he ranted and raved. Finally, when he realised no one was listening, he'd run out of steam, then one of us – Letty liked doing it – would hang up on him. After about a month, he stopped calling and then Connie and Ari seemed finally to relax.'

Alice brushed some crumbs from the red and white checked tablecloth into her hand, then got up to shake them into the bin. She didn't sit back down, but instead took a broom from behind the door and began loudly sweeping the tiled floor.

'Then what? Alice?'

She stopped and stood with the broom in her right hand.

'Mae, love, it's not my place. What about your parents? What's the big secret about them? You've said not a jittery jot about them since you first stopped here. Classic case of homophobia-itis, is it?'

'It's more subtle than that.' Mae folded her arms and sat back on the dining chair. 'My mum loves men. She's obsessed with how *strong* and complicated and *different* to women they are. Which is funny, 'cos my dad's not like that at all. She doesn't understand how I could not be attracted to the opposite sex and she wants to get to the root of it, like it's a problem she can help solve. *Why* am I gay? Maybe I just haven't met the right guy yet?' She felt herself getting angry and noticed that Alice had started sweeping again.

She put her elbows on the table and leant forward to try and keep Alice's attention. 'The fact is, my mum wanted a handsome son-in-law she could be all giggly and flirty with and secretly fancy a bit. So she's not homophobic exactly, but she's quietly disappointed. And I can hear it in her voice every time we speak, and I can see it in the way she looks at me. Both my parents wanted me to have the big family they never did, and of course they reckon that now I'm a lesbian, they'll be lucky if I have a couple of cats. Forget about grand-children. But what gets me is they'll never *say* any of this. I'd rather they'd shouted and screamed at me when they found out, I'd rather they'd kicked me out, told me how they really felt. But they're so fucking repressed.'

'Would you listen to yourself!' Alice leant the broom against the wall and shook her head disbelievingly.

'I'm serious. At least if they'd been honest and told me it was a problem, I could have fought back, but it was all just swept under the carpet.'

'Sounds like they're doing their best from where I'm stand-ing. You try coming out in Yorkshire in 1973. You young queers today, you don't know you're born, quite honestly.'

'I did it!' said Ari proudly, poking his head around the kitchen door. 'Your boudoir awaits.'

Ari said goodnight and Mae remade the bed, because he had used a duvet cover as an undersheet. Tucked up finally beneath pale pink cotton sheets and an old patchwork knitted blanket that smelt of log fires, she stared up at the ceiling.

Aunt Alice's cottage felt like home. But she couldn't stop thinking about everything she still didn't know about this complicated family. Was their silence all that different from her parents'? Why did everyone think she needed protecting from the truth?

Under the heavy covers, sleep came quickly, her anxieties picked up by her subconscious and pushed into dreams.

Mae played with Letty all the following morning while the others prepared lunch and did their Sunday chores. They sat reading comics together at the kitchen table and Mae was amused to watch Ari attempt to help his aunt cook.

'Stir the stew, love, it's sticking,' Alice said to him.

'Yikes, sorry,' Ari said. 'I was miles away.' Alice raised an eyebrow and took the wooden spoon from his hand, knocking it expertly three times on the rim of the saucepan for emphasis. She replaced the lid and turned down the burner.

'OK, well go and help your mother with the housework instead.'

Connie was doing her best to tidy up, moving piles of things from one surface to another – she wasn't lazy, she just didn't know how to do it, and neither did Ari. They'd had a housekeeper for so long. He tried to tackle the chores Alice gave them with enthusiasm,

'Yep, no worries, on it now,' he said in a flurry of faux-busyness. When Alice shouted up the stairs, 'You'll need to empty the hoover,' Mae burst out laughing and Letty joined in.

'You know your big cousin is up there right now on the internet looking up "What is empty the hoover?"'

'Should we help him?' asked Letty sweetly.

'If we do, he'll never learn,' Mae replied.

'Too right!' said Alice from where she was standing at the stove. 'They're not Park Avenue princesses any more.'

By bridging the gap between Ari and Connie's flaky uselessness and Alice's brusque stoicism, Mae realised that she helped everyone make sense of their odd little set-up.

The cottage felt like a cosy old cardigan that fitted perfectly. Any style was accidental. Books, papers and unopened letters covered every surface. Mess normally made Mae nervous, but there was a laid-back sense of order to the chaos. The tatty Chesterfield sofas were so dense with cushions there was barely space to sit. Throughout winter, Alice lit the log fire in the living room. The house overlooked a meadow of wild flowers, which would bloom in spring. It was idyllic but escaped twee because, like Alice, there was nothing contrived about it. The house was just joyfully itself.

Mae liked how warm and uncomplicated Ari's aunt was. She was a teacher, a single mum since her wife left her, and she always seemed genuinely pleased to see Mae. Even after the previous night's conversation, when Alice had seemed annoyed with the way she'd spoken about her parents, there was no awkwardness or tension. Alice said what she meant and meant what she said, and that was like fresh air to Mae.

Ari evidently adored Alice too. He'd watch her busying around the kitchen the way you might observe an animal on a wildlife show, building its nest. She dressed comfort-first. Occasionally, when she had a date, she'd pull something surprisingly spectacular from her wardrobe, like a velvet gown, then ruin it with clashing knitwear and sensible shoes. No one could really believe that she and Connie were sisters. Alice would say: 'Connie got the brains *and* the beauty. I got the boobs.' And even though nothing appeared even similar about them, once they'd finished eating that afternoon and Mae had washed the dishes and joined the family by the fire in the living room, the two women took each end of a thread as they talked, untangling their childhood.

'I was telling Mae last night about the joy of coming out as a lesbian when we were young.'

Connie popped another tab of nicotine gum into her mouth. 'Oh, my sister was the talk of the town. She was so different and she just didn't give a shit.' Ari's mother had picked up a pretty flawless American accent, but occasionally a northern vowel slipped through.

'Still don't,' piped up Alice, who sat cross-legged on the armchair while Connie, Ari and Mae were in a row on the sofa opposite.

'I must have been six at the time, and Alice comes down dressed for the school dance in one of Pa's suits. You should have heard the way our folks shouted at her, all these words I didn't understand.'

Alice threw another log on the fire; it spat sparks before the flames grew and began to dance. 'It was that night I said, "Mother, Father, I'm a lesbian *and* I'm a feminist *and* I'm taking Stacey Toogood to the dance."'

Connie wrapped her gum in a tissue so she could take a sip of coffee.

'Alice, I hope you won't mind me telling the kids this, but she never made it to the dance.'

'Let's not spoil a perfectly good evening with all that non-sense, eh, Con?' Alice smiled tightly and Connie nodded. Ari reached across Mae for his mother's hand. Mae stared at the fire and felt her cheeks flush pink. She was embarrassed that she didn't understand the depths of whatever it was genera-tions of this family had endured.

Letty was bored of all the sitting around and talking. She was turning somersaults on the carpet, and Connie, who had the least patience of them all, snapped, 'Please, Letty, for goodness' sake, stop it.'

Letty looked embarrassed, and Mae felt in that moment that she had more in common with this six-year-old than she did with the other adults.

'Let's go play in your room together,' she suggested.

Connie took a cigarette and her lighter from the packet she kept on the bookshelf.

'Popping out for a smoke,' she said, disappearing.

Letty pulled Mae towards the door.

'I'll meet you up there,' Ari called after them.

In Letty's messy bedroom, Mae expertly erected a den. A duvet cover draped over the end of two small armchairs made for a good tent, and they filled it with cushions and blankets and the contents of the washing basket. Mae turned out the overhead lights and closed the curtains, and she and Letty sat in the warm glow of a torch, hugging their knees and pretend-ing to be explorers setting up camp in the jungle for the night.

'Why do you always look so serious?' Letty asked out of the blue.

'Well ...' Mae said, suddenly conscious of her general resting expression, which was often mislabelled 'moody'.

'Honestly, it's just my face. We've spent hours together playing today, do you really think I'm serious?'

'No!' squealed Letty. 'You're so silly and funny!'

'Exactly. Never judge a book by its cover,' Mae said. Letty looked confused. 'Give people a chance to show you who they are by what they do, not how they look.'

They heard a slow clap coming from outside the den.

'An excellent life lesson,' said Ari, without a hint of sarcasm. They watched as his silhouette circled the tent.

'Come in,' called Letty, who had been beside herself with excitement since Ari and Connie turned up at her door one Thursday after school and announced that they were moving into the attic for the foreseeable future. When Ari told Mae about their arrival at the cottage, he recalled that the first thing Aunt Alice said to them when they pulled up was: 'You bloody took a taxi all the way from Heathrow?'

Ari ducked under the sheet and threw himself in and on top of the girls, a tangle of limbs and three octaves of laughter.

'I'm going to get pudding,' said Letty, urgently scrambling out of their makeshift tent, taking the torch with her and leaving Ari and Mae lying next to each other in the dark.

Being involved in Ari's family felt like a secret part of their friendship that no one else shared, and that was comforting, until Mae remembered this feeling of being deep in herself and letting Freya join her there. Then she felt a creeping anxiety that she would ruin what she had with Ari in the same way.

'The night we met, you told me you wanted kids. Was that true?' Ari asked.

Mae was surprised he'd remembered the details of her ramblings.

'Yes,' she said instinctively. 'I don't like to admit it, as I know it's what my parents have always wanted from me. Then when they found out I was gay, it was like, oh, OK, Mae's never going to have kids now, let's add that to the pile of stuff not to talk about. But I always wanted a big family, the opposite of mine. I imagine having this little crew of kids who use me as a climbing frame, and we have a secret handshake that we try to teach their other mum, but she never does it properly like we do.'

They lay still, uncertain about what should happen next. Mae tilted her head towards Ari and asked, 'You?' He took longer before answering.

'I want to be a parent. A good one. Honestly, I've realised living here with Letty that I want it more than anything else. I know it seems silly to think about it now.'

'Does it? Why? Because we're young, or because we're queer?' She carried on before he could answer. 'I fantasise about it a lot. I want kids before I'm thirty.'

Ari had never imagined meeting someone gay, someone his own age, who like him saw parenthood in their future with the absolute certainty of a nineteenth-century bride. He and Mae had arrived at this desire from such different places. But family, *home*, was the place where their wild opposites met. Realising this laid out a new cartography between them.

'Wow. Honey, we're going to have to widen our net if we only have nine years to meet our life partners. I think you've slept with every single gay girl in the city, and I don't get the feeling any are potential co-parents. Meanwhile, I've barely *winked* at anyone eligible.'

'Why do you think I'm so desperate to get to London! I need to find the other mother of my child *and* my sperm donor.'

A strange intensity hummed in the silence that followed. Mae wondered if they were thinking the same thing: that they each had what the other needed to make this future a reality.

Chapter 9

New York, a year or so earlier

All through winter recess, Professor Scott emailed Ari sad dick pics that were badly lit and always had some giveaway of his happy home life lurking in the background – a birthday card by his bed, his-and-hers robes on the back of the bathroom door.

'I can't talk! I'm with my folks,' Ari whispered through clenched teeth when he called him for the tenth time that day, 'just to hear your voice'. It wasn't that the professor was unattractive, or even old, that bothered him most. It was more that he wanted love as much as sex.

Sure, Ari took something good from an older man being kind to him, seeming so *interested* in everything he thought and felt. His own father had never once asked him anything beyond the rhetorical 'What is wrong with you?' But no, no, everything else, all the staring, and the 'I saw this and thought of you' gifts, and the lent books and late-night phone calls . . . He wished he could close his eyes and cover his ears like he did during gross bits in movies.

He had vowed to end their affair before spring semester

started but had put off administering the final blow. It was now the third of January, and classes resumed on the fourth. He'd have done it sooner but the Scott family were upstate for Christmas and so he hadn't been to the Closet for almost a month, and amid all the season's social gatherings, he'd almost forgotten how much he dreaded the weekly rendezvous.

His parents were out at a charity gala when Ari sat down on a Philippe Starck Ghost Chair in the dining room, opened a new message on his phone and typed, *Srsly this has got to stop.*

He was wondering if he should at least spell out 'seriously' when the elevator doors opened and he heard his father shout, 'You make out I'm some kind of *monster*! Do you think I want to be this angry? You do this to me. You flirt with every man that comes near you like a twenty-dollar whore.'

'Randolph, please, not tonight. Can we just not. It's been a lovely evening. We both had a good time ... '

'You call that a good time!'

The door to their bedroom slammed and Ari felt his heart quicken. It would be better in the morning, he told himself, as he had done almost every night since he was old enough to be scared. *Tomorrow it'll be better.* He looked down at the message once more and hit delete. The feeling he got when he was with the professor was something toxic he could control the dose of. As self-harm went, it was neat and efficient. He needed it.

Instead he phoned Elliot.

'Love!'

'Hey,' replied Ari. 'Happy New Year. Look, I'm sorry I've not been in touch. You know what the holidays are like.'

'I do. I do. Mommy's social calendar is so demanding, and

she has me coming with her to all her galas and goodwill missions, which I *want* to, of course, but my film's not going to edit itself. And Chesterton is beautiful and all but it's not home any more.'

Elliot really could talk and talk. Ari took a breath, giving the conversation a wide berth. In the space, Elliot said, 'I've missed you, Ari.'

'About that,' Ari paused. Coughed, sat on the sofa and looked up at the high ceiling. The apartment had a meanness about it at night. 'I think we should start the new term fresh. Maybe not hang out as much. Explore, you know. We don't want to be tied down so soon.'

'Are we splitting up?'

'I don't think there's anything to split up – that's kind of my point.'

'Oh,' said Elliot, deflated. 'What a shame.'

'But we'll still be friends, yes?'

'Yes,' Elliot said in a low voice, after waiting a beat. Then he whispered as if in agony, 'Of course. I'll see you on campus.'

Ari hung up, not feeling that he'd ended things with the wrong person *exactly*, but that the weight had shifted and now it was more comfortable to carry. And so the affair went on. John Donne, champagne, bad sex, good grades. Without Elliot, he gave himself up to his teacher instead. He felt nothing. He let the professor love him and he tried not to hate him back.

By the end of the spring semester, maybe they were getting sloppy, or maybe Ari didn't care enough about the consequences of getting caught. The Tuesday following Memorial

Day, they met in the bodega under the Closet, after class. The professor ordered a Reuben, and Ari secretly gagged watching him eat it, yellow mustard caught in the corner of his mouth as pastrami slapped his lips. Ari himself preferred the light-headedness of not eating. His teacher could be a little handsy, and Ari noticed the woman behind the deli counter observing. She must have seen Professor Scott eat that same sandwich with countless different boys over the decades.

The school year was almost done and everything was winding down, including their vigilance. After a session in the Closet, which Ari performed on muscle memory rather than engaging in anything like reality, Professor Scott walked him downstairs and out into an early summer evening. They lingered on the stoop. He stuck his hand in Ari's back pocket, not wanting to let him go.

Ari knew something was wrong, a few days after this last hook-up, when he walked home from the library to find his mother standing on the street outside their building with the doorman and six enormous trunks. It was a steamy June afternoon and the rain had only just stopped. Connie was biting her bottom lip and looking anxiously at her watch.

'You're here,' she said, crumpling in relief.

'I am,' Ari said. 'What's happening. Where's Dad?'

'He's at squash. We're going. Give me your phone.'

He fished it out of the inner pocket of his satchel to see the home screen dense with, missed calls and messages. In the library, he was completely absorbed in writing; it never even occurred to him to check his cell.

Connie snatched the device from his hand before he had a chance to read anything. She put it in the pocket of her faux-fur gilet and motioned to the doorman to hail two cabs.

'Where?' Ari said. 'We're going where?' His heart was racing, knowing that if his dad saw them out there making a scene, he'd be seriously, quietly and then volcanically mad.

'England,' she said firmly as their bags were heaved into the boot and the back seat of the two cabs. 'Get in. I packed all your things.'

As he was driven through Manhattan to the airport, his hot breath steamed up the windows, making the city blur past like a seventies movie transition scene. At JFK they didn't speak all the way through security. It was only in the first-class lounge, once Ari had downed one glass of champagne at the bar and brought two more to the small circular table overlooking the runway at which his mother was drinking a large gin and tonic and cracking open pistachios with her manicured nails, that he thought it wise to ask what the hell they were doing.

'I know, Ari. Everyone knows.' She sighed and gently shook her head as a 747 trundled to its final stop outside.

Ari thought he was gliding through life like a jet leaving no trail, in a cloudless sky. Nothing he did mattered or meant anything. He watched himself at one remove and couldn't fathom what it was that everyone knew, or why anyone would care.

His mother looked at him despairingly.

'Do not tell me you are having to think about this.' She always sounded her most British when she was angry.

Ari pressed fast rewind on the last six months and then caught it, finally. He felt the space where regret should have been. 'The professor,' he said, picturing the soft lines on his doughy white face and the curly grey hairs that sprouted from his ears. He couldn't have been any less worth it.

'There was a video of you and that man . . . your teacher . . . standing outside an apartment block in the Village. It was released online. I got sent a link to it by one of your so-called friends' parents. Your father will see it tonight, as soon as he turns on his computer, and when he does, he will want to kill us both. We're going to stay with my sister Alice in Yorkshire. We'll be safe there.'

Connie told him that the video had been released anonymously. Someone with a camera, most likely a film studies student because it was emailed to the full NYU liberal arts faculty list. Perhaps they just happened to be passing when Professor Scott had taken hold of Ari and kissed him. She speculated that the student was either motivated by a moral compass or a grudge over a grade, or, she scoffed, 'because this might be the most watched short he'll ever make'.

She showed Ari the video on her laptop. He thought he looked grotesque, like the airhead mistress in a movie. Oh God – they zoomed in – he was horrifying; a fake smile, a coquettish wink, and Professor Scott was all over him. He'd seen enough. Shame took root. It would grow twisted and deep before breaking the surface.

Two hours after take-off, once dinner had been cleared away and the few other people in business class were donning their eye masks for some sleep, Connie lowered the screen that was dividing their twin seats.

'Hello,' Ari said.

'You're a good boy,' his mother said.

He raised one eyebrow.

'A good human then,' she said. 'But I couldn't leave Randolph.' She closed her eyes for what felt like a long time, and when she opened them, she was crying. 'It was my choice to stay and it has dimmed the light in you, and for that I am so, so sorry.'

'Don't be,' Ari said quietly. 'I don't deserve it. I killed everything good you gave me. I did it to myself and now I am just numb. I'm a ... a human-shaped thing without a soul.'

'Oh for goodness' sake, please, Ari, don't be so dramatic. You did something stupid, OK. You did a lot stupid. But he was your teacher. This is on him. Not you. Nothing has been *killed*, and that's why we're going to England. I'd left it too long – something like this was bound to happen eventually. I'm your mother and it is my job to protect you, and I've failed. But that stops today. You need to be who you are. Not made to feel ... what is it you said, numb? Because of your father and what he does to us. And now, with this *video* on the loose online, it's the end, one way or another.'

The seat-belt sign pinged on and the overhead lockers started to shudder. Ari gripped the armrest. After a few minutes, the turbulence got so severe a drinks trolley came careering down the aisle and crashed into the bulkhead. And then the plane dropped suddenly, and his stomach flipped. The plane bounced up again and dropped. Someone behind them screamed. It levelled out, still shaking like a tin can caught under a train. Ari felt panic flood his body, and with that fear, he remembered how much he wanted to live.

At last the plane rose above the rough air and he relaxed his clenched fists. Connie smiled at him as if she had always known it would be OK.

Chapter 10

Leeds, May 2015

Ari leant against the Books4U shopfront and waited for Mae's shift to finish at six. He watched as a woman in a polyester skirt suit sat on the steps of the office across the street and swapped her heeled court shoes for flats. A teenage boy on a BMX did a wheelie and shouted, 'All right, tranny?' at Ari, who was dressed for the night ahead in a gold lamé vest top and cut-off jean shorts. He removed his pink-hued sunglasses to deliver the kid a withering look.

The boy cycled back for another wheelie, on the pavement this time, and fell off at Ari's feet. As Ari offered him his hand and pulled him up from the floor, he saw all the closeted longing in the boy's eyes and smiled. 'You're good,' he said.

Mae marched out of the bookshop, removing the name tag from her white shirt with one hand and undoing its buttons to reveal a high-necked white vest with the other. She didn't stop to acknowledge Ari. He fell into line and she started talking as quickly as she was walking.

'Straight people! Honestly. There was this couple today, asking if we had anything on relationships. Don't sound patronising, I said to myself. I mustn't be rude or sarcastic. I'm trying to take Trace's constructive criticism on board, Ari. I really am.'

He loved Mae's stories of being reprimanded by her manager. Trace was a stickler for customer service, and Ari found it hilarious that she told Mae she intimidated shoppers. He did an impression of Trace despite never having met her: 'Smile, smile, smile, Mae! You're scaring the children.'

'Right, well, this woman and her boyfriend were testing in every sense. Are we talking *Anna Karenina*, or *Men Are from Mars, Women Are from Venus*? I asked politely. She said the thing was, they were "up for experimenting" but didn't know where to start and thought maybe there was a book that would inspire them more than the World Wide Web. Then she starts saying she thinks she might fancy girls but she doesn't know where to start with that either. I sent her to the LGBTQ section and him to Sex and Psychology, and do you know what they left with? A fucking Jamie Oliver cookbook.'

Ari laughed, but it bothered him that Mae could be so dismissive of people who didn't have their sexuality as figured out as she did. He would normally have let it go, but with half an eye on what he planned on telling her soon, he ventured, 'What makes you angrier, that they didn't know books or didn't know if they were one hundred per cent straight?'

Mae slowed her pace as they turned onto her street and looked at Ari quizzically. 'It was just a funny story.'

They were at the door to her flat. George, the old locksmith, was pulling down the shutters for the night. 'Evening, lovebirds,' he said.

'Evening, George, and again, we're both gay!'

'And a gorgeous gay couple you are, lass.'

'Did George just call you a lez?' Ari stage-whispered.

'Funny,' said Mae, pushing the heavy steel door that opened onto a dark and musty-smelling hallway. They climbed the narrow staircase to her bedsit, and once inside Ari put his moment of irritability down to having skipped lunch.

'I'll have you know Trace awarded me employee of the week today,' Mae told him proudly. She hung her shirt on a hook by the door and headed straight for the fridge.

'No way!' said Ari, taking his favourite spot on the chair next to the open kitchen window, where Mae's herb garden was turning into more of an allotment.

'Yep. I am officially Books4U's most efficient and accurate shelf stacker. Even if I do still need to work on what Trace calls "a lack of bubbliness". So there.'

Mae had no problem smiling around Ari. She couldn't help herself. She took an ice-cold glass from the freezer and opened a beer with a tantalising hiss. She poured it into the frosty glass and Ari sighed.

'Shit. Sorry. Um, I bought some Cokes especially. Let me just ice a glass.'

'It's cool. I'm just messing. Enjoy your beer. Long night ahead. What are the options?'

Mae picked up her phone and perched on the edge of the kitchen table. She began scrolling through her messages.

'OK, Sam wants us to go to Kween, obviously. We've got guest list at Fibre. That new place in the Calls is saying we can have the whole VIP area and invite whoever we want if we stay at least three hours. Oh, and it's disco night at Majestic and the promoter says he'll give us a stack of free drink tickets if we go 'cos he wants to get the gays there.'

'I vote Kween,' said Ari.

'Because Sam's going?'

'Nooooo. Because they let me dance on the podium.'

'Why don't you just get with Sam already? Surely this whole no-sex thing has lasted long enough. And I see the way you look at him. Why keep denying yourself?'

'OK – thought experiment. How would you feel if we did start dating?' said Ari, deflecting. The truth was, he'd made a promise to himself because he figured he'd only hurt someone if he allowed them to get close to him. But he hadn't hurt Mae – not yet, at least – and he was beginning to feel that maybe he *had* changed. Maybe he was ready, and now, with desire for Sam licking its flame against his skin, he wasn't pulling so quickly away.

'I'd be fine about it,' she said defensively. She hopped off the table and began preparing their supper. She took place mats from the cupboard under the sink, along with cutlery and her two plates, and arranged the settings opposite each other, like they were an old married couple. Ari scooted his chair over from by the window to his spot at the table. He could tell she was picturing him and Sam as boyfriends by the way her shoulders were hunched tensely forward, and as she slammed a saucepan of water onto the stove to boil, he could also tell she wasn't fine about it.

She stood over the pot while the pasta cooked, her back to Ari. He looked at his empty white plate and wondered intently how she would cope if he slept with as many people as she did. She would not have the patience to listen to the details of his conquests like he did hers. If he fell in and out of people, navigating the obstacle course of their feelings, veering from mad lust to boredom in a matter of days, Mae would call him reckless and cavalier. She got the ice-cold beer *and* the hot sex. He missed life's extremes.

'It's not fair.'

'What's not?' She spooned ravioli in a butter and sage sauce onto his plate, then served herself before sitting opposite him with a look of such fraternal concern on her face that he relinquished his irritation.

'I guess what I mean is it's so easy for you. I feel like you trust yourself deep, deep down and you know you're always gonna be OK. Like, you walk this tightrope but there's a huge net underneath to catch you if you fall. That's why you can sleep around and treat girls badly.'

'I do not treat girls badly!'

Ari spoke softly when he said, 'You're kind to them, sure. But you still sleep with them then basically tell them you don't want a relationship and that's the end of it.'

'It's called honesty,' Mae snapped. She suddenly wasn't hungry. She moved the pasta around on her plate then put her fork down.

'OK, well. What should I do, Mae? I like Sam. A lot. He's golden. He's sunshine. He just glides through life in a way I could never . . . And I like how he's big, you know, in every sense. I'd like to know how it feels to have him hold me. And that's kinda scary. Because what if I fuck it up, then lose him as a friend? And who knows maybe I lose you too.'

Mae rocked back in her chair, arms behind her head. She looked deep in thought. After a moment, she brought the front legs of the chair back to the ground with a thump and, as if she'd cracked it, said confidently, 'You should go for it. Would I be jealous if you started going to the cinema with Sam and not inviting me? Yes! Is that your problem? No. But let *me* be your safety net.'

Satisfied with her speech, she wolfed ravioli into her mouth and pushed the plate away. She was still chewing when she said, 'Now I know you're rich and sober, but free drinks mean a lot to a poor lush like me. So we're going to Majestic. And then we'll find Sam.'

Ari wasn't embarrassed by his trust fund or the fact that the divorce was set to make his mother a millionaire, but Mae – in cahoots with Alice – did enjoy mocking him for it. The joking about silver spoons and 'Her Majesty' only occasionally crossed a line, because really, everyone was grateful for Ari's generosity. He and Connie paid Alice's mortgage each month, and Ari always offered to pick up the bill or finance a taxi home when he was with Mae. She wasn't too proud to take his handouts when she needed them.

'And who are we avoiding tonight?' he asked, playfully provocative.

'No one! Other than the usual. Oh, and do you remember Ace? The new door bitch at Fibre. She's been messaging me all week since we hooked up.'

'She was cool, though. I thought you really liked her?'

'I did. I do. But she's not exactly life partner material, is she? So, like, what's the point?'

'You're twenty-two is the point. But with you and girls, like you said, it's "the one" or "everyone". Is there not a middle ground?'

'Between rampant monogamy and raging promiscuity, you mean? Who wants to be in the middle ground, Ari? *Boring.*'

'You know what's more boring? Being so black and white about everything you miss out on the colour.'

He'd felt his frustration buzzing around him like a persistent wasp since he'd met her from work. He'd been batting it away, but perhaps despite Mae's earnest promise its sting was inevitable. Mae tried to laugh, and Ari could tell she was hurt.

'Sorry,' he said.

'You're the one missing out by abstaining from *everything*, living like you're some gay nun on the run. I'm living my life in full colour, thank you very much. I'm going to get changed. Would you wash up?'

Bickering wasn't something they'd ever done before, and Ari felt strange and self-conscious about their fight as he cleared things away. By the time Mae had put on black denim shorts and DMs, keeping the same white vest she'd worn under her work shirt, only now accessorised with three silver chains of various lengths and thicknesses, he wished he could hold down the delete button and watch their last lines disappear.

Instead, he looked up from where he now sat on the floor by her bed and wolf-whistled.

'Hot masc twink nineties baby butch, yass.'

Mae looked approvingly at his efforts to tidy and held out her hand to pull him up.

'Let's do this,' she said, and they headed out into the handsome half-light, walking arm in arm to the gay village, an anchor and a shipwreck.

Chapter 11

September 2006

On Ari's first day as an eight-grader at Park Avenue High, he'd taken a place at a desk next to Lilly Scott. She seemed cool, introverted and not like the other girls, who were all fashion brats with Vivienne Westwood handbags. Lilly had a blue streak in her hair and bit a pencil so hard that it snapped.

Shortly after registration, an alarm wailed through the hallways.

'OK, kids,' said the homeroom teacher calmly, 'just do what I say and please stay quiet. This alarm means there's a threat of violence in the building. Boys, I need you to move the desks up here to barricade the door. The rest of you hide behind your chair like this.'

Ari forgot that 'boys' meant him, so he knelt on the floor next to Lilly and flipped his chair so it became a shield. He wasn't worried. The thought that someone might want to kill him was nothing new.

'I'm Ari,' he whispered.

'I'm scared,' Lilly said, turning to him with a look of sheer panic on her face. He realised she wasn't joking.

'OK, chill,' he said. 'It's way more likely to be a kid slitting their wrists than a shooter, don't you think?' Then he felt something warm and wet pool around his ankles.

That was the end of Lilly Scott, socially speaking. You can't piss yourself on your first day of high school and survive it. Especially not when it was a false alarm. Ari quickly realised that being friends with this nervous, interesting girl would be the end of him too, so he kept his distance as day after day she was annihilated by bullies and became even more withdrawn.

Towards the end of the school year, when Lilly's blue streak had faded back to blonde and Ari had been assimilated into a pack of mean girls who treated him like a gender queer pet they could dress up and play with, he found himself alone with Lilly in detention for persistent lateness.

They sat next to each other, looking at the blackboard at the front of the class on which was written their detention assignment: Write two pages about the importance of timekeeping.

'I'm sorry my friends are so unkind,' Ari said quietly.

'Those girls you hang out with? They're not your friends. They don't even like you, you know,' whispered Lilly. 'Not really.'

'I know,' said Ari. He leant over and drew a smiley face in the top left corner of Lilly's notebook. 'But I don't mind. They help me survive here, and that's something.'

The teacher at the front of the classroom hissed, 'Shh! No talking.'

Lilly took a much-chewed pencil from her bag and ripped a page out of Ari's notebook. On it she wrote, We could be secret friends?

Ari nodded, then mouthed, 'OK.'

He wrote two pages on the ephemeral nature of time in thirty minutes flat. He handed the paper to his teacher with a flourish and left the detention room. Lilly remained there, her head now slumped on the desk, staring vacantly into space. When Ari waved, she didn't respond.

Ari knew how it felt to disappear deeper and deeper into yourself for protection as Lilly had done. But as long as he was popular, school was a breeze compared to life at home. His status as a friend to everyone, as a pretty boy the girls carried with them like an accessory, kept him safe. He wasn't unkind to Lilly, but he watched as people he called his friends were, and that – he realised now – was worse. It was weak. He would smile at her in the hallway, try to talk to her in the lunch line. But she acted like he wasn't there.

Once he slipped a note into her locker. *Hey, secret friend, want to go to a bookshop after school?* She never answered.

Mae would say all the right things if she knew about the affair. Or she'd try to. But it would change the very foundations of who she thought he was. And that would change everything. Ari had to tread carefully. Because there was something else, something more urgent he had to tell her first.

Chapter 12

Leeds University, May 2015

By the time Ari had decided that he would date Sam, Sam had started going out with a second-year rugby player. He resigned himself to this fact with a blankness Mae mistook for stoicism. She was his champagne and his cocaine now. She complimented him, held him, called him babe. What more did he need?

They were the unofficial king and queen of the scene, always the right side of a velvet rope. Doors opened for them. They didn't queue. Ari felt greater than the sum of his parts with Mae by his side. As they walked through the city streets together, they tallied the admiring looks they got from strangers.

After a midweek night out at Kween when it was *almost* warm enough for the first time since term began to not need a jacket, Ari gave Mae a piggyback for the short walk back to hers. Once inside, she sat on a chair and he knelt before her to unlace her boots. She placed her hands on the top of his head. 'That girl I was kissing, Sindy, she told me she was bisexual.'

'It seemed like you two really hit it off. Now you're telling me that's why we had to make such a sudden exit? The DJ hadn't even played my song yet!'

'Freya is the problem. She wasn't clear, you know. I thought she liked girls. I thought she liked me.'

'Mae, you were kids. You were still figuring it all out. It's different now. Sindy liked you or she wouldn't have been eating your face off.'

'That's my point. By our age you should know for sure if you like red wine or white wine best. It's a cop-out to say you like rosé. I don't want to drink bisexual wine. It tastes of penis.'

Here we go again, thought Ari.

'Everything's spinning.' Mae pulled off her socks with such force she almost fell from the chair. He helped her out of her clothes and onto her futon. He poured a big glass of water and left two aspirins on the stack of books next to her.

Ari took his time getting ready for bed. He thought about how Mae coveted boys' haircuts, their strong arms, flat chests. But she'd never be attracted to someone of the opposite sex. Kinsey would have had her holding up the gayest end of his scale, and the fact that Ari was somewhere closer to the middle felt like it was creating a distance between them.

'How wasted are you? Are we talking a nine? Or a seven?'

Mae took a big gulp of water and downed the painkillers. She lay down and closed her eyes,

'Um ... it's a six, I think. Yeah. Six. Why?'

'Because,' Ari said slowly, drawing out each syllable before launching into his next sentence in a mad rush of words, 'because I'm actually not gay, I'm pansexual, and I think you should know and I'd like you to stop being so obtuse about people who aren't one hundred per cent one way because it hurts my feelings.'

He waited tensely for her response. Mae inhaled, then exhaled a deep rumble of a snore.

The next morning, Mae was freshly washed and smelt performatively masculine thanks to the combination of Active Sports shower gel and Pure Energy antiperspirant. By the time Ari woke up, she was dressed in jeans and a white shirt, which she appeared to have ironed, and was sitting at the table reading, a highlighter pen poised in her hand. Sunlight streamed restoratively through the open window, and he caught wafts of mint and basil from the pots on the sill. She had been out to buy croissants and a bunch of peonies, and when she saw that he was awake, she poured him a cup of coffee.

'You really didn't hear anything I said to you just before bed?' asked Ari sleepily.

'Oh God, sorry, I literally conked as soon as my head hit the pillow. Was it important?'

'Yes, actually,' Ari said, feeling determined to have this conversation and deal with the consequences. 'I wanted to talk to you about something,' he said nervously, sitting up in bed. He watched Mae sense the change in atmosphere and close her book. She walked over to sit on the edge of the bed next to him and said as nonchalantly as she could muster, 'OK . . .'

'Last night. You seemed really pissed that Sindy was bi.'

'Was I? Oh. I can't really remember, but I didn't fancy her anyway.'

'I'm starting to find some of the things you say and don't mean to, or don't remember ... I'm starting to not be able to let them go any more.'

'Right,' said Mae dismissively, glancing at the clock above the bed. Sam would be arriving to study with them any moment.

'So you know I've never said I'm gay.'

'Haha. You're not about to tell me you're straight, are you? Can you imagine!'

'Not exactly. But I am pansexual.'

Mae seemed to swallow that fact as bluntly as he'd delivered it. She coughed and adjusted the way she was sitting so she was directly facing him.

'I'm not joking,' said Ari.

'Wow.'

'It's no big deal. It shouldn't be a big deal, I mean. I like people, simple as that.'

'You've had sex with women.' Mae said it like a statement, but Ari took it as a question.

'A few.'

'Who?'

'No one you know, obviously. Girls back in New York. Why does it matter?'

'Girls. Hmm.' Mae pulled a pillow to her chest and shuffled towards the edge of the futon.

'Oh seriously? You're edging away from me now?'

'It's just weird, Ari. I'm a girl. You shag girls. It changes things.'

'I don't "shag" anyone right now. I cannot believe you're being this basic about it.'

'So that time you basically flashed me, when we'd only known each a few months . . . '

'C'mon, that was nothing to do with any of this. I just wanted you to see me.'

'But rather than tell me something true that night, when we were supposed to still be getting to know each other, you thought it a better idea to get naked. Nice, Ari. Thanks for that.'

'I knew you wouldn't be able to cope knowing that being queer is different for me.' He was exhausted and confused suddenly.

The doorbell rang. Mae threw the pillow at him and ran to the intercom.

'Come on up,' she said, sounding as fake jolly as her mother often did.

A minute later, Sam poked his head cautiously around the door. 'Um, I'm here for study club,' he said, pretending to be nervous, then barged right on in wielding two brown paper bags containing a fast-food breakfast.

'Paul won't let me eat McDonald's, says it's poison. But I'm like "There's only room for one fittie in this relationship and that's you, babe. Leave me to my McMuffins."' Sam leant in to kiss Mae on each cheek.

'Having a nice lie-in there, Ari? Bit of me time? All right for some.'

Ari sank under the sheets with embarrassment. His aborted conversation with Mae hung in the air.

'I actually got some croissants, if you want one instead, or as well?' Mae said perkily. Ari wondered if she was in fact a soccer mom trapped in the body of a fuck boi.

'Oh lovely, lovely, lovely, how nice, what fun,' he said at an alarming pitch. He threw the sheets off and stood up theatrically. 'I'm going to shower. To be continued,' he added, looking pointedly at Mae.

As Ari flounced into the bathroom in his underwear, Sam took a seat at the table and began unwrapping his greasy breakfast on top of Mae's pristine notebook.

'What's got into *her* this morning?' he asked, biting down on a hash brown.

Mae sat down opposite him and whispered, 'Did you know Ari was pansexual?'

Sam finished his mouthful, then dabbed his lips with a paper napkin. The question didn't seem to faze him. 'No, I did not, but it doesn't surprise me. I've seen the way he looks at girls like he wants to devour them. Not unlike certain other—'

'Oh my God, gross!' said Mae loudly, then fell back into a whisper. 'He does not look at girls. I would have noticed,' she hissed.

'You two are so close you can't see the full picture. Zoom out, babe. Anyway, so what? I used to think he looked at me like that too, but nope. Miss Ari is all about the pre-game, as Paul would say, not the match.'

Ari emerged from the bathroom dressed in an oversized tie-dye T-shirt. He'd pulled his hair into bunches for a reason not even he was sure of.

'I'd better get my books out,' he said. 'Study club waits for no man.'

What was left of the morning slipped quietly into the afternoon. Sam's intrusion into their intimacy had turned the tension down. Ari flipped the pages of *Structural Poetics* but was really running scripts in his head, deciding on the perfect combination of words to continue the conversation with Mae as soon as Sam left.

By early afternoon, he was in a frivolous mood that masked his anxiety. Mae was on the verge of snapping at him, he could tell. He'd taken a dance break and was voguing while holding a cold egg McMuffin, which fell on the floor when he mimed opening a mirror compact.

Sam played along, clicking his fingers in appreciation. 'Category is . . . femme queen finals revision realness!'

'Please tell me you're not going to eat that,' said Mae.

Ari took a bite, enjoying her disapproval.

After that, they worked on their separate assignments. Mae was finishing an essay on Judith Butler; Ari moved on to reading *Gender Trouble* so that he could start that same essay. Sam was preoccupied with a doodle that had spread across the entire A4 page of his notebook and included cartoon versions of Mae and Ari and their names written in a perfectly rendered type he'd designed himself. Sam studied English because it was the closest thing to art his banker parents would approve of. But really, he wanted to be a graphic designer, and all this unpicking of texts was a frustrating distraction from the career he knew lay ahead. He just needed to pass his degree. He didn't care about his marks, unlike his exhaustingly intellectual friends.

They had moved to the floor, sitting with their lower backs flush against the edge of Mae's mattress. Sam was in the middle. He wore his hair in tight cornrows normally, but since reading a biography of Basquiat, he had styled his hair into three tall peaks. If Ari had met him in New York, he would have thrown himself at him. He was enjoying the way Sam's leg accidentally touched his. But Sam was boyfriend material and that was the problem.

After about three hours, Mae was bored and Ari knew it. She washed up everything, threw the fast-food wrappers in the bin, dried her hands and sighed loudly. Without Mae sitting the other side of him, Sam had shifted subtly closer, and Ari jumped up, thinking of rugby-playing Paul and the fact that he had vowed never, ever to touch another person's man again.

'I'm shattered,' Mae said, yawning.

'I should go,' Sam said, looking between Mae and Ari like a detective in a TV show suddenly figuring it all out. 'I'll leave you to it.'

'Oh, you know us gal pals, Sam. We'll probably just braid each other's hair and exchange mood rings. We will certainly not be having a conversation about why Mae cannot fathom the nuances of sexuality despite having just written a two-thousand-word essay on the subject.'

'Okaaaay,' said Sam, grabbing his things and walking backwards towards the door. 'See ya then.' He gave an awkward wave and left.

Mae began pacing from the kitchen sink to the bathroom and back again. 'Thanks for making me look like a total bigot in front of Sam. *That* is exactly the problem, Ari. I don't care if you're gay, or bi or poly or pan or whatever. I hate labels. And it's 2015, for God's sake. Of course I understand that not everyone fancies just one gender. I'm not my mother!'

Ari had only seen Mae react so strongly when she was

expressing an opinion about something outside of herself. He was shocked by her passion.

'Sorry, since when did you not like labels? You live for them! Just look at your spice rack – Mae, you literally have a label maker. And what difference does it make really? Why do you *care* so much about my sexuality?'

She stopped walking and sat in the middle of the room, hugging her knees to her chest. Ari crawled back into bed and pulled the stupid scrunchies out of his hair, letting it fall to his shoulders. He felt as if he couldn't move from his spot even if he wanted to. The conversation had spiralled into its worst-case scenario.

Mae said, 'I *care* that you are the best friend I've ever had, and the past few terms have been so good.' She had tears in her eyes. 'But you've lied to me about something intrinsic to you. I know there's all this other stuff you're not telling me, but surely "Hey, when I do have sex, I do it with girls too" is an easier thing to be honest about than whatever it is you're hiding that happened in New York.'

'I'm not *hiding* anything,' said Ari, anger prickling his skin. Mae scoffed.

Ari ignored it. 'I guess I was right to be worried about how you might react when you found out anything about who I was before you.'

'This is a lot to deal with right now,' said Mae, standing up and brushing invisible dust from her trousers.

'You made the assumption that I was gay. Yes, I never told you otherwise, but you never asked.'

Mae placed her hand on the kitchen counter to steady herself. It was true Ari's celibacy had selfishly suited her.

'It's a mess,' was all she could muster.

Ari knew he'd used Mae as a shield from his sexuality and all the past mistakes that were a result of it. But facing this truth intensified his self-loathing. He took it out on his friend instead.

'A mess! Oh, sure. This, the truth about me, it doesn't fit into your neat little world, where everything is planned out: "Tonight I will go out and have fun. On Tuesday I will eat tofu for dinner. My best friend is my rock, he's there for *me*, he's always A-OK. He's gay just like me." I'm not your rom-com GBF, Mae, here with a shoulder to cry on and a cute wisecrack. I thought you *knew* me, but you just want to stick one of your stupid labels on me too.'

'How can you expect me to know you when you don't tell me anything real? You involve me in your life, your family, but there's this whole side of you that you've kept a secret and—'

He cut her off. 'Because you liked it that way. Don't ask, don't tell. It worked for both of us – you can't pretend it didn't.'

Mae stood over the bed, looking down at Ari, who hadn't moved an inch. His heart beat heavily in his chest and a hot rage swirled with the incoherent singing of a drunk man on the street outside. They hadn't left the bedsit all day and he felt that the walls were closing in.

'I'll call Mom, she can probably be here to get me in an hour,' he said, reading Mae's mind and feeling for the first time ever that she didn't want him there.

'Stay,' she said, unplugging her phone from where it was charging on the floor. She rapidly fired off messages that received the instant beeps of replies. 'I've plenty of places I can go.'

She quickly gathered some clothes together, then disappeared into the bathroom to change in private.

'You don't have to hide,' Ari shouted after her. 'I'm not looking at you like that, Mae, Jesus!'

'No, Ari, *you* don't have to hide.' She reappeared in her work clothes so she was ready for her shift in the morning, and threw the door keys onto his lap. 'Leave them with George when you go.'

She left without saying goodbye. Ari felt stupid, sitting in Mae's bed like a puppet without its master. He buried his head in her pillow and inhaled her absence.

Chapter 13

It had been a week since Mae had spoken to Ari – long enough to have flipped her Sapphic Icons wall calendar from May's Radclyffe Hall to a more 'summery' Anne Lister. When she got home from work on Saturday evening, the white nylon shirt clung clammy to her chest. She couldn't wait to take a shower and wash away the sticky feeling of regret that had followed her all day.

The flat was stuffy; she opened the window, noticing with a wince the sweat patches at her armpits. She poured herself a glass of water from the tap and sat at the kitchen table, ready to give form to the words that had been swimming around her head as she stacked shelves and tried to smile at customers. It was then that she noticed a postcard had been pushed under the door to her flat. On the front was a Hokusai illustration of a wave about to break.

M. Do you see me? Am v convinced by your ability to
ignore my existence even when I'm literally staring right
at you across an exam hall. I could say sorry for not
telling you sooner, for not being the person you wanted me
to be. You fitted your idea of me so neatly into the spaces

in yourself. I get it, it was never about my sexuality, it was about you and how you see the world. You're the kindest, most gentle person, but when you're not being that Mae, you can be so closed-minded. You talk about your perfect future but you can't just teleport yourself there from here; it's a journey with twists and turns and you've got to give in to the getting there, allow the terrain to change you like I have. Find me when you're ready. And good luck with finals. Ax

Oh, that is rich, thought Mae, ripping the postcard in half and throwing it across the room. How dare he lecture her, turn this around so she was the one in the wrong. Ari had lied to her, he'd made her think he was gay when he wasn't, and God knows what had happened in New York, but it was something so bad that he had to cross the Atlantic to run away. He'd ghosted all his old friends. Hadn't been in touch with them once and wasn't bothered. And *she* was the obtuse one. What a joke.

She released her fingers from their tight fists and fetched her phone from her rucksack. Opening a new message, she typed: *Closed-minded?! That's the most hurtful thing you've ever said to me. Now I feel shit about myself AND you. Great. We're both assholes. We probably need some time apart. M*

Her thumb hovered over the send button, but she caught sight of her watch and pressed save instead. She only had an hour to freshen up and pack for a weekend at home. It was her mother's birthday, and although her dad had tried to plan a spectacular surprise party, Janet had soon found out and taken over operational duties, much to Michael's chagrin. Ari had been due to attend; it would have been the first time he'd met her parents or seen the shudderingly average house on the dullest street in Snoresville, Cheshire, where she'd grown up. It was probably for the best he wouldn't be coming now, she thought.

Thanks to her terrifying efficiency, she arrived at the station with time to buy a coffee. As the train sped south, she watched the landscape blur past and thought more about what she stood to lose if she sent that message. By the time she'd finished her black Americano, she felt a new mood wash over her with the caffeine high. Her knee jiggled uncontrollably as she wrote – but didn't send – a different message: *It's only been a week and I'm missing you! Wish Connie was driving us to the cottage right now, instead I'm going home alone wondering who I'll be without you. You're right – I care about your sexuality because I thought that was at least a part of you I understood, when so much else is a mystery. Mx*

Mae's dad drove a big family saloon, which struck her as ridiculous given the size of their family. As she walked into the car park, still wondering which, if either, of the messages to send to Ari, he toot-tooted the horn three times and waved enthusiastically through the open window. Mae slumped into the passenger seat.

'So what happened with Ari? Tell your old dad. Why is the guest of honour not coming after all the fanfare?'

His kindness made her uncomfortable. She turned on the radio, flicked fast through the pre-set channels and turned it off again.

'We argued, that's all. And I feel angry with him.'

'Because . . .'

'Because he didn't tell me something really important. And then he made it seem like it was my fault.'

'When was this?'

'Like, a week ago.'

'Oh Mae, that's no time at all. Seems that you both need some time to take the heat off. Then you must talk to each other. It's the secret of every good relationship. Call him in a few days, but if he's as decent a chap as your mother seems to think he is, he'll call you first.'

When they pulled into the driveway, Michael manoeuvred himself over the gearstick to give her one of his hugs. There was no escape. But once she relaxed into his soapy smell, she remembered she didn't hate it.

'Thanks, Pa,' she said, and her voice cracked.

The following evening, once the house had been cleaned to within an inch of its life and the champagne glasses were all standing to attention on the kitchen counter, Janet said, 'Darling, you're gloomier than usual.'

Mae was sitting on the sofa with a plate of Swiss rolls on her lap and her head in her hands.

'What's wrong? Is it girl trouble?' Janet plumped a cushion and sat down next to her. 'I'm a man's woman myself, as you know, can wrangle them like wild horses, but I've read enough books to know it can get very intense between two women.'

Mae cringed and spoke through gritted teeth. 'I appreciate it. But I'm fine. There is nothing for you to psychoanalyse on my behalf. Thank you, though.'

'How is that darling boyfriend? Devastated he couldn't come to the party. Desperate to meet him. Such a tragedy for the women of the world that a man so *charming* isn't that way inclined.'

'Ari isn't *inclined* any particular way, Mum, and I never said he was. You just assume because we're friends that he's gay.'

'Oh,' Janet replied, nodding sagely. 'He's one of these bisexuals then, is he? How *interesting*.'

At that moment, Michael came into the living room with the Henry and began vacuuming the carpet. 'Lift your feet up, ladies,' he ordered as he shunted the hoover across the floor.

'Not exactly,' said Mae. 'He's attracted to people, not genders. Anyway, it doesn't matter. We had a fight.'

'Say again?'

'A fight. We had a fight,' she shouted over the loud whirring.

Michael pulled the plug from the mains. In the abrupt silence, Janet curled her legs under her on the couch, making her look like a tiny bird in its nest.

'It was a tiff, nothing more, I'm sure. You two are young and passionate and you'll figure it out. I've every faith. You haven't had a friend like him since Freya.'

Michael quietly backed out of the room at the mention of Freya's name. Mae could have done without the reminder. She'd been trying hard not to conflate the loss of her first crush with the fact that she hadn't spoken to Ari for a week and had no idea when she would again. Of course, her mother could always be trusted to say the wrong thing at the wrong time. She took the plate into the kitchen, where her dad was pouring himself a large glass of wine.

'Don't tell your mother,' he said, and took a gulp. 'Can I interest you in a glass, kiddo?' He looked at her hopefully. He was desperate to connect, but Mae didn't have it in her.

Guests started arriving then, the women smelling of perfume and the cheeky gin they'd drunk while getting ready. Their husbands, wearing their 'fun' shirts, thrust bottles of wine into Mae's arms while asking how she was getting on at university and if she was seeing anyone. She expertly batted away small talk, without – she hoped – appearing rude and directed the squawking crowd that loitered in the hallway like it was the toilet queue at Kween into the living room. Janet was already shimmying to the Buena Vista Social Club CD Michael had insisted on as warm-up music.

Mae settled into a corner by the open French doors, from where she could enjoy the breeze and be just out of the way enough to show her face without being in the firing line of her parents' friends. She undid the top button of her own fun shirt – a preppy yellow chambray that Janet had deemed 'unusual' – and tried to think her way out of what had happened with Ari. If she just forgave him, everything would go back to normal. But did that make her a pushover?

Ari thought of her as robust, as someone who spoke her mind. Maybe if she sent that needy, pleading, soppy message, he'd be disappointed in her. She knocked back the last of her red wine and squeezed past the couples who were dancing in that jerky, finger-clicking way people over fifty danced, to top up her glass in the kitchen. Her mother was holding court but excused herself from the conversation to follow her.

'Are you having a good birthday, Mum?' Mae threw some empty beer cans in the bin before opening a bottle of Malbec.

'Sandra said she's not had this much fun since Alan's retirement bash, which ended up with car keys in a bowl, so Lord knows what *she* expects.'

'That doesn't answer my question. Are you having a good time?'

'You know me. I'm happy if everyone else is happy.'

'So you're saying that because I've had an argument with my best friend and I'm justifiably upset, you can't enjoy yourself? I'm spoiling your party.'

'That's not it at all, Mae.'

Mae rolled her eyes and muttered, 'So selfish,' but decided not to push it as she normally would have done. It was her mother's birthday, after all.

Janet was whisked away by an effusive friend and Mae walked out into the hallway to check if car keys had been put in a bowl. Finding out that Ari fancied girls was one thing; finding out her parents were swingers would be quite another.

The doorbell rang and she opened it expecting more late arrivals. It was nine p.m. and their small house was already overflowing with people. Her mother certainly was popular. She opened the door and saw a giant bunch of white roses on two skinny legs. He lowered the bouquet. They said each other's name at the same time, and it sounded ridiculously like 'marry'.

And then he said, 'Hello, handsome.'

'What are you doing here?'

'I decided I couldn't possibly miss the party of the century.' He pressed his cold cheek against hers and said softly, 'And I missed you.'

'Who is it, darling? Do get them a drink tout suite.' Janet

appeared, her skin now gleaming like a glazed doughnut from dancing.

'Happy birthday,' said Ari, and handed over the flowers, looking ready to impress.

'Oh my word, what a wonderful surprise! You must be Ari – I'm so happy you came. Mae has been an absolute Eeyore without you. Now you two kiss and make up or do whatever it is you people do and then come back down. Ari, my daughter tells me you are *the most* fantastic dancer.'

Ari didn't have a chance to respond as Mae dragged him upstairs to her childhood bedroom. She shut the door and wedged a chair under the handle so no one could get in, just as she'd done whenever Freya used to sleep over, then turned on a lava lamp so the embarrassingly childlike decor would be less visible and pushed him onto the single bed. She sat on the pink inflatable armchair opposite and stared at him in silence.

When it looked like he was starting to notice that she still had glow-in-the-dark stars stuck to her ceiling, she said, 'You're right. I need to be the person I think I'll be in the future . . . I need to be her now. I only really like myself when I'm with you.'

Ari slipped off his velvet jacket. He was wearing a V-neck tank top and had a mauve feather boa tossed around his neck.

'Is this OK?' He looked down at himself. 'I wasn't sure what the dress code was, but I figured "semi fabulous" was acceptable.'

'You look good,' said Mae, then after a beat she added, 'Thanks for coming.'

'I'm sorry for what I said. It was silly to write you. We should be able to talk, right? This is us!'

'Listen, I've been trying to figure it out. And here goes. My fear ... my biggest fear is that if you were intimate with a woman, you'd have something together we never could. It makes me irrationally jealous.'

'What if I fell in love with a guy? How would that be any different?'

'Well, I guess I'd be jealous about that too. But that's something I can't give you.'

'Mae, you have to let me spread my wings at some point, like I do you. OK? You've not met anyone you're really into and maybe that makes it easier for me. But I don't need you to stay distanced from people because you're worried it'll hurt me if you get too close. I want you to find that connection. What *we* have is different and it's special, and whoever either of us falls for in life, we won't ever have with them what you and I have with each other.'

Mae was silent, taking it all in. She was grateful for her wise friend's ability to cut through the white noise in her head and speak in a language she understood.

'We should go back down. I feel really bad that I've been a dick to my mum. I tend to take things out on her and I suppose it's not always fair.'

'Aha,' said Ari, removing the barricade from the door. 'Progress.'

In the kitchen, a flock of middle-aged women flapped around Ari with coos and aahs. They all wanted to touch his hair, which he'd pulled into a half ponytail, and they all wanted to play with his feather boa. He lassoed Janet with it and the ladies screamed with laughter. Mae watched. She felt proud that Ari could bring so much joy when he carried such a shadow.

When she finally got to stand next to him, Ari said, 'I really did miss you,' and everyone around them seemed to disappear. Mae shuffled from one foot to the other and looked away to hide the fact that she was grinning.

She looked at him finally and said, 'Come here, then, you screaming heterosexual.'

'I'm not *not* gay,' he said, slotting into her open arms for a hug.

She stroked his head maternally and whispered, 'I know. I like you for who you are. I even like the bits I don't understand or know about yet.'

When the time felt right, they pulled away from each other.

'I've spent a lot of time on my own these past few days,' said Ari. 'Honestly, forty-eight hours felt like weeks! I've realised that (a), I am desperate to go out and *dance* again, so Janet best get ready because this party is about to pop *offf*. And (b), I want to tell you what happened in New York. I don't need your help to forget it. I need your help to face it, so that I can move on.'

'You don't have to,' said Mae, and she meant it. She was accustomed to Ari's secrets now, and not knowing about his past was easier, emotionally, than having to engage with it. She clung to the version of him she'd constructed like a raft in a storm. She checked herself, shook her head. 'No, sorry, of course. You should tell me if you're ready. I need to stop being your enabler. I'm sorry, Ari.'

Mae's dad sidled in between them. 'The great Ari Hines, I presume?'

Ari curtseyed. 'This is she,' he giggled.

Michael laughed and shook his hand. 'Your presence has been requested in the living room. My wife wants to "do" Diana Ross with you. I'm just looking for the CD.'

'But of course. It would be an honour,' said Ari.

Some hours later, once Mae had sent her parents to bed and cleaned the entire house, with Ari's well-meaning if somewhat unskilled help, they sat at the kitchen table where she had eaten breakfast before school every day. They were exhausted. Mae had taken a shower and was ready for bed.

'You're so lucky,' said Ari, looking around the room, which hadn't changed since they moved in in the 1990s. 'You must have had such a nice life growing up.'

'I guess. But Connie told me about all the designer clothes she used to buy you.'

'It's not the same. Mae. Yes, we were rich, we had a fancy apartment and I had a closet full of Gucci and Chanel. But . . . ' he put his head in his hands, 'I never felt safe.'

Mae, sensing where this was going, pulled her chair closer to him. Her hair was brushed into a side parting, and in her pyjamas she looked so innocent, Ari felt he was about to tell her Santa didn't exist.

'My dad was abusive. He hit Mom sometimes, for as long as I could remember.' It was the first time he'd used that word, 'abusive', and as soon as he said it, he worried that he didn't have the right. Maybe it wasn't as bad as he remembered. And it was such a strong term, when the truth was that he and his mother *had* wound Randolph up. If he shouted or lashed out, it was never for nothing. Ari shook his head – the self-doubt and insecurity was his dad's voice, with all this distance between them, asserting his control.

'Did he hit you?' Mae asked quietly.

'No. Not exactly, but it came close. He didn't need to, because I knew what went on behind their bedroom door. I heard the noises and saw the bruises. He put me down a lot, called me names. He frightened me.'

'Ari, I'm so sorry. That must have been awful.'

'It made me do some fucked-up things to cope, put it that way. I've told you I drank a lot and did drugs. Coke mainly. The worst. But it helped me forget about home and forget myself too. Then, when I got to NYU, I got in with this crowd who were so much better people than I was. This sweet boy called Elliot fell in love with me, and I think I was an asshole to him. I think I broke his heart. I tried to quit partying, and Elliot and his friends helped, because that wasn't their jam, but it wasn't enough. I still had this wild drive to self-destruct. I don't know ... to hurt myself maybe. So when my sixty-year-old creative writing professor came on to me, I didn't say no. Even though I was repulsed by him. And before I knew it, it was a full-blown affair. He was married, and to a woman, no less. And he had kids ... One of them was in my class at high school. Lilly. That's a whole other story ... '

Mae had listened without expressing any opinion of her own for what felt like the first time in their friendship. Ari scanned her face for judgement.

'Anyway, someone eventually recognised us and caught us kissing and, ya know, fooling around – stupidly, on the street. They filmed it. And then they emailed it to the faculty list, as well as the entire student body and their registered guardians.'

'Oh my God,' said Mae. She hadn't expected all the answers she'd spent the past year searching for to come tumbling out of Ari at her kitchen table. It was almost too much to bear. She covered her face with her hands.

'When Mom found out, she got us straight on a flight out of the city, because once my father saw the video ... Well, he would have taken it out on Mom, and it would have been bad, Mae. Real bad.'

He exhaled a tidal wave of relief, then laughed and wiped latent tears from his eyes. 'I honestly don't know why I didn't tell you all that sooner.'

'I wonder ... maybe if it was a kind of Stockholm syndrome,' said Mae tentatively. She was so aware of blurting out something stupid in her nervousness. She gave him space to speak, and when he didn't, she continued, 'You were in love with your captor. And your captor was your secret. I don't think you were ready to escape.' Ari had to admit, the secrets had kept him company and provided a messed-up kind of comfort. But he was grateful now to be freed of it.

He took Mae's hand and said, 'So Mom and I disappeared. No one knew we'd come to England, though Dad worked it out soon enough. I was kind of dating Elliot, for a while, even though I didn't want to be, and if I think about it, I feel terrible for ghosting him. That's why I blew it with Sam. And why he thinks I'm not into him. I was so ashamed of those relationships. Elliot, the professor, they were both so wrong and twisted. But you know ... Sam is the first guy, ever, really, who gets me, even though he doesn't know any of this. I feel like he sees it, and it's OK. Anyway. I've no idea what mess I left behind. In all the drama of leaving, I lost my phone. I thought if I didn't tell you about it, my past would disappear too. But it hasn't, it's growing like weeds through the cracks.'

Chapter 14

They both passed their English degree with first-class honours. Ari's was a higher mark, but he didn't tell Mae that. Sam scored an internship with a digital design start-up in Bristol and moved there as soon as he finished his last exam; he didn't wait around for results.

At his leaving party, held in a pub in Headingley, he cornered Ari. 'Something's going on with you two, something's changed, and I know I'll never get it, but whatever it is, you seem lighter and Mae seems less angsty and I'm happy for you both.'

Ari shuffled and stared at the floor. He had decided not to tell Sam or anyone else what he'd shared with Mae. It all felt too soon and too precious and he couldn't face it spreading like wildfire among their year group and leading to all sorts of probing questions and concern.

Sam reached over and gently lifted Ari's head with his hand. He brushed a strand of long hair off his face and looked him confidently in the eye.

'If you ever want to ... Me and Paul aren't cut out for long distance, so I'll be footloose and fancy free ... if you ever want to visit. Or even, like, call me for a chat. You know where I am.'

Ari wanted to do both those things. He felt Sam's strong, tender hand on his face and pleasure shivered under his skin.

Suddenly Mae bounded up behind them with a pint in one hand and a can of Red Bull in the other. She thrust the can towards Ari and drunkenly leaned into him.

'We're going to miss you, Sam, aren't we, Ari?'

Ari smiled. Overwhelmed with what he felt but couldn't say, he turned and walked towards the door of the pub.

'I better go after him,' Mae said.

'I know,' replied Sam tersely, before disappearing into the throng of his friends.

That night, Mae went home to the cottage with Ari. She sat quietly in the back of the car as Connie drove them there. Ari took the front seat and bristled with the sense that he'd just ruined his last chance to tell Sam that he liked him. Mae reached forward and squeezed his shoulder. Ari relaxed. Mae's intervention, though typically obtuse, had saved him from having a difficult conversation. Sam, he figured, could wait.

While Ari was in the shower that night, Mae sat in the back garden with Connie, watching her extinguish cigarette after cigarette in an empty plant pot.

'Ari told me about what happened in New York,' she said carefully, unsure how his mother might respond.

'Oh, I thought he might have. He's been less mopey recently. Well, that's good. About time, I say!'

'I'm so sorry that you—'

'Don't, Mae,' snapped Connie, sharply inhaling smoke. She breathed out and added, after a beat, 'Please.'

Chastised, Mae stood up from the wall where she was sitting next to Connie. She looked up at the moon and the bright blanket of stars and felt again the weight of a world she would never fully understand. Connie reached for her hand.

'Wait here. I have something for you,' she said, and threw her still burning cigarette into the pot. Mae stubbed it out after she left, and a few minutes later, Connie returned holding what looked like a small bird in her hand. It was a mobile phone. She handed it to Mae.

'This was Ari's. He thinks he lost it, but I took it and hid it because I felt he needed a fresh start, without being pestered by those so-called friends of his about what happened with that teacher. And I didn't want his father harassing him either. But ... '

She held the phone out and Mae took it, carefully.

' ... it's been long enough for the dust to settle, and it may be there are some people he needs to reconnect with. That boy he was dating. Elliot? I know he felt bad for disappearing on him.'

'Is it charged?' Mae asked, and Connie laughed.

'Always so practical, my dear. Yes, I charged it. Just tread carefully with Ari. It might be a lot for him, going back there I mean. You'll need to steel yourself. But you're tough, Mae, and I can see how much you love him."

Once Ari had gotten over the fact that Connie had had his old phone all this time, he realised he was quite grateful that he'd had a reason not to engage with the world he'd left behind in New York. Mae suggested that for peak 'moving on' symbolism, they should perform a purging of the past the day before their graduation ceremony.

It was her idea to take the train to the coast and turn on the phone. Face it all, then hurl it into the sea, she said. The plan was to consume every message sent by his old friends and piece together what happened after he left the States. The phone had sat like a grenade in Connie's desk drawer for this long; it made sense to make an occasion of detonating it.

Ari was wearing an oversized chiffon shirt and cut-off denim shorts. It was one of those hot days that left him flabbergasted by the UK's lack of adequate air conditioning. They took a sweaty train packed with families who had loaded up push-chairs like pack horses: beach toys; colourful buckets and spades; every kind of inflatable; and kids hanging off the front, back and sides. Ari watched a toddler scramble onto her dad's lap to look out of the window. The man held onto her as she stood up and pressed her nose to the glass.

'What can you see?' he asked, and the child sprang into his arms as the train suddenly plunged into a tunnel. Her legs wrapped around his chest like a baby monkey, head nuzzled into him, eyes squeezed shut.

Ari experienced a childish, jealous longing. But did he want to be the kid or the parent? It felt, somehow, like both.

Mae wore a black T-shirt and board shorts. She had a crop top on underneath that flattened her small breasts, so her torso looked taut and muscular. Her hair was longer than it had been and fell softly around her face. Ari thought it looked pretty, but would never dare use that word.

They arrived in Scarborough at midday and needed the

crowds to disperse in order to best stage-manage what they had to do. Mae had it all figured out. Ari was nervous, but at the same time it was like they were gearing up for a scene in a schmaltzy teen drama, which made him feel like it was all just pretend anyway.

They queued for fish and chips from The Codfather. At the counter, Mae covered hers in vinegar, while Ari revelled in the attention he got by asking the woman serving if she had any Dijon mustard. Only he could manage to be so outrageously other in a small-town chippy and still leave not just unscathed but with 'Bye, duck, come back soon,' and 'You'll have the mushy peas next time!' as he sashayed out through the door. Mae, as usual, followed him with her head down like she was his publicist on the Oscars red carpet.

They ate side by side on a bench looking out to sea. Overhead, white gulls were dotted across the sky like punctuation marks. Ari watched a family overestimate the temperature of the water and, after dipping their toes, run squealing back to their towels and fortress of stripy wind-breakers. He felt the uncomfortable pinch of his bare skin against the wooden slats of the bench.

Mae opened her rucksack and pulled out a sarong. They both stood up silently and she laid it out for them to sit on. Mae picked the batter from her fish and just ate the flesh. The amount there was to say had rendered them both speechless. By four o'clock, the people on the beach were thinning out; the kids needed feeding and the wind had picked up.

'Shall we?' said Mae. She took Ari's hand and led him onto the rocks, which they hopped between before making their way down to the sandy water's edge.

'That rucksack makes you look like the leader of a lesbian rambling association. You do outdoorsy so well.'

'Yes, please. Dream job,' she replied, while tenderly laying the sarong out on the beach. She'd also packed snacks, bottled water, tissues and an extra jumper, as she'd guessed Ari would wear something inappropriate and need it for the journey home. Ari took out the phone and held it like it might explode. He kept his eyes closed as he pressed the button to turn it on.

The world that Ari had left behind cascaded onto his phone screen via 108 messages. With Mae by his side and his toes digging into the damp sand, he scrolled to the bottom of his inbox to work his way through them in the order they were sent. Mae silently read along with him. At first they were mainly from Professor Scott, getting progressively more desperate:

My love. Where are you? I'll leave my wife. We can be together. We can tell the world xx

Don't do this to me. I'm broken!

Ari, I love you. I left her. I'm in the studio. Please. Come back to me.

You tramp, you whore. You've ruined me. I hope you're happy. No one will ever love you like I did. I'm deleting your number. I will never forgive you.

In between there were missives from Elliot, who was heartbroken in a softer, floppier way than the professor. He asked what he'd done to deserve this. He loved Ari, he wrote, he missed him, he missed him, he missed him.

Then, after it became clear to his correspondents that Ari

and his mother had gone AWOL, there was another message from Elliot, who appeared to have pulled himself together: *Ari, I hope wherever you are you're OK. I have to tell you something. Call me.*

And then, three days later: OK, *I'm not sure if you're getting messages, or checking emails. Shit, Ari, I'm not even sure you're alive. But I know you went to school with Lilly, Prof Scott's daughter. Maybe she was your friend??*

In between, there was a message from Maddox delivered with her trademark charm: *FYI, word on the street is a kid named Elliot filmed you and sent the vid. Will let u know if verified.*

OK, *double verified. What a bitch. Srry.*

Ari said, 'That spineless piece of . . . ' But the next message he read severed his sentence. It was Elliot again.

I'm sorry to be the one to tell you this . . . Lilly took her own life.

Ari was reeling. The news that his ex had betrayed him was nothing compared to the suicide of his old classmate. Mae looked at him with terrified anticipation, not knowing how he was going to react. Her instinct was to fix things, find some answers, so she used her own phone to search Lilly's name on the internet. She found a story on Wellesley College News. She scanned the article, then gasped. Softly she read out the last line: 'Please speak to your college counsellor if you'd like help at this difficult time, or visit www—'

'For fuck's sake, Mae, stop. I don't need the web address.' There wasn't enough room inside him for his feelings. He had no choice but to pull on his shoes and run, off the beach and back to the train station, not stopping to remove the pebbles, his long shirt billowing behind him.

He ended up going to York, because it was the next train to leave the station. From there he used the bank card he'd pushed into his back pocket just in case to buy a ticket to London. Two hundred miles felt like the right kind of distance. In London he would be neither good nor bad. He'd be no one.

Each time he closed his eyes on the long train ride, he heard Mae's voice reading that news report and pictured the message from Elliot in its incongruously cartoon-like bubble: *Lilly took her own life.* By the time he arrived at Euston, it was nine p.m. and darkness had seeped into the edges of the long summer day. He phoned home. Alice answered cheerily,

'Now, it's your graduation tomorrow, Ari, you promised that you and Mae wouldn't go wild. I hope you're on your way back for an early night.'

'I need to speak with my mother,' he said, feeling the rage pool in the pit of his stomach. 'Now.'

He heard Alice whisper, 'Something's wrong' and pass the phone to Connie.

'Mom, I need you to tell me the truth. Did you know?'

'Know what?'

'Did you know that Lilly killed herself because of me?'

There was a rich silence. A sigh. Connie said nothing, then whispered in a stunned monotone, 'No.' Louder now, her voice shaking, she said, 'No! Ari, of course I didn't know. But Jesus, it wasn't your fault. She must have been sick. You didn't make her do it.'

Ari hung up the phone and bit his bottom lip until his eyes watered with the pain.

*

Alice turned the living room lights on and sat next to her sister on the sofa.

'The professor's kid, Lilly, she took her own life not long after this ghastly business with Ari and her dad came out,' said Connie.

Alice stared at her in disbelief. 'And I expect Ari blames himself.'

Connie nodded sadly. 'But I honestly didn't know! I would have told him.'

Alice scoffed. 'Would you? Really? I think you would have wanted to protect him from it just like you always do. But Connie, you have to be honest with that boy now. About everything. After all he's been through, he deserves to know the truth.'

Ari had heard people in Leeds talk about a gay club in London called Heaven. Outside the station, feeling a swirling mix of betrayal and grief, but also a frightening focus on his own annihilation, he hailed a black cab and hoped it was a famous enough place that the driver would know the way.

'Sounds about right,' said the cabbie through his half-open window, looking Ari up and down.

He was dropped by Embankment Tube and had to run to the cashpoint and return to pay the driver before joining the queue for the club. He had taken out £200, and pushed the wad of notes into his pocket. Once inside, strobe lights hit him like slaps. He felt the night inside him, a heavy black, sharp pinpricks like stars.

Now he was in the centre of the dance floor, his body loose from the MDMA he'd scored in the toilets. He swayed, giving himself up to the crowd, letting himself fall into it. He wasn't thinking or feeling anything. He was a dream, a memory. Nothing was more solid than the skittery trance music. *It's my fault Lilly died.* He found his way into one of the dark nooks by the coat check. A man was staring at him as if he'd placed an order and was waiting to be served.

He said, 'You look lost.'

'Maybe I am,' said Ari leaning his back against the clammy stone wall. He'd taken off his shirt and tied it around his waist so it hung over his shorts like a skirt. He could still feel the stones and sand from the beach in the bottom of his shoe.

'I'm Oliver,' said the man, and Ari tried to focus on this new face.

He was actually very handsome, if a little older than Ari. He held out his hand, but instead of shaking it, Ari grabbed it and placed it on the side of his face.

'Kiss me,' he said.

'Say please,' said Oliver.

They were pressed up against each other. Ari took in Oliver's chinos and blue Oxford shirt, undone at the collar, the only nod to the fact that he was at a gay club and not a business meeting.

'Please,' said Ari.

It was the first time in years that he had felt another person's lips on his own. Oliver took a fistful of his hair and pulled it as they kissed. He tasted of menthol gum. Ari worried that he himself tasted of salt: fish and chips, tears, the sea and sweat. He felt the need to apologise.

'Your hair is so long,' said Oliver.

Ari smiled. 'You like it?'

'Sure.' Oliver smiled, then asked for Ari's phone. He punched in his number, saved it and said, 'Call me tomorrow,' before disappearing into the crowd.

Tomorrow. Fuck. Tomorrow was graduation. It was already six a.m. Ari was due to introduce Mae's parents to his mother, Alice and Letty for the first time, and have lunch at a fancy brasserie before the ceremony. Mae had booked the table months ago.

He felt dizzy. He swallowed and tried to concentrate, retracing his steps to the exit, where he was regurgitated back out onto the street. He squinted in the early-morning sunlight. People in sportswear were racing to their pre-work gym classes. He shuddered and imagined his aunt getting up right about now to iron his graduation dress shirt.

He felt his stomach flip, a numbness at his jaw. He had to vomit. As he retched over a pile of kebab wrappers in a trash can, his scrunchie, which had as loose a grip of his ponytail as he had on his life, slipped off into the rubbish.

He grabbed his phone and read a message from Mae, then called her number. When she answered, he didn't need to say a thing; she told him exactly what to do.

Mae was so focused on sorting Ari out, she had forgotten all about her parents' imminent arrival. When her phone next rang, it was Janet.

'Mae, dear . . . yoo-hoo, it's ten a.m. Your father and I are at the station, and I'm afraid we are not *au courant* with this municipal city centre and would rather appreciate some guidance. Are we to wait here?'

'Mum!' Mae said in frustrated disbelief. 'I sent Dad all the details, including a map to the restaurant. You're hours early! I was supposed to meet you there. As per the email.'

'Michael!' Janet shouted. 'Your daughter says she sent you all the necessary information.' Mae knew she'd be giving him *the look* and her father, affably flustered as usual, would be fishing his glasses out of his jacket pocket and attempting to open his emails on his phone.

'OK, stay where you are. I'll come and find you and take you to Harvey Nichols. You'll be happy there for a bit until I'm ready.'

On her way out the door, she phoned Ari to check he was on the 9.30 from St Pancras. If he was, they could just about pull off their graduation plans as if nothing had happened.

Three hours later, Mae sat in a sharp baby-blue suit at the head of a long table in the window of Brasserie Nantes, the poshest, blandest, most parent-friendly place she could think of. Letty was on her right, reading a comic, Aunt Alice was on her left, wearing an odd ensemble of black silk dress and mohair cardigan.

'I wanted to wear my tux, but Connie said I looked like a waiter,' Alice whispered.

Mae caught her mother watching from the other end of the table; she raised an eyebrow as if to say *how dare you share secrets with my daughter.*

Connie looked flawless in a white Stella McCartney trouser suit and Jimmy Choos. Mae had to stop herself from staring. Conversation had been stilted and painfully polite. The fact that Mae shared jokes and a casual familiarity with Ari's family had made Janet behave as a strange parody of herself, out-glammed by Connie and unsure how she and Michael fitted into this peculiar dynamic. Just as Mae was running out of ideas for how to keep everyone talking, Ari, immaculately dressed in a black suit he'd bought from the department store opposite the station on Mae's instruction, snuck up behind her and clasped her shoulders.

'Well don't you just look ravishing, darling!' he said, too loudly. He'd scraped his hair back into a neat ponytail with the scrunchie he'd fished out of the trash. Mae noticed his sunken eyes and pallid skin as he enthusiastically shook Michael's hand, then planted a kiss on Janet's cheek. 'The mother I wish I had,' he said with a laugh in his voice. Janet shook her head, embarrassed but also glowing with pride.

'Oh, you silly boy, you don't mean that,' she said, avoiding Connie's eyes.

Ari sat down, but then promptly jumped back up again. 'Will you excuse me for just one moment?' He bolted for the bathroom.

Mae awkwardly excused herself too, leaving the world's most unlikely combination of people to find something – anything – to talk about.

She ducked into the men's without anyone noticing. Ari was talking quietly on the phone.

'I've got to go, but I will, I promise,' he said quickly before hanging up and looking forlornly at Mae through the bathroom's mirrors.

Too preoccupied to ask who he was talking to, she handed him a tote bag containing a bottle of deodorant, some wet wipes and aftershave. Ari felt hot tears run down his face.

'Thank you,' he said, gripping the sides of the washbasin and bowing his head. Mae placed her hand on his back.

'I've got you,' she said with comforting certainty. 'And Ari, it wasn't your fault. You know that, right?'

He looked up and met the reflection of her eyes again. He felt as if he was sinking into the comedown of all comedowns.

'Mae. I've an idea and I need you just to say you'll think about it. Ten years from now, longer even, when we're – when I'm – less fucked up, there's something amazing we could do together that would make all this darkness go away.'

He turned and whispered in her ear. Mae smelt the night on him, sour and unknown, but she didn't pull away.

'I'll think about it,' she said.

Morning

Summer 2030

Could this have been how it was always written? Mae wonders. The end or the beginning.

Palm fronds litter the pool.

Was there a great stone where her life was chiselled from the start and everything else that happened was pulled back inexorably; a moon, a tide, to the curve of its letters and the story told?

A lilo in the shape of a giant ice cream has found its way into the shrubs that divide the lawn from the fields beyond. It is all a mess.

She should have taken the cushions in. Obviously a storm was coming, but in the chaos she forgot. Now they lie scattered across the grounds, like stepping-stones sodden with rain. She gently presses the heels of her hands over her closed eyes. The sun is fresh. The children are asleep. She notices the wet grass on her bare feet for the first time and shudders. Tidying up out here can wait. She takes a gulp of the cool air. Now there isn't a cloud to be seen. Like it never happened. She smiles to herself – how quickly the sky forgets.

She turns back towards the house and tiptoes quickly through the garden, careful to avoid slugs. It is going to be a brighter day regardless.

The kitchen was the first room they renovated together. It is large, with white floorboards, and two big skylights over the island. There is an old Aga that only Mae knows how to work. She opens the windows and surveys the dinner table, which was abandoned mid meal last night. Still the shock of four chairs where there should be five. A glass was knocked over and red wine pooled like a wound on the white tablecloth. Mae rolls up the sleeves of her pyjamas and begins scraping plates into a bin under the counter. She feels too old for a hangover. These days three drinks are enough to push her into an unpleasant heaviness the next day. But she didn't even have a glass of wine with her meal, she recalls indignantly, so this must be something else. Loss, probably. The burden of absence. A month has passed since the funeral, but it is as raw as the day it happened.

Seeking distraction before her thoughts spiral, she turns on the radio. What the kids call 'old school' but she still considers pop music splices open the thick atmosphere that lingers. This house has a way of holding a grudge; the movement of light through its rooms seems deliberate. The old beams in the ceiling can oppress one day and feel comforting the next.

It was never going to be easy, owning it between all five of them, but it is a sturdy cottage, a survivor, and in the corner of a village where Virginia Woolf once lived, it seemed like the grounding, creative presence they all needed in their lives when they bought it four years ago. After much back and forth, they settled on a style blandly considered contemporary British, but interior design by committee was as complex as everything they did together. *The Moroccan flourishes were a compromise; Ari wanted a place in Marrakech, but Mae insisted it was too far and the logistics of their already illogical families would have made regular visits impossible.*

She stacks the crockery methodically in the dishwasher, then finds a clean glass and pushes it against the water dispenser in the fridge door. Ice whirrs and crunches then topples in. She tries not to look at the photo just next to her hand, stuck on with a magnet, oblivious, when it was put there, to its future poignancy. She feels the violence of the portrait's aliveness. Eyes shining, an easy smile.

She ignores the bright ache of grief, and instead, memories of last night begin to creep into focus. With them that spent, empty feeling that descends after a colossal row. All the words have been shaken out of her, and now she doesn't know what to say or where to start. She takes a sip of cold water, turning so she doesn't have to face the photo. A figure catches her eye through the open patio doors. Ari has emerged from somewhere that couldn't have been his bedroom, or she'd have heard him on the stairs. He is standing at the edge of the pool wearing a black bathrobe that barely skims his knees.

Mae downs the rest of her drink and turns on the dishwasher. She must talk to him before the others get up. She is searching for her gardening sandals so she can go back outside when the baby cries. It is six a.m. Adrienne is certainly punctual, and consistent with it: unlike her parents. Instinct kicks in, and Mae sets off to fetch her, but halfway up the stairs she stops, turns and runs towards Ari.

'Addie's awake,' she shouts from the patio. 'She's crying.'

He darts inside, brushing past without meeting her eyes.

*

The table still needs to be cleared, but Mae has almost finished washing the silver cutlery when Ari appears next to her at the sink. The baby is tucked under his right arm and pressed snugly against his bare chest where his robe gapes open. August grips his left hand. She reaches his waist now. 'I'm four but I'm five when it's my birthday,' is what she says when asked her age. Mae recognises that urge to always stretch ahead to the next and the next milestone. She was the same until it felt like there was nothing left to want.

The children, as always, lift their mood.

'Goodness me, what a mess!' Ari says for his daughter's benefit. 'Those naughty fairies must have broken in and had a big ol' party last night and forgotten to clean up.'

He winks at Mae, and she softens, feeling the instant ease of his approval. She crouches down to kiss August on her cheek.

'Good morning, kiddo.'

'Can I have strawberry jam with my toast?' Augie asks in reply. 'But not the yucky yellow one, the sweet jam. The red one. The one I like.'

'We're on it, boss.' Mae salutes. Her knees crack as she stands up.

Ari puts Adrienne in a wicker crib by the hearth of the old fireplace that separates the kitchen from a large room no one knew quite what to do with, so they called it 'the salon' and mainly use it for dancing at parties. He cuts the bread. August runs out into the garden.

'Don't go near the pool,' they both call after her.

Mother and father. Those titles are as limiting as girl and boy once were. But how can language express the endless, unfolding strangeness of parenting? 'We're transitioning,' was how Ari put it in the early days. Their identities were shifting, becoming. A sense of body, self, sexuality made strange by all this nurturing.

'I've put one load in the dishwasher. The rest . . . ' Mae sighs.

'I'll do it later,' he says kindly.

'The tablecloth's a goner, though, have you seen the stain?'

'Whose fault was it? I don't remember.' Ari butters the toast and Mae passes him the correct jam.

'Everyone's, no one's. The usual. Let's blame the wine glass – it threw itself over.'

She holds out a chipped white plate from the collection Ari's aunt donated after the wedding, and he slips two crustless slices onto it.

'August! Breakfast!' he shouts as he sets her place at the patio table and fetches a cushion. Mae slumps down on the seat opposite. Augie is busy rolling down the grassy bank in front of the pool.

'Shall I leave her?' asks Ari.

'She'll come when she's hungry.' Mae can't pretend any longer. 'Ari, listen. I'm so sorry about last night.' She bites her lip.

He pulls out the chair next to her and sits, keeping his eyes on his daughter. Mae turns to face him. He is ageing annoyingly well. While she was once thin like him, her pleasingly androgynous body revealing nothing overtly female, now she feels her hips betray her. The years spent trying to conceive have left their mark, with a softness where her abs once were. All Ari has to show of the life that has passed between them is a few silver strands that shimmer among his long black hair.

'You're doing that scary staring thing. Do I have something on my face?' He brushes the dark stubble on his cheeks, then says matter-of-factly, 'There's an extreme intensity radiating from your aura right now. Dial it down, please, handsome, it's barely half past six.'

Mae laughs. 'You know I scowl when I'm tired,' she says. 'And I'm so tired.'

'Listen, I overreacted at dinner,' says Ari, pretending not to notice the dark circles under her eyes, and the way her body has crumpled over the patio table. 'Sometimes it comes out, you know, in that way. But I need you still, I do need all of you.'

Mae sits up straight now so she can reach an arm around his shoulders and lean into him, smelling the familiar richness of his skin. She whispers, 'I shouldn't tell you what to do with the kids. You're fantastic.' August rolls down the hill once more, then stumbles to her feet. She clocks the grown-ups watching her and runs towards them.

'I know you can't help it. And I appreciate it,' Ari says just before the child throws herself onto his lap. He lifts her into her seat, and she begins ferociously devouring the cold toast.

'When a person dies, I know it's true they don't come back,' August says frankly between mouthfuls. Ari gets up and stands behind her so she can't see his sudden tears. He strokes her hair from her face.

Mae looks away. Moments like these could floor her for the rest of the day, and there is too much to do. She smiles at Ari as if to say, 'You've got this,' and goes back to cleaning the kitchen. She checks on the baby and listens for movement upstairs. Someone will soon wake up and offer her the hug she needs.

After a few moments, Ari says 'Mae?' drawing out the vowels into a question as he walks quietly into the house with August trailing toast crumbs behind him. 'I was thinking perhaps I should go. Take the family. Your idea, it's just too soon. It'll never work.'

'Go where?'

'To New York. Now the funeral's done and we've had this ... this healing. Like, maybe it's the right time to go back to how things were before the accident.'

Give. Take. It has always been the same with Ari, Mae thinks. For someone so fluid, the options he hands her can be so binary. Go. Stay. She feels a wave crash through her. Push. Pull. Nothing has really changed. She still needs him like air.

'Tell me not to and I won't.'

'No, you tell me.' Mae takes a deep diver's breath. 'Tell me if there's any other way for us to live now, Ari. Because I cannot conceive of a future without you.'

PART 2

Chapter 15

London, February 2019

Mae was the first person in the office. She kicked the snow off her black boots and hung her leather jacket in a cupboard. No coats on the back of chairs! That was a rule. There was a stack of newspapers on her desk; she pushed them to one side and put down the Americano she'd bought from the canteen before taking the glass lift thirty-two floors up to *Edit* magazine's vertiginous City HQ. Even after three years of making this journey countless times a day, five days a week, first as an intern, then as a staff writer and now as a junior editor, she still gripped the rail and felt her legs wobble, unable to look out at the view of London as she soared up to an obnoxious height above the city. It meant that by the time the doors pinged open to her place of work, she was flooded with cortisol, her breath quick and shallow, a cold sweat prickling on her skin. After a hit of caffeine, she was at a level of frenetic energy that powered her through until lunch.

The day had started in grey marl but slipped into something brighter. It was 8.39 a.m. according to the big clock over the as yet unmanned reception desk. Mae bundled her gloves into a ball, sipped her coffee, then took the first broadsheet from the top of her pile and opened it with a brusque shake. She scanned each spread for story ideas, then licked the ink-stained tip of her left index finger and quickly turned the page. When a story caught her attention, she ripped it out carefully and placed it in her 'cuts' pile, ready to pitch as a feature idea to her boss – the only other person in the office who read the papers and didn't just scroll for news online.

She was engrossed in this ritual when the new intern crept up to the desk next to her. Mae had been tasked with training Reeva and had accidentally befriended her.

'You'll notice I'm barefoot,' said Reeva. Her sad little toes peeked out from under the soaking wet cuffs of her trousers.

'Hmm. I do, now you mention it.' Mae was used to her friend's daily dramas. Reeva was only nineteen and had won the internship after writing what the editor-in-chief, Virginia 'V' Bates, had called a 'powerful and moving piece' about losing her mother at the age of twelve. She'd hand-delivered it to V's house, asking for a break. In other words, she'd got the job on merit, not because her best friend's mum had pulled in a favour with the fashion editor. Mae was grateful, if embarrassed, by how easy Connie had made it for her to work at *Edit*.

For months after graduating, Ari was still furious with his mother. He felt that he should have spent his year at Leeds racked with guilt for pushing poor Lilly to suicide, not skipping around the city with Mae, writing pretentious essays and dancing on podiums at gay clubs. He hated that Connie had, for so long, kept him from the sadness he deserved to feel.

Even if it was true that she hadn't known the extent of what she was hiding by concealing his phone, he blamed her for denying him this painful awareness of the truth.

With anger wound tightly around his heart, he fell into a relationship with the man he'd met in Heaven.

In the months after graduating, when Mae had left Leeds and he continued to live in the cottage, withdrawn and seething and barely speaking to Connie or Alice, he took the train to visit Oliver in London every weekend. They would go to the cinema or eat at a steak restaurant Oliver liked near his law firm in the City. But Oliver wasn't 'sceney', as he put it. He'd only been dragged to Heaven that night on a straight mate's hen do, he explained. And so, the pair never went to the kind of queer venues where they might run into Mae.

Mae was living in a bedsit in Croydon, interning at the magazine and volunteering at a local queer youth club. She was too exhausted to even try and make social plans with Ari. But they spoke every night about bigger things, things that felt as heavy and promising as sacks of gold. First on the to-do list was getting a place together. With Ari promising to shoulder most of the rent, they were looking to be as near to Soho as they could find.

And then there was the crazy, scary but also thrilling prospect that one day, before they were both thirty, they would – as promised – have a child together. They discussed every hypothetical detail, explored every possible scenario, including how it would work if one or both of them were in relationships. This wouldn't be a problem, Ari had insisted. In fact, he joked, the more parents the merrier. Mae felt that in theory it was a brilliant idea, but it was *her* body, and the thought of it changing and growing, bringing an inescapable softness, was hard to reconcile with the person she knew herself to be. Still, the more they talked, the more it seemed like something that in six or seven years she'd be ready to embrace. And working at the youth club was a regular reminder of the easy contentment she felt taking care of children. When she pictured creating a family with Ari, it was like being wrapped in a warm blanket; comforting to be so sure this was the life that awaited her.

'My love, big news. We're pivoting,' was how Ari had put it when Mae phoned almost eight months after she'd moved to London to say she'd found a perfect flat for them just off Carnaby Street.

'So, Oliver has asked me to move in with him, and I know you're gonna be mad but Mae, please. It's been over a year. This is a good thing for me. He makes me happy – you see that, right?'

She'd met Ari's boyfriend only a handful of times and found him handsome for sure, but honestly, she told Sam when he asked for the gossip, he was way too average. It would never last.

But since Ari had let Mae into the darkest corners of his past, she felt a new confidence in their connection. She wanted him to know she didn't need him in the same way she once had. She was building her own life in London. So she said with an affected ease, 'If you think that's what'll make you happy, who am I to stop you. I guess I better get used to living in Croydon for the foreseeable. There goes our fabulous Soho life!'

'You sound pissed.'

'Well, I'm doing my best not to.'

'I know you hate it when plans change. But this doesn't change *the* plan. We'll still get there. This is just for now. The child we'll have – that's for ever, right?'

Mae laughed. 'Sure,' she said. But she was worried about how Oliver would factor into their future. Ari hadn't told him about the promise they had made to each other, but he would if they were still together a few years from now he assured her. For the first time, Mae heard a niggling 'what if' in his voice that night. It occurred to her that so much potentially stood in the way of their idea ever becoming a reality.

Mae took a personal interest in helping Reeva get a permanent position on the magazine to atone for her own privilege in this respect. She'd only been interning for a year when she was offered a staff writer job with a decent starting salary. And then six months later V promoted her to junior editor. It meant she had to quit volunteering at the youth club, and she missed it, but she barely had time to take care of herself any more, let alone devote her spare energy to needy teens.

After rolling her eyes at Reeva's latest disaster, she said, 'You've got your interview today. What the hell happened? There's no way V will even let you in her office looking like this.'

'Obviously I know that,' Reeva tutted. 'Basically, I got a seat on the Tube for once and my shoes were wet from the snow, so I took them off and put them by that little heater thing under the seats to dry. And then I was reading that pamphlet of poems you lent me, by that friend you're always on about. And anyway, I looked up and it was my stop, so I ran off and forgot I didn't have my shoes on.'

'OK,' said Mae pragmatically. 'Here's what I want you to do. Go into the fashion cupboard. Take the cheapest-looking pair of shoes from the shelf on the wall to the left. Do not take them from the right-hand shelf, whatever you do. It'll be fine, there are no shoots today – no one will notice they've gone. Just bring them back – clean! – tomorrow.'

'I could just pop to the shops and buy a pair?'

Mae shook her head despairingly. 'You work for a fashion magazine. The last thing you need to do is spend your own money.'

Reeva gave her friend an ironic salute and shuffled off.

'Hang on!' Mae shouted after her. 'The poems. What did you think?'

'Brilliant. I mean, look what they did to me!' She pointed dramatically at her bare feet and continued on her mission.

Mae felt a kick of excitement as she turned on her computer. She needed the day to go as smoothly as possible so she could leave on time. She had a date with Ari, and it had been a long time since she'd seen her best friend.

Reeva emerged from the fashion cupboard wearing a pair of unremarkable black flats.

'Good choice,' said Mae, putting down the paper she was speed-reading. 'Now let's practise your interview quickly. I'll be V.'

She sat up straight in her swivel chair, crossed her legs and affected an air of feminine grandeur. Reeva stood in front of her and tugged nervously at the ends of her bobbed black hair.

'Who would you put on the cover of *Edit* if you were in charge?'

'Um, I've never thought about that. Er . . .'

Mae broke character. 'Think about it! You'll need a whole list; she's bound to ask that.'

'Yeah, all right, will do. Mental note.' Reeva tapped her finger on the side of her head and smiled. Mae nodded her approval.

'And do you consider yourself a *words* person or a *fashion* person?'

'I don't consider the two mutually . . . mutually . . .'

'Exclusive,' prompted Mae like a proud mum watching the school play.

'Yes. Because as Diana Vreeland said, "Where would fashion be without literature?"'

Mae spun around in her chair. 'Nailed it!' she said, putting her hand up for a high-five. 'You've got this. Just remember a few things about V . . .'

Reeva looked up, then urgently at Mae. She shook her head, her eyes wide and panicked. But Mae was on a roll.

'First, don't be boring. She can't stand anything dull. Don't mumble, and remember to make eye contact. V hates to think that people are scared of her, even if they are. So don't fiddle with your hair like that. What else? Try not to put yourself down, but don't be too confident. Don't expect her to laugh or smile; she has this thing about her teeth, not that she'd admit it . . .'

There was a loud 'ahem' from behind her, and she turned to find her boss, the formidable Virginia Bates, standing with her arms folded and an eyebrow raised.

V took a car to the office, so she didn't need to dress for the weather like regular people. She was wearing a custom-made soft pink suit, a white shirt with an oversized collar buttoned up to the neck, and her signature square black-rimmed glasses. Mae's stomach flipped as it always did when she saw her.

V smirked. 'Oh, that is rich, Mae. Surely you, of all people, wouldn't have a problem with my resting bitch face, you're not exactly Miss Congeniality yourself.'

'It's not a problem!' said Mae, backing herself into a corner. 'I like it! I mean, yes, I'm the same. I'm flattered you noticed.'

'I noticed.'

'Thrilled, in fact.' People were quick to cast V as the cliché ice queen. The fearsome female leader who wouldn't stand for bullshit. She could be bad-tempered with anyone not working hard enough or fast enough; she loathed posers and cast out those who were in the business for the perks and prestige. She had grown up on a housing estate in south-east London. As a child, magazines had given her a reason to dream. Now she believed their purpose was to open the door to a world people might not normally have access to and invite them in.

Mae had seen V explain this during industry awards speeches a number of times, and it never failed to send a shiver down her spine. It didn't stop her believing their job at the magazine was merely entertaining and frivolous compared to the important work she still planned to do one day, but watching V in alpha mode was extremely sexy. *Flattered you noticed ... thrilled in fact* – had she really just said that to her boss? She felt her cheeks flush at the memory.

V was the first mixed-race woman to run a magazine of *Edit*'s magnitude in the UK, increasing its sales year on year until it was the most powerful title on the news-stand. She was also the youngest, working her way up to the top job before she was thirty. Mae understood that she still wanted to be part of the team. She enjoyed banter and knowing the details of her staff's dating lives and dilemmas, but Mae was the only one brave enough to engage with her on this level. She wasn't intimidated by her. She saw through the tough exterior and recognised something about her boss that no one else did: V was lonely in her corner office. And despite everything she had achieved, she wasn't happy.

'For the record, I don't give a fuck about my teeth. If anyone around here was actually as amusing as they thought they were, maybe I'd have a reason to smile more. Try harder. Both of you. See you later for our interview, Reeva. And Mae's right, you must stop fiddling with your hair.'

At 3.47 p.m., the whole London *Edit* team, including the most senior executives, and the entire New York and LA bureau received an email entitled: *MISSING!* In it, the fashion director, Raven, who had personally typed and pressed send on only a handful of emails throughout his illustrious career, implored whoever had *STOLEN* the limited-edition Elane Bocella shoes from his shelf in the fashion cupboard to return them immediately. He would be reviewing the CCTV footage, so the culprit had nowhere to hide. The shoes were due back to the brand, and Bocella's temperamental director of marketing was threatening to pull the issue's advertising unless they were in Milan by tomorrow morning. This would not do at all. The value of the shoes was €5,000, the value of the advertising was £70,000. The note ended with a line of exclamation marks, and then a single 'x'.

Reeva, who hadn't yet read the email, was walking through the office to the beauty desk, holding two bouquets of white peonies in her arms, musty water dripping from the stems onto the shoes.

Mae jumped up from her desk and ran over to her. 'Let me help you with those,' she said loudly. Taking the extravagant bunches from her, she leaned in to whisper, 'Check your inbox. And don't panic, I'll fix this.' She knew that the fashion director had the power to have Reeva removed permanently with little more than a flick of his wrist. V was too busy to fight for her and no one else would care. She was just an intern.

Mae threw the flowers at a beauty assistant and followed Reeva back to her desk. All the colour had drained from the girl's face, making her pillar-box-red lipstick take on a ghoulish hue.

'I'm gonna vom,' she said.

Mae sat down next to her and began unlacing her own boots. 'Just wear these. It's a whole nineties vibe; don't worry, it works. Now go. V thinks early is on time.'

Reeva stomped self-consciously towards her interview, turning to blow Mae a kiss and whisper, 'Thank you.' Mae hid the shoes in her rucksack until she could work out what to do. It would take Raven, or his long-suffering assistant, at least a day to discover how to actually get hold of the CCTV as threatened.

The only thing for it was to confess that *she* had taken the shoes so they wouldn't need to look at the footage. She had acted the fool in front of V once already today and survived. She was confident she could charm her way through another ridiculous episode.

Reeva was beaming when she returned to her desk. The interview had gone better than expected. V had said she saw a lot of herself in Reeva and offered her a job as her PA. It wasn't the junior writer role Mae wanted for her friend, but it did mean Reeva would be V's closest confidante, *and*, Mae told her, if she made herself indispensable, V would be a powerful ally throughout her career. The editor was known for promoting her personal assistants after a few years of service.

Mae waited until the office was almost empty. February was a big month for parties. People often put external meetings in their diary at three p.m., so they could disappear early and pop home for a power nap and a shower before hitting the circuit. Reeva gave her a hug before leaving.

'I'm literally still shaking. I can't believe it. I thought it would be a hustle for me to get anywhere, ever, you know a mad hustle, but it happened just like that. Thank you, Mae. I'm *honoured* to be your token straight mate.'

She bounced out of the door to meet her boyfriend in the white trainers she'd finally had a chance to buy from a nearby shop.

Mae tidied her desk so it was ready for the next day. She grabbed her jacket and slung the bag containing the shoes over her shoulder. She did a sweep of the office to check no one was hiding in the corner booths, and once confident it was all clear, she knocked on the glass door to the editor's office.

V was hunched over her bespoke teak desk, poring over page proofs. She faced away from the view, so that the city throbbed in anticipation of night behind her. Glancing up, she took off her glasses to rub her temple.

'Tough day?' asked Mae, genuinely concerned.

'You could say that.' V lifted her head to take in Mae's presence. For a twenty-six-year-old, she exuded a compelling confidence. Her white-blonde hair fell over her face in an effortless quiff.

'What can I do for you, Mae?' V said, momentarily flustered. 'I'm surprised you're not already propping up a bar somewhere.'

'Is that really what you think of me, Virginia?' Her boss's full name tasted forbidden in her mouth. Mae's eyes sparkled as she gave a flashy, practised grin. She noticed V press her lips together to suppress her own smile, and run a hand through her curls.

'What do you want? I'm busy, and contrary to popular belief, I do actually have a life outside this office that I'd like to get back to at some point this evening.'

Mae took a seat on the low sofa opposite the desk and recounted the shoe saga, replacing Reeva's role in it with her own. She opened her bag and placed the fabulously expensive pumps on a cushion next to her.

'*Voilà.*' She waited for a response.

But V didn't say anything. Instead, she picked up the phone, looking directly at Mae and shaking her head mockingly as she did so.

'Raven, I've got them. Long story. No! No! Look, I don't have time now. They're here. Yes, they're fine. OK, OK, I'll sort it – they'll be on a flight to Milan tonight. I know. And goodbye to you too.'

She put down the phone, then turned to look out of the floor-to-ceiling windows. Lights were flickering off in the surrounding tower blocks. Cars left trails of orange on the road below. It was a misty and glamorous winter night. Mae wasn't sure whether she should leave.

'What do people say about me?' V asked quietly.

'Does it matter?' Mae said soothingly.

'Somehow, tonight, yes.'

Mae looked at her watch. She really ought to get going to meet Ari at the top of Old Compton Street, but she couldn't step away from this moment.

'Well, I guess most people think you're pretty fierce, in every sense of the word. A bit scary. And, I don't know, cold?' She wanted to say something right. 'But I think you're amazing. Honestly.'

V scoffed. 'You don't know me.'

'Maybe. But I think I get you ... I really do.' Mae stepped towards the window where her boss was standing. Without meaning to, she glanced down, and her legs began to shake. Involuntarily she reached out to steady herself on V, who clasped her wrist softly and didn't rush to let go.

They stood next to each other in silence, Mae felt her skin tingle where V's cool fingers pressed into her flesh. A magnetic charge pulled them apart and both women shuffled awkwardly in the shock of it.

Without turning to look at Mae, V said coolly, 'Cancel your evening plans. You're going to Milan.'

Chapter 16

It was the only time in the history of their friendship that Mae had stood him up. She'd called him as he'd stared at the reflection of himself in the train window, London's suburbs edging in and out of focus as he sped towards the city. Before the train plunged into a tunnel, he'd caught something about Milan, something about her boss and a tragic apology that made him feel even worse. He got off the train at Victoria, crossed the platform and went straight back to Clapham Junction.

Ari had kept in touch with his family since he'd moved in with Oliver, but it was clear he didn't want to *really* talk. He'd visited them in Otley a few times but had been so withdrawn and spiky the whole atmosphere of the cottage shifted. He still blamed himself for Lilly's death and his mother for keeping him from finding out about it sooner.

Oliver would be pleased his plans had been cancelled at least, especially an evening with Mae. Perhaps it was too much to ask for his boyfriend and his best friend to be buddies. Life would be easier, logistically, if they could at least pretend to enjoy each other's company, but the dynamic between the three of them never worked.

*

Mae often thought of the time she had been invited for dinner after Ari had officially moved in with Oliver three years ago. Standing on the doorstep of his small townhouse in Clapham with a tote bag over her shoulder carrying a bottle of expensive sparkling wine and a cheaper bottle of red, she gave herself a talking-to before pressing the bell. 'Smile. Don't judge. Living in SW4 does not make him boring. If Ari likes him, I like him.' The doorbell played a jingle. Mae frowned, then adjusted her face – it had to be ironic.

Ari had grabbed Oliver's hand and dragged him upstairs from the kitchen so that they could open the door together. His boyfriend was wearing a pale blue polo shirt and blue jeans – Ari hoped Mae would be generous in her assessment. Earlier, he had slipped a white silk kimono, with an embroidered tiger on the back, over the black trousers and vest he wore while cooking, but when Oliver scrunched up his nose and shook his head, he'd hung it back in the closet.

'Babe, you look hot, why ruin it with a granny gown?' Oliver had said before smiling in that hundred-watt way that made Ari's knees go weak.

In the narrow hallway, Mae and Ari pressed themselves together like the rough and the soft sides of Velcro. Mae's hand instinctively went to the back of Ari's neck. His head found its place on her shoulder and they breathed each other in. Ari released himself from his friend's grip, conscious of Oliver's eyes on them. He giggled nervously.

'Great to see you again, Olly,' Mae said, trying her hardest to match his catalogue model grin with a tight smile of her own.

'Oh Mae, he prefers Oliver. It's just his thing, I thought I'd told you,' said Ari, looking adoringly at his man and placing a condescending hand on Mae's shoulder.

Oliver gave him a nod of thanks and gestured to Mae to come in.

Ari had been conscious the kitchen looked as if it had come straight from a show home and was lacking any of what Aunt Alice would call *character*. Oliver put the sparkling wine in the back of the fridge and told Mae he too was sober.

'It's fine,' said Ari, noticing that she was fidgety and nervous and needed a drink. 'We've no problem with you enjoying it.' He took the bottle back out and handed her a glass, then poured sparkling water into a jug of ice.

Oliver whispered something in Ari's ear, then said kindly, 'Of course not.'

While Ari attempted to cook and Mae tried not to notice he was cutting the carrots in batons when circles would have been better, Oliver sat opposite her at the kitchen table and fired out questions. She didn't know any other lawyers so figured this was just what they were like. She enjoyed the interrogation, because saying things out loud about herself was a way to confirm them. She felt good being the person she told Oliver she was. He was artful in the way he avoided talking about himself.

Ari quietly predicted her answers to each of his boyfriend's enquiries and was pleased he guessed them all correctly, apart from her response when asked about the internship at the magazine he knew she loved.

'It's silly and meaningless really. It's so superficial, I think I'll leave soon. What I really want to do is work with kids,' she said, and he decided not to chip in. He was enjoying half listening to the easy back-and-forth between them. They were so different, but there was a core, he felt, that they had in common – a ruthless pursuit of a good life maybe. A confidence? Or was it that they were two people who made him feel looked after? He stirred the sauce.

At that moment, Mae agreed that Oliver was dashing and definitely not boring. She understood why Ari had seized on the opportunity to move in, even if she did find the decor rather drab. She was pleased the red wine was a screw top so she didn't need to ask for an opener before sheepishly pouring herself a glass then hiding the bottle behind the giant pepper grinder on the table.

Just as the conversation was running out of steam, Ari said, 'Here we go,' and plonked down a big dish of vegetarian lasagne. He hoped it was to everyone's taste, he said; the cheese sauce had gone a bit lumpy despite following his aunt's instructions not to stop stirring.

'It's delicious,' said Mae after taking a mouthful.

Oliver said nothing, but made a face that Ari was starting to recognise.

'Babe? What do you think?'

'It's really nice. Sorry, I'm used to meat, so it's, you know, a bit lacking in that respect, but it's lovely. Thanks for cooking.'

Ari felt his posture slump. Mae noticed, and after downing her glass of wine and pouring another, more boldly this time, she placed a protective arm around her best friend and said, while locking eyes across the table with Oliver, that it was perfect.

They ate in silence for a while. Ari suddenly felt the

pressure of the evening as an unbearable weight and counted on Mae to lighten the mood.

'So, Oliver,' she said pointedly. 'Tell me something, anything about yourself now you've been subjected to my full download.'

'Nothing much to tell. I'm a boring lawyer who got lucky and scored a beautiful boyfriend.' Ari rubbed his foot against Oliver's leg under the table and smiled bashfully.

'Oh, I don't believe that for a second. If Ari's into you, there must be more.' She took a gulp of wine. 'Are you out to your parents? When were you happiest? Last gig you went to? Favourite character in *Friends*? Rather die by an arrow through the chest or a gunshot to the head?'

'Mae!' Ari interjected. 'I don't think any of us need to know that.'

'It's fine,' said Oliver. 'I can handle her.'

'Handle me?' asked Mae, caught off guard.

Ari looked embarrassed.

'Um, sorry, since when do I need "handling"?' Mae was talking louder than she realised.

'You're drunk,' said Oliver.

'You're a dick,' said Mae, and then gasped, surprised at herself. 'Sorry.'

Ari began scraping plates into the bin. Mae and Oliver stared at each other across the table. Oliver smiled, like he'd been right about her all along.

'Ari is sober. He doesn't need this.'

Mae felt the injustice of his comment corrode inside of her, and started gathering her things.

Ari dried his hands calmly on a tea towel. 'Don't go, this

is just a stupid misunderstanding. Why don't we all go up to the living room and watch a film or something?'

'No thanks,' said Mae.

'No thanks,' said Oliver, imitating her tone.

As she walked up the stairs to leave, Ari not coming as quickly as she would have liked after her, she heard Oliver shout, 'A gunshot to the head. I'd take the gunshot.'

At the door, Ari pleaded with her not to go.

'Oliver is just super stressed at work. He's tightly wound. You get that, right? You liked him, I know you did.'

Mae was confused. She had liked him, and then she'd called him a dick. Whatever had happened was bound to have been her fault; she'd polished off the bottle of sparkling wine and most of the Malbec on her own. But she still wasn't drunk enough to not feel embarrassed.

'Oh man,' she said forlornly, 'I really fucked up, didn't I?'

They heard soft footsteps on the stairs and Oliver appeared smiling apologetically. He had bright yellow washing-up gloves on each hand and held them up in a gesture of peace.

'Fancy coming to help me?'

Ari felt so grateful he would have done anything for his boyfriend. What pulled him deep and close to this man was a love like he'd never felt before.

At the sink, Mae dried the dishes Oliver passed her with the utmost efficiency. 'Are you this good at everything you do?' Oliver asked with a friendly laugh in his voice.

'She totally is,' answered Ari for her, feeling giddy now with the reconciliation.

Mae was sobering up. She looked at the gorgeous man standing next to her and couldn't recall why she'd turned against him. Then Oliver began scrubbing encrusted vegetables from the lasagne dish, and she pushed the sudden clarity of what had happened to the back of her mind.

She wanted to like Oliver, and she liked how much Ari liked him. But in the time that had passed since that night, instead of a closeness developing, distance had pressed its way between them, slowly and quietly, until Ari kept Mae in one orbit and his boyfriend in another.

Chapter 17

The Monday after her ridiculous twenty-four hours in Milan, Mae arrived at work before eight, knowing that V would already be at her desk, making her final amends to pages before they went to press.

She barely noticed the tiredness that loitered at her edges, so steely and singular was her focus. She zigzagged quickly between the rows of desks, unzipping her leather jacket and shaking the rain from her hair. No games, she said to herself, repeating the advice Ari had offered when, instead of going out to one of the five parties she'd been invited to in Milan, she'd spent the night in her luxury hotel room on the phone to him. He'd urged her to be honest; if this crush felt different, and was seriously reciprocated, she was to behave like the high-functioning emotionally intelligent adult person she was and not fuck it up.

The venetian blinds in V's office were closed. Mae knocked on the glass door, then, without waiting for a response, opened it a crack, mustered her resolve and walked confidently in. V dropped the croissant she'd been about to take a bite of onto a page proof, looking more ruffled than Mae had ever seen her.

Mae dived straight in. 'Things are . . . weird, in a good way, between us, right? It's not just me?' She struggled to catch her breath after power-walking from the Tube station. She gasped and carried on. 'Just to be clear, I'm into it. Because I'd be mortified if you thought I wasn't. And if I've totally misread this whole thing, then please don't fire me. Pretend this conversation never happened. I just wanted to say I am fully enjoying the, er, the mood between us. Just so you know. Just, um, just let me know next steps, OK? All the best, kind regards.' She began backing out of the office.

'Just, just . . . ' V smiled softly. She was mocking Mae in a friendly way that defused the intensity. She regained her composure and scooted her chair so she was on the same side of the desk as Mae. '*Just* sit down a second, would you.' She gestured to the other chair. 'You're making me nervous. I wasn't expecting such an entrance.'

Mae perched on the edge of the seat. She felt wired. She pulled off her jacket and scratched at her neck, which was burning with a stress-induced heat rash beneath her white cable-knit jumper.

V was wearing a faux-leather midi skirt. When she crossed her legs, Mae noticed that the soles of her knee-high black boots were completely clean; they had never touched a pavement.

She said, 'Thanks for offering such . . . clarity. I suppose I was beginning to be concerned that we were crossing a line.'

'No lines were crossed. Honestly.'

V looked at the framed *Edit* covers on her office walls. She seemed to be weighing something up. Mae checked her watch, worried that her colleagues would soon be arriving and she'd have to explain why she'd had such an early audience with the editor.

'Would you like to have a drink with me tonight?' V asked, as if it was no big deal. 'There's a pub near where I live in Brixton where we won't bump into anyone. The Talbot.'

'You live in Brixton?'

'Yeah, I grew up there, why?'

'I figured you had a place in Primrose Hill like the rest of them.'

'I'm not like the rest of them.'

Mae winked. It was an instinct born from decades of meaningless flirtations. *Shit.*

'Did you just wink at me?'

'Sorry. Bad habit.'

V shook her head in pretend disapproval. 'Eight?'

'I'll see you then,' said Mae as casually as she could, sending strict instructions to both eyelids to behave. She tossed her jacket over her shoulder and opened the door to the office hoping her raging flush would cool down before anyone noticed.

That night, they sat at a small table next to the jukebox until closing time. V wasn't wearing her glasses, and out of the harsh lights of the office she looked more like a normal thirty-seven-year-old than a woman who the *City Times* had claimed 'held the future of media in her hands'. Mae would not let her buy the drinks.

'I'm treating you like any other girl I'd go out with, and I always pay on the first date. We can split it on the second, but it's what I do. It's important to me.'

'So this is a date?'

'Of course.'

'Ha! Mae, you are so blunt. It's very refreshing. I spend my days with people who are too insecure to just say what they mean; nothing is ever a clear yes or no. It's exhausting trying to work out what it is they want.'

Mae was tempted to say, *Well what I want is to kiss you*, but instead took a sip of wine and wished she'd stuck to beer. She felt giddy and was mustering every iota of self-control to appear attractive and mature. They hadn't spoken about work once. V had told her about her family. She'd never met her dad, or any of his relatives. Her mum, Leah, hadn't remarried, and she had two older brothers.

She said that working in an industry where at her level she was one of only a handful of women who weren't white and straight and privately educated didn't help the feeling she'd had since she was a child that she didn't fit in. She had to work harder than everyone else to get where she was and had sacrificed friendships, relationships and fun for success. She told Mae that she had recently been thinking a lot about what she'd lost by achieving so much. She was sad that her team believed her to be so unapproachable, but the persona was well-established protection. It was only Mae, eleven years her junior, who'd ever seen through it.

Mae listened intently. She wanted to understand more about V's life, her childhood – she wanted the stories no one else knew. But when it came to offering a glimpse into her own family life, she was embarrassed by her parents' blandness. Instead, she told V all about Ari, maybe too much about him, from why he'd fled New York to how unsure she was starting to feel about his boyfriend. She was conscious of the time suddenly and worried she was being boring. V had little patience for rambling anecdotes, and if you were talking in a meeting and she picked up her phone, it was the equivalent of being played off stage by the orchestra at the Oscars; you had no choice but to stop mid flow.

'I feel like I know Ari better than you.' V lightly touched her foot against Mae's leg under the table. She hadn't taken her phone out of her handbag all night.

'Sometimes I feel like I know him better than me too,' Mae said.

Over the next few weeks, Mae and her boss met secretly at the Talbot after work as often as V's schedule would allow, and they texted every day in between. There was a comforting regularity to their correspondence. Even on her busiest days, sometimes during meetings with her publisher, V would find time to reply appropriately to Mae's idiosyncratic missives. Since Oliver had come on the scene, Ari was far less quick to respond to his friend, and many of Mae's texts to him were left hanging pathetically in little green bubbles. She liked having someone to validate her, to say, simply, 'I see you.'

To cover their backs, she had saved V's number in her phone as 'Brenda', and she was 'Barb' in V's. Their texts were sweet and flirtatious but in no way reflective of the rampant longing Mae felt when they were together. In the office, around others, they barely spoke. Mae kept her head down in meetings when V was reprimanding the team about one thing or another, for fear she'd make eye contact and be unable to help giggling like a love-struck teenager.

*

One morning, after a night spent shivering in the garden of the Talbot until last orders, pressed close on a picnic bench, kissing like crazy and talking about things that seemed to blaze with importance, V called an all-staff meeting. She stood at the head of the boardroom table with a stack of paper.

'On each of these printouts is an email from one of you explaining why you are filing your work late.'

She picked up the first sheet, scrunched it into a ball in her fist and threw it at the wastepaper basket on the other side of the wood-panelled meeting room. It hit the wall behind and fell in. She looked at Mae in a silent 'Yesss!' while everyone else collectively flinched as if it had hit them.

'I need you all to understand that you are part of something bigger than yourselves.' She screwed up another piece of paper and chucked it powerfully across the room. 'What you do, however small, matters.'

She repeated the action over and over again, scoring twelve of sixteen slam dunks (Mae was counting).

'Every detail of your work *matters* because it adds up to something incredible, so if you don't think it makes a difference that you're a day late with your copy, you're wrong. You're letting everyone else in this room down. And you're letting our readers down.'

She made a ball out of the last sheet of paper, then walked slowly over to the bin, held her arm out over it and dropped it in. The room let out a sigh of relief. Mae put her notebook up to her face to cover her smile.

'Am I making myself clear?'

There was a chorus of mumbled yeses.

'Reeva, please see that all the paper is recycled. OK, every-one, back to work.'

Mae had never once missed a deadline. She hoped that made her look more smug than smitten as she joined her colleagues in skulking back to their desks. Reeva walked past dragging a big blue wheelie bin, and said, 'What a woman, eh?' with an emphasis Mae couldn't quite interpret.

Mae had been secretly seeing V for almost a month, and their ritual of after-work drinks held firm, with the addition of regular illicit assignations in the office at a safely deserted seven a.m.

One particularly bleak Wednesday morning, Mae arrived at work, hung up her jacket and went straight into the beauty cupboard to fix her hair in the well-lit mirror. As she reached for a pot of expensive wax, she knocked a vial of glitter onto the floor. She cursed and tried to brush it off her hands, but flecks had already found their way onto her face and clothes. She checked the time. V would be waiting in her office by now, blinds drawn, door locked. She tried to kick the silver glitter into the carpet, to no avail. In a rush, she put the empty pot back on the shelf and – giving herself one final check in the mirror – made her way quickly to her 'appointment'.

'Hello, you. It's been a while,' said V after opening the door to Mae, kissing her on the lips and hurrying her in. It was a joke. They'd only been apart nine hours, having spent the previous evening drinking white wine spritzers and sharing a bowl of chips at the pub before V had to leave to finish a sales presentation.

Mae laughed generously. 'I missed you.'

Despite the late night, V looked like she'd fallen straight out of a cruise collection fashion spread, wearing a floral print maxi dress with a pale blue blazer and neon-heeled court shoes. A Chanel clip held back a stash of soft curls, and her Birkin bag was tossed carelessly on the sofa, its mouth open.

Twenty minutes later, she said, 'You're very good at that,' as Mae lifted her head from between her boss's legs, noting how much she enjoyed praise of any kind.

'Can I get a promotion?'

V wriggled back into her underwear and extracted Mae's white vest from the muddled pile of clothes at her feet.

'Get dressed. You're lucky to be keeping your job at this rate.'

'Yes, boss.' Mae wiped her mouth with the back of her hand and hopped up from the floor. She kissed V quickly on the cheek and pulled on her tight black jeans, then brushed the creases from her shirt and shrugged it back on over her vest, preparing to switch into regular work mode.

'Hey, Mae, wait. Before you go. Enough of this before-work thing, don't you think? It's a wonderful start to the day, but I have a nice house, with an actual bed. Why don't you come and spend the weekend?

Mae hadn't wanted to be the one to suggest evolving their routine of pub chats and pre-work sex in the office, because the whole relationship felt as precarious as a champagne glass on a dish rack. But she was thrilled that V had initiated the change of pace, and fell into easy acquiescence. As she pulled the door closed behind her, she heard V call Reeva.

'I need the lint roller. My jacket is somehow *covered* in glitter.'

*

Later that day, Reeva marched over to Mae's desk.

'Hey! V wants to see you at five about your story ideas.'

Reeva was serving executive realness. She was revelling in her role as personal assistant to the most powerful woman in publishing, and Mae was proud of how quickly her confidence was growing.

'She's got a hard out at six, so best keep the pitch short.' Reeva removed a fleck of glitter from Mae's cheekbone with her little finger. 'Glitter is a real shitter, isn't it? Gets everywhere.'

At five minutes to five, Mae entered V's corner office and sat on the uncomfortable sofa that had served as a bed for them that very morning, waiting for her boss to finish a phone call. She held a file of cuttings but was keen to suggest a story she wanted to write more than anything else.

'You have to feature the advertiser. I don't care that you think it's ugly; if their clothes are not in the shot, no one is getting paid this month, so sort it out.' V slammed the phone down and took a moment to shift gears. 'Hey, sorry,' she said. 'I really want to hear your ideas, just let me ... ' She jumped up, slipped off her heels and began running on the spot, punching the air.

Mae watched bemused for five minutes while V dropped into squats and then press-ups. The blinds were open now, but no one in the office dared to be caught noticing this bizarre routine.

'Thanks, that's better.' She put her shoes back on and perched on the edge of her desk, breathless, motioning for Mae to get on with it. It was weird being a lowly employee again.

'OK, so this is a piece I've really wanted to write for a while now. It means a lot to me personally and ... '

V looked at her phone.

'Uh, right. There's a charity called FAM. When I first moved to London, I volunteered at one of their LGBTQ-focused youth centres, and it was so rewarding bonding with these kids who had been through so much but showed such resilience and were fun and full of life and hope. Honestly, they inspired me to stay in London and enjoy my life . . . '

'I thought you stayed because you got a full-time job that a million girls would kill for?' countered V.

'Well, yes, obviously there was my whole *Devil Wears Prada* story arc.'

'The one where you end up shagging the Devil, you mean?' V looked at her provocatively, and Mae pretended to scowl.

'You're making me lose my thread! I'll have you know I've worked hard on this pitch,' she said.

'Sorry,' said V kindly. 'Do continue.'

'So FAM offers support and mentoring for kids who have lost their parents or suffered abuse or been kicked out of home . . . '

'Mae, *Edit* is a fashion magazine – what's the angle?'

'The angle is that these young people are the future, and isn't that what we're all about – what's next? Plus, some of them are so insanely talented and make all their own clothes and desperately want to work in fashion. I plan to spend some time with them at the project, getting to know the older teenagers and profiling them as "ones to watch". The piece would showcase them but also highlight the struggles of a non-profit and the lifesaving work FAM does for young people who have fallen through the cracks and been abandoned by everyone else in their life. FAM is in dire need of funding; coverage like this could be really great for them.'

'Write it and I'll see if I can make it work in the Real Life section as a point-of-view report. But it's got to be brilliant. I don't want the others thinking I'm giving you special treatment.'

Chapter 18

Mae was shouting into her mobile phone when she blustered into the restaurant. Ari watched people on the tables around him stop mid conversation to stare at her. He'd noticed how, since working for the magazine, she took up more space; she looked like someone you wanted to impress. He had arrived half an hour early so that he could sit with his tonic water and fresh lime, enjoying the weight of the glass in his hand.

He swirled the ice and thought about how good cold gin used to taste, and then the inevitable spiral of shame sank him back to Lilly, dead. He dug the sharp edge of his thumbnail into the skin on the inside of his arm, a private patch of pain that he hid beneath his long sleeve.

'We don't give copy approval. Ever. Virginia is very clear. I'm sorry if that doesn't work for your client, but this is editorial. It's journalism. We have to tell the story how we see it.' She hung up abruptly. 'I'm so sorry I'm late,' she said breathlessly. 'I can't even begin to explain how publicists have become the bane of my life.'

'Try me,' Ari said, leaning precariously over the candle on the table to hug her.

'Wait. You look incredible!' Mae looked him up and down.

He swung his long black locks from one shoulder to the other. 'She's free!' he joked.

He had relished the opportunity to dress up that night. It had been a while since he'd worn anything but the clothes Oliver said he looked good in – pastel colours, V-necked sweaters, blue jeans. As he'd swished through the hangers of bejewelled, opulent fabrics on his side of the wardrobe, he'd recalled how it felt to slip on a silk jumpsuit, say, and the freedom that came with it. I've missed this, he'd thought as he zipped up his Chelsea boots and caught a glimpse of a person he actually recognised in the mirror.

'Can I get you a drink?' A waiter appeared out of nowhere; just like the restaurant, she seemed to take herself very seriously. The staff all had the same muscley tattooed arms, making the small plates they delivered look even smaller. Ari knew Mae would say she wasn't drinking in order to keep him company, but he hated the thought of spoiling her fun so he jumped in to order her a mojito.

'Eurgh, you know me so well!' she smiled, and he felt a deep release in the comfort of her presence.

After ordering, they looked at each other, silently reconfiguring the algorithm of their friendship. They were used to being alone together, but now their lives were expanding, zooming further and further out from a tight focus on the two of them.

'Oliver sends his love.'

'Seriously?'

'Yes!' Ari sighed and popped a single arancini in his mouth. Something unexpected exploded on his tongue.

She waited until he'd swallowed before asking, 'So come

on then, how are you really?' She might have grown more assertive since working at *Edit*, but Ari noted that the fashion world's grace and subtlety had yet to rub off on her.

He considered the truth, telling her how it felt, really, to wake up each morning and have memory upon memory take up its place in his mind: his dad's clenched jaw as he breathed in loudly through his nose; the soft, wispy bristles of Professor Scott's beard tickling his cheek; Lilly sitting alone in the cafeteria at school while his friends laughed at her. Even after so many years, these thoughts still rose to the surface before any good thing had the chance.

But as he looked at Mae's eager face across the table, he wondered how he could possibly describe the weight of it to her. How could he make her understand how disgusting he felt until Oliver rolled him over and pressed himself on top of him, his heavy chest on his back, his hands pulling his hair so his head arched upwards. Then he felt better. Mae had her own life now, and Oliver was his.

He smiled, which he hoped was enough to imply he was totally fine, and said, 'Oliver really wants to get together again soon, but *we* can hardly find time to hang out at the moment, let alone making time for you, me *and* Oliver. We'll have lots of fun together very soon. I promise.' He popped another arancini ball in his mouth.

'They're so good, right?' Mae seemed to want to change the subject as much as he did.

'Delicious,' he said 'Now. Tell me about work.'

She launched into a story that sounded like one of his mother's. Something about people he was vaguely aware were celebrities. As she spoke, he found himself remembering all the times he and Mae had held Letty's hands and spun around in a circle in the garden at the cottage. Letty's feet would lift up off the ground and she would shout, 'I'm flying, I'm flying!'

When Mae stopped talking, he threw in a lacklustre 'Fabulous,' hoping it would cover for his daydreaming.

'Ari, were you even listening to me?' She rolled her eyes at him playfully, but he could tell she was a little offended.

'I guess I was just thinking ... it doesn't sound very *you*, working at *Edit*. I know it's a great job, and there are bits of it you enjoy. But you were always so sure you wanted to work with young people, really change something, make it better. And I'm just not sure that's something you can do at a fashion magazine.'

Mae looked hurt. She stabbed a piece of burrata with her fork and put it quickly into her mouth.

'I'm sorry, Mae.' He shook his head. 'I don't mean to be critical.'

Defensively she said, 'I hear what you're saying. But actually, I'm working on this big piece about FAM, and the kids there, and giving them all that publicity could really make a difference. It could help get them more funding. So it's not like I've just abandoned all my morals for the gilded cage. And anyway, give me a break – I'm twenty-seven. Can I just enjoy whatever *this* is for a minute?' She gestured to the space around her, which was heaving boisterously. Everyone else seemed as excited as she was to be there, eating tiny morsels of food as nineties R&B blared from speakers.

'Are you asking my permission? Because you don't need it, Mae, I just want you to be happy.'

'I want to know you don't think I'm a sell-out,' Mae said

with a shudder of vulnerability that he'd not seen since she'd moved to London. She dabbed her lips with a napkin.

'Of course I don't. I'd never think that. But I know you, and soon *Edit* is not going to be enough, and then I'll be really excited to see what you'll do next. But for now, sure, enjoy! Why not? You're young, you're hot, you're *in* it. Just don't forget little old me, scribbling away at my crappy poems, never making anything of myself, while you're off gallivanting with the fabulous glitterati.'

'I do not gallivant. And Ari, "fabulous glitterati"? Are you sure you're a poet?'

He laughed.

'Seriously though, you know I think you're an incredible writer. And look, I made some calls through work and there's this agent—'

'No!' Ari shook his head. 'What did I tell you about trying to help me? The work isn't good enough yet, and if I'm going to make it as a poet, I have to figure it out myself.'

'Please just take this.' She handed him a business card, and he held onto it for a second before placing it in the loose pocket of his cardigan.

'Seriously, send her some work. They're *great* poems, Ari. You're never going to feel like they're good enough to share with the world. You just have to take that leap.'

'Oh, she does not leap,' he tutted at her playfully.

'I beg to differ. Talking of which – let's go somewhere I can watch you dance.'

Mae signalled for the bill, but the manager came over to say the meal was on the house, and she hoped Mae might consider featuring the restaurant in the next issue of *Edit*. Ari watched as his friend complimented the food, the ambience, the manager's beautiful dress – was it vintage? She pressed a twenty-pound note into her hand as she thanked her again, then they barged their way through the milling crowds and outside into the warm night air.

'I thought I was the rich one. Since when can *you* afford a twenty-pound tip?' he said, with mock outrage.

'I can't! But it was the least I could do.' Mae laughed. 'See ... I am doing *some* charity work at least.'

Now that they had the space to, Ari threw himself into Mae's strong arms and she held him.

'I missed us,' she whispered into his neck.

He threaded his right arm through her left and they walked through Soho Square.

She took him to three private parties, each more decadent than the next. Ari knew Mae would want him to be his most exuberant, so he rallied for the occasion and tried not to think about how much easier this world was with a glass of champagne in his hand.

He lost himself in dancing as Mae swayed next to him – half accomplice, half bodyguard. It felt so good to move his body, to spin and drop and vogue. They danced for hours and hours, until the crowd had reached its peak and he recognised that moment when it was as good as it was going to get. Everyone was on the right side of wasted, looser, shifting into a new, freer place.

The possibility of sex hung like dry ice on the dance floor. A mood was rising, and Ari was blazing bright. He was the best dancer, and people were pulled inexorably into his aura. Mae was on her fourth, or was it fifth cocktail; she said hello to people she knew through work and proudly introduced Ari as her best friend. He watched amazed as she expertly handled small talk with each new character.

'Great to see you,' she said to a grand dame with long bleached-blonde hair and gold grillz in her teeth.

'I'm impressed.' He nodded with arms crossed.

'I know she's iconic.'

'No, silly, with you and the way you're chatting so *seamlessly*. I thought hell was other people?'

Later that evening, at a warehouse party for a fledgling fashion label, Ari got so lost in the music that it took him a while to notice Mae was no longer next to him. She was lying on one of the luxuriously dressed double beds that lined the perimeter of the dance floor, deep in conversation with a drag queen wearing a lampshade as a hat. Behind her, a skinny girl with big eyes and a buzz cut massaged her shoulders. Lying across all of them as if she was really trying to sleep was a model Ari recognised from the front cover of Mae's magazine (to which he dutifully subscribed). One of the model's arms hung off the side of the bed and the other reached up to stroke Mae's face.

Mae waved him over and everyone scooched up to make space. He was enjoying himself and took a moment to realise it. He leant back into the tangle of bodies and felt his mobile phone in his pocket dig awkwardly into him. He pulled it out and looked at the screen. There were twenty-seven missed calls from Oliver. Fuck. There was just one text message. He opened it up:

Call me.

He jumped up, feeling a childish panic in his chest.

'What's wrong?' Mae sounded anxious.

'What? Oh God, it's fine, I think. It's just Oliver, I have to call him.'

'It's only one a.m.'

'I know, but I forgot to check in with him earlier and I didn't think we'd be out this late. I'll just be a minute, OK?'

Mae surveyed the party, which was beginning to look bedraggled.

'Come on, let's go – you can call him in the cab back to mine.'

Ari was embarrassed to talk to Oliver in front of Mae – he knew she could be judgemental – but he didn't have a choice.

'Oliver, sweetie, I lost track of time. I know, I'm sorry. No, nothing. Just dinner and Mae wanted a few drinks after. Yep, yeah, I'm heading back to hers now. Come on, don't be like that. I said I'm sorry.'

The phone line went dead and Ari sighed in annoyance.

'What were you apologising for? You've done nothing wrong.'

'Oh, I know, I know,' he said lazily. 'It's just easier to apologise. He was worried about me, that's all. He'll have forgotten about it by tomorrow.'

He knew it wasn't malicious. His boyfriend loved him, and he enjoyed that he was a little protective. Mae shook her head, no doubt holding in what she really thought, and Ari was relieved. She didn't understand what it was like to be in an actual relationship. Silence rested between them.

'I think this thing with V might be something real,' she

said then, gazing out of the window at the city cloaked in moonlight.

Ari raised his eyebrows in a silent 'Ooh . . . '

'And I don't know what to do because I like her *so* much. The real reason I'm happy at work and not looking to move into the charity sector like I always planned is that I get to see her and talk to her and sit so close to her. Sometimes I can smell the brand of washing powder she uses, and it sends me crazy.'

Ari had never heard her talk about someone like this. There was Freya, the girl from school . . . and that was where the list ended of people who had held her attention for longer than a week. She'd been at best satisfied, or amused, by her university girlfriends, and none of them had lasted beyond three dates.

'It really feels like it could be something proper, you know? The vibe is so easy between us.'

'Vibe with a capital V, eh? Well then I'm happy for you.' He put his arm around her and she rested her head on his chest. They listened to the radio in the cab, which was tuned to late-night love songs, all the way back to Mae's front door in the depths of south London. Ari insisted on paying.

'It's always been my job to get you home safely. Let's keep at least one thing the same.'

Mae put three different keys into three different locks and opened the door to her block. There was a dodgy-looking lift but they took the stairs and were out of breath by the time they reached the fourth floor and walked along the corridor of identical metal doors to number 437. Ari felt bad that he hadn't been to her flat more often. It was almost a replica of her place in Leeds, but upgraded. She had similar art to that which was on the walls in her bedsit, except now it was professionally framed rather than taped up.

She still had a herb garden perched on the windowsill, although it wasn't thriving. The old futon had been replaced with an actual bed, still perfectly made but with crisp white linen sheets. And she'd filled her shelves with beautiful ceramic crockery. Mugs, bowls and plates were piled up. She noticed him looking.

'I have friends now!' she joked. 'Anyho, I figured you'd want a shower, so I left a towel and some stuff out for you. You can go first.'

Ari used a tiny amount of the miniature bottle of body wash she'd given him. It smelt of her. As the warm water trickled down his back, he decided being with Mae was more intoxicating than anything. If only he could feel this way for ever.

By 2.30 a.m., they were both washed, hair combed, moisturised and in clean pyjamas, like a couple of rosy-faced kids ready for story time.

'It's nice to see you happy,' said Ari as he peeled the duvet back ready to get in. Mae was crouched on the floor next to him, pulling something out from under the bed. It was an air mattress and a foot pump. He refolded the corner of the duvet without her noticing and realised then just how much he'd been looking forward to lying next to her. He stood, unsure what to do with himself, while Mae vigorously inflated his single bed.

'There,' she said, breathless from the exertion. 'I thought you'd probably prefer this now.'

'No, I mean sure. Yes, thank you. My own bed.' He felt sad.

She found clean sheets and threw him one of her pillows. The distance that the past few years had forced between them had, thought Ari, been good for his friend. She'd learnt to like herself without him. But he felt he'd shrunk in comparison, disappeared by another increment into himself, his poetry, and life with Oliver.

He sat on the edge of his mattress and thought about Lilly. It was a habit. Last thing at night, like clockwork, shame crept across his skin like the first prickles of a fever. He had been complicit in her bullying at school. He had slept with her father. She had killed herself. It didn't take a detective to figure out the role he'd played in her tragic death. He wanted to scratch at the shame until it bled. Instead he sat on his hands and said:

'I love Oliver, he's what I need . . . stable, and I know how to handle him. We have good times together.'

Mae looked dubious. 'Can you be open with him about what happened to Lilly?'

'Oh, I wouldn't want to. I don't think he'd have much patience with all that, and anyway, I'm done thinking about it.'

They both knew that wasn't true.

'I'm not going to forgive myself. Ever, probably. But I've got to move into the future, and there will be *things*, you know, *plans*, that will readdress the cosmic balance of life.'

'Like becoming a majorly successful poet with a mega book deal?'

'Yes, and . . . ?'

Mae nodded, aware of what he was alluding to. 'But

there's Oliver to consider too, now, maybe even V or whoever else we might end up with. Where would they figure
in the plan?'

A whistling noise prevented an answer, as all the air
escaped Ari's mattress and he slowly sank to the floor. They
both giggled.

'Guess you're in with me after all.'

'Guess so!' He curled up next to her and fell asleep with
the words from a song he'd heard in the cab playing on a loop
in his head: *It must have been good, but I lost it somehow.*

The next morning, they said a hurried goodbye at the Tube
station and took separate lines – Mae off to work, where she'd
have to manage the flashes of desire, the looks, the secret text
messages all while keeping on top of her deadlines, and Ari
headed home to face Oliver's mood, which was bound to be
a certain flavour of foul. He would pick up ingredients for
truffle pasta on the way, and a bunch of flowers.

It was dusk when he heard Oliver open the front door and
let it slam behind him. It was a sound that always took him
back to the apartment in New York, where slamming doors
was used as punctuation. He shuddered. The daffodils he'd
bought looked pathetic in a glass jug.

'Hey, babe! I made you dinner!'

Nothing. Oliver stomped upstairs. Ari followed. He stood
opposite his boyfriend in their bedroom, the thick carpet
blended with the walls so that it was a cocoon of beige.

'I missed you. Sorry for last night, I should have called.' He
took a step forward and Oliver turned away. Still not speaking.

Ari stood staring at the back of him for a while longer,

noticing the way he wore a smart work shirt one size too small so that it stretched taut across his muscles. Then he walked softly out of the room and down to the kitchen, where he ate alone in truffle-infused silence.

Chapter 19

One Sunday morning in June, Mae sleepily stretched out her right arm with the intention of finding V's toned body and pulling her close. Instead, she patted the expensive duvet cover and wondered if she was making her breakfast in bed; working; or doing something else entirely.

Mae had discovered a computer server's worth of biographical information about her lover over the past few months, but she still found it impossible to predict how she might behave in any given moment. And because there was no threat of creeping boredom, she had for the first time ever slept over at a woman's home and not left with a shifty excuse about a non-existent cat needing to be fed. She wasn't dreading the inevitable ennui that crept in around this time with other girlfriends. Everything about being with V was exciting.

When she'd first visited V's discreetly palatial home, she'd discovered so much to file under 'too good to be true'. She had a wine cellar and a Nan Goldin original; there was a big garden (Mae had no idea people in London had gardens) where V grew vegetables, which she would often set about digging and planting and watering in the middle of the night, as it was the only chance she got. She had an entire wall dedicated to photos of her family. There were black-and-white pictures of her two older brothers, their kids' drawings, letters and post-cards; she kept a stack of politics magazines on the large glass coffee table, and they actually looked like they'd been read. To top it all off, the sound system was wired into every room.

V's house was a hundred times more stylish than Oliver's shrine to mediocrity. Not that it was a competition, but given that Mae and Ari were now both sleeping with attractive, successful grown-ups, comparison was inevitable.

Mae slid out of bed and opened the big white shutters and then the windows to diffuse the musty scent of sex and champagne. She walked into the en suite bathroom wonder-ing why the black-and-white marble felt so warm under her bare feet. *Heated floors!* She added that to the list of things she never knew she needed. Having fixed her hair and brushed her teeth, she ventured downstairs to get her answer. It was, of course something else entirely. V was in the living room, standing on a vibrating platform in leopard-print Lycra leg-gings holding two small dumbbells. She spoke into a headset. 'Yeah, I'll see you later. I'll ask her, I promise. I know, I'm sure she's dying to meet you too.'

She hopped off the Power Plate and into Mae's arms. Mae traced the smooth, contoured outline of her hips and kissed her, feeling the dewy spritz of sweat on her face.

'Sorry, I'm disgusting,' said V, pulling away and looking for her towel.

'You are absolutely not,' said Mae, pulling her back and kissing her hard to prove the point. 'I have so many questions right now, but in lieu of WTF are you doing on *that*? I'd like to ask who you were talking to and about *whom*.'

'My mother. And you. She wants you to come over for Sunday lunch.'

Mae bit her bottom lip, a habit prompted by even the slightest discomfort.

'You've told her about us?'

'Yeah, I tell her everything. She thinks you sound "impressive".'

'Uh huh. OK.'

'Is that a problem?'

'No. Sorry, it's just a lot to process. One minute I'm fucking my boss, the next I'm meeting her mother. We've not even spoken about what this *is* yet. And you're ready to go public?'

'Going around to my mum's is hardly stepping out on the red carpet at the *Edit* Awards, Mae. Look, what we have is something special. Different. *You're* different. You're the best thing that's happened to me for a long time. Yes, we have to be careful at work, but you know my mum is my best friend.'

'I didn't realise that meant you would have told her all about us. I haven't even filled Ari in properly yet.'

Everything had been going perfectly as far as Mae was concerned. The secret element added a sexy subversiveness that worked. Well, it worked for her. Now she felt a familiar instinct to retract; a cold rush to hold V back, to say something cruel and stop her from liking her this much. But no, she told herself, V wasn't like the girls at university. She was everything she had wanted from a partner and a life then, and now that it was inching into focus as a reality, her head was a muddle. She was hungry, and V looked so distractingly beautiful.

'Let's eat something,' she said, leading the way into the gleaming stainless-steel kitchen. 'I'll cook.'

As she cracked eggs into a frying pan, she heard V's disappointment in the way she pulled a stool out from under the kitchen island, sat down and slowly turned the pages of the Sunday newspapers. The oil spat. Mae cut two thick slices from a loaf of ciabatta.

'You fit into my house so well,' V said quietly, without looking up.

Mae sighed. It was all so perfect. Why did she feel this gnawing urge to destroy it?

'Let's avoid calling for the U-Haul just yet, though.' She laughed, but it sounded less kind than she'd meant. 'We cannot be those lesbian clichés, right? It's only been four months.'

They ate in silence. When she'd finished, V pushed her plate to one side and looked at Mae quizzically. 'You've always said you wanted this. No games. An open book. But what page are we on now? Are you saying what you really mean or are you saying the thing you *think* you should feel?'

The observation was acute. Mae was embarrassed, so she said, with fake certainty, 'I can't make it today, but please thank your mum so much for the lunch invitation.'

'Fine. No big deal. Just a stupid family tradition anyway. You've probably got better things to do.'

V's tone was pleasant enough, but Mae could tell the mood had tilted. Power was switching between them like an electric current. At work tomorrow she would feel edgy and insecure. V would sashay through the office in six-inch Jimmy Choos and a bodycon dress demanding copy, pictures and answers on her desk. But right now, Mae owned the next move. She did the best she could to pull things back onto an even keel.

'I actually better go and work on my story for you. I haven't forgotten it has to be *brilliant*.'

She left V tidying the kitchen and got dressed quickly. She splashed cold water on her face and checked her hair. Then she picked up her book from the bedside table, her wash bag from the sink, her underwear from the hallway floor. As she put these belongings into her rucksack and pulled the zip, she felt as if she was taking something of herself back, closing it off.

'OK, I'm going to head. I've got to transcribe a ton of interviews for the FAM story.' She poked her head around the kitchen door but couldn't meet V's eyes. She noticed her shake her head sadly, but ignored it, instead offering a faux-cheery 'Bye, babe.'

The sun was bright as she walked to Brixton station, the sky a minty blue. She noticed the weight of her bag on her back and adjusted the straps. By the time she got to the Tube, she was sweating under her denim jacket. She stopped to take it off and was assaulted by the noise of a preacher wearing a beige suit and carrying a Sainsbury's bag. He shouted into a microphone attached to a large portable speaker.

'Put your ear down to the Bible and hear Him bid you go and pull sinners out of the fire of sin. Put your ear down to the burdened, agonised heart of humanity, and listen . . .'

Women pushing buggies swerved around her, children screamed, a man asked if she wanted to buy weed. She held her jacket under one arm and walked down the stairs to the ticket barriers. Her head throbbed, and all the way home she wondered why she had left. She could have worked in V's home office, they could have had lunch with V's mum, gone home and watched that French lesbian movie they were both excited to see. But no, here she was back in Croydon, putting the key in the door of her empty flat.

It was stuffy inside; the air smelt of the flowers that had died in a vase while she'd been away. She poured the murky water down the sink and shoved the stems into the bin, dried petals falling to the floor as she did so. She sat at her kitchen table and tried to work, but her head still ached and she felt a creeping sense that she'd messed up. She stared at her mobile for a while, working up the courage to phone V and apologise for being so weird. Her girlfriend was right; she was backing away, scared of the intense intimacy that had grown between them. She made the call.

'Hey.'

'Hey.'

'Are you going to say anything, Mae? I'm super busy with all these proofs I've got to get through before LA next Thursday.'

'Are you not going to meet your mum, then?'

'I cancelled,' said V.

'I'm sorry. I panicked. We should have gone together.'

'Well, it's too late. And anyway, we both have to work.'

'Wait, I didn't know you were going to LA?'

'I'm sure I told you. I've got to schmooze Ana Palomo. I want the exclusive on her coming out, and with these big Hollywood actors it's all about building relationships. I need her to trust me, and to trust *Edit* to tell her story.'

Mae quickly googled Ana's name. Despite working at the magazine, she had little interest in celebrity and found it hard to differentiate one famous actor from another. Her laptop screen displayed a page of images of a beautiful Mexican woman with long wavy auburn hair, naturally full lips and big dark eyes. She didn't seem to wear make-up, even on the red carpet, and she was even more stunning for it.

She clicked on a picture to make it bigger. 'Oh my God, her breasts!' she said aloud.

V laughed in spite of herself. 'Yeah, I know. She's pretty incredible. She's just come out as queer. Plus she's a humanitarian *and* she's just completed a master's degree in philosophy and literature.'

Fuuuuuuuuuck, Mae thought. And V was about to spend three days with her in her Malibu beach house. Great. Jealousy grabbed hold of her heart and twisted it into an ugly shape.

'Is it really too late with your mum? How about dinner? We could take her out somewhere fancy.'

'That's so not her style. Look, it's fine, forget it.'

But Mae felt desperate suddenly to see her girlfriend. To conjure up a closeness before she ran off into the arms of a glittering queer star.

'How about I make it up to you by hosting you tonight for a change. I'll invite Ari, it's about time you two met.'

'Whoa, easy there. Are you sure it's not too soon for me to be meeting your bestie?'

'Touché,' said Mae with a smile in her voice. 'I'm so sorry for freaking out. It was stupid.'

'OK, I'll come, but you'll have to get me a car. I'm no snob, but Croydon!'

'Hey, I'll have you know Kate Moss grew up here.'

*

Oliver was travelling for work, so Ari was pleased to get a spontaneous dinner invite from Mae. He said he'd bring dessert but only remembered as he entered the small elevator up to Mae's apartment.

V was already there when he arrived. She opened the door and Ari said:

'I'm afraid I come empty-hearted but full-handed.'

V looked confused.

'I mean empty-handed. Full-hearted. I forgot to bring dessert basically.'

He took a step back to admire V, who was wearing Céline trackpants and a matching fleece hoodie.

'Gorgeous!' he declared, kissing her on both cheeks. She ushered him in, and Mae appeared from the kitchen with the biggest grin on her face.

'Isn't she?' She shot a quick wink over to her girlfriend, who had curled up on the sofa, determined not to lift a finger, as Mae had insisted.

Ari embraced his friend, then sat next to V on the tiny sofa, their knees touching. Mae handed them both a zero-alcohol beer.

'It's a school night,' she said by way of explanation.

'Has she always been this much of a square?' V asked Ari.

'Oh sure. This is nothing. She probably has all her clothes ironed and laid out for the morning . . .'

'And her little packed lunch ready-made in the fridge,' added V. They both laughed.

'Hey, I can hear you mocking me!' shouted Mae from the kitchen. But really, she was thrilled they both knew her so well.

Ari and V filled the small flat with their combined riches. It was like a treasure chest had been prised open and was spilling out its spoils. Mae was worried they might cancel each other out, or there wouldn't be room for two such vibrant personalities, but instead they made the other shine even more. She herself was quiet for much of the night. She served an Ottolenghi salad with French bread and cheese. She even whipped up a fruit salad for pudding after Ari had been typically flaky and forgotten to bring something. But she was happy being a fly on the wall as her two favourite people in the world talked about fashion and literature and New York. It was like listening to a brilliant radio show.

Ari helped her tidy up while V flicked through magazines in the living room.

'Soooo?' whispered Mae when they were in the kitchen.

'I adore her,' Ari enthused. 'If you don't marry her one day, I will.'

Mae flicked water from the washing-up bowl at him. 'Hands off, hetero.'

'Seriously, though, she's fabulous.' Then he whispered, 'Have you talked to her about our plan? About the B word?'

'Jeez, give me a break! It's only been four months. No! Have you spoken to Oliver about it?'

'No, but that's different.'

'Is it? Why?'

'I don't know,' Ari said huffily, and walked back into the living room declaring it was time he called a taxi.

'Yes, I should be going too,' agreed V, and soon enough, Mae had waved them both off at the door. She'd asked V to stay over but had known she'd refuse. She was in her leisure wear and had to be home to dress in her fashion armour on Monday morning. Ari wouldn't stay either. He said Oliver would be back early the next day and he wanted to be there for him.

The silence without them was strange. She looked out of her living room window, as V and Ari strode across the road arm in arm and ducked into the back of a silver Mercedes. Her flat felt empty and sad. So she picked out her clothes for the morning, made her packed lunch and went to bed.

When V left for LA on Thursday, Mae felt terrible about the holding pattern she'd left their relationship in. They'd been going somewhere fast, but now, despite successfully deploying her best friend to help patch things up after their argument, she wasn't so sure.

She distracted herself with work, finally finishing her big story. But she noticed the lack of V's gentle attention. Her heart sank as she returned to her desk from a lunch break spent on the phone to Ari, assessing the extent to which she was self-sabotaging. Office life was dull without her secret girlfriend. She jiggled her mouse to wake up her computer, and at the top of her inbox was an email from the founders of FAM.

Subject: Your story

Dear Mae,

Thank you for sending us the draft of your brilliant article about our charity and the profiles of our inspiring young people. We found it extremely moving to hear you capture the kids' struggles so authentically. You seem to have a deep understanding of what FAM is about, and we're honoured that you took such an interest and that you share our passion for providing brighter futures for the city's most disadvantaged young people. With this in mind, we wanted to make you aware that we're currently recruiting for a marketing role, and wondered if it might be of interest. A stretch to think you'd leave the glamour of *Edit* for a charity such as ours, but more information about the role is attached just in case.

Warm regards,

Nicole

Co-founder of FAM

It hit Mae like daybreak. If she got that job, she'd be able to quit *Edit*. And that opened the possibility of being honest about her relationship without worrying how it might be perceived. Which opened up ... well, *everything*. She could finally stop getting in her own way.

She had to reach V to tell her she had it figured out. To tell her she was all in. She loved her and wanted the world to know it. Mae called her from her mobile in the bathroom, the only place you could expect any privacy at *Edit*. But V's phone went straight to voicemail. Of course it did; she was in Malibu with Ana Palomo. Mae wondered how far she would be willing to go to get the cover exclusive.

Chapter 20

Oliver had been chatty and good-tempered for the first weeks of June. He had surprised Ari with theatre tickets, had taken him for dinner at a fancy Asian restaurant up the Shard and a steakhouse by Tower Bridge. He bought him books that he'd researched online and thought he would like. He kissed him on the lips before he left for work, said *I love you* like it was easy. He sent him cute messages throughout the day.

He was fond of saying that being made partner at his law firm was unprecedented for someone so young, though Ari knew what he really meant was for someone so gay. If Oliver was happy, it made Ari's life easier. But it also meant he didn't have a purpose, something to fix in the same way he did when his boyfriend was in one of his sulks.

The start of summer was passing slowly. With Mae so preoccupied with V and her new job at the charity, and generally throwing herself head-first into life, one day dragged hot and lonely into the next. Ari found himself the outlier with Oliver's friends. He'd worked so hard to fit in his whole life, contorting to be the kind of person other people wanted him to be. It made him angry that there was something so complexly contrived about his boyfriend's straight-acting friendship group; that for the first time ever, he wasn't sure of his place in it.

Ari had no interest in the Cricket World Cup, but Oliver insisted on hosting viewing parties at the house for every big match. Jon and Lloyd, Billy, Frank and someone called Dobsy for a reason Ari didn't understand but assumed was a weird British thing, came over with six packs of beer and steaks to barbecue.

Oliver's garden was more of a luxury concrete yard. Plastic shrubs that didn't even try to look real sat in terracotta pots in each corner. The sun beat down on the white flagstones and there wasn't so much as a parasol to offer any shade.

Billy hissed open a Foster's and handed it to Ari, who slapped another slab of meat on the grill and said, 'No thanks, Billy. Still don't drink.'

'Ah, mate. I always forget that about you two.'

'I've noticed.'

Across the yard, Oliver was laughing at something Lloyd had said. It must've been a bit rude, because he shook his head and gave his buddy a friendly push. Ari caught his eye, and when Oliver smiled back at him, he felt addicted to his boyfriend's attention. He could never get enough.

He flipped the meat. 'OK, boys, I've got one steak well done here.'

'Who's the pussy?' shouted Dobsy.

'That would be me,' said Frank, sheepishly handing his plate to Ari.

Frank was Ari's favourite. The only one who'd ever asked him anything about his writing.

'Thought you of all people would know how to take your meat, Frankie boy,' said Lloyd.

'It's how I like it.'

'It's how I like it,' Dobsy mimicked in a high-pitched voice, and the others laughed sharply. Frank rolled his eyes.

'Get over yourself.'

Lloyd was drunk. 'I'll have mine nice and rare, Ari. Rareback, you could say. Raw as Oliver tops.'

'Gross,' Ari muttered under his breath as he seared the flesh on one side then the other. Oliver winced but offered no comeback.

'Nothing gross about two hot-blooded homosexuals doing it how the Lord intended,' said Lloyd.

Ari was sweating. His polo shirt clung to his chest under his apron. He hoped Oliver would say something kind. When he didn't, Ari flopped the bloody steak onto a plate and offered, mischievously, 'Oh, but Lloyd, I'm not a homosexual. And why would you assume Oliver is the top?'

The background chatter stopped abruptly. The men all looked at Ari, who wielded his spatula theatrically then loosened the belt of his apron and pulled it off over his head. He put down the cooking utensil so he could undo his hair from its ponytail and ran his fingers through it while everybody stared.

'I'm pansexual.'

Jon said, 'Are you fuck!'

'Which one's pansexual again?' Frank asked innocently.

Dobsy opened another can. 'It's when you're a massive slut and sleep with anyone, right?'

The men had inadvertently formed a circle around Ari. The barbecue smoked behind him as a string of sausages burnt to a crisp.

'He's taking the piss,' said Oliver, walking over to Ari and putting his arm tightly around him. He leaned in for a kiss and whispered, in an ominous tone, 'We'll talk later.'

'Match starts in three minutes, boys,' said Jon, checking his watch.

'I'll get the TV set up.' Oliver pushed open the French doors and began fiddling with the remote that turned on the large flat screen in the conservatory. Lloyd, Billy and Dobsy followed, taking their seats on a black leather sofa that Ari thought so disgustingly naff it was almost cool. Frank was the last to head inside.

'Is it true, though? Have you slept with women?'

Ari pressed the apron he'd been clutching since his outburst into Frank's arms.

'Will you take over the grill, please? I don't feel well all of a sudden.'

He walked back into the house through the side door to avoid the others. They were shouting, 'Come on, England!' as if it would make a difference. He snuck up to the bedroom and lay on the bed fully clothed. The curtains had been shut all day, the windows open. He took a few deep breaths and fell asleep.

When he woke up, it was night and Oliver was coming out of the bathroom.

Ari rubbed his eyes and said groggily, 'Sorry about today. I should've told you about my actual sexuality before blurting it out like that, but your friends, they're all so . . .'

His boyfriend was silent.

'Oliver? Are you listening to me? I thought you wanted to talk? It doesn't change anything that I'm not gold-star gay.

It shouldn't make an ounce of difference. And the truth is, I only ever slept with like two or three girls in New York when I was wasted. I just get fed up with everyone assuming things about me.'

Oliver got into bed and immediately turned off the side light, so the room was plunged into darkness. He rolled onto his side, and when Ari reached for him, he pushed his hand away.

This time, Oliver was silent for a week. They shared a house, they shared a bed, but he refused to even look at Ari. Now this *is* unprecedented, Ari thought, rising to the challenge of winning back his love. In the evenings, he heard Oliver talking and laughing on the phone with his buddies, but Ari felt like a ghost. Oliver acted as if he wasn't there – with dead eyes, he looked straight through him.

After four days of being ignored, Ari began to wonder if he did actually exist. He wrote in his notebook, reassured by the marks the pen in his hand could make on the page.

The Closet

> you will find me
> at the bottom of the sea
>
> past coral and reef
>
> beside clocks bent
> in time you'll see
>
> through the dark

and find encased in oak
bound in chains

near consumed by an octopus

the old groan of the cupboard
full of seaweed and crab

here in the suffocating wreck

you'll find me fangtoothed
ink-eeled
narwhal-tusked cracked
on the back
of an urchin's shell

filling a void only you
could create –

don't
stop

don't stop
I let you find me

in my state of resistance
full of the ocean's salt

but I'm ready
I'm ready for sweetness

The silence was finally broken in bed one night. Oliver said into the darkness, 'We should cut your hair.' The words hung heavy between them, echoing in the aftermath of seven silent days. Ari had said, in a moment of desperation, that he would do anything to make it better. He had not anticipated this. He thought of Mae, who told him he was beautiful, and of how Letty liked to brush his hair and take strands between her fingers, interweaving them into thin plaits.

He knew that its length, even when tied up, made him look different to other men. He knew it marked him as other. People weren't sure which of their stereotypes applied to him and this meant he had been free. But what had he done with that freedom?

'OK,' he said, and Oliver rolled onto his side, pulling him close. Ari felt the relief of a battle having ended, then the unsatisfying niggle of not knowing who had won.

The next morning, he sat shirtless on a chair in the kitchen. Oliver stood behind him. The blunt kitchen scissors made for an awkwardly inefficient guillotine. After some hacking at the thick black length of hair gripped in his left fist, it came off and he held it up as if it were the spoils of a hunt. He used clippers to shave off the remainder in neat strips, until Ari was unrecognisable.

'Hey, sexy!' said Oliver, rubbing the palm of his hand over the fresh fuzz like you might an obedient dog.

Later, when Oliver was in the kitchen whistling jauntily as he made them a chicken salad for lunch, Ari locked the door of the downstairs bathroom and looked at himself in the circular mirror above the sink. He turned his head slowly from side to side and wept, feeling that a part of him was lost for ever.

Chapter 21

He kept his hair clipped short, and the perky, easy-going side of Oliver emerged again. Ari was enjoying the novelty, if somewhat at a loss for how to *be* around his boyfriend when he wasn't trying to make amends for something he had done wrong. Every time he caught his reflection, he felt a complicated mixture of satisfaction and pain.

It seemed like a good time to suggest Oliver accompany him to Otley to meet his family for the first time. Oliver said they all sounded 'lovely' whenever Ari told him about life at Aunt Alice's. He'd avoided having to explain why he'd left New York; it would have just fed into his boyfriend's narrative that he was a fuck-up. He couldn't expect someone like him to understand. Oliver had asked about his father, but Ari just said they weren't in touch and didn't see eye to eye, and Oliver nodded as if that explained everything.

He was surprised that Oliver was looking forward to the trip. He called Connie the night before they set off. Partly to warn the family about Oliver's various allergies and partly to apologise. He understood what it was like to be on the receiving end of icy indifference now. And he'd behaved like that with them for too long. He felt a rising compassion for his mother.

'I'm sorry I cut you out, Mom,' he said after exchanging pleasantries. 'I suppose I felt you'd robbed me of all the guilt and pain I deserved to feel about Lilly's death by keeping my old phone, my one anchor to that life, hidden from me.'

Mentioning Lilly's name out loud made him feel faint. He sat down at the kitchen table, pleased that Oliver was still out at work.

'I was trying to protect you,' said Connie, sadly. 'I could never have predicted that something so awful would have happened, but honestly, I'm pleased you were able to enjoy your time in Leeds without the heaviness of it. I have wanted to talk to you, to tell you it wasn't your fault. But you've been so distant. We could have *connected*. We could have got through this. But I didn't know how to reach you even when you were here with us.'

He pressed his bare feet against the cool metal of the chair leg, catching his balance. He remembered the slammed doors. For him it signalled the end of a confrontation, but his mom would be slammed in the other side. He never knew really what that meant for Connie, had never dared fully comprehend it.

'You know your father sent me an email. Says he's in treatment for his issues. Sounded contrite enough, or at least he said all the right things. I'm ashamed to admit, I was tempted to message back. I don't talk to you about what it meant for me to leave him, because no one needs to be burdened by their parents' emotions like that, but Ari, just understand that Randolph has a power over me, and although I hate him so, so deeply, there's a terrible kind of love there that I just can't shake. Alice slammed the laptop down when she saw me hit reply. Almost severed my fingers.'

'Mom, I'm sorry. I know you've always shielded me from your suffering. I do see it. But please don't let Dad weasel his way back into your life. You're free now.'

'When you've been in a relationship like my one with your father, you're never free. I hope to God you don't ever need to realise that yourself.'

Ari felt weary of the constant dull threat of conflict with Oliver; he didn't have the mental capacity for a fractious relationship with his mother as well. And shit, she had been through so much – he was grateful she had never pulled him deeper below the surface.

'Just promise me, no more secrets, OK?' he said.

She didn't respond at first; then, after a minute, 'I can't wait to see you and meet Oliver.'

'Me too, Mom. See you tomorrow.' He hung up, and Connie's refusal to meet his promise lingered in the silence.

Early the next morning, Oliver drove Ari to Yorkshire in his haughty four-by-four, playing a 'how to succeed in leadership' audiobook the entire way.

Connie, Aunt Alice and Letty were waiting on the porch as the car crunched over the gravel driveway. Ari couldn't predict how they would feel about his boyfriend; Oliver was the first lover he'd ever introduced to them. He wanted to prove that after the professor, he'd found someone stable, someone normal. Someone who took good care of him. Because Mae had made her views on Oliver quite clear, he hoped for his family's approval even more.

When he hopped out of the passenger seat, all three looked a different shade of aghast. Letty said what they were thinking:

'Ari, what have you done to your mermaid hair?!' She burst into tears and ran upstairs without even acknowledging Oliver's presence.

'Doesn't it look smart!' said Oliver as he affectedly air-kissed Connie and Alice.

Ari felt burdened by his family's palpable disappointment, but also loyal to his boyfriend and aware that this was a test he needed to pass.

'Yeah, I'm really into it. I love it, in fact. Brand-new me.' He kissed Oliver brightly on the lips. Alice edged them out of the hallway and into the living room, where no one was yet comfortable enough to sit down.

'What's up with Letty?'

'She's been like this a lot since you left. She misses you so much. We all do,' said Alice, plumping a cushion. 'How's Mae? We haven't spoken in a bit. I gather she's got a new girlfriend who she really likes for once.'

Ari could feel the air around Oliver tighten at the mention of Mae's name. 'She's seeing someone, you're right, and she quit the magazine. She's working for a charity now and is super busy. We just don't really have a chance to meet up.'

Glances shot between Alice and Connie. Oliver, noticeably irritated that the conversation had so quickly turned to Mae, asked if there was anything he could do to help with dinner; it was clear from his tone that the enquiry was rhetorical.

'No, no, you go on up to the attic and settle in,' said Alice.

'Connie's on the couch tonight so you can have it all to yourselves.'

Oliver hauled his wheelie case up the stairs and Ari said he'd be there in a minute. As soon as Oliver was out of sight, the women enveloped their boy, squeezing him tight. Connie rubbed her hand against his shaved head.

'Was it his idea for you to cut your hair?' she asked.

'Of course not!' Ari said. 'I wanted a change.'

'So?' said Ari when he creaked into the attic to find Oliver sitting on the bed, about to open his laptop. 'What do you think?'

'About what?'

'My family!'

'They're sweet. They're nice. What do you want, a medal?' Oliver laughed.

Oliver's parents were called Rose and Donald. He phoned them every other Sunday. They were Christian. They knew he was gay, but it was never discussed. It had never needed to be. And when Ari pushed the subject, Oliver had said, 'You don't discuss being straight, do you?' There was little suggestion that Ari would be taken home to meet them any time soon.

Aunt Alice had pulled out all the stops. The best crockery was laid out on the table, and she'd made starters, and garlic bread, and a big pot of pasta with home-made pesto. Letty was wearing a dress and had designed little name cards for the seating plan, though Ari caught her changing her mind last minute and putting Oliver at the opposite end of the table to her. Everyone was on their best behaviour. This is jolly, he thought, hearing Mae's sarcastic delivery in his head.

After dinner, they played charades and Oliver did his very best to mime 'Flower Fairies' without having to actually hop about and flap his wings like a fairy. No one laughed. Everyone wished Mae had been there instead. But it could have been a lot worse was the general, unspoken consensus.

Ari kissed Oliver on the lips once they had packed the car and waved goodbye the following afternoon. As they pulled out of the driveway he reached over and placed his hand on his boyfriend's crotch, applying just enough pressure to imply he owed him something. When they were on the motorway, he broke the silence between them.

'Any feedback?' he asked with a curious laugh in his voice.

'Your mother is very beautiful,' said Oliver.

Ari smiled to himself and relaxed into his seat, and then Oliver added:

'But it seems like she's let herself go.'

Ari spent the rest of the journey pretending to be asleep.

Chapter 22

Ari had a feeling he would be indebted to Oliver for the trip despite his appearing to have enjoyed it at the time. And just as expected, the line *I drive you all the way to Yorkshire and you can't even ...* was now regularly deployed. He settled into it and did his best to repeatedly show his appreciation, mainly through being available for sex, cooking, shopping and organising the cleaner to come twice a week.

It meant that when Sam messaged to say he'd be in London for the weekend and wanted to get 'the old Leeds crew' back together for a grand farewell, Ari wearily accepted that it would be impossible for him to go without it causing a huge crack in the already shaky ground he was on with his boyfriend. Oliver was too busy even for his own friends at the moment. There was no way he'd be persuaded to join Ari and a bunch of people he'd never met at a gay pub.

Mae phoned on her way to work. 'Can't you just come without him? V isn't up for it either, but she just said to have fun and not get too wasted. I've told her what Sam's like.'

'Oliver is not as chilled as V, surely we've established that. He thinks everyone from uni had a crush on me, which let's face it isn't entirely untrue, and he'd be mad jealous but too proud to admit it, so he'd just be an ass about it. It's not worth the stress, Mae, honestly.'

'But Sam is moving to Sydney! How do you think he's going to feel if you don't make the effort to see him before he leaves?'

'I'll call him to explain. When has Sam ever been bothered about anything?'

Mae sounded exasperated when she said goodbye, but she was sensitive enough not to push it.

Ari didn't call Sam to explain. Instead, once Oliver had left for work, he took a deep breath, knowing that the next eleven hours were all his.

He put on a silk kimono and wrote while lounging on the sofa. Then he closed the living room blinds and slipped out of the robe to dance naked to Donna Summer, the soft cushion of the carpet beneath his bare feet. He felt bored, and *bored* quickly tripped into angry. Mae had always had it so easy. She'd never needed to compromise or prioritise anyone but herself. He pinched the soft skin of his inner arm, digging nails into flesh until the sharp pain shifted to a dark pleasure. He hadn't seen his best friend in person for months. She was so occupied with V and her work, and she had no idea. No idea at all that he hadn't just moved on. What had happened to Lilly haunted him still. Connie had betrayed him by hiding his phone. Elliot had *really* betrayed him. At least Oliver was loyal. Ari felt listless, guilty, ashamed. He hated the magnolia paintwork and the leather sofas. The only things hanging on the walls were television screens.

'Where's the art?' he shouted pointlessly. Really, he longed to see Sam. But Sam was single now and Ari didn't trust what would happen if he looked into his dark green eyes and felt his kind arms around him again.

In an attempt to distract himself from this line of thought, he fished the business card Mae had given him out of his wallet, found his laptop and, sitting naked on the sofa, emailed a selection of poems to the agent with a brief, self-deprecating note. He was about to shut his email down when a new notification popped up on his screen.

From: Dr Hines, Randolph
Subject: Son

Dear Ari,

This is not an easy message for me to write. Since you and your mother left, I want you to know that I have changed. I've been in therapy and as part of that journey I need to confront the roots of my anger. I have come to London because I need to talk to you. I'm staying near the South Bank. You can reach me on my cell or email. I'm here for as long as it takes to hear from you. I know you won't want to see me. But I have something very important to tell you.

DAD

Ari wondered how much he'd considered the sign-off, maybe tried a few different versions before switching to caps and typing those three final letters. Panic fell through a chute in his chest. Adrenalin set him to high alert and a cold sweat drenched his neck and back as if it had been lurking under his skin in anticipation of this moment.

He remembered the advice he had given Connie; he imagined Aunt Alice telling him to delete the message, to not give his father the chance to feel better about himself by making amends. He didn't deserve it, she'd say. But he was in the mood for pain. The more discomfort he felt, the closer he was to being absolved for Lilly's death. He regularly daydreamed about trials that measured his personal suffering against hers. He added up everything that made him feel bad and subtracted anything that made him feel good, and always the conclusion was that he needed to feel worse. He responded straight away to his father and said he could be outside the Royal Festival Hall in an hour.

He gave himself no time to think about what he would wear, let alone what he would say. He pulled on a pair of Oliver's ugly cargo pants, a plain black shirt, put on his helmet and cycled to the South Bank. Outside the main entrance, twenty minutes early, he took a moment to gather himself and catch his breath. He watched a yellow tugboat on the river. The sky was clouding over. He unclipped his helmet and hung it over his handlebars. Brushing a hand over his sweaty head, he felt the loss of his hair like grief.

'It looks good, kid.' His father, also early, was suddenly standing next to Ari, taking in the view. 'I barely recognised you.'

Ari was annoyed at being on the back foot already. He had wanted to make him wait and watch him a while before walking over and saying something clever. It took him a minute to turn and look at him.

'I regret it.'

'I know a thing or two about that,' said Randolph without missing a beat.

Ari scoffed.

His father was thinner. He looked shabby. His stubble was unkempt, and he wore an oversized Yankees sweater.

'Let's walk,' said Ari, and he positioned his bike so that he wheeled it between them, finding comfort in it as a shield and also an opportunity to escape quickly at any moment.

'You know, I would go fishing with my father twice a year . . .'

'At the Lake House in Connecticut. Yes, I'm aware, Dad. You told me that story every Sunday when I went to my dance class.'

'OK, well what I didn't tell you was I hated it. I never caught anything. Not a single fish. My father made hook bait out of chopped-up worms. He'd give me my own box at the start of every trip. We'd cast at the same time, my line always falling short of his, and then I'd sit there next to him, on a wooden stool, in silence for hour after hour while he reeled in rainbow trout and I didn't. "Bad luck, son" was all he'd say as we packed up to head home. It was the same every time.'

'When do you get to the bit about beating your wife?'

Randolph flinched and carried on.

'One afternoon, before we got into the car to head to the lake, I caught my dad in the garage, tipping some kind of white powder into my box of bait. He didn't see me, but I watched him. And do you know what I did? Nothing. I carried on fishing with him for another year until I left for college. Sitting there when I could have been at the movies with a girl, knowing I wasn't going to get a bite.'

'And of course, you assume it was sabotage, because the possibility that you simply weren't good at something doesn't even occur to you.'

'He had to win, Ari. That was the deal. And he did what-ever it took.'

'I am living for this metaphor, truly I am. Two men and their rods. But was this a speech you felt would in any way endear you to me? Look, Dad, I've got nothing to lose here. I don't care what you think about me any more, you don't control me. You can hate me all you like and it means noth-ing, because *you* mean nothing to me. I won. Don't you get it? I won.'

They stopped to let an impatient jogger overtake them. Ari wasn't sure his father had actually taken in what he said.

'I'm flawed. Like my father was and his father before him,' Randolph continued. 'Being a parent doesn't fix you, Ari. I've been doing a lot of thinking over the years since you and your mother left. I've been in anger management because my temper was not good for me.'

'You have got to be kidding! Wasn't good for *you*? What a joke. What about us? Do you tell your therapist what you said to your son? Or that you hit Mom? Or do you just talk about your mean daddy messing with your tackle?'

'I understand you're feeling frustrated.'

'Do not therapise me. You have no right to be here. This is my city now. I'm happy and you cannot reappear in my life and expect me to listen to this shit. You haven't even said sorry.'

'You don't look happy.'

'Fuck you, Dad.'

They had stopped walking and were standing in the garden under the OXO Tower, facing each other. Ari put his helmet back on and swung his leg over his bike.

'Wait. Son, I *am* sorry. I'm sorry for all of it. And everything you don't know, I'm sorry for that the most.'

Ari gripped his handlebars. One foot was on the ground, the other on the pedal. He was ready to push off and pretend this farce had never happened. But what didn't he know?

'I am literally out of here in thirty seconds.'

'OK, well . . . It's complicated, but I was infertile.' Randolph looked at the floor and kicked up some dirt. He dug his hands into his pockets and turned towards the river. 'I *am* infertile. Doctors diagnosed me years ago. It's not a good feeling. Imagine being a man and not being able to do the thing you are biologically made to do.'

Ari was confused.

'I didn't want anyone to know. At first I blamed your mother. Thought it must've been her fault we weren't getting pregnant. And you know what our friends are like. If we wanted to be part of that world, be somebodies, get the invites and the ins, we had to have a family. And I had a reputation to uphold. I couldn't be *weak*. Imagine what the guys at squash would say if they found out my junk was, well, junk. I'd have been a laughing stock.'

Like in the millisecond before a crash, Ari knew what was coming and there was nothing he could do to protect himself from it.

'Your mother should have told you this. But as part of my healing, it's important to me that you know. Ari, you were adopted.'

Chapter 23

Reeva carried a bottle of white wine and two glasses back from the bar and squeezed in next to Mae on the tatty Chesterfield in the furthest corner of the pub.

'It's not the same at *Edit* without you,' she said.

Her jet-black angular bob had been cut shorter than usual and her fringe was so blunt it framed her forehead like a ruler.

'There's no one for all the fashion girls to flirt with now, so they're buzzing round like bees on heat.'

'I'm not sure that's a thing,' said Mae, frowning in a jokey way.

Reeva smiled and Mae decided not to tell her she had red lipstick on her front teeth.

'Anyhoo. How's your new mega meaningful career? Putting us all to shame doing something important. Saved the world yet?'

Mae laughed and poured them both a glass. 'Cheers,' she said. 'To new starts.'

V had thought it a good idea for Mae to take Reeva for a drink to suss out if she knew they were a couple. She wanted to meticulously stage-manage their announcement and needed to be sure nothing got out before the big reveal. She planned to claim that they'd only got together once Mae had left the magazine, thus avoiding any accusations of unprofessionalism. Certain people were after her job and looking for any reason to throw her under the bus, as she saw it.

'I've basically been tasked with saving the charity. Raising its profile and getting enough donations to keep it afloat. The work they do is so important, it would be devastating for the kids if they had to close.'

'Don't I know it,' said Reeva. 'When Mum died, FAM was like a second home to me. They got me into creative writing – paid for my extra tuition. I wouldn't be where I am today without them.'

'I had no idea you'd been part of the project, Reeva! Why didn't you say?'

'I suppose I've just tried to shut the door on that part of my life, you know. Move on. It's not something I talk about. So I kind of forget that I can. V knows about my mum and stuff, but the fact that I was in care while my dad sorted himself out, well, it's not exactly on brand for *Edit*, is it? We're more about the free handbags than the free school meals.'

Mae felt the discomfort of her privilege like a punch in the gut. She took a large gulp of wine and screwed up her nose. It was warm and not very nice.

'Are you enjoying working for V still?' She looked closely for a reaction.

'Ups and downs,' Reeva said, her face revealing nothing more. 'She's tough and expects a lot from me, but it's fun in the main. And I'm learning tons of stuff, like did you know you can get fat frozen off your hips?'

'V does not do that!'

Reeva nodded and smiled with just the left corner of her mouth.

'Wow,' said Mae, incredulous.

'Oh yeah, I know all her secrets.'

'Do you?' asked Mae quickly.

Reeva opened the bag of crisps she'd bought and offered them to Mae before taking one herself. 'I do.' She looked Mae in the eyes and licked the salt and vinegar from her lips.

Mae coughed nervously and asked after her old colleagues. Reeva gave her just enough detail for it to feel like a catch-up rather than a gossip fest. They finished the wine and Mae said she'd better get back – she was due to run a drama workshop with FAM's LGBTQ group early the next morning.

'Shit, mate, that's rough. We're hosting a breakfast for the Paris editor at the Wolseley. I'm not sure we're gonna be able to be friends any more. You're a bit gritty for my liking.'

Mae laughed. The wine on an empty stomach made the blood rush to her head when she stood up. She retrieved Reeva's white Puffa jacket and held it open for her.

'Thank you, sir,' said Reeva, slipping her arms into the sleeves.

'I do miss all the fashion and silliness,' said Mae as they walked through the pub and out onto the streets of Soho. 'The only freebie I've got since joining FAM is a mouse mat that says "You Do You" on it.

'Want to share a cab back to Croydon? I can get one on V's account. She lets me expense a couple a month.'

'Oh, um, I've actually moved.'

'Where do you live now, then?'

Mae's brain was sluggish; she couldn't think fast enough to lie. 'Brixton,' she said stupidly.

Reeva was looking out for a taxi, her head turned towards the oncoming traffic, so Mae missed any flicker of acknowledgement. She wolf-whistled and waved her arm and a cab pulled over in front of them.

'Right then I'm off,' she said, hugging Mae. She felt like a marshmallow in her giant jacket. 'Tell the boss I'll see her tomorrow.'

'Great to catch up,' said Mae, closing the taxi door. It was only as she crossed the road to the Tube, a sobering breeze dislodging strands of hair from her quiff, that she realised the significance of Reeva's last words.

In bed later, Mae said, 'She knows.'

'Fuck.' V was unusually stressed. 'I knew it.' She put down her book and looked up at the ceiling as if it was the chandelier's fault. 'I'll have to talk to her tomorrow.'

Since Mae had moved in at the beginning of September, V's previously minimalist bedroom had taken on a more eclectic feel, with the piles of old university textbooks Mae couldn't bear to part with how occupying the nook under the window. A framed Polaroid of her and Ari outside Kween stood on the bedside table where a scented candle used to be. V was surprisingly tolerant of her trinkets. 'If they mean something to you, they mean something to me,' she had said when Mae carried her cardboard boxes of books and memorabilia along with five black bin bags full of clothes into her new home.

'She's as loyal as they come. I really don't think you need to worry.'

'Do you understand what's at stake here, Mae? Everything

I've worked for. We agreed we'd wait six months after you left to come out as a couple for a reason, remember?'

Mae wrapped one arm around her. 'I get it.'

'Do you?'

She pulled her arm out from between V's back and the pink velvet headboard. 'Sheesh, why does everyone have so little faith in my ability to empathise. Yes! I understand. But we knew this was a risk when we first got together. You weren't worried then.'

'I didn't know there was a plot to oust me from my job then. Sorry, I don't mean to be like this. I'm just tired. Let's get some sleep.'

'Honestly, I wouldn't say anything to Reeva yet. Trust her; she adores you.' Mae kissed V on the lips and turned out her bedside lamp. She lay on her side and V snuggled into her concave spaces. Mae stroked her bare thighs.

'V?'

'Mmm . . . ' she responded sleepily.

'You don't get fat frozen off, do you?'

'Oh my God! Reeva! I had one appointment, OK? One! And you think I should trust her?'

V had left for work by the time Mae's alarm went off at seven a.m. In the kitchen she'd left a smoothie in the blender with a yellow Post-it note stuck to it:

Sorry for being moody. I'm making you dinner tonight, be back by 8? Brenda x

Mae noticed happiness like perfume on her wrist that she'd forgotten all about. She grabbed her rucksack from a hook in the hallway and rushed out of the door. It was a dark grey, blustery morning and an unexpected downpour threatened her good mood. She pulled her denim jacket over her head to protect her hair and ran to the bus stop – her white boots were a regrettable choice.

The top deck of the bus was as steamy as a sauna. She sat in her favourite spot at the back and stared out of the window. Twenty minutes later, she was untangling her earphones when Ari called.

She answered without letting him speak. 'Hey, I've been meaning to give you the T from Sam's drinks. Jules hasn't changed. Still annoying. Sam said you never called. Think he was pretty upset you didn't go ...'

Ari was silent. She pressed the bell and stood amid a crush of people in wet coats on the stairs, waiting to get off the bus. The woman in front opened her umbrella by accident, causing a chorus of profanities.

'One sec.' Mae pushed herself through the rush-hour crowd as if it were a rugby scrum. She walked hurriedly off the main road and onto the cobbled alleyway where FAM occupied a converted Methodist chapel and the offices above it.

'Ari? What's wrong? Why aren't you saying anything?' She was on the steps of the building, kids pushing past her into the hall. Her half term improv class started in five minutes.

'Will you meet me later?' Ari asked flatly.

'Ah, shit, I can't. V's cooking me dinner.'

'Oh.' Ari sounded devastated. His voice cracked. 'Don't worry then.'

Mae changed her mind quickly. 'No, I'll be there. Of course. Where?'

'Meet me under the hut in Soho Square?'

'I can make it by six,' said Mae. She knew V would understand. Whatever was wrong was something more important than skipping Sam's drinks, that was for sure.

All day she worried. What she wanted was for Ari to tell her he was breaking up with Oliver, but knowing him it would be nothing so simple. Her improv class descended into chaos when a sixteen-year-old boy mimed performing oral sex on a banana.

'Well what did you expect me to do with it, miss?'

'Not that, Benjamin. Anything but that!' The rest of the group fell about laughing.

She was surprised that almost twenty of them had signed up for her class, and wished she'd put a little more thought into planning it. All the staff at FAM, even those in executive marketing roles like Mae, had to spend a certain number of hours with the young people each month.

Nicole, the CEO, had been watching, and said afterwards that she'd handled the situation well.

'You're a natural with these kids, Mae, and you know sometimes you've just got to laugh. They like you, but most importantly they respect you. I think it's because you look as if you could beat any of them in a fight, then when you speak, you're just the nicest, funniest girl. If that's how you identify?'

'As nice? Or funny?'

Nicole looked embarrassed and Mae felt bad. 'Girl, yes. Mainly. Good of you to check, though. Listen, I need to leave a bit early tonight. Can our meeting wait until tomorrow?'

At 5.30 exactly, she dashed out of the door and took a bus to Tottenham Court Road.

She first recognised the long khaki mac that Ari wore every autumn. His head was bowed and his shoulders hunched. It was October and the day had burned out quickly. Mae was walking fast towards the middle of the square, then stopped abruptly. Ari hadn't yet seen her, and she looked at him with a mix of fear and dread curdling in her stomach. Why had he shaved his head? It was the first thing she asked, her shock trumping any attempt at sensitivity.

'Ari! How could you?'

He looked so crushed she didn't push him for an answer, just stared at him a bit longer, trying to make sense of this gaunt, sad-looking boy.

'God, I'm sorry. I was shocked. It's OK,' she said finally, sensing the seriousness. 'I'm here.' She wrapped her arms around him and he folded himself into her. He cried quietly at first; then, when he couldn't catch his breath, he began sobbing so loudly that passers-by noticed.

It took about ten minutes for him to get enough of a grip to say, 'Mae, I'm adopted. My mom and dad adopted me from Romania.'

They sat on a bench and after some moments of shocked silence Ari told her what he knew.

'So they lied to all their New York friends, saying Mom was pregnant and they'd be moving to the UK for nine months to be nearer her side of the family. My dad. *Randolph.* He of course would have boasted that Harley Street had the best OB-GYNs in the world. It made sense. No one questioned it, apart from Aunt Alice. She knew all this time too.'

Mae was reeling as she tried to make sense of this new information whilst anticipating how Ari was feeling about it.

'They spent six months holed up in what Dad called "a really top-notch" spa resort in Zurich before travelling to Romania, where they had – and I quote – a "dreadful" few weeks staying in the best hotel they could find, and after meetings with various intermediaries they were presented with a baby. Me. My biological parents are dead, so I can forget about tracking them down. And any other issues I am to take up with Connie. According to him, it was all her idea.'

'You need an ice cream,' said Mae, feeling instantly ashamed of the childishness of the suggestion but bereft of any alternatives. She had to practically drag his forlorn body into Bar Italia, where she sat him at the back and ordered gelato with chocolate sauce.

Ari smiled faintly. 'It's nice to be looked after,' he said. 'Oliver didn't want to hear any of this last night. To be fair, he's working on a really important case, which I get . . . '

He told Mae that he didn't know much more about the adoption and wasn't sure if he wanted to, but that he'd never let Connie and Alice off the hook for keeping it a secret. 'I can't talk to them about this – at least not now. I just have to slam the door on it. It's too much otherwise.'

'But Ari, look where silence has got you. Shutting your family out isn't the answer.' Mae had a pang of guilt about her own parents. She thought of the almost daily messages her mother sent her, which she never seemed to have the time to answer. She remembered the rambling voicemails from her dad that she still hadn't listened to in full. She wasn't sure she believed her own advice. But Ari wasn't paying attention anyway.

'If Mom . . . if Connie had just told me, it would have explained so much.' Every time Randolph looked at him with such obvious hatred and disgust, he was seeing his own failure as a man, Ari reasoned. It made sense that his father hated him.

'My instinct was right,' he continued, licking the spoon after demolishing two scoops of vanilla. 'The problem was never that I was queer, it was that I was *here*, that I existed in my father's life at all.'

'Will you tell me why you cut your hair?' Mae asked, trying her best to remove all judgement from her voice.

Ari took a deep breath as if coming up for air, and seemed to notice that Mae was not a part of him, but separate and sitting opposite carefully eating a Baci brownie.

'Please? Was it Oliver? Did you do it for him?'

He nodded sadly, then looked away, tears filling his eyes once more.

'Eurgh! You do realise he's force-fitting you into his life like a piece in a puzzle that's in the wrong place.'

'Don't do this. Not now.'

'But how can you stay with him, Ari? I'm sorry. I've tried to keep my mouth shut for so long, but you have got to be able to see it.'

'I see it. But I love him. I want him to be happy. I chose to cut my hair. He didn't hold me down. I wanted to do it. I want to please him. I'm sorry that's hard for you to understand.'

Mae had once been able to slip into Ari's feelings as if they were her own. But the way he felt about Oliver was a stark reminder that they were not a single consciousness. His depths were unknowable, and this caused her a crushing sorrow.

'I don't know how to help you through this when Oliver is holding you back from me.' Mae downed her espresso and reached urgently across the table for Ari's hand.

'Don't worry about Oliver. He's mine to worry about.' Ari pressed his fingers between hers and gave a reassuring squeeze.

'Why don't you come and stay with me and V tonight? We can talk more.'

Ari nodded, then got up and went outside to call Oliver. 'I'm not asking for his permission, before you say anything. I just need to let him know.'

When he returned to the table five minutes later, Mae could tell he'd been crying again. But she bit her tongue.

'If Oliver ever asks, which he won't, you were helping me edit my poems tonight, OK?'

'Fine,' she responded flatly. She couldn't stop herself from adding, 'But why you need to lie about staying over is beyond me.'

He pretended not to hear. 'Oh, anyway, I forgot to mention amid all the *draaaama*, that agent you hooked me up with wants me to do a book or something. I told her I'm thinking about it.'

'Finally! That's so amazing. I'm thrilled for you.' Mae gushed, thankful for the change in mood.

They stood up and she held him fiercely. She left a ten-pound note on the table and Ari looked at her quizzically. Outside the café, Soho was dressing for dinner.

'I had sex with the barista,' Mae whispered. 'Before V, of course. And I never called her back.'

The lights were set to ambient and V was waiting in the living room, reading competitor magazines, when Mae got home with Ari shuffling sadly in behind her.

'Sorry to miss our dinner date.'

'Don't worry,' said V, laying the latest issue of *Rouge* on her lap. She had changed from her workwear into a robe and bundled her hair under a headscarf. 'To be fair, I've always known you'd drop me for Ari in a heartbeat.'

'Ah, come on, it's not like that,' Mae said, bending to kiss her cheek. V smiled, but Mae knew there was a hint of real jealousy behind the joke.

Ari gave V a hug and thanked her for letting him stay. V rubbed his shaved head, but as Mae had messaged to warn her in advance, she made no comment. He took a seat in the rocking chair opposite the fireplace.

'Come here.' V patted the spot next to her on the sofa, and Mae pulled off her work shirt, adjusted her black vest and slumped down, sinking blissfully into the softness that surrounded her. V reached over and untangled the silver chains around her neck

'So tell me, how is our beautiful boy?' she then asked Ari kindly. 'We're sorry we've not had you over sooner. It's been too long. Unlike your hair.'

Nothing important was complicated with V. While Mae spun thoughts around her head, twisted them into little knots that seemed impossible to undo, her girlfriend would take the same problem and gently work at it until a solution revealed itself. She would loosen a mass of emotions with an easy tug.

V's face quickly changed into a mask of genuine concern as Ari filled her in on the adoption. Mae added her own sense of betrayal, which was nothing compared to what her best friend was experiencing, but nonetheless, Connie, Alice and Letty had felt like family, and she was shocked that they could have kept this a secret for all these years. V listened patiently, but she might as well have not been there. Mae and Ari were looking at her, but really they were talking to each other. At half past ten, she excused herself, explaining that the top-floor spare room was made up, and she'd see them in the morning.

After they'd said goodnight to V, something in Ari shifted. His eyes narrowed as if focusing, and he sat up straighter.

'Since I saw my dad yesterday, something has been spinning around my head. It's louder, so much louder than everything else. I want to be a parent, Mae. I want to have a family. I want it so, so much.' The usual soft growl of his American accent took on a sharpness. 'Oliver won't have anything to do with it, I promise. I want to make it happen with you. And with V, of course. Do you think she'd be up for it?'

It had been a long time since they'd first fantasised about starting a family together, and now Mae wasn't sure if this was something she wanted or if it was what she knew Ari wanted. Those had been one and the same thing for a long time.

She crossed her legs and bit her bottom lip.

Ari continued, 'You don't need to worry about Oliver, I know that's what's putting you off.' He was frantic, and the tears started to fall down his face again. 'I'll split up with him. Or I'll have him sign a contract when we get to that point, relinquishing all rights and responsibilities.' He focused in hard on his future family rather than the one that was unravelling around him.

Mae realised she was tensing every muscle in her body as he talked. Ari was wild with this desire and it scared her. But there was something true beneath the madness that she had to admit felt right. She unclenched her toes and tried to relax her shoulders.

'I don't think this is the best time, but ... OK, yes. The answer is still, is always, yes. I want to have a baby with you. One day.'

A floorboard creaked outside the living room door. V entered, looking furious.

'I was just going to remind you to blow out the candles,' she said, striding over to the coffee table, then the mantelpiece, then the bookshelves, blowing them out herself. Without saying anything more, she left the room. Darkness and lemongrass-scented smoke hung in her wake.

V appeared to be meditating when Mae climbed into bed next to her.

'Can we talk?' she mouthed, gesturing for V to take off her headphones. V closed her eyes and exhaled so deeply it sounded like the sea. Mae removed her necklaces and put them carefully in the little dish on her bedside table. When she looked back, V had stopped meditating, put her glasses on and was staring expectantly at her.

'I'm guessing you heard ... everything?'

'If by "everything" you mean that you and Ari are going to have a baby together, then yes. Jesus, I don't know what I'm finding harder to process: Ari's shaved head, his adoption bombshell, or the fact that my girlfriend is having a baby with a man I barely know. Have I been transported into an episode of *EastEnders*?'

V was witty when she was angry or emotional. It was what her whole work persona was built on and served as a useful defence mechanism. But here in bed with Mae, the tone misfired and they both felt it.

'You don't *barely know* Ari. You two get on like a house on fire.'

'That's not the point, Mae!' You two have this whole life planned, this future . . . Where do I figure in it?'

'Ari and I made a kind of promise to one another back at university. I suppose we wanted to know that we would share something important one day – that something would come out of this love we had for each other. And I was waiting to talk to you about it, because the more I fall in love with *you,* the more scared I am that I'll have to make a choice.'

V turned on the bedside lamp. She took off her glasses and rubbed her eyes, then lay on her side, resting her head on the crook of her elbow. She smiled softly at Mae.

'I take it you *were* planning on telling me, then?'

'Oh my gosh, yes, of course! I was building up to it. I just wanted to wait for the right time so we could talk about it properly. Because I don't want to lose you, V. I know it sounds a bit mad. I'm twenty-seven. But I've always wanted kids someday.' Mae looked up at the ceiling, but she felt the intensity of her girlfriend's eyes on her in the soft light. 'And I guess because Ari found out he was adopted, and all the other issues he had growing up, he wants to be the kind of father he never had. There's more of an urgency to the plan for him now.'

'What about you, Mae? Because "someday" and "now" feel like very different places.'

'Yes. But they're inching closer for me, I think. I want to be a parent. I always have. Honestly, I don't know why. It's like this longing deep inside me. And it was something we'd planned to do by the time we're thirty and I guess we're almost there. I've sometimes worried I'm too queer for it. And Ari almost definitely is.' She closed her eyes.

'That's sad. And also not true, Mae.' V pushed herself up and leant against a stack of pillows behind her. Mae rolled onto her front, pressing her face into the mattress. She had laid herself bare and now wished she could disappear. She felt V's cool hand on her naked back.

'It's all the crap around parenthood that turns it into a big hetero-fest,' V said calmly. 'Being a mother is what you want it to be. It makes total sense to me that you'd have a family. Yes, you're young. Don't remind me! But you aren't like others your age. I've seen how you look after people.'

Mae's voice was muffled. 'Did you ever think about it?'

'I've sometimes pictured myself with kids, but that longing you describe, I don't have that. And I know for sure that no way do I want to grow a baby inside me. None of my exes were family types themselves, so I threw myself into my career. To be frank, until this very second, I've not really thought that much about it.'

'But it doesn't scare you?'

'It scares me that it might be something you'd do without me.'

Mae slowly rolled onto her back. She pulled V on top and wrapped her arms around her.

'I'm so sorry you found out that way. I should have told you sooner. But ... do you want to be part of it now, like part of the conversation, I mean? Obviously the actual doing of the thing might still be a long way off.'

Chapter 24

I know you adopted me.

These were the only words Ari had spoken to his mother in weeks. He'd ignored all Connie's attempts to contact him, but still wrote long letters in his most legible handwriting to Letty, and she sent him back pressed flowers from the garden and notes on pages ripped from her school books that always ended with: *Connie is really upset and wants to talk to you.*

After signing with the literary agent, an impressive woman called Basma in her mid-twenties who was a rising star in the publishing world, Ari had deadlines. She told him his poems were raw and vital but also that he needed to quit moping and get on with it. Her energy reignited something he had buried deep. *Take up space*, she had told him. She gave him equipment for a makeshift home studio and insisted he record himself performing a poem and talking about it at least once a week.

He waited until Oliver had left for work, then put on a black silk shirt dress and stood in front of the camera feeling more confident than he'd done in years. His thick dark hair was growing back fast and he fashioned it into curtains. He smudged a charcoal-grey eyeliner along his lower lids, which made his big brown eyes look, as one boy wrote in the comments after Basma posted the first video to his new social media account, 'soulful and sad ♥'.

When Ari watched back the videos, he liked what he saw. This persona felt truer than the person he'd become in real life. Oliver wasn't interested, beyond being irritated that the tripod was kept in his walk-in wardrobe. He didn't have time to watch what Ari created but still authoritatively declared it self-indulgent. Ari didn't need his approval. With Basma's help, his audience grew from a few literary fan boys to hundreds, then thousands, and after a reading went viral just a month after his first post, his follower count hit 40,000.

'So a while ago, I found out my parents aren't my parents. Biologically speaking.' He looked into the dark lens and spoke as if he was alone with Mae and it was only her listening. He went on to introduce his latest piece, which gnomically hinted at the violence of his upbringing, by explaining that the shame wasn't in the fact he was adopted, but that it had been a secret. 'No good comes from hiding,' he said, having rehearsed his lines in the mirror before hitting 'record'. He took a pre-planned breath. 'Self-loathing festers in the unsaid.'

He was processing the revelation that he had started life in a Romanian orphanage by being violently honest about it with the thousands of strangers who were drawn to him online just as their university friends had been paper clips to his magnetism. He read and responded to almost every comment and nurtured a community, many of whom felt alienated by their family and had grown up not fitting in. He enjoyed the power of a following. Mae was being more attentive than she had been all year, but she hadn't mentioned 'the plan' since

V had overheard them chatting about it. Virtual thumbs-ups validated him in a way he'd been missing.

When Basma informed him that he'd secured a two-book deal with a major publishing house, Oliver supposed this meant more lolling around in pyjamas writing.

'Please don't show off about it,' he said. 'It's really not attractive.'

Ari normally let such feedback roll off him like raindrops on Gore-Tex, but this hurt.

'Fine,' he said boldly. 'I'll make a plan to celebrate with Mae and V instead.'

Ari liked V a lot. She could be decadent, loud and funny, and she was glamorously camp. She was in the centre of fashion but somehow managed to rise above its pretentiousness to understand it as art and as commerce, and Ari, having witnessed his mother's own fall from grace in that same world, respected her for it. He enjoyed watching how easily she and Mae worked as a pair. It was a surprising match on paper, but the more he got to know V, the more he realised the thing that anchored them was the same. They were both somehow substantial. They didn't fill each other's gaps; as a couple they were wholly themselves. V would reduce Oliver to a quivering schoolboy given the chance – she was far sharper and more intelligent than he was. So was Mae, come to think of it. But she couldn't control her emotions the way V had learnt to.

'So what *do* you like about this guy?' V had asked him once.

'He's there for me, I guess. And . . . I don't know, it's complicated. He satiates something I need. And he's hot. It just is what it is. Changing anything feels too complicated.'

V had looked at Mae, who shook her head in response, as if to say, 'Don't go there.'

His friends never passed up an excuse for a celebration. The Saturday after he'd shared the news, Mae told him to meet them at seven p.m. in their local Italian restaurant in Brixton.

Oliver can't make it. But sounds fabulous! See you there, handsome ;-) xxx

He'd texted Mae an excuse for Oliver out of habit, even though everyone knew he wouldn't have come.

When he closed the front door behind him that evening, he felt bad for having abandoned his boyfriend. He crossed the street and looked up at the house. It was dark, apart from a single white light coming from the bedroom on the second floor. He watched Oliver, topless, hammer-curling weights in front of the mirror. Even from this distance he felt desire stirring, and fought the impulse to run back upstairs and throw himself into Oliver's arms, to beg him to consume him and take him away from himself. He was still staring when Oliver stepped straight in front of the window and pulled the curtain across. If he noticed Ari there, he gave him no acknowledgement.

It was a quarter to seven. Ari ran as best he could in heeled boots to the station, and once on the hot Tube, clattering through deep, dark tunnels under the city, he shifted his head out of Oliver's world.

He followed the directions Mae had sent him to a small restaurant adjacent to the market. He wove through busy tables and down some stairs. He saw Letty first. She was blowing up balloons. Mae and V rushed to his side and linked his arms.

'Don't freak out, but your mum's here too. And Alice.' Mae winced, as if expecting him to lash out.

They guided him around a corner to where his mother and Alice sat next to each other at a long table. Ari saw his aunt squeeze Connie's hand in support.

'Everyone here cares about you so much, Ari, and we are all so proud of you,' said V, and Ari looked at her like she had crossed a line.

'We wanted you to be able to celebrate with the people you love,' said Mae from his other side.

Ari still hadn't spoken when ten-year-old Letty skipped up to him and put her hand out for their secret handshake. He couldn't not.

'I took the day off school to come to London,' she said after the final high-five.

'I hope you don't get in trouble,' said Ari, genuinely concerned.

'I don't care if I do.'

Alice got up from the table and now stood behind Letty, ruffling her hair.

'Ari, we *had* to come. We needed to talk to you. When Mae rang and told us about your book deal, we were so chuffed. We said, "Right, that's enough, we've got to see our boy," and Connie, well, she'll tell you, she's been desperate. We've been watching all your videos and we miss you so much.'

Letty pulled her mum away to help with the balloons, and a waiter popped his head in to see if anyone wanted drinks. Ari left Mae and V to order and sat down next to Connie, who was nervously chewing nicotine gum and pretending to read the menu.

'I thought you hated pizza,' he said.

'People change.'

'Do they?'

'Well, your father evidently has. Can you believe he's in therapy?'

Ari was silent. The others took their seats at the table but talked among themselves.

'He had no right to put all that on you. I wanted to tell you the whole story and I was waiting until I thought you were ready to hear it.'

Through gritted teeth Ari hissed, 'Please don't pretend you were protecting me. It barely washed the first time, Mother. This was a lifetime of a lie.'

Connie clenched the menu in her hands. 'I so wanted you to be mine. If you knew you didn't come from my body, I worried you'd have a reason not to love me as much. And if I lost you ... It was just too unbearable to even think of.' She spoke in an urgent whisper so that Ari had to lean in close to hear. 'Your father hated me, blamed me even though it was in black and white on the medical records that the reason we couldn't get pregnant was all down to him. And once we'd started the lie – not telling anyone; disappearing off for nine months; coming back to New York with a baby – it was too late. You grew up so fast. I often thought about telling you, but whenever I tried, I couldn't find the words. Having that secret with your father became one of the few things that kept us close. I worried what would be left without it.'

He let his mother's words wash over him like warm water, easing the pain. He looked down the table to Letty, who was holding court. She had roped V into demonstrating what happened at a fashion show, using her knife and fork as the front rows and a pepper grinder as the model.

'Let's order!' he said loudly.

Mae jumped up, elated, and sandwiched herself between mother and son, bending down to put her arms around each of them. When the waiter returned, Alice asked him to take a photo and handed him her first-generation digital camera.

'You can look at the little square at the back, see,' she said. 'Now, eyes up, everyone – I want a nice family portrait.'

Ari said 'cheese' and wondered what Oliver would be doing right now, and what subtle warning would be waiting back at home.

Beneath the table, Connie passed her son a letter. 'Read this, another time, then ask me anything. Anything at all,' she whispered. 'I'll fill in any gaps. You might not have grown in my womb, but you grew in my heart. Never, ever forget that.' She reached for his hand and he opened his palm in a silent forgiveness.

Letty was exhausted from the long trip to London, so after dinner, Connie and Alice bade everyone an emotional goodbye so that they could get her to bed in their hotel. Ari wanted to put off going home as long as possible. Mae and V needed little convincing to accompany him to the pub.

The three of them cut a curious picture as they marched down Electric Avenue. Ari and V were roughly the same height and equally finely bedecked. V wore her weekend casual jeans with four-inch heels ('These are my running shoes,' she'd told him), and Ari had on silk harem pants, sandals and a crop top, with a black denim jacket tossed over his shoulders for modesty. It was a *fuck you, Oliver* outfit. Mae had made an effort too, dressed in black cigarette pants and a white shirt with the top three buttons undone and the collar half turned up. She stood between them like their security detail.

Not drinking had started to feel less and less necessary for Ari and he'd begun to wonder why he was bothering to keep up his sobriety. Oliver seemed very keen for him not to drink, but secretly he treated himself to the odd glass of wine when he was feeling happy and in his own company. At the Talbot, V asked what he wanted.

'I'll have a gin and tonic and I don't want anyone making a fuss about it. I've dealt with enough tonight. OK?'

'Ari—'

'I said no fuss.'

V asked, 'Any particular gin?'

'The most expensive.'

Three gin and tonics later and he was feeling the warm undoing of alcohol in his bloodstream. What was it Mae had said about stopping before you had the urge to have one last drink? He'd try that, but he wasn't even close yet. The girls shared a bottle of red and quickly became woozy with booze and the emotional intensity of the evening. Mae squeezed inelegantly out of the booth to go to the bathroom and Ari rested his head on V's shoulder.

'You're wonderful,' he said.

'You too, Ari.' She bent her head and her curls fell in his face.

'I suppose I should say sorry for you finding out about our plan that way.' As soon as he spoke, he regretted it.

'Our plan?' V lifted her head and Ari sat up straight.

He felt a nihilistic impulse to say the next words in his head out loud.

'The plan for Mae and me to have a baby together one day.'

There. It was done. He'd started something or ruined something. He wondered how long he had until Mae reappeared. V's body language changed. She turned so that she was looking at him iris to iris and took a long, deep breath.

'Yes. It wasn't a great thing to overhear in my own house. But Mae explained. And I suppose you want to know what I think?'

Chapter 25

The night of the *Edit* Awards was also the annual FAM talent show. Mae had arranged for the older kids to put on a dance performance and had invited reporters from local papers. She wasn't supposed to have favourites, but ten-year-old twins Luke and Lewis were special. As soon as she was introduced to them at the after-school club on her first week as the charity's marketing manager, she saw something of herself and Ari in each of them.

Luke was a nascent drag queen, but despite watching endless online tutorials, and FAM using precious funds to get his make-up kit started, he still hadn't mastered contouring. Lewis was quieter, more sensible, and too serious for a kid. But he came alive around female attention and was allegedly dating two thirteen-year-old girls from school at the same time.

'It's a nightmare, miss,' he'd said to Mae one afternoon when she'd popped in to see the kids after working in the office above the community centre all day.

'Please don't call me "miss", Lewis, it's creepy. And it seems that you need to dump one or both of them. I'll help you write a message – give me your phone . . .'

The brothers were incredible dancers. They'd never had any formal training but could move their bodies in ways that Mae could hardly fathom. They had been in the care system since they were born and had accepted that they would probably never be adopted now. Their current foster carer was 'nice enough but proper dull', they said. Mae had to be careful not to give them too much attention around the other children.

For the talent show, Luke was performing 'It's Raining Men' in drag and Mae, via V, had arranged for one of *Edit*'s regular make-up artists to do his face. Lewis was fronting a hip-hop routine with some of the other boys, and when he backflipped across the stage, Mae couldn't bear to watch. Afterwards there was a party that she begged the project leaders not to advertise as a disco. 'No one will come if you call it that,' she insisted.

She had time to take one twirl on the dance floor with Luke before getting changed out of her jeans and hoodie into the Prada suit V had arranged for her and jumping into the sleek black car that was waiting outside the centre. She would pick V up from the office on the way so they could walk the red carpet together as a couple for the first time.

Mae felt nervous. Reeva would still laugh, shake her head and mutter, 'I just can't believe you thought I didn't know,' whenever Mae mentioned V's name, but that wasn't why. No, she was nervous because Ari would be receiving a New Talent award and doing a poetry reading at tonight's ceremony and Oliver was accompanying him.

When V slid into the cream leather seat next to her, she filled the car with a rich, velvety scent. 'You smell like sex,' said Mae, nuzzling into her bare neck.

'Is it too much? I did three spritzes, I normally do two.'

'It's perfect.'

'Look at you!' said V, turning to her. 'I knew dusty pink would be a great choice. You scrub up well, pretty boi.'

'I hope I don't let you down.'

'You're a heart-throb and you know it. The entire *Edit* team had a crush on you. I'm scared to let you out of my sight tonight.' She leant over and kissed Mae on the lips. 'Can I run my speech one last time?'

It still floored Mae that her girlfriend was so beautiful. When she was dressed for a work occasion, she exuded such an aura of glamour and celebrity Mae couldn't quite believe that she was the same woman she'd woken up next to. As the host of London's most star-studded annual party, she was looking resplendent. She'd spent the afternoon in hair and make-up, being dressed by her favourite stylist, who had secured her a very in-demand Erdem gown for the occasion. She seemed to glow as if the spotlight was already on her.

Reeva was waiting for them at the venue, a disused factory by the river in south-east London. She wore an earpiece and wielded a clipboard like a Viking shield.

'Alpha One is in the building, repeat, Alpha One has landed.' She spoke into a walkie-talkie.

'Don't I get a code name?' said Mae, giving her friend a firm hug.

'You're the First Lady tonight – how does it feel, mate?'

'Not sure yet.'

Mae ran around and opened the door for V. She took her hand and the two of them were escorted by Reeva to the start of the red carpet. They were attacked by flashes from the waiting paparazzi, and in front of the step-and-repeat, blinded by the glare of lights, Mae began to lose a grip on what her facial muscles were doing.

'Am I smiling?' she whispered to V through clenched teeth. 'I feel like I've gone into rigor mortis.'

They turned to face each other, and as soon as their eyes met, they burst out laughing. That was the picture that would be splashed all over the society pages the next day, announcing that 'the editorial ice queen has melted thanks to new squeeze and ex-writer turned charity worker'.

Inside the cavernous old sugar warehouse, blue and purple lights swished from floor to ceiling and models mingled with actors, fashion designers, writers and artists. V had made a point of inviting every single member of staff, including the receptionists and Jason from IT, who milled around the edges looking conspicuously normal. As she was whisked off by Reeva to have her brief audiences with the most important guests, Mae reminded her that if she happened to bump into Ari and Oliver, not to mention anything about their plan.

'As if I don't have enough to think about tonight,' V replied, trying to modulate the annoyance in her voice.

Mae fought her way through a gaggle of the *Edit* team, who swarmed on her demanding she spill about her relationship with V. 'We heard you were doing it in the fashion cupboard,' said one beauty editor.

'Who made the first move?' asked another.

Raven rolled his eyes. 'At least she's approving all my shoot concepts at the moment, so whatever you're doing, keep it up, hun.' As he turned with a flounce of his LV cape, Mae heard him say under his breath, 'I give it a year.'

An announcement was made for everyone to take their seats for dinner, but Mae hadn't yet seen Ari and wanted to wish him luck. She knew he'd be nervous. When she scanned the table plan, however, she realised that she was, of course, seated next to him. V was involved in every tiny detail of planning.

Ari and Oliver walked towards her. They were holding hands and wearing matching tuxedos. They looked like the December picture in a 'hot boys' calendar. Mae was pleased that Ari was growing his hair back.

'How bonkers is this!' he squealed, giving Mae a quick self-conscious hug. Oliver slapped her on the back like she was an old pal.

'You must be so proud of him,' she said.

'Of course I am,' said Oliver. 'Not that he needs any more fans.'

After the entree, V made her speech. Mae knew it off by heart and was unconsciously mouthing along. The room erupted in applause, and V said it was her great honour to introduce a close personal friend, and an exciting new voice in literature, Ari Hines.

When Ari leant in to air-kiss V and take the glass slab embossed with his name, she whispered something in his ear that made him smile in a way Mae had only rarely seen. He nodded and hugged her again, and when he said, 'Thank you,' she could tell it was for more than the award.

Mae couldn't take her eyes off her favourite two people in the world on stage together. It was as if they'd been put there just for her. She could have stared at them all night. It had only been four years since she'd pushed Ari onstage at gradu-ation to collect his degree. He'd been broken and wretched that day. Now he was back, not to his fullest or his brightest, but he seemed at least happier; his success had coloured in one of his empty shapes.

Basma jumped up out of her seat, wolf-whistling and clapping loudly. Mae was too transfixed by her beloveds' combined star quality to move, but out of the corner of her eye she noticed that Oliver had his phone hidden under the table and was replying to what looked like a work email. She got up then and clapped for both of them.

Once the applause had died down, Ari performed a poem. The audience carefully held its breath until the last line, when the silence snapped and the atoms in the room shifted in the aftermath.

He remained bouncy and excited throughout the evening. He was itching to dance, but first had to be whisked backstage for photos. Mae was finally reunited with her girlfriend, and they kissed passionately in the middle of the room because V was tipsy now the scary bit was over, and because 'Fuck it, it's what everyone wants to see.' She knew the power of pleasing the masses.

Oliver was pointedly charming. He was well versed in how to behave with important people. He complimented V on her speech, thanked her for the fantastic party and said warmly, 'I must let you go.'

'He seems perfectly nice,' said V as he disappeared into a throng of people by the DJ booth. 'Are you sure you don't want to give him another chance, Mae?'

'No way.' Mae had to shout over the music, which had

been cranked up for the after party. 'Look, over there, he's heading to the coat check. He's leaving without Ari! He wants to sabotage the night – he can't bear Ari getting all this attention. He's going to leave, and Ari will spend the rest of the night anxious about what he's done wrong this time. He's so controlling and I can't stand to watch it any more. Hold my drink.' She thrust her champagne glass into V's hand and strode over to the exit, just as Oliver reached the door.

'I cannot believe you're doing this to Ari. Tonight! After everything he's been through recently. Are you not even capable of basic kindness?'

'You have no idea what I'm capable of.' Oliver shrugged on his coat and wrapped a Burberry scarf around his neck like a noose. 'You all have fun.' And with that he left.

Mae found Ari dancing with the winner of Best Actress, a fifty-year-old Spanish woman in a black halter-neck dress. She'd kicked off her heels so she could keep up with his moves, and the two of them seemed so in the zone with their seductive, rhythmic circling of each other, Mae didn't want to interrupt. Basma sidled up next to her. 'He's hot property right now,' she said proudly.

'He's no one's property,' said Mae, who was beginning to think she might have had a better time if she'd stayed at the FAM talent show.

Basma looked shocked.

'Sorry. I know you didn't mean it like that. I just worry about him. People have a way of turning Ari into who they want him to be.'

Sensing he was being talked about, he extricated himself from his dance partner.

'Where's Oliver?'

'Oh, um, I don't think he was feeling well,' Mae said. 'I caught him at the exit. He had to go home.'

Ari looked dejected.

'What an incredible night.' Basma attempted to change the subject. 'Everyone is raving about you, and I just spoke to a promoter who wants to talk about a tour.'

'Did he say it was his allergies?' Ari asked Mae. 'It's the dry ice, I think. I'd better go after him.'

'Don't you dare!' said Mae and Basma at the same time.

Softer this time, Mae said, 'This is your night. Celebrate. Oliver will be fine.'

Ari stayed, but the party had gone from him. Mae knew he wasn't really present. She hated seeing him like this, but if she pushed him, he pulled away, and it was safer to keep him close.

In the car home with V, she asked what it was she'd whispered to Ari up on the stage that had made his face light up with such joy.

'What do you think?' V said with a smile, before resting her head on the window and falling asleep.

The next day, Mae had been up for an hour when her phone rang. Since moving in with V, she'd established her own weekend morning ritual – seeing to the garden, making a big pot of coffee for them both, and sitting at the marble kitchen island to read the stack of newspapers she still scanned for story ideas, despite no longer being a journalist. V did her exercise regime and took work calls. They didn't bother each other until at least eleven a.m., when they would meet back in bed to have sex then discuss what to do with the rest of their day.

Mae hoped it was Ari on the phone letting her know he'd got home OK after last night. But the word *MUM* flashed up on the screen, causing her to panic. She and her mother spoke once a week, on a Thursday morning, before Mae started work and Janet hosted her discussion group. Phoning outside of this window was for emergencies only.

'What's happened?'

'I think that's for you to tell me, dear.'

'Am I on speaker phone?'

'Yes. Your father's here. Say hello, Michael.'

'Hello, Michael,' said her father in the background.

'I don't know what you mean, Mum.'

'Well, Sandra from book club has just sent me a link to a picture of you on www dot what the hot dot com and you appear to be having a delightful time with a young woman who the caption refers to as an "editrix".'

Mae groaned. She'd been planning to tell her parents about V when she next saw them in person. She wanted to pre-empt their questions and concerns before they embarrassed her by saying them out loud.

'I've tried to tell her it's not the same as a dominatrix,' her father called from a different room. 'But you know what your mother's like when she gets an idea into her head.'

Mae took a deep breath. 'Her name is Virginia. She is the editor of *Edit*, and then after I left, she ... she became my girlfriend.'

'Well. We'd like to meet her, wouldn't we, Michael?'

'Yes, of course we would love to meet her, and she's

welcome to bring all her whips and cuffs,' he chuckled down the line.

'Dad!'

'Michael. You are a naughty boy. Why don't you bring her along to my annual festive nibbles, dear?'

Mae reluctantly agreed, and felt her hangover dial up a notch.

Chapter 26

V walked up the driveway in front of Mae's parents' house, with her girlfriend dragging her feet through the gravel next to her. Mae had been dreading this day. They carried a handle each of a heavy Harrods hamper, which Mae hoped was at least the next best thing to turning up with a charming boyfriend on her arm.

Mae had met V's mum months ago and seen more of her than her own family ever since. Leah Bates was in her mid-sixties and had spent her working life as a nurse but was now rediscovering her passion for true crime and crochet whilst enjoying her retirement. She refused to take money from her daughter, who had offered countless times to buy her a bigger flat or pay for a holiday. She liked things just the way they were. Mae had warmed to her instantly, as she had done with Connie and Alice. She felt relaxed and comfortable around other people's mothers in a way she never had with her own, who operated at a pitch that she found impossible. She'd seem sullen or cross when she simply lacked the energy to match Janet's preternatural cheer.

Mae's family home was in a cul-de-sac, where she'd taught herself to skateboard at the age of ten. There were patches of snow slowly melting on cars in the driveways. She was embarrassed by the toytown architecture, the pebble-dash, the too-green Astroturf in front gardens. Lace curtains were twitching more than usual at their arrival.

Something strange happened to Janet's face when she flung open the door and saw her daughter and her new girlfriend. It went from a big forced grin to complete surprise and back again.

'Well! What a gorgeous pair you make! Wonderful! Wonderful! And look at your *hair*, Virginia ... Isn't that just wonderful!' She reached out an arm. Mae dropped her side of the hamper and stepped protectively in front of V, giving her mum a perfunctory hug.

Janet, as Mae had warned, began by telling V about the terrible fate of a friend-of-a-friend who had yesterday 'passed on' after discovering he had a lump in his testicle.

'She likes to kill the vibe from the outset so it can only get better,' Mae said, ushering V into the hallway.

V sounded like she meant it when she told Janet how lovely her house was. Photographs of Mae as a child, looking like a tomboy from an Enid Blyton book, lined almost every wall. And there was a framed *Edit* issue featuring her first cover story in pride of place above the piano.

'I thought your parents didn't *get* your old job,' V whispered in her ear as they passed.

'They didn't, but my mum still likes to boast about it. Now she says I run a charity, as if I'm Melinda Gates.'

They walked upstairs, nodding a polite hello to various middle-aged women in sparkly Christmas shrugs en route. V smiled at them all and said, 'Nice to meet you.' She had been in rooms with some of the most intimidating people in the world, so when Mae asked if she was OK for the fourth time in as many minutes, V snapped, 'It's not the Met Gala, babe. I'm perfectly fine, honestly.'

Upstairs, Mae pushed open a door with a *Keep Out* sign crudely nailed to it. Her parents had kept her old bedroom untouched since she left home for Leeds at eighteen, in case she ever needed a place to stay. V entered as if walking into an art installation and looked carefully at the space, searching for meaning.

'Classic baby dyke posters, right?' said Mae. Sharleen Spiteri was above her desk, Leonardo DiCaprio as Romeo by the mirror. She threw herself onto the single bed and motioned for V to join her.

'You're a different generation to me, remember,' V said, taking a seat on an inflatable purple armchair instead. 'All I had on my walls were certificates of achievement from school.'

'Cute,' said Mae. She hugged her pillow. 'I remember practising kissing on this. Can you picture me here? Crying onto my crystals about my unrequited crush, mood ring a persistent blue, listening to Texas and reading *The Well of Loneliness?*'

'I think we'd have been friends. Though you were way cooler than me. It's nice to see this side of you. You're so cagey about your family.' V got up from the plastic armchair with a loud squeak. 'It's as if the thing you want to hide is the fact you've got nothing to hide.'

Mae laughed flippantly. 'Let's go meet my dad.' She jumped up and kissed V briskly on the lips.

She knocked four times, twice fast, twice slow (their secret code), on her father's office door.

'Come in,' said a friendly voice. 'Maybe baby! How are you? And this must be Virginia. You know I once had a great-aunt called Virginia. Terrible drunk.'

'Hi, Dad,' said Mae, and V stepped forward to shake his hand and introduce herself properly.

'I told your mother I was looking for something, but I've been hiding up here for an hour. She's in full flow, I find it easier to get involved once she's settled down a bit.' He turned to V. 'Janet considers herself quite the hostess.'

'I see where Mae gets it from then.'

Janet called up the stairs. 'Mae, darling, would you help me with these vegetarian sausage rolls? I have no idea what to do with them.'

'Just read the instructions on the back, Mother.'

'Righto, sorry,' shouted Janet.

V gave Mae a quizzically disapproving look.

'OK, I'm coming, Mum, one sec.'

Alone with Mae's father, V felt an unfamiliar flicker of nerves.

'Do you drink whisky, Virginia?' he asked.

'I do now,' she laughed.

She perched on his mahogany desk and Michael pulled his office chair round to face her. He smiled warmly and handed her a glass, then took a dusty bottle of Laphroaig from a shelf and poured.

'She's certainly sounded jollier on the phone since she met you. And Mae is rarely jolly. I hope we can get to know you, and maybe get to know Mae better too in the process.' He gave her a smile, unaware of the sadness etched in it. 'Cheers.'

V clinked her glass against his and wondered why Mae

chose to involve herself so deeply in Ari's dysfunctional family rather than embrace the love of her own.

In the kitchen, Mae removed a tray of vegetarian sausage rolls from the oven and tipped them onto a silver platter. Janet's hands were inside oven gloves, but she'd been distracted by her friend Frances, who was showing her photos of a new grandchild from an album she kept in her handbag.

'Of course, I suppose you won't have grandchildren of your own?', said Frances sadly.

'That's rather an assumption, dear,' said Janet, wafting her oven-glove paws dismissively.

Mae stood between them with the platter. 'Can I interest you in a sausage roll, Frances?'

Frances bit into one and screwed up her face. She spat it out into a napkin. 'Will you be getting any pets, Mae?' she asked, wiping her mouth with the back of her hand. 'Perhaps a little cat would be nice company in the absence of a family.'

Mae took a deep breath and walked away, so she never heard Janet say, 'Don't be so ridiculous, Frances. You have no idea.'

V was surrounded by jauntily bedecked ladies all asking her questions about being a magazine editor. Mae pushed through the circle around her. 'Might I steal Virginia away for a moment.' She took her by the hand and pulled her into the laundry room. There was a bundle of Michael's shirts waiting to be ironed on top of the dryer, but it was otherwise immaculate. The smell of fabric softener reminded her of childhood.

'I can't stand these people. I was just with my mum in the kitchen and she and one of her book club cronies were talking about how sad it was that I'd never have children. Suggested we got a cat!'

'Oof. Your dad's great. I like him.'

'He's on his best behaviour.'

'And your parents' friends seem nice enough.'

'Let's have one drink, then go.'

'That feels rude, Mae. They've gone to so much effort.'

'Trust me.'

They snuck back into the kitchen, and Mae ladled two big portions of mulled wine into glasses.

'There you both are!' Janet was now sufficiently lubricated. 'You really do make a fantastic-looking couple.'

Mae mumbled something under her breath.

'It's lovely to meet you properly, V. I really hope we can see more of you now.'

'Oh please. Why, so you can parade us as a curiosity in front of your uptight friends?'

V looked as shocked as Janet by the vehemence of Mae's outburst.

'I'm sorry if I've said something wrong.' Janet started to flounder.

'You haven't,' said V kindly. 'I'm having a lovely time.'

'We're going,' Mae said, downing her mulled wine and taking V's still steaming mug from her hand.

'But you've only just arrived! At least say goodbye to your dad.'

On the train home, V seemed pensive.

'Sorry that was so painful,' said Mae.

'It wasn't painful. You were. You change so much around

your parents it's awkward for everyone. Mae, you are so lucky. Think of someone like Reeva. Or those boys at FAM you always talk about, Luke and Lewis. What they would give for a home life like yours.'

Mae blushed and looked out of the window.

'I don't want to make a thing of this, but it was . . .' V searched for the right word, 'disappointing to see how dismissive and unkind you were when they obviously adore you.'

Mae bristled, annoyed that V hadn't come away with the same feeling she had. 'My mum just *loves* men. She talks about them like they're these mythical creatures women can never fully understand but must revere nevertheless. She tries so hard to hide the fact that she's gutted I'm not bringing a handsome boyfriend home who she can flirt with and adore.'

V cut her off. 'She struggled with your sexuality, and granted, that's unacceptable. You should all have addressed it at the time. But rather than talk to her openly about it now, as the emotionally mature adult person you are, you present this weird, incomplete version of yourself. As if you're still the sixteen-year-old caught kissing what's-her-name . . . Maxine in your kitchen. And your dad. You talk about him like he's this bumbling fool, but he's sharp. He totally gets you. From my perspective, it's you who misunderstand your parents. And I reckon you need to sort that out in your head before we go into this baby thing with Ari.'

Mae thought about this the rest of the way home and guilt kept rising to the surface. She pushed it back down and it popped up again like a plastic bottle in water. As their cab pulled up outside the house, she sighed so loudly it sounded more like a groan.

Inside, she enjoyed the instant shock of calm her new home hit her with. It smelt like subtly scented candles. The lighting was neither too bright nor too gloomy – it was an ambience she'd never be able to afford herself. In the hallway, she stood in front of V's wall of beautifully framed family photos. Then she sat down on the bottom step and began trying to compose a message to Janet. She scrolled back up through the texts her mother had sent her over the past few months. Most, she noticed had gone unanswered.

Read this in Good Housekeeping. Interesting!!! Janet had sent the message weeks ago, but only now did Mae decide to click on the link. It was a story about different lesbian mums and the ways they'd had their children. The photos showed smiling women with their arms around each other, cradling a newborn baby, or with the back of a toddler's head in the foreground. Mae scanned the article cynically, trying to imagine what Janet would have thought about the couple who used an anonymous donor from a Danish sperm bank.

Interesting. At first, she took the comment as pejorative and patronising. But with V's words ringing in her head, she began to wonder if her mother had meant it that way. Was it a clumsy attempt at connection? Was this Janet's way of opening up a conversation, and had she simply shut it down with her silence?

V asked her to move so she could head upstairs to bed. Mae shifted towards the wall to let her pass. 'You're right,' she muttered, looking up at her. 'As usual. Dammit. It's so much easier to hate my parents than hate who I am with them.'

*

The next day, Mae phoned Michael and Janet, apologised for her abrupt exit, and asked if they'd like to spend Christmas at her new place, with V and her mother Leah. There was a big spare room, she said, and they'd have their own bathroom. Janet was quiet for so long that Mae worried she hadn't been able to brush off her behaviour yesterday as she usually did.

'Mum? What do you think?'

'Gosh, sorry! We'd absolutely love to! I just can't quite believe you've invited us,' she sniffled into the receiver.

'I know. I realise that. I'm sorry, I should make more of an effort. I *want* to make more of an effort now. Maybe we could, like, get to know each other a bit more.'

'Well I'll have to help, I can't have you doing it all. I'll bring pigs in blankets and I can batch-make my eggnog.'

'Mum, please. No fussing, or I'll revoke the invite.'

'Mae!' shouted V from the other room. 'Be nice, remember!'

'We'll be delighted to have you. I'll be in touch with the details. See you on the twenty-fourth.'

On 23 December, just after the *Edit* offices had closed for the holidays and Mae was winding down activities for the kids at FAM, though she'd arranged for the centre to stay open in case anyone needed a place to escape to, V's phone rang in her handbag under the coat rack. Mae fished it out for her and ran with it into the kitchen, where V was making mince pies.

'It's Reeva, should I answer?'

V shook the flour from her hands. 'Yes, put it on speaker phone. It must be important for her to call on my day off.'

'Boss, I've got bad news. Is Mae there with you?'

'Hi, Reeva!'

'OK, good. There's going to be a coup. I've just heard from Raven's second assistant, who was talking to his first assistant when it slipped out. Raven is making a play for your job. He's got the publisher on his side. Says it's his relationships with the fashion houses that are bringing in all the ad revenue and he's had enough of playing second fiddle to a . . . to a woman like you. I'm sorry, V. He's threatening to walk and has testimony from the advertisers that they'll pull their spend when he does. The big boss is flying over from New York and they're going to corner you after the Christmas break. Make you and Raven apply for the job, and you know Raven will already be working on his pitch, or paying someone else to work on it.'

V seemed strangely calm. In a crisis, she always went into herself and became singularly focused.

'I'll come over,' said Reeva. 'We can start work on your game plan tonight.'

'It's the night before Christmas Eve, Reeva. You're not going anywhere. Unless you want the company, of course?'

'I'm at the boyf's family for the holidays.'

'Right then. Stay put. Enjoy yourself, relax and let me think about this. Let's talk after the big day, OK? And thanks, as always, for looking out for me. You're a good soldier.'

Mae was shocked. 'What do you need?' she asked.

'I need to get through Christmas with our families. And then I think I'm going to need a new baby.'

Given the conversations they'd been having with Ari ever since the Edit Awards, Mae wasn't sure how literally V meant this. She felt anxious momentarily. It was too soon, surely. Without Edit, V would need an all-consuming project. A big job. But no, she wouldn't want to hop straight from being a magazine editor to being a mum. Although Mae pushed the thought out of her mind, the possibility lingered like the sweet earthy scent of their Christmas tree.

Back in early December, Ari had been booked on a two-week reading tour of the East Coast of America. Oliver acted like he'd chosen his work over him, and called him selfish for agreeing to go. At first, Ari felt terrible about it and asked Basma if he could cut the trip short, or if there was a budget for him to fly back halfway through to check on Oliver.

'Are you fucking joking?' was her response.

Because of this, by the time he returned to London, the couple's normally tepid relations were down to freezing, and Ari was exhausted from trying everything in his arsenal to make it better. So there wasn't much to lose when he suggested that given everything he'd been through with his family this year, he'd like to go back to Otley for Christmas. Oliver was invited, but if he didn't want to come, Ari would happily go alone.

Oliver hated Christmas. He didn't want a tree because the pine needles fell into the cracks in the floorboards and were a nightmare to get out. He had no desire to see his own family, nor his boyfriend's for that matter, which put Ari in an impossible predicament. He had to choose between leaving Oliver alone on Christmas Day and disappointing Letty, Aunt Alice and his mother as he had done for the past five years. In a flash of clarity, he booked a train ticket to Leeds. He was wrapping presents and keeping out of Oliver's way when Aunt Alice called his cell phone.

'Ho ho ho! Not long now!' he answered excitedly.

'Ari, the place has flooded. We've had terrible rain these past few days and it's all come through the roof. There's a lake in the living room. The whole village is in the same boat. Actually, I wish we were in a boat. It's a nightmare. Your mother's clothes are ruined, she's beside herself. You're not going to be able to come for Christmas. We're being put up in a local B and B by the insurers while it's sorted.'

'Oh Alice, I'm so sorry. That's awful. Is Letty OK?'

'She's being a drama queen about it, as you can imagine.'

'We'll be together next year, whatever happens. You have my word.'

He felt so sad after saying goodbye that he instinctively dialled Mae's number.

'Spend Christmas with us!' Mae said without hesitation once he'd filled her in. 'Call Alice back right now and tell them all to get a train down to London tonight. We've already got my parents and Leah coming. What's three more?'

'Will you check with V first?'

'Babe!' Mae shouted. 'Can Ari, Alice, Connie and Letty join us for Christmas too?'

He heard V in the background: 'Of course, though some-one will have to take the sofa bed.'

'We have three spare rooms. It's not a problem. Come over tonight if you want. It'll be fun.'

'Such fun!' said Ari hysterically.

Ari hadn't told Oliver about the flood, or the change of plans. He knew how this would play out.

'Everyone will be sad not to see you, but we can do some-thing really special for New Year's together instead.'

'You're still going?' said Oliver in disbelief.

'Yes, of course.'

'Wow,' he said, narrowing his eyes.

'What's the problem? I'm spending Christmas with my family like ninety per cent of the population, and as I said, you're very welcome.'

'You do what you think is right,' Oliver said snappily.

'I will,' said Ari.

It was the bravest he'd felt in a while. He finished packing his bags and called a minicab. When it was outside, he quietly ran downstairs and flung himself into the back seat. As the car drove over Albert Bridge, which was all trussed up in sparkling lights, the idea of splitting up with Oliver in time to start the new year was becoming increasingly appealing.

V's house was now Mae and V's. She was contributing towards the mortgage payment each month despite V telling her she really didn't have to. Ari found it strange that people who weren't from money cared so much more about the fairness of giving and receiving it. Oliver liked to be the breadwinner; he enjoyed the status of paying for everything. He had no idea that Ari's trust fund was spilling over now he was earning from his writing too. He would find it emasculating that his poor orphaned writer boyfriend was sitting on a fortune. And Ari had to admit he enjoyed the secret that he was rich. It felt like his superpower. He could leave Oliver any time, buy a house of his own, travel the world, disappear. And yet he still chose to stay.

The cab stopped abruptly outside number 11 Grove Street. What good was a superpower if you never used it?

Ari thought. He heaved his suitcase and four bags of presents from the boot. There was a wreath on the front door. It was festive but understated so as not to upset the neighbours. Inside, Mae had gone wild with the Christmas decorations. Ari looked appreciatively at the real holly and ivy that wound its way up the stair rail, and the big paper stars that hung delicately from the edges of V's framed artworks. Both women were at the door to greet him, and V said, rolling her eyes and gesturing at the decorations: 'It's all her, of course.'

'You love it,' said Mae, smiling. 'It's tasteful, as promised! But yeah, OK, I got a bit carried away.'

Ari put his arms out to hug them, and was pulled into the fold of femininity he so missed. He liked the way they fussed over him, taking his coat, leading him to a nest of cushions on the big sofa. Mae offered him a glass of mulled wine. He was drinking more regularly now. It no longer led to blackouts or a quagmire of despair, but he still tasted a sharp kind of shame with each sip and was conscious that Mae moderated her own intake around him, keeping an eye on how much he topped himself up. He wasn't sure whether to be embarrassed or appreciative of this, so settled for something in between.

'I'm afraid my parents are already here,' Mae said. 'Mum is adamant I told her to come on the twenty-third, when we all know I said Christmas Eve. She pretended to be terribly sorry when she rang the doorbell an hour ago. V and I were in no way prepared for her arrival, but she has settled herself in comfortably nevertheless.'

'Janet!' shouted Ari, jumping from the sofa.

'Oh, is that you, Ari?' came a plummy reply from the kitchen.

Mae followed Ari out of the living room and watched as her mother threw herself at him. Ari picked her up so that her feet lifted from the floor.

'It's wonderful to see you again! It's been so long.'

He put her down carefully and Janet blushed. She seemed to come alive around male company in a way that had always made Mae cringe. Ari extended a hand to Mae's dad, but Michael pulled him in for a hug instead.

'Ari, my friend. Happy Christmas.' He patted him on the back, and when Ari emerged from the embrace, he was grinning in a way Mae hadn't seen for a long time.

V appeared with a tray of champagne.

'It's not too early to celebrate, is it?'

Janet clapped her hands and squealed.

V's mother arrived the following afternoon, and Mae felt certain that *her* mum was comparing the natural friendship Leah had with V to the stilted performance of a relationship she and Mae were guilty of. Ari neutralised the intensity between the two matriarchs and their daughters by being delightfully solicitous. By four p.m. on Christmas Eve, Janet – flighty and insecure – and Leah – stoic and unpretentious – had, thanks to copious refills of wine, met each other somewhere in the middle. After supper, they played Scrabble on the kitchen table while Michael snored in a chair by the fire and Ari, Mae and V finished prepping vegetables for Christmas dinner.

'I see you've learnt how to peel a spud finally,' teased Mae. She stood in between Ari and her girlfriend at the kitchen counter, feeling childishly giddy with excitement. Ever since the three of them had begun talking about having a baby together, sending the occasional text message with name ideas, sharing links to articles about co-parenting and queer families, V had become as invested in the plan as they were, and she loved how Ari so elegantly made space for her in their friendship and their future.

'Darling, I'm a veritable Martha Stewart these days. Oliver loves a Sunday roast.' The mention of his name brought Mae back down to earth, but before she could make some snide remark about him, the doorbell rang.

'Oh Lord,' said Ari. 'They're here. Let the games begin!'

Mae wiped her hands on her apron, which displayed an image of a naked male torso and ran to welcome her guests. Letty barrelled straight into the hallway, declaring the house the coolest she had *ever* seen.

'I literally can't believe you have pink steps!'

Mae bent down to hug her. Letty's cheeks were cold and she smelt of cheese and onion crisps.

'I missed you, Letty Bear.' When she stood up, Alice enveloped her, wax Barbour mac damp with rain.

Connie was the last inside. She inhaled through her nose and said, breathing out, 'Ah, Diptyque candles, the eau de success.'

Mae laughed. 'It's Baies. Are we a terrible cliché?'

'Quite the opposite, dear.'

Mae initiated an air kiss, knowing Connie wasn't a hugger. 'Come on in and meet everyone. It's a full house.' She led them through to the kitchen and sat at the table with Janet and Leah, pretending to admire their Scrabble words while surreptitiously watching the way Ari embraced his aunt and cousin then hung back polite but aloof with Connie. She noticed her mum's eyes darting from person to person; she would be worrying about where she fitted into this dynamic, accepting that Connie now occupied the chief diva slot more authentically than she herself could.

It would, Mae assumed, bring out the worst of Janet's character as she battled for attention and felt the need to prove her worth among such big personalities. She had been thoroughly briefed on not mentioning Ari's adoption, but Mae assumed it would only be a matter of time before she wouldn't be able to help herself. Their eyes met and Mae forced a smile that Janet matched in insincerity. The next forty-eight hours were going to be a ride.

She started to regret her decision to host Christmas for such a group of complicated and wildly incompatible individuals. And then she saw the way her girlfriend stood so poised and confident amid the muddle of bodies, radiating calm despite being desperately anxious that her role as editor-in-chief of a magazine she had nurtured from its conception was being snatched away from her. Virginia Bates handled life with grace. It made Mae feel that together they could survive anything.

Michael was roused from his nap by the high-pitched chatter. He peeked his head around the kitchen door and said, 'I must still be dreaming! A bevy of beautiful ladies has suddenly appeared.'

'Dad!' Mae dropped her head into her hands.

V engineered the greetings as expertly as she had at the *Edit* awards, offering a conversational gambit or morsel of information with each new introduction.

Alice said, 'I can't remember the last time I was called a lady! Haha. Nice to see you again, Michael.' Then she turned to Ari. 'Come to think of it, where's Oliver? He'll top up the testosterone in the room.'

'Oh, Oliver's doing his own thing.'

There was a sudden silence. Everyone looked at the floor, the walls, anywhere but at each other, until Letty said, 'Phew! He's terrible at charades.'

By eight p.m. on Christmas Day, the house was a mess of wrapping paper, abandoned glassware and small bowls of crumbs where snacks had been. V had let Michael choose a record from her collection to play. He placed the needle carefully on the vinyl's outermost groove, and as Nina Simone's voice pierced the warm pine-scented air in the living room, he reached out an arm to his wife, who sat slumped against Alice's broad shoulder on the sofa.

'I've had too much trifle, dear. It wouldn't end well,' she said.

He twirled over to the fireplace, where his daughter and Letty were ripping bits of tissue paper into tiny pieces and dropping them into the flames, which rose and danced higher each time.

'Will you have this dance, Mae?'

'Oh my god, Dad, no, awkward.'

V had accompanied Connie into the garden so she could smoke *sans* judgement, or else one of them would have felt sorry enough for Michael, who had drunk almost half a bottle of whisky on his own, to take up his offer. Leah was washing dishes. She insisted she wanted to do it. V explained that she was an introvert, and it was actually her excuse for some alone time after a heavy social day. So that left Alice. She firmly shook her head when Michael looked at her expectantly.

Ari, who had been sitting in the armchair in the corner of the room, reading a book on voguing and the history of the ballroom scene that V had given him, stood up and bowed theatrically. 'It would be an honour.' He placed his hands on Michael's waist, and Michael took his shoulders and led him inexpertly in a slow dance. Ari looked tired. He closed his eyes and let himself be guided around the room in stately circles. Mae turned her head from the fire to watch, feeling a swirling cocktail of embarrassment and love.

'The room's spinning,' said Michael, and Ari pulled away, gently escorting his partner to the sofa.

'I think it might be time for us to retire,' said Janet, patting her husband patronisingly on the knee.

'We should hit the sack too, Letty, it's been a long day.' Alice heaved herself up and brushed the crumbs off her Christmas jumper. They all hugged goodnight, looser and more intimate with each other now.

Alone in the living room, Ari pulled Mae into him.

'That was lovely.' He was wearing suit trousers and a white silk pussy bow blouse, though the bow had long since come undone. Mae had bought a new gold velvet lounge suit for the occasion.

'What did I miss?' asked V, her heels clacking loudly as she walked through the door. She hadn't taken them off all day. Mae was astounded. She somehow looked as well put together in her long black chiffon dress as she had when she first got dressed that morning.

'Ari and Dad just had a romantic moment.'

V didn't seem to need any more detail. 'Mum's gone up to bed. And Connie said she wanted a bath.'

'I guess it's just the three of us then.' Ari sighed and collapsed onto the chaise longue. The girls followed suit, slumping onto the large mid-century sofa opposite.

'It shouldn't have worked, but it did,' Mae said, reaching for her now warm glass of white wine on the coffee table in front of her.

'Our families, you mean?' asked V.

'Our *family*,' said Ari, smiling. 'Don't you think it felt like we all somehow belonged together?'

'You know what, it did,' said V, picking up the thought, ready to run with it.

'I don't think my parents have had a better twenty-four hours, like, ever. They seemed so happy.' Mae took a sip of wine and handed her glass to V, who finished it in a single gulp.

'See. It makes sense we'd have a child together,' said V.

'Whoa. That escalated quickly.' Mae laughed nervously, guessing where the conversation was going.

Ari said, 'Yes, V! I'm so happy to hear you say that, because you know I couldn't agree more!'

Mae sat back as Ari and V leant forward.

'We can make it work however we want,' Ari continued. 'That's the beauty. The whole parenting dynamic is totally up to us. I don't think I've asked you this yet, V, but would *you* want to be pregnant?'

'Gosh, no. Mae's already said she's taking that one for the team.'

Mae felt unduly sober all of a sudden.

'Oh, right, yeah, I guess I did say that.' She wilted.

With excitement rising in her voice, V said, 'So, we've got a mum and the other mother. Ari, what does that make you? Dad or donor?'

'I'd love for the child to know it was connected to me. But dad feels a bit loaded for me at the moment. I don't know, though – I guess they can call me whatever they want. And if you two were doing the day-to-day parenting, I'd be cool with that. I wouldn't need to be involved in *everything*. Just the big stuff.'

V nodded slowly, thinking.

This plan had been Mae and Ari's secret. Over the years they'd held it carefully as if it could break. Now that there was a third person involved, it was becoming less precious. V was giving shape to the unsaid and asking all the difficult questions they had skirted over ever since first whispering about it in the dark. Mae watched her girlfriend talk, not interrupting, but letting her find her way to what it was she really wanted to say.

V stood up and Ari took her spot on the sofa to be nearer Mae. She began pacing the room like a film actress who knew all her marks but had decided to improvise, and no one dared stop the cameras from rolling. 'If the publishers think Raven can do a better job editing that magazine than me, let him try. *Edit* was my baby. But if we have a *real* baby ... We don't need to rush this, I know. But why not start trying sooner rather than later? We've been talking about it for long enough. My notice period is six months. I'll use it to set up something new work-wise.'

Mae imagined her becoming a TV pundit or a motivational

speaker. She was too revered and well connected to drop into the Rolodex of nobodies. V sat down between Ari and Mae and took both of their hands.

'Come to think of it, I'll pick up with Ana Palomo about producing that film with her.' Mae raised her eyebrows and V gave her hand a firm squeeze. 'I can take the baby on set, answer emails while it's in one of those pouch things. And anyway, my mum will babysit. She'll be thrilled. Mae, this could be so perfect.'

Mae knew that Ari was thinking the same as her. Their dream of a future was now in someone else's hands, and it was spiralling, happening in a way they would have struggled to ever initiate themselves.

'So, next steps?' V was in boss mode. And Mae, despite her reservations about the timescale, had reverted to an eager-to-please employee.

'Contract?' she said. 'Start looking into clinics? Agree on when we start trying.'

V nodded. 'But before any of that, we need to talk to Oliver. He'll be part of this whether we like it or not.'

'The elephant in the room,' said Mae sombrely. The tea lights on the mantelpiece began to flicker out, one after another.

Ari thought for a moment. 'It's simple. I'll end it with Oliver, it's the only way. It might take me some time, but you've always been right, Mae, he's not my forever; you two are.'

'Hark the herald angels sing,' said V, at an unfamiliarly manic pitch. 'A true Christmas miracle.'

'An immaculate conception!' added Ari, and Mae felt a strangeness deep where his seed might soon grow.

Noon

Summer 2030

It's space they agree they need, so Ari drives the girls to Brighton beach. There is no elegant way to manoeuvre a stroller over stones, but he is halfway now between the promenade and the sea, and he doesn't believe in going back. It is easier to pull than it is to push, so he bumps the baby along behind him while August darts ahead, stopping every now and then to inspect shells. The sun needles his back. Mae would have brought the suncream.

'Papa, I found treasure.'

Ari stops to catch his breath and gather his hair into a pony-tail. He tries not to look fed up as his daughter walks purposefully towards him, arm outstretched. She drops a bottle top into his open palm and he clasps his fingers around it, feeling the sharp edges press into his skin. He squeezes it harder.

'Take care of this for me,' she says, and runs towards the shore.

Grief is such a cliché. Whenever tears warm in his eyes, he wonders how after everything he's still so goddam sentimental. Memories stack up like gifts under a Christmas tree. He'd set a match to the pile if he could.

When he reaches the wet edge of the shingle, Ari checks that

Addie is still strapped into her little cocoon. He adjusts the yellow romper, which has slipped off her shoulder in the commotion, and pulls a pacifier out of the pocket of his denim shorts, slipping it between her perfect lips before she can even think about crying.

These children are the product of every swerve, choice and mistake. All of it led him to them. He sits down on the stones. A wind farm, Tippex-white redacting the blue, puts a prosaic stop to the horizon. And although it is a shame how it spoils the view, Ari can't help but be grateful for a reason to not gaze off into endless space.

He crosses his legs and August stands in front of him, squinting because the sun is in her eyes. She looks like Mae when she scowls.

Nature. Nurture. He conjured his family into existence with a spell, it sometimes seems. It may as well have been sorcery.

The sea air is helping to clear his head, in spite of the heat. He takes a deep glug of it and exhales slowly. He thinks about Mae. She is always right. It's frustrating, but true, and she never could wear it lightly, moving around him with the confidence that came from knowing she was his punctuation. She gave his sprawling syntax a tone and, more often, a period. Recently, though, it feels as if all the words have been cut out and stuck back together like a Dadaist poem. Not even Mae can bring the clarity he needs.

Ari rarely raises his voice, but last night something broke inside of him, and he shouted. It sounded so unfamiliar, and the way the others shrank because of it, scared of the power he forgot he had, made anger rise even hotter in his chest.

He recalls saying, 'I didn't realise this was a competition. Who lost the most. I'll start a tally, shall I?' Fuming, he pulled a pen from his shirt pocket and was about to start writing on a napkin when a hand reached across the table and snatched it from him. That was when the wine glass was knocked over. He remembers now.

'I have a right to feel fucking sad,' he screamed at them. He was trembling, and self-conscious that he'd started something he'd have to see through.

'We all do,' Mae said quietly and with such weight that the others pushed back their chairs and, avoiding eye contact, slipped away into the margins of the house.

'This is the problem with you. You want us to feel the same way about everything,' Ari shouted so that they would still hear him. 'Grief even! Has it occurred to you that people need to process what happened differently? You can't manage everyone's emotions. No wonder they just left.'

That was when his shoulders shuddered, and a big messy sob rose from the pit of his stomach.

Mae looked cross, and she shook her head as she said, 'There are other people now who need us more than we need each other. Our children.' Then, rattled by her feelings, she spoke louder. 'How do you expect me to be fully present with them when I'm trying to be whatever it is you need me to be as well?'

'I don't need anything from you any more.' They are the last words he can remember spitting at his friend before downing the rest of the wine in the bottle.

A pack of squabbling seagulls nosedive for a discarded chip. August skips in and out of the surf in front of him. Adrienne sleeps. Parenting is a precarious balance, a kind of dance. He always thought it would come naturally because he wanted it so *much, and yet he struggled to find his flow. And it isn't like he is a single parent, far from it. There is always someone else who has a way of doing it he can fall back on, and that is probably stopping him from figuring it out himself. But he is a father. The father. And it doesn't take long for that idea to spin his mind back to Randolph. He feels a jolt as his thoughts realign, making space for the metallic scrape of pain.*

'August, sweetie, come have a drink. Here's your water.' His voice doesn't carry, or she is wilfully ignoring him. He doesn't dare leave the baby even for the couple of seconds it will take to run to fetch Augie and bring her back. He doesn't dare move the baby in case she wakes up and he's fucked the routine again. It is a familiar conundrum with the two of them. He looks around as if the beach might hold the answer and catches the eye of the chip-eating woman next to him. She smiles, taking him in, filtering the situation in a way that makes sense to her.

'Mum's day off, is it?' she laughs. 'I'll keep an eye on the little one while you get her. Go on.' She nods patronisingly towards the sea.

He often advises Mae to pick her battles. Not everything needs to be a thing, he tells her. But screw it. He flashes the stranger a kilowatt smile. 'You're so kind,' he says emphatically, then undoes his long hair and flicks it behind his shoulders. As he stands, the woman looks up at him expectantly. 'Oh, and actually I am the mum.' He savours her confusion for a moment, then runs to August, swoops her into his arms and spins her in a circle. They walk back to Addie in her stroller and the woman promptly departs.

'Have a fabulous day,' he calls after her.

What it means to be a parent is the only thing that keeps

expanding and letting in more light since the accident. He can be everything and everyone for the children. Where that leaves him as a person and as a lover and as a friend is not something he's sure he'll ever understand.

PART 3

Chapter 27

London, January 2022

It was Blue Monday, the day that for some pseudo-serious reason had been anointed the most depressing of the year. V was standing at the kitchen island in front of her laptop, aggressively deleting all the press release emails that referenced what she called 'another ridiculous made-up day designed entirely to commoditise our misery'.

'I don't know how many times I have to tell these PRs I don't work for *Edit* any more, they still track me down and inundate me with this crap.' She slammed the delete key again.

It was early morning and still dark outside. Mae finished frothing the milk at the coffee machine, then sidled up to V and placed a steaming matcha latte next to her. She kissed her cheek, which was flushed either from her five a.m. workout or from the spiral of rage her inbox was now sending her into.

'It seems I'm pregnant,' she whispered.

As V drove them to Clapham to tell Ari the good news in person, Mae flicked between radio stations trying to find something that set the right mood. A delicate happiness hung between them. She opened the passenger window as they sat in rush-hour traffic over Battersea Bridge. The blast of cold air made her feel alert suddenly to the poignancy of this journey. Was being conscious of memory in the moment, and feeling nostalgia for a real-time event, like breaking the fourth wall on life somehow? she wondered. She began to imagine herself remembering the scene five years from now. It was a shame she couldn't get the soundtrack right.

'Mae, honey, could we just have a bit of quiet,' V said, turning the radio off from the controls on the steering wheel. Mae reached across and squeezed her girlfriend's thigh. V had sent her mug of bright green matcha flying over the countertop when she had jumped up to congratulate Mae earlier. But beneath the excitement, they were both nervous. Ari still hadn't broken up with Oliver, and that felt like the last piece in this puzzle. So much depended on it.

Ari was getting ready to leave for Stockholm and stopped packing to answer the door. Without saying anything, Mae slipped the positive pregnancy test into his hand.

'I'll end it with Oliver,' he said determinedly after a tearful embrace. Mae and V knew he'd been trying to end things for a long time, but life with his boyfriend was too familiar to climb out of easily.

'I'll do it now, before my trip. It's going to be messy, and God, he's going to think I'm choosing you over him, but . . . '

'Ari, that's exactly what you're doing.' Mae shot him a look and he crossed his bare arms. 'It's what you said you'd do years ago.'

He hopped from one foot to the other to keep warm. He wasn't really listening.

'I can't believe this is actually happening, we're doing it!' Then, after a steadying breath, 'Look, let me worry about Oliver, I'll do what I need to do, I promise. This is *everything*.'

Mae had barely moved; the shock of it all was only just hitting her. Ari was so tied up in what it meant for him and Oliver, he hadn't even asked how she was feeling. He kissed her dramatically on the forehead, and the thing they'd been working towards for so long, that now belonged intrinsically to her body, was somehow all about him.

'*This* is everything I need now.' He rubbed his hands over where Mae's stomach probably was under her bulky winter coat. He said, 'I've got to catch this flight, but when I'm back and when it's all sorted with Oliver, which it will be, let's celebrate with V, OK? A baby! Wow. This is wild. Wild!"

She pushed his hands gently off her and looked at him searchingly. He was too excited to notice the distance in her body language. He hugged her again and she turned to walk back down the steps and into the car.

When V asked why she looked so sad, Mae couldn't explain it. Desire and fulfilment were two very different states to shift between overnight, she was realising. V turned on the radio, attempting to lighten the vibe, and the DJ announced that it was *officially* the most depressing day of the entire year. Mae laughed half-heartedly. The morning felt deflated of its specialness, and she was going to be late for work.

Ari skipped upstairs to his office and placed the pregnancy test on his desk, its two perky parallel blue lines smiling from behind the little cut-out window.

It was a 'mental health day' at Oliver's work, and he had

the day off for some self-care, which meant he was at home watching action movies on the sofa in his tracksuit, with a bag of beef jerky between his legs and a can of Diet Coke within reaching distance on the coffee table. 'Who was that at the door?' he asked.

'Oh, just the postwoman,' Ari shouted casually from the landing. He slipped his passport into his jacket pocket and zipped up his case.

'Time for a coffee before you leave?' asked Oliver. 'There's something I've been meaning to chat to you about.'

Ari checked the time, and as it was so rare for his boyfriend to suggest such a thing, he agreed.

He was surprised that Oliver reached for his hand as they walked around the block to their local café. Oliver wasn't a fan of rubbing their sexuality in people's faces, as he put it. But as the street was deserted, he had evidently deemed it safe to express a moment of affection. Ari couldn't help but enjoy the pressure of his soon-to-be-ex-boyfriend's fingers between his own.

'I actually was hoping to talk to you about something myself,' Ari said, trying to make sure his voice didn't give anything away just yet. 'But you go first.'

They joined the queue for takeaway coffee, and Ari noted that men in Clapham seemed to think a gilet under a blazer was acceptable winterwear. Oliver said, 'I've put the house on the market. I figured it was time we upgraded, and I've seen this place on the commuter belt towards Tunbridge Wells. It's got a huge garage and it's a new-build so it's mega high spec.'

Ari had been so engulfed in the plan with Mae and V, so sure it would be easy to leave Oliver when he really, really had to, that it hadn't occurred to him that his boyfriend might have his own plans for their future. Oliver so seldom wanted to talk about anything beyond the here and now that Ari had quite forgotten he was capable of it.

'And look,' added Oliver casually, 'I know about your little secret.'

'You do? Fuck. This was not like how I'd expect you to react.' Ari reached into his pocket for his wallet to pay for the coffee, but Oliver swooped across and tapped his credit card on the machine before he had a chance.

'I know you've been chatting to that old dude you had it off with at college. The creepy professor. I saw an email, and honestly, I thought it was sweet what he was saying. How he's sorry he used you, he was a sex addict, blah blah blah.'

'Oh, that. Yeah, um, I guess it was good of him to reach out. Why were you reading my emails?'

'I'm not jealous, if that's what you think. I looked up a picture of him, and he's old, like some gay version of Ian McKellan.'

'Ian McKellan *is* gay.'

It was too cold to linger on the street, so they started walking back to the house. Ari took a sip of his espresso. Hot and bitter, it scalded the roof of his mouth.

'Oliver, I'm not sure about moving house. I don't think I'm cut out for the British suburbs.'

'Oh right, yeah. Forgot you were so up yourself for a second there. You think you're so clever, don't you, *I know everything about actors, I'm some cultural fucking genius.* Well bully for you.'

'Oliver! No! Oh my God, that's so not … I just, I don't

know if we're on the same page about this move and about the future generally. You never want to talk to me about it.'

'Don't worry, I'm not asking you to go in on it with me financially. How could I ever expect my poor poet to be able to contribute at all to our life.'

'I've never said I'm poor, Oliver. I can afford to buy a house, that's not the issue.'

'Ha! You've got no idea. You can't even pay for our coffees; do you seriously think your little nest egg, as you call it, is gonna get you a million-pound house in a desirable area?'

'Actually, yes, I do. But I can't talk to you about this now.' Ari opened the front door and took out his phone to order a car to the airport. 'We've got way more we need to discuss. I've got to catch this flight, though. When I get back, let's have dinner or something. We can go to the steak place you like. I'll explain everything.'

The thought of telling Oliver that Mae was pregnant with his biological child filled him with dread. He'd mentioned the plan once, casually, and Oliver had scoffed and said confidently that it was never going to happen.

'My cab's outside. I'll see you in a couple of days,' he said as breezily as possible.

'No kiss?' Oliver replied with an irritated laugh in his voice. Ari pretended not to hear and closed the door quietly behind him. It was only as the taxi was pulling into Gatwick's North Terminal that he remembered the pregnancy test lying like a sorcerer's wand on his writing desk.

Of course, V knew how to tentatively celebrate something, and she was determined that Mae should retrieve the happiness she'd felt that morning before Ari complicated it. The dinner she prepared while Mae relaxed and tried to push her anxieties about Oliver out of her mind was pitched perfectly. Hot dogs, fries and champagne served in front of the big screen in the snug. She had a choice of Oscar-contender screeners for them to watch as they ate, and there was a tray of chocolate brownies in the oven.

'Consider this a "marking the occasion but not getting too excited yet" party,' she said as she fed a DVD into the machine. 'It's a shame Ari isn't here.'

'I thought I was supposed to feel overwhelmed with joy and full of magical optimism at this point. But you know, we've been talking about it for so long and planning it and going over and over parenting contracts and predicting who will feel what and what our roles will be and how much of a dad or not-a-dad Ari will be, and that's all up here.' Mae tapped the side of her head. 'But now it's all here' – she lifted her plate from her lap to touch her stomach – 'and it just feels scary, I guess. That shift.'

'Oh sweetie.' V licked the salt from her fingers and pressed pause on the TV remote. She turned to Mae. 'I know it feels scary and strange, and let's not forget that your best friend has been saying he'll leave Oliver since that Christmas over two years ago. Two years, Mae! If you think about it, we've normalised a very strange situation—'

Mae interrupted defensively. 'Yes, but he always promised if and when there was a pregnancy he'd do it. Straight away. And he is!'

'I know, I know,' V countered softly, placating Mae's prickly tone. 'All I'm saying is that it added an extra emotional burden to our plan, and now it's worked, and we trust that Ari is doing what he promised. It's just part of why you, why *we* aren't frolicking over rainbows right now.' She topped up her champagne and poured a splash more into Mae's half-glass. The smart watch on her wrist began to vibrate. *Unknown number.* She hit answer, and because all her devices were synced with the house's sound system, Oliver's monotone boomed out of the speakers by the fireplace.

'Did you actually think you could steal my boyfriend's sperm without me finding out?'

The women looked at each other in panic and shuffled closer on the sofa. Watching the flames in the hearth, her voice surprisingly level, V replied, 'We thought you knew. Ari said you wanted nothing to do with it.'

They could hear Oliver pacing back and forth. 'You are *terrible* people,' he said. 'The worst, most selfish, spineless individuals. I always knew it.'

Mae had started shaking. She instinctively placed her hand on her stomach, as if her newly implanted embryo might be scared too. V wrapped an arm around her protectively.

Oliver raised his voice. 'I know you've tricked Ari into this, and you're going to use him like everyone else in his life has used him. It was one thing when this was your ridiculous pipe dream, but now you're actually . . . ' he spat the word, 'pregnant.'

'Why do you even care what we do if you've broken up?' said Mae, feeling bolder now. She tried to stand, but V stopped her with her arm.

Oliver seemed to gasp, then disguised it as a sarcastic laugh. He breathed heavily for a moment, then said, 'It's funny that just a few hours ago we were discussing moving to Tunbridge Wells, then, isn't it? Funny that Ari wants to take me for dinner to discuss *our* plans for the future when he gets back. And what's this – a text sent at five forty-three p.m.: "Miss you, O. Kiss kiss." Ari and I are still very much together, and if you have this baby, I will *delight* in always being in your life too.'

As if she had just realised that removing Oliver from their home was possible, V hung up.

Mae burst into hot, intractable tears. 'No. This can't be right,' she sobbed. Despite evidence to the contrary, she refused to accept that Ari had done anything wrong.

It was V who composed herself quickest and called their friend. He begged them not to freak out. He could explain, he pleaded.

Ari was in the green room of the Berns hotel in Stockholm, about to step out on stage under a disco ball to read from his second collection. He had developed a slick routine, interspersing poems with stories from his past. Sharing his secrets with the world meant sharing the shame and the pain too. Oliver called it airing his dirty laundry. But Ari was addicted to the disclosure now; he felt a visceral uplift like ecstasy every time he revealed a morsel of trauma to his fans, and they in return showered him with love and support. He didn't care that other people, his mother, his father, the professor, might have their own side of a story. He took the wheel of the narrative and drove it where he wanted before anyone else had the chance.

'Let me speak to Mae.'

'I've told her to lie down. She's in a state, Ari. We both are. It was horrible.'

'I'm so sorry. That was unforgivable,' Ari said. His pre-show jitters had swollen into full-body anxiety. He slumped down against the wall and hugged his knees.

'This is *your* fault, Ari. Oliver is ... Oliver. But by not being honest with him, or with us, you did this.'

'I was going to going to break up with him. I just felt so happy earlier. And he had this whole idea about moving house. I couldn't.'

Mae hadn't been able to relax, and now she got up from the bed and walked slowly downstairs. She stood behind V and said softly, 'I'll speak to him.' V sighed despairingly and passed her the phone.

'Was the text real? You miss him?'

'No. I mean, yes, it's habit. I was going to split up with him. I just had to find a way, but now, of course, now I just have to ... Mae, I'm so sorry.'

'But will you do it?'

Ari sounded wounded but certain when he said, 'I promise. I don't want to be with him any more. You know that, Mae. But Oliver is a drug, it's not easy.' His voice cracked. 'And I've been weak. But I'll move all my things out as soon as I'm back. It's over, please believe me.'

'It'll be OK, Ari,' she said, and looked imploringly at V, who nodded in resigned agreement. 'We love you. Good luck with the show.'

Ari powered through his performance on muscle memory. Afterwards, he had Basma cancel his remaining dates and change his flight home to the next morning. He would have gone straight to Mae and V's but had to pick something up first.

Oliver was sitting in bed with a smug smile on his face when Ari, who hadn't slept and was functioning now on pure adrenalin, walked into the bedroom, opened the drawer of his bedside table, removed the still-sealed letter his mother had given him and, without acknowledging Oliver's presence, left again. He resisted the urge to slam the door behind him.

He had always known Oliver was dangerous. He'd lived with that fear, that tension because he felt he deserved it. But his friends did not. He walked around the rest of the house wondering if there was anything more than the letter and his notebooks that he wanted to take with him. There was nothing left that he cared about. He could buy anything and everything he needed. Except, that was, for his clothes, his real clothes. The ones he rarely wore with Oliver.

He walked back upstairs to the bedroom, flung open the door and shouted, 'In case you're struggling to compute what's happening here, it's over. I'm starting a family with Mae and V, and you ... you will die sad and alone, in Tunbridge fucking Wells.'

Oliver turned off his smile, his face fell and he looked suddenly ashen. Realising Ari was serious, he jumped out of bed and began begging him to stay. He fell to his knees, he wailed – a sound Ari imagined came from the darkest part of his soul. But Ari stayed focused. He pulled all his favourite clothes from their hangers and threw them into a suitcase. It took less than five minutes. When he was finished, he slammed the closet door. Then, in a lightning bolt of rage, he smashed his fist into it. Oliver sat on the carpet with his head in his hands.

'I hate you,' Ari seethed. It felt so good he shouted it again, louder, and then finally he screamed, 'I always hated you.' Then, his hand throbbing from the impact, he picked up his suitcase and left.

Chapter 28

They were waiting for the three-month scan before telling anyone else. Ari moved in temporarily. The house became a temple to their secret. V lit the log fire in the living room every evening when she got back from the office she shared with Ana, who didn't even seem to know they had an office and was never there. The hearth reminded Ari and Mae of winters at Aunt Alice's cottage, and they settled back into the comfort of being together. The three of them would stay up late, talking, playing cards and making plans. A country house was floated as an idea – it would be somewhere Mae and V could escape to for a break from childcare, leaving Ari on daddy duty. But more than an escape, it would be a home – a place they all shared and could design for the family they were to become. Mae was reading *The Waves*. She said they should look on the south-east coast near where Virginia Woolf lived. She promised to devote some serious time to scouring property websites.

Ari often fell asleep on the sofa, watching the logs in the fire throb from red to amber then finally black. When he woke up, he was never cold, because one of the girls would have crept down in the middle of the night to cover him with a duvet and slip a hot-water bottle under his feet.

One of his favourite topics of non-baby-related conversation to have with Mae and V was about wasting what he called his best, his *hottest* years trying to satiate a sociopath. There were only so many ways they could tell him to move on, and he tried. He channelled his regret into a manic wellness regime. He made the girls green juices every morning, and as they were both out at work all day and he'd postponed the rest of his tour, he researched 'nutritional meals for early pregnancy' and spent his days shopping and cooking, in perpetual avoidance of dealing with his feelings. He'd also started doing an online yoga class for pregnant people, but hey, he said when challenged, why shouldn't he also be 'at one with his body at this precious time'?

Mae was pregnant for eight weeks before she started bleeding. Barely at all at first, so it was possible to think there was nothing to worry about when she went to sleep that night. Then, as the sun seeped through the shutters, it became a labour, and with a deep moan it was a gush of indisputable loss. She was turning back into who she'd been before, but her body felt changed for ever. Every cell ached for what it was letting go.

It was deemed an early miscarriage, but Mae had been pregnant long enough to have confessed, 'I wish there were more examples of people like me "carrying". I feel like my only option will be to start wearing Breton tops and leggings and cradling my stomach, saying things like, "We're hoping for a boy. Boys are so much easier."'

It was long enough for them to have started building the foundation of an agreement to raise this child 'together but apart'.

It was long enough for names to have been vetoed and villa holidays discussed. It was long enough for them all to have felt that they were parents 'to be'. It was long enough.

It was long enough.

While V drove Mae to hospital, Ari lay in his bed in the spare room and opened, for the first time, the letter Connie had given him.

Dear Ari,

I wanted you so much. I saw your picture in a brochure the orphanage mailed to us. You were three months old and you had these big dark almond eyes that looked straight into the heart of me. I was so worried someone else would take you before we made it out to Bucharest to meet you. Your father was a nightmare the entire nine months we hid and secretly went through the process of adopting you. No doubt you can imagine.

We were driven out of the city to the orphanage. It was a big modern block, not a scary building from a Grimms' tale, which was what I was imagining. It was clear you'd been looked after. You were in a cot with two other babies when I first saw you. You were playing with a rattle and I remember how those other babies were watching you and smiling.

A woman in a bad-fitting pantsuit was showing us around, and when she picked you up out of the cot, you looked right past her and reached out to me. Ari, I can't tell you how my body felt alive, gloriously, when your tiny hand grabbed onto my necklace and I took you in my arms for the first time. I was flooded with so much joy and safety. Even then, with you I knew I could be more than myself. You were power and hope and happiness, all bundled up into a stained yellow onesie.

Everything we were told about your biological family is in the documents I've mailed you. Your parents were academics. They died in a car crash shortly after you were born. You were in the back of the car, and according to the medical reports, when the police found you, you weren't even crying. There was no one else in the family that could look after you; I believe attempts were made to reach out to grandparents, aunts and uncles, but no one came forward. If you want to find your Romanian relatives one day, I will support you however I can.

Now to the hard bit. Why didn't I tell you all this sooner? A secret like this grips onto your roots like knotweed and it's so tangled and thick and buried, there's no way out. Life was hard enough with your father. Being accepted by his awful network because we had a 'perfect' young family just like them gave me some support. But more than that, the truth is, son, I needed you to believe you were all mine because without your love I don't know what I would have done. You took care of me even before you could talk. OK, the violence never stopped, but it was bearable with my baby. I couldn't risk a part of you, even a tiny part of you, being elsewhere. Love, real love, can feel like it comes from the darkest cavern of us. It pulls us below the surface and it lives in that deep, secret place.

My blood is yours, Ari, my flesh, my pain, my joy. What I mean to say is, I am your mother.

He refolded the three thin sheets of paper. He carefully placed them back in the envelope and lay down. He put the letter on his chest and fell asleep with his hand over it, his heart beating through his mother's words.

Chapter 29

March, with its promise of new life, seemed to mock them. As a scattering of daffodil shoots emerged in the Brixton garden, Mae carried her loss alongside a restless hope that it would work if they just kept trying. Balancing these two thoughts was a heaviness that flattened every day.

Snow fell. It wasn't enough to settle on the ground, but flakes gathered on the skylights in the loft, which had been earmarked as the baby's room. One weekend, Mae lay on the guest bed up there and watched the icy patina melt as the sun crept over the house at noon. The daffodils survived. They were nature's stoics, said V. In a few weeks they would be trumpeting their cartoon yellow snouts, all bright and cheery as if nothing had ever tried to stop them.

The mood in the house had tilted, and no one knew how to get back to the easy rhythm they'd established. They barely spoke of the baby they'd lost, because really what more was there to say than *for forty-nine days we believed so fully in something that barely existed, and in spite of everything we remain willing to believe again.*

*

In April, Ari moved into a cold and unlovingly furnished apartment in Peckham to give his friends space. It was the first time he'd ever lived alone. Unlike Mae, who had always cherished her own company, he couldn't stand the sound of his footsteps echoing down the empty hallway. He hated that there he was, the same old Ari, in the mirror every morning. Was it possible to be bored of yourself? he wondered. He contemplated downloading a dating app, but worried how his commitment to monthly ejaculations might be affected by casual sex. So instead, when he wasn't writing, he would scroll through social media photos of Sam's life in Sydney. The activity, which was now more of a compulsion, was one of the only things that stopped him from thinking about the baby they had lost, that stopped him from obsessing about Lilly and wondering why Professor Scott kept emailing to ask for his forgiveness. All these things spun on a constant rotation around his mind. But then there was Sam. Always a port in a storm. There were pictures of smiling co-workers who obviously adored this big-hearted Brit, beach selfies, cocktails and – Ari's favourite of all – Sam holding a friend's baby up high above his head.

Ari never commented, of course. They'd not been in touch since he'd ghosted Sam's London drinks. Nevertheless, he took a great pleasure from Sam's joyful life. It seemed so different and so distant from where he and Mae had ended up. He drank it up like sugary coffee, yet the buzz didn't last long.

They took a break to let Mae's body recover. But she was keen to get back to the process as soon as the doctors allowed. Ari made more donations at the sperm bank, flicking between the straight and the gay porn on offer in the discreet basement room. 'Take your time,' the nurse would say, but he didn't have all day. When the pot was still empty after twenty minutes, he closed his eyes and thought of that picture of Sam topless in a beachside café. A gold chain gleaming against his brown skin, almost hidden behind a thicket of chest hair.

Done.

The sperm was frozen in vials.

They tried again in June, July and August. Each month Mae's period came before she had the chance to buy an early detection test. Life ticked on in an ersatz of usual, but on the bus to work, in the shower, and mostly in the time between turning off her bedside lamp and falling asleep, she allowed herself a silent, selfish grief.

'I think we should switch to IVF,' V said one dark morning in October as rain lashed the skylights and they moved around the kitchen swerving each other's singular silences. She poured the last of the coffee into Mae's cup and put the cafetière in the sink. 'I know you said it was too medical, and you'd hate what those hormones would do to your body but, if you think about it, it's efficient, and you like efficient.'

'OK,' said Mae, nodding to herself decisively. 'I didn't want to do IVF because it felt less natural. But IUI is hardly the romantic conception of my queer dreams. I mean, what is *natural* about going to a clinic to have sperm shot into you through a catheter? Efficient. Yes. Let's be more that.'

*

When they started the treatment later that month, V offered to do Mae's twice-daily injections for her, but Mae wanted to tough it out, not make it into a bigger deal than it needed to be. When Ari asked how it felt sinking a needle into her own flesh, she said it was 'actually quite fun' to avoid any further concern. The truth was, she loathed how heavy and sluggish she felt. She didn't recognise the softness that had enveloped her body. She missed her flat chest, her muscular shoulders, the curve of her biceps when she accidentally happened to flex them in front of the mirror. But the sacrifice would be worth it . . . eventually.

Even with the help of IVF, over the next seven months Ari's sperm and Mae's eggs failed to do the one primeval thing they were supposed to and merge into a viable embryo. But then, just as hope was becoming harder and harder to hold onto, an egg – one of nine collected during her most recent procedure – was successfully fertilised and made it to day five, when it could be implanted into her uterus. The doctor showed them a blurry black-and-white picture of the divided cells. Ari inspected the image and said to Mae, 'She has your eyes.' They giggled, but V looked disapproving and asked the doctor, seriously, what the odds were that it would work this time.

'It's impossible to say for sure, but this is a good-quality blastocyst. We can do the embryo transfer now and hope for the best. I'm afraid there's not enough space for you both to be with Mae during the procedure, though—'

'Of course,' Ari interrupted. 'I'll wait in a café.'

*

An hour later, they left the clinic. It was a softly sunny afternoon and the pavements were covered in trampled white blossom like confetti on the steps of a town hall after a wedding. 'I feel good about this,' V said. She helped Mae with the zip on her jacket as she spoke. 'This wasn't just a shot in the dark. It was a good-quality embryo, placed in the *perfect* place in your *beautiful* uterus . . .'

Mae pretended to gag. 'Ew, no thanks, not those words, please. You know I'm squeamish,' she said.

V squeezed her hand. 'Beautiful uterus,' she whispered again, teasing. Then added, 'Hey, I was the one that saw it, up close on that screen while you had your eyes squeezed shut, and it was amazing – trust me.'

They held hands and walked towards Marylebone. Mae saw herself in V's oversized sunglasses whenever she looked her way. She smiled at the reflection and allowed herself a moment to enjoy the strange swell of pride that came with the knowledge that she was carrying an actual embryo inside her like a secret stash of treasure, containing both her genes and Ari's. Life created in a test tube and now placed in the optimum position in the depths of her body.

'Science has given this minuscule amalgam of cells every chance it can to make it. Now it's up to me,' Mae said, while spontaneously hailing a passing cab.

'I thought we said we'd meet Ari for coffee?' V protested as the taxi made a U-turn.

Mae flashed a quick smile. 'I think we need to go home and consummate this conception as a matter of urgency, don't you? Ari will understand.'

*

It was cold for spring. Mae took her old pilot's jacket from the back of her wardrobe and started wearing it every day. The two-week wait passed in a banal agony that got sharper the closer they were to the test date. Time was measured in cycles now. Round and round it went. Mae thought about the definition of madness – doing the same thing on repeat but expecting a different outcome. Fertility treatment was madness. Because even after everything she believed it would work. The amount of money their limitless hope was costing them was obscene.

Since leaving *Edit*, V had been brokering deals in her new creative partnership with Ana Palomo. They had started a film production company and secured funding for a documentary about Ana's life. But V's heart didn't seem to be massively in it, Mae could tell. However, it was filling an *Edit*-shaped hole in her girlfriend's life, and she had no intention of rocking the boat by mentioning her concerns. More to the point, the injections of cash V received when various contracts were signed more than compensated for the lack of a monthly pay cheque, and made another £10,000 IVF cycle a possibility in a way that was out of reach for so many of their lesbian friends. They were embarrassed to tell anyone how many times they had tried; the bill was astronomical, but the fact they could afford it was most shocking of all. Ari said again and again that money was no object. He'd cover it all if V wasn't so proud. But no amount of money could change the outcome of their endeavours. The sheer magic of biological coincidence was what it came down to.

For Ari, who was grappling with the realisation that he had been born poor and it was a dark mix of luck and tragedy that had made him rich, and for V, who had earned every penny in her bank account by hard graft, the fact that money wasn't enough was no surprise. It was only Mae who was outraged that they couldn't throw more cash at the problem to fix it. She came to realise over the months and months of 'failure' that her upbringing as neither rich nor poor, with parents who were not wildly successful nor abject failures, coupled with her own middle-manager salary, had made her the least aware of the paradox of actual wealth.

A day before she was supposed to, Mae peed on a stick in the disabled loo at work, and after a minute the word 'pregnant' appeared on the display. She phoned V, and then Ari, and because she was so excited, she almost phoned her mother but stopped just before pressing call as she'd have to explain so much.

The consultant advised caution. 'Let's do the blood test tomorrow,' she said.

The three of them arrived back at the Harley Street clinic two days later for the blood test results. They were buzzing with nervous energy. Ari said he'd browse Daunt Books and meet them after the consultation, conscious of giving Mae and V space to do things just as a couple sometimes. They'd discussed this during one of their late-night 'Co-parenting: the Ground Rules' sessions, and he'd agreed it was important.

Inside the clinic, Mae and V sat on identical rococo armchairs, facing each other, smiling. The waiting room had been carefully styled so as not to trigger any of its emotionally fraught visitors. The artwork hinted at the possibility of new life – butterflies, birds' nests, two gender-ambiguous hands entwined. No actual babies.

As she sat there, Mae thought that if this pregnancy ended in miscarriage as the last one had, she couldn't put her body through another cycle of internal ultrasounds, injections and suppositories, not to mention the egg collection procedure, which was redeemable only for the small pleasure of its mind-obliterating sedation. Her stomach was covered in bruises. But a positive pregnancy test was good news. She had to remember that.

Their names were called, and she suddenly felt a sinking dread.

Dr Granite sat in front of Mae and V at her desk on the first floor of the Regency townhouse that was known, imaginatively, as the Stork.

She smiled briefly, then said, 'I'm afraid the results of your HCG blood test have come back, Mae. It's what's known as a chemical pregnancy. We'd expect levels to be over twenty-five by now and yours are at eight.' She then launched into a monologue about fertility not being 'an exact science', reiterating that 'the sperm you are using has a very high motility. The quality of your eggs is low for your age . . .'

Mae found it hard to focus. She felt V's hand reach for hers and watched as she took a tissue from the box on the desk to dry her eyes. Why was she crying? Nothing made sense. Her head ached with all the information.

'Based on the patterns of your treatment up to this point, we must accept it as a possibility that you may not achieve a viable pregnancy, although of course you are welcome to continue to try. I'm very sorry that this has been the outcome.'

It took Mae a few minutes to process what she was being told, but then it was twisting, angry injustice that she felt rising from where her feet pressed on the ground to the very top of her head, which all of a sudden was so heavy it slumped forward and she rested it in the palms of her two hands.

V reached her arm around Mae's shoulders. 'We'll find another way.'

Mae laughed sarcastically and sank deeper into her chair. Ari was probably at that very moment buying them *What to Expect When You're Expecting*. Was it still a loss if she'd only been pregnant for a day? Was she entitled to grief this time? It wasn't even a miscarriage, it was a phantom. She was quiet. Her face pale and serious. Pregnancy was the only thing in her life she'd ever failed at. Emotions played out on V's countenance in a way Mae's perma-frown tended to hide. She looked up at her girlfriend's face. V's eyes were swollen, and red from crying.

'This is not your fault, Mae.'

'It seems like it is.'

She was already pulling up the drawbridge on the big, messy feelings that threatened to hit. To indulge them would be to invite in chaos, be overwhelmed by something she couldn't control. She chewed her bottom lip and withdrew into herself. She felt a narrowing, a sharp slicing into pieces of a mass of emotions that were more like thoughts than feelings.

Dr Granite chipped in unhelpfully, suggesting that V, even though she was 'not the optimum age', try carrying the child instead, as if that had never before occurred to them.

'No,' said Mae protectively. 'The sheer fact that my girlfriend contains all the component parts to make a baby should not pressure her into feeling that she has to, Dr Granite.'

V started to cry again, and Mae threw the doctor an accusatory glance. V stood up and seemed to remember the power of her height in heels. Mae offered her the handkerchief she kept in her back pocket, but V refused.

'I'm fine,' she said to the room. 'We're fine.'

Dr Granite shook their hands as she ushered them out of her office.

Ari bounded along Harley Street swinging two dark green plastic bags full of books. He'd been browsing the self-help section when he'd discovered a hardback, published earlier that year, called *Grief and Other Stories*, written by his old NYU professor. He looked at the author picture on the dust jacket and felt a pang of nostalgia for Professor Scott. He wasn't quite as gross as he'd remembered. He bought the book, along with six parenting-related titles that the pregnant shop assistant had gladly pointed him towards.

He stopped when he saw V leaning against the wall outside the clinic. Mae was pacing up and down nearby. If she kept moving, she could ride the wave of V's feelings rather than be pulled under by them. Ari dropped the bags and ran towards her.

'What is it? What's happened?' He cast a desperate look between the two women. Mae froze in front of him. V turned her head so he wouldn't see her cry. Neither of them could bring themselves to tell him.

Finally, with sadness darkening her voice, Mae said, 'There's no baby, Ari. False alarm. I'm sorry.'

He was silent at first, careful not to gazump her feelings with his own. Then he reached out his hand to V and pulled both women into his arms. Passers-by crossed the road to avoid the unusual helix of bodies. They slowly unravelled.

'But it's *us*,' Mae said, wiping Ari's tears away with the back of her hand while V dug around in her handbag for a tissue. 'What else are we meant to do with this love?' Ari shook his head in disbelief. 'The baby was the thing. I was so sure it would work this time. I was stupid to be so confident.' Mae collapsed back into his chest.

'We'll try again,' he whispered, but he was vacant and untethering himself from the two of them before their eyes. He said they all needed some space so walked, alone, towards Regent's Park. He stopped to leave the bags of parenting and pregnancy books on a bench, slipping only *Grief and Other Stories* by Professor John Scott into his satchel before setting off on the long walk home, with a new idea taking shape in his mind.

Evening

Summer 2030

'Where is everyone?' Ari is surprised to find only Mae home once he has barrelled through the white picket gate and along the stone path, pushing open the front door with his shoulder. She is sitting in a cerise velvet armchair, waiting for him. He leaves the stroller in the hallway and starts up the stairs because August has conked out in the car and if he puts her straight into bed now, fully clothed and covered in a sticky patina of orange popsicle and suncream, she may just sleep through the night.

'They're shopping, apparently, but I figured they'd go out for a burger or something after. Clearly keeping out of our way.'

'How rude,' Ari calls down from the landing.

Mae takes off her reading glasses and stands up to go to Addie, who is chattering happily to herself. The temperament of this child! she marvels as she unclips her from the pram and lifts her high above her head so that she laughs excitedly. Adrienne is now the most chilled of them all. The realisation makes her sad. She brings the baby carefully down into the crook of her arm and gives her head a quick self-conscious sniff.

*

Nappy, pyjamas, bottle; she settles Adrienne with military efficiency. Lights out, lullaby, gut punch of grief. It's funny, she thinks, when people asked how she felt after the miscarriage and the chemical pregnancy and all those months of it just not working, she wished she could make it sound more complicated, but the answer really was so absurdly simple and, she supposes, pure, that it was almost embarrassing to admit. She was just sad. And now another loss, years later and different in so many ways to what she endured then, but still that same dull sadness.

Ari is finishing up a call downstairs. He's taken her spot in the armchair and completed her crossword.

'OK, honey, don't rush back. Love you, sure, bye.' He places his phone on the lacquered table beside the chair. Mae sits on a newly upholstered chaise longue opposite.

'Don't tell me, the boys wanted to go bowling?'

'They just booked into a lane – they'll be home by ten.'

'So then?' Mae coughs awkwardly.

'So then . . . twelve down was "palimpsest", by the way,' Ari says. Mae looks genuinely annoyed.

'I would've got that.' She feels a wave of nausea and gasps. It is never going to be normal.

Mae is pregnant. They found out on the morning of the funeral, and the news settled like oil on water, not quite mixing with the moment but there, a film on its surface. Could he really leave her now? She wanted to make them a family – different to the one they'd planned, but a family all the same. It would be queer and unruly and like nothing anyone had a precedent for. Parents and children, several of each, and now another baby.

But something, or more accurately the memory of someone, is holding Ari back.

It's rare that it is just the two of them these days. And although their partners and children are knitted into the warp and weft of their friendship, the moments they find themselves alone are as charged as they ever were.

'What does it feel like?' Ari nods vaguely in the direction of her stomach. Mae's hands instinctively clasp it.

'Weird. You know.'

'I don't really,' says Ari, inching forward on his seat.

'Well. It's all I ever wanted from you and now it's the reason you're leaving.' The thing inside her is more parasite than foetus considering what its existence threatens to take from her. But she would never let this ugly thought take shape in words.

Ari pulls at the dark stubble under his bottom lip.

'Last night, you asked me what it was I wanted. But we had an arrangement, remember. An arrangement you were very keen on us all sticking to. And now one of the people who made those promises is dead. It's out of respect for that that I . . . I can't be here and be in the background like you always said. It won't work. And it was a good life I had in New York; the kids' other grandparents are there, and my publisher. I know things are different now, but maybe I'm grasping for something that feels the same.'

'But nothing is the same, Ari. I thought we'd had our happy ending. It was all so neatly tied up, and now it's unravelling. What I'm proposing has you in the foreground, right next to me.'

They called 'cut' but life had kept rolling. There was a time four years ago that Ari wishes he could have set in amber. Except happiness doesn't exist in stasis. He realises that now. And so, we move.

'And so, we move,' he says aloud without the context of his thoughts. Mae looks confused. 'I mean, if I went back to New York with August and Addie, maybe that's our happy ending. Your baby doesn't need a father.'

Ari had given Mae the greatest gift for her birthday. A sperm donation at a London clinic. One last shot, he wrote in her card, and it was signed by all of them. And now, like a mad joke, she is pregnant.

Before the accident, Ari had his unconventional family unit and she had hers – different configurations, but just as queer. They met at their house in the countryside four times a year, and there were trips to New York on top of that and ad hoc visits to London by Ari and his clan. Distance and closeness in perfect measure. They were the best of friends, a pack of five adults and their assorted offspring. Then came the phone call in the middle of the night to say there had been an accident. And now there are just four parents, and the life Mae is growing feels like a cruel and terrible mistake.

Silence buzzes with the intensity of their thoughts. A key rattles in the front door. They hear a ripple of laughter. A lone female voice rises above three baritones. The others are finally home.

PART 4

Chapter 30

New York, February 2024

After a week of snowfall black sludge now covered the sidewalks. Ari was on his way to a book signing in the Village. He applied his trademark eyeliner each time the taxi stopped at traffic lights.

It had been almost a year since he'd left London, and he missed his best friends so acutely that if it hadn't been for the book deals and live events and readings Basma kept bringing to him for sign-off, he would have found it hard to get out of bed. His agent knew full well that it was only Ari's sense of loyalty to his army of young fans that was keeping him emotionally afloat.

The cab approached the bookshop, where a line of queer teenagers snaked out of the door and around the block. Boys with floppy hair and long necklaces, girls wearing vest tops and sporting sharp fades waited for Ari to arrive. He would tell his sad stories, read his poems and write notes in their books. Ari asked the driver to drop him on the street parallel so he could walk for a bit to gather himself and sneak in the back door.

When he stood up, his height in heeled boots gave him a

boost of conviction. He smoothed the creases from his black silk shirt and tossed his hair behind his shoulders. He walked purposefully to the end of the street and back again, taking deep breaths. His satchel swung by his side. Finally he was ready to perform.

Mae had said she understood why he left, but she didn't really. The truth was, when the word *infertility* became a wall to demolish in every conversation, and Mae and V sank into a world of loss and disappointment that Ari wasn't sure he had a place in, he had drifted deliberately from the apex of their life and returned to New York.

The inconceivable failure of their plan had come between him and Mae in a way neither wanted to admit. They barely spoke now. And when they did, it felt forced and unfamiliar. It felt like a break-up.

When he had first moved back to New York, Ari craved Oliver's all-consuming attention. He pinched the skin on his inner arms with his fingernails. It provided a release, and the marks faded in a few hours, unless he pressed harder; then they would leave a tiny half-moon of a bruise. The same impulse that had him desiring everything that was toxic about Oliver also led him to almost send a message to his dad at least once a day. Why not pile up the pain? he thought. Engulf me in it. Take me beneath its swell.

'Pull yourself together, Ari. Sort it out for Letty's sake. That girl idolises you. Enough of the wallowing.'

Connie could be harsh, but he needed it. With her help negotiating on the phone from the UK, he had secured a warehouse apartment in Williamsburg within a week of arriving back. He'd outsourced the interiors, remembering the pleasure of having and spending his own money, and ended up with a semi-minimalist, bit-too-masculine, exposed-brick kind of bachelor pad that felt cool but bore little resemblance to his own taste. It was fine for what he needed – a space to figure out who he was without Oliver, and without Mae, and V and the future they'd planned.

And now, nine months later, he was a professional wallower. Award-winning. Critically acclaimed. He snuck into the back of the bookshop, where Basma was waiting for him. Looking in the mirror in the tiny bathroom that doubled as a broom cupboard, he realised his eye make-up was all wonky. It didn't take much for Ari to spiral into feeling stupid. His success was a joke, he didn't deserve it. Kids looked up to him but he was a fuck-up. He'd driven someone to suicide, he'd wasted so many years of his life in a toxic relationship, and his one chance of starting a big queer happy family of his own to atone for everything ugly and wrong he'd ever done was over. But worst of all, he'd lost the fullness of his friendship with Mae. He dabbed a wet tissue under his eyes and made it worse.

Basma poked her head round the door. 'Two minutes, Ari.'

He took a last look at himself. He was cashing in – turning real feelings into anecdotes he told to make people feel sorry for him. He wished he could go back to Leeds, when the future had felt like a brilliant shining possibility.

'I'm ready,' he said sombrely, then walked out on stage to a gush of applause.

*

After the show, Ari spoke to his fans and signed their books on autopilot.

'Hey, friend, who should I make it out to?' he asked without looking up. A familiar voice answered.

'John Scott. *Professor* John Scott, if you don't mind?'

Ari froze, reluctant to meet his eyes, but when he did, the professor smiled and said, 'It's good to see you, Ari.'

He looked well, Ari thought, like he'd had a *Queer Eye* makeover – trimmed goatee, good spectacles, a well-fitting shirt half tucked into dark blue jeans. He wasn't at all as vile as he remembered.

Ari still hadn't spoken. Instead, he took his pen and with a shaking hand wrote, *Dear John. I'm sorry for everything. Ari x.* He closed the book without him seeing the message and handed it back. There was a line behind him, so the professor stood to the side to let the next person have their audience with the poet.

'Wait,' said Ari. 'I read your book and I . . . Would you like to have a drink with me when I'm done here?'

After the show, they walked through the Village together. Down Christopher Street to Hudson River Park. John said he was avoiding bars; he had pulled himself back from the brink of something terrible and needed to stay away from the kind of dark, soulless places he'd lost himself in after Ari left and his daughter died. Ari was taking slow, careful steps that traced the topography of his old life as they talked. He remembered how kind and gentle John had been, and with a now familiar serving of shame, how insolent, thoughtless and entitled he'd been in return.

They sat next to each other on a low stone bench facing the water.

'I want you to write something different in my book,' said John, taking a fountain pen from his shirt pocket. He removed the lid and handed it to Ari along with the book open on the page he'd signed.

Ari made a sound like a laugh and shook his head. 'I know, "sorry" is a worthless crumb of a word really. I wish I could find a way to tell you how bad I feel every time I'm alone or close my eyes even for a second. The horror of what I did is overwhelming. I can't actually believe you're sitting next to me right now.'

'Ari, look at me,' said John, turning to him and placing a paternal hand on his shoulder. 'You have nothing to be sorry for. I fell in love with *you*. I was your tutor and I abused that trust. You were vulnerable and I should never have taken advantage of you like that. I had a problem. My shrink says a sex addiction, but my ex-wife calls that a lousy excuse. I am of a different generation to you. I think that's why I was so attracted to youth – you're all so good at being gay. I hid my homosexuality because I didn't know how it could ever be anything but a sordid secret. Now, thanks to you, it's out in the open and I'm starting my life as a gay man, and that's good, Ari. It was terrible of me to have affairs, but it was the only way I knew how to be myself.'

Ari watched a girl on rollerblades glide in effortless circles. 'But Lilly ...' The words caught in the back of his throat. 'Lilly died because of me.'

'Lilly killed herself because she was sick. She had debilitating depression and it had been that way for a long time. We tried every kind of drug and therapy and still she would fall into the darkest places. It was chemical and there was nothing more any of us could have done to save her. Her suicide wasn't your fault. Nowhere near. Please believe that.'

Ari pressed the palms of his hands into the cool stone bench and tilted back his head. Dusk was turning the sky blood orange. He felt an atavistic moan rise in his chest but he pushed it down and loudly exhaled.

'Thank you,' he said. His pen was poised to cross out his first inscription. 'But actually I'd like you to keep this as it is.' He closed the book and handed it back to the professor, who took it reluctantly. 'I can't forgive myself for what I did to her.'

'It wasn't you, and it's no good for any of us if you think it was.'

'No, I don't just mean what happened after we ... you know. I mean before. At school. She was bullied by people I thought were my friends. I never stood up for her. I watched, and my silence was complicit. You can't absolve me of that, John.'

'Perhaps not. But I can tell you that Lilly spoke very highly of you. She said you were kind to her. She could see your pain, she said. And she always thought you could have been friends. Had she been more functional, I imagine that might have happened. But she was too sick, too fragile – she couldn't handle friendships. You listened to her, she said, and Ari, that was kind. So please, this has been a great tragedy, but I have chosen for it to not define the rest of my life. And so should you.'

When Ari got up to walk John back to the subway, his legs felt weak and shaky, his head light. So much of the idea he'd built up of himself as an adult had been contingent on the transgressions of his youth. The emotions he'd felt as a consequence of this had become the bedrock of his creativity. These feelings had held him back but also propelled him forward. Now the pieces of his past were realigning, and an unexpected lightness washed over him. He dared to smile.

'You called me a harlot.'

'I believe it was "whore". And yes, not particularly imaginative of me. Terribly embarrassed by all that; you caught me at rather a nadir.'

'Forget it.'

'I've learnt that's not always best.'

'OK, well don't worry about it then.'

'Fine, I shan't. And promise me you will stop worrying too. You are a glimmering gem of a person. But there's a darkness that doesn't belong with you.'

Chapter 31

August 2024

There were not enough vases. Mae tutted to herself as she arranged the buxom bunches of flowers that she'd bought in the market into the five vessels she could find. It was weird that between her and V they had an abundance of stuff but she'd started never being able to find what she needed. The flowers were not so much a peace offering as a joy offering. She wanted the fullness of life back in their world. She wanted colour and fun and that wild glamour they'd once enjoyed.

V was working flat out. She was rarely home for dinner and always so stressed. Mae had decided she should make an effort for her, and so had left work early to push through the crowds at Brixton market on a sweltering August evening to buy up all the lilies and dahlias and irises and roses still on sale. V hated carnations, said they reminded her of a first and only boyfriend, so Mae bought everything but.

She had just about found a home for every stem when V arrived.

'It looks so gorgeous in here,' she said, giving Mae a kiss

on the lips for the first time in a while. 'Wait, it's not our anniversary, is it?'

'Nope, just a regular Tuesday. How was your day?'

'Don't ask. Honestly, this project is spiralling and I'm just not getting the support.' Mae bit her lip. She felt annoyed at how quickly stress and negativity had entered the house.

Ana Palomo was bankable, and that was the main thing, but she was also a wild card. And as much as people in Hollywood knew that her name on their film would guarantee its success, she spread high drama thick on every project. V was the ice to her fire as a co-producer, bringing cool negotiation tactics that she had honed in the gilded cage of fashion magazines, sharp business instinct, and the kind of reliability and track record insurers liked. Together they became a powerful duo, with V determined to help quash the 'spicy' Latina stereotype her business partner had been lumbered with. This woman studied philosophy and literature in between filming commercials for a diet yoghurt brand; she spoke five languages; there was nothing predictable about her.

Their first film was a documentary about Ana's rise through the Hollywood ranks, set against the wider narrative of her parents' undocumented status and their journey to Miami from Mexico in the 1950s. It had been picked up by a major streamer for a summer release and was already getting awards buzz. They'd landed a cover of *Variety* magazine; the two women stood back to back and the headline read: *Hot Stuff! Meet Hollywood's Latest Power Couple*. Mae refused to admit she was bothered by it, but really the image made her gut twist. V tried to brush it off, saying the editors simply didn't have the language to contextualise two successful gay women of colour any other way. The magazine was relegated from the coffee table to the stack in the downstairs loo.

It wasn't that Mae didn't trust V with Ana, more that she had spent enough time with the actress at parties to know she had zero boundaries and was completely, brilliantly impossible to second-guess. She had once referred to Mae and V's 'perfect queer life' in a way that sounded alarmingly bitter. But Mae didn't want to believe she had anything but their best interests at heart. 'I don't think it's working out between you two, babe, you've got to admit it, right?'

'We don't need to be best friends,' V snapped, then apologised. Calmer, she continued, 'But she needs me, and I know she doesn't like to admit that. She's complicated, Mae, but harmless really. We just have to be able to tolerate each other to keep making great work.'

Mae pushed her worries about Ana to the back of her mind and began moving vases of flowers into the kitchen, the living room and the snug.

The *Variety* splash was the tip of the iceberg. Beneath the surface, nothing between Mae and V had been feeling right, and it was going to take more than a hundred pounds' worth of market flowers to fix it. Insidiously, since they'd stopped trying for a baby, they had started to bicker. V accused Mae of sulking and said there was nothing stopping them having a baby any number of other ways. Mae replied it wasn't about a random baby; she'd wanted a family with the two people she loved most in the world.

She felt V was using work as a coping mechanism. She'd thrown herself into Ana's life story at the expense of their own. V meanwhile claimed not to have been defeated by their failure to conceive and said that Mae had given up too easily. When they did spend time together, Mae tended to ignite an argument as quickly as a match tossed into a pool of oil.

Time was no longer measured in IVF cycles. Now it stretched like a tensely pulled line and without Ari around, each day felt strange and unsettled.

One positive that had come out of her conscious uncoupling from Ari and the slow drifting apart from her girlfriend was that Mae now saw Janet and Michael at least once a month. She would invite them to London to catch an exhibition or a play. They would always arrive impossibly early, and her dad seemed unable to walk down a single street without reading out loud the words on every advertising billboard they passed. It drove her mad, and even Janet always ended up walking two metres in front of him to avoid the commentary. But Mae enjoyed that simply *being* with her parents was getting easier, as well as the fact that she was in some small way broadening their minds with these cultural excursions.

She liked to do activities with them so they could talk about the things they had seen rather than anything more personal. Mae certainly didn't want to involve them in the detail of her life – a fact that V found increasingly irritating on the rare occasions she joined them.

'It's just wild to me that they don't even know we want kids,' she would inevitably say during the taxi ride home. 'Are you embarrassed to admit you failed, or that you even tried?' Mae wouldn't usually answer. The truth was, she didn't know.

*

Ari emailed Mae a long, heartfelt narrative about once a month. She'd reply with cursory updates, hoping on the one hand that her best friend was still racked with guilt for leaving, and on the other that he was happy. He had been right: space and time apart had helped soften the serrated edge of her feelings. She tried not to care what he was doing every day, and she knew he was fighting the compulsion to tell her.

What made Mae happy without Ari at the centre of her universe was the weekly mentoring sessions she ran with Luke and Lewis, who were now almost fifteen. She helped them with their English homework after school on Thursdays. It was their secret; as the head of marketing for the charity, she was supposed to spend less time with the young people they helped and focus more on business affairs. But the tutoring satisfied something in her – a need to take care of people that had been left like a scraped knee without a plaster in her best friend's absence.

The twins' combined energy – Luke thoughtful, ethereal and camp, Lewis simpler, but stoical and unselfconsciously charming – evoked something that Mae missed. She resented having to leave their most recent tutoring session early to accompany V to her London premiere on a boat on the Thames. Luke had been sulky and quiet all session. His brother was worried about him and had told Mae in confidence that he was barely eating.

Reluctantly she said, 'I'm sorry, boys, I've got to go to get to this party on time, but let's pick up on *Romeo and Juliet* next week, OK?'

Luke perked up at the suggestion of glamour. 'Wherefore

art thou, Mae? Get thee to the party,' he said, packing away his books. 'But first, tell me *everything*. What are you wearing and *who* is going to be there?'

'I'm not sure what I'll wear,' she lied, knowing full well that Reeva would have prepared a rail of options. As V's personal assistant, Reeva's loyalty was with her mentor more than the magazine. And she'd been offered a large pay rise to leave *Edit* and support V in her new job.

Mae said to the boys, 'And it's a boat party, so I guess it'll be quite fabulous. I'll tell you all about it next session.'

'You should really go now or you'll get stuck in rush-hour traffic,' Lewis said anxiously after he'd looked up on his smartphone how long it would take her to get to St Katharine Docks. 'You're cutting it fine.'

She left the centre with the boys, and they wolf-whistled when they saw the car with blacked-out windows waiting for her on the street outside.

'It's all right for some!' said Lewis.

'Ooh, she *fancy*,' said Luke.

Mae ignored them. 'Finish the play! Don't just read the York Notes.' The driver put her bag in the boot and Lewis closed the door of the passenger seat behind her. She wound down the window. 'And wait, I'm sorry I said Juliet had it coming. Lack of communication was a big part of her downfall, granted. But love and death, pain ... I mean, it's complicated. We'll discuss it when I'm back.'

'Adieu!' said Luke dramatically, pulling his rucksack onto both shoulders. The car pulled away and Mae turned so she could watch the brothers safely cross the road.

*

The boat left the dock at seven, and by nine, its cargo of A-listers were loosening their bow ties and slipping off their heels. Once it dropped anchor in Greenwich, it was rocking with the kind of wild abandon conjured only when money, power, fame and ambition mixed like an ice-cold martini.

Mae snuck away from the dance floor, where she'd left V talking to someone important, and walked down onto the outdoor lower deck. She was wearing a Tom Ford tuxedo that had been tailored to fit her perfectly. Her shoes were old black brogues – the wrong tone and the wrong shape for the suit. She felt awkward in them, like they betrayed the fact that she spent her days working at a tiny desk above a community centre and making tea for people who said things like 'Ooh, I think Nigel brought in some Bourbons for everyone.'

She was unlacing them so she could dangle her feet through the safety railings when she felt someone's presence behind her. Assuming it was V, she turned with a bored look on her face ready to ask how long till they'd be returning to shore. But it was Ana. She stumbled a little as the boat bobbed on a wave, and Mae jumped up to help her steady herself.

'Hello, darling,' said Ana. 'What are you doing down here all by yourself? Has that naughty girlfriend of yours abandoned you?' She seemed drunk; not as drunk as she had been known to get at parties, but the strap of her red Valentino gown was hanging loosely off her shoulder, and Mae recognised the way her eyes flickered as she tried to focus.

'Nothing really. Just needed some peace. It gets a bit much after a while.'

'Tell me about it,' said Ana, lifting the long hem of her dress so she could sit on the deck where Mae had been. Mae sat down again, putting a few inches between them. But Ana closed the gap and their bare feet touched in the darkness. Mae felt the fizz of desire.

'I've got to find V,' she said in a panic, fumbling to get her socks on, pulling on her shoes and not stopping to do up the laces until Ana was completely out of sight.

V was on the upper deck talking to a male model called David. Mae swooped two glasses of champagne from a passing waiter and downed them in quick succession. She channelled her pent-up sexual energy into a passionate kiss that took V quite by surprise and left David reeling.

'Oh yeah,' he said, 'I'm into that. You ladies are hot.' He leaned in closer.

The three of them spent the rest of the evening laughing and flirting together as Mae tried to forget the space that had wedged itself between her and V. David asked them if they'd like to come back to his. He went to get more drinks while they thought about it. Mae pushed herself up against V and, somehow pitching her voice perfectly between seductive and serious, said, 'Fuck it. Why not? Maybe this is what we need.'

'Oh Mae, I don't know. It doesn't feel like either of us are in a great place right now. Is this a good idea?' V was unsure.

David was at the bar, looking vacantly at the shore and nodding his head awkwardly to the beat of the music.

'You know, I've been so certain about my sexuality for so long. So sure I would one day carry a child. I'm so boringly black and white about everything – Ari told me that once. Maybe I should challenge *everything* I always thought was certain about myself. Plus It's basically a free round of insemination, and you never know.'

V nodded, quickly grasping the intention behind Mae's rash rationale. 'What's the right thing to do? What's the best way?' She was tipsy and giggled excitedly. 'We're such fucking *good girls*, Mae. But you're right, look where that got us. Maybe we need this?'

Mae was feeling nicely woozy, and she was bored of being so miserable. She leaned close to her girlfriend. 'OK, you take the lead, but I'm not going to his place.'

Once the boat had sailed back west and docked at Embankment Gardens, David followed Mae and V like an eager lapdog to the Savoy, where they were spending the night. V dimmed the lights in their riverside suite, then pushed Mae onto the queen-sized bed and straddled her, white silk jumpsuit pulled tight over her thighs. She undid Mae's bow tie and the top few buttons of her white shirt, then invited David to do the rest. Mae closed her eyes. She felt V's soft hands stroke her face, felt her mouth kiss her neck. Then she felt David's big sausage fingers struggling at her chest.

'Sorry, these are fiddly little buggers,' he said.

Mae opened one eye, then the other, and burst out laughing. When V started laughing too, David looked at the two women and then began giggling, which started them off all over again, this time with tears running down their faces.

'Take it I should go?' he said graciously when they'd all gathered themselves and sat like naughty children on the edge of the bed.

'Sorry, mate,' said Mae, getting up to hold open the door. She shook his hand and pulled him in for a fraternal pat on the back. 'I'm just definitely massively gay. It's nothing personal.'

'Come here,' said V after he had gone. 'That was a really stupid idea. It was reckless. If hilarious. And I'm sorry I encouraged you.' She expertly unhooked Mae's cufflinks for her and placed them on the bedside table.

At two a.m., they ordered a pot of mint tea, which arrived on a vast silver tray with a plate of petits fours. Mae was so embarrassed by the display of ostentation she practically threw a ten-pound note at the tired-looking boy who had delivered it. They sat up in bed, not speaking, but processing the madness of the last few hours and the unhappy months that had got them to this place.

'Tonight was your big night, V. The film is incredible.' Mae kissed her cheek. She lifted her cup from the tray that rested on the duvet between them, took a sip, then sighed. 'I'm sorry about the world's worst threesome.'

V laughed and poured them more tea.

'I'm not sure what's going on with me. There's something else that's been playing on my mind, I think.'

V tilted her head. She looked as though she was struggling to stay awake.

'I'm worried about Luke. Lewis came to see me before our tutoring session earlier and said he barely leaves his room any more. His foster mum laughed at him in drag, and ever since he's stopped even trying.'

'Just when he'd mastered make-up!' said V, startled back to alertness.

'Exactly.'

Behind the heavy drapes, the sun would be rising in a few short hours. Thankfully Mae didn't need to be at work until ten on a Friday.

'He was growing so much in his performances and in him-self, it was lovely to watch. Lewis says he's bunking off school and that he seems really sad all the time. I feel like I need to do something, but it came up at a meeting that I was giving the twins too much attention, so I'm loath to.'

It was V's turn to say 'Fuck it' now. She topped up both their cups from the heavy silver teapot and appeared momen-tarily lost in thought. 'This kid needs your help. Why don't you invite them to stay over this weekend? We can plan some fun stuff to do together and have a heart-to-heart with Luke. It'll be fun.'

They did have spare rooms, lots of outside space, and a sound system that Lewis was bound to call 'sick'. V would need a DBS check and there would be much paperwork, but Mae knew how to get the approvals she needed in days rather than weeks. She laid her head on V's bare chest and her eyes fluttered closed with the pull of happiness.

The twins were dropped off by their foster carers for a 'res-pite break' a few days later. Mae worried that her glamorous girlfriend wouldn't have the first clue what to do with fifteen-year-old boys, but as usual, V astounded her. Mae hung back and watched as she instantly made them feel at home.

She laid down some ground rules in the strict voice Mae used to swoon over when they worked together. She showed them how to operate the speakers and the mood lighting and told them to feel free to play their own music. Mae fetched fizzy drinks and big tubs of crisps from the kitchen and smiled as Lewis attempted to teach V a complicated dance move. Her girlfriend rarely showed this playful side of herself.

She kept it well suppressed at work; even at the parties she frequented, she never really let her guard down and enjoyed herself. Only Mae, Leah and occasionally Ari had experienced V at her silliest.

Mae assembled a pizza oven in the garden while V organised the toppings.

'Boys, I need help, I think there's a piece missing!' she called through the conservatory doors. Lewis popped his head out and offered to take a look.

'Thought lesbians were supposed to be good at DIY,' he said with a cheeky grin.

'Not funny.' She rolled her eyes and handed him the screwdriver. 'But it's nice to finally have a man about the house.'

After dinner, the four of them sat around the firepit, which Mae had allowed Lewis to build and light, seeing how happy the task seemed to make him. Luke had been quiet, and once the flames were dancing in the warm September evening, it was V who asked him what was up.

'I dunno,' he grunted.

'C'mon, Luke, you do,' encouraged his brother sweetly.

'It's just I'm shit at drag. I'm a laughing stock. I watch all these boys my age online and they're so pretty and they can do this incredible contouring and I'm just some chavvy kid in care with no money to buy the brands they have and ...' He burst into tears and instinctively fell into Lewis's arms.

'I really like Peppermint. I think she's cool,' said Lewis, rubbing his brother's back.

'I do too,' said Mae. 'And she's just getting started.'

V shook her head. 'Hang on, you're definitely not a "Peppermint".'

'V!' Mae shot her a look.

'No, I'm sorry, but that name isn't right for you, and maybe the character you're creating isn't either. Luke, drag isn't about being someone you're not. It's about revealing a side of yourself, inhabiting an identity that somehow expresses who you really, truly are. And from what Mae tells me, you've lived too much of life to be so sweet. We can help you find your true drag spirit, but you're going to need charisma, uniqueness, nerve and talent – and frankly I'm getting none of that from you right now. So buck up, little queen, we start work tomorrow morning. Who's in?'

V held her hand out and Mae put hers on top, then Lewis, and finally Luke added his delicate hand to the top of the pile. 'Let's do this!' said V, and Mae fell in love all over again.

In the company of the boys, she felt closer to her girlfriend than she had done in months. V opened her wardrobe and make-up cupboard to Luke, who Mae had never seen so ecstatic. She gave him her time and expertise, and by Sunday evening 'Minerva Fontaine' had been born. The twins left early Monday morning. Their foster dad tooted the horn of his white van from the street, and the boys reluctantly picked up their backpacks and parroted an overly polite thank you that Mae imagined had been drilled into them by the various carers they'd had throughout their lives. Later, while tidying up the chaos their stay had created, she and V felt the boys' absence acutely. Neither of them dared mention it.

Chapter 32

Mae had wanted to sneak into Ari's London reading unnoticed, so as not to distract him, but V had worn her highest heels and a sequinned Dolce trouser suit. They had also invited Luke and Lewis to join them, and if it wasn't V's outfit turning heads, it was the handsome identical twins by her side. Mae normally enjoyed the attention they commanded as a foursome, but this evening all she could think about was Ari.

She pushed open the door of the Soho shop and was greeted by the sharp, comforting smell of books. Her eyes adjusted to the low light and the air-conditioned calm. She was transported back to her part-time job in Leeds, and the sweet satisfaction she felt on stacking each new consignment of novels in their place on the shelves, knowing that Ari would be waiting for her outside at the end of the work day with the next eight hours stretched before them, abundant with possibilities. She had liked the spines to line up perfectly. Trace used to call her 'finickety'.

As she led V and the boys through the display tables towards the back of the store, where rows of chairs had been squeezed in between the shelves for Ari Hines's reading, she stopped to neaten up a pile of new releases. She heard his voice before she saw him.

'"A friend is a second self, so that our consciousness of a friend's existence ... makes us more fully conscious of our own existence." I wish I'd come up with that, but it was Aristotle.' The audience chuckled politely.

Mae and V took the last two empty seats on the back row and the twins stood behind them. Mae realised she'd been holding her breath, and thinly inhaled. Lewis placed his hand on her shoulder and gave it a friendly squeeze. Ari looked well, less pale and thin than when she'd watched his last live-streamed video. He wore his pleated silk Issey Miyake trousers with a tight-fitting black T-shirt, which she knew meant he'd been working out. He cleared his throat.

This poem
– after Adrienne Rich

you are reading this poem in your future
on the cliffside next to the knuckle of the moon
beside your wife watching
your daughter draw her own atlases
and plant stars ready to
soar

you are reading this poem in our future
in a house made of books
wooden tables packed with candles
and I am still your sleeping beauty
drug-dead and dreaming

ready for your kiss to breathe
life back into my lungs

every day will be a Sunday
the smell of potatoes roasting
the table scattered with crayon-fingers
chess pieces our children will grow sunflowers
in the garden dance with firebirds
make cities in the snow

you are reading this poem in my future
on the edge of an hourglass
crocodiles clapping outside my window
whispers floating under the curtain

there the haunt begins

you
having taken any and every form
lapping in the abyss I am not alone
I submerge myself
and the crocodiles lay their heads
on my stomach and plait my hair
I no longer have to wash my heart

I am she I am he I am
home.

V was crying. She reached for her girlfriend's hand, but
Mae pulled it away, feeling anger as an understudy for grief.

V looked hurt and confused by her reaction, but Mae was processing so much she didn't know how to explain.

Luke bent down and whispered between their heads, 'I think I'm in love.'

The reminder of his presence shook Mae out of herself for long enough to laugh, and then mouth, 'I'm sorry' to V, who was gathering her things, getting ready to leave.

Officiously V said, 'I'll drop the boys home – we told the foster parents we'd have them back by eight.'

'But you'll come to the after party still?' Mae asked in a shaky, pleading voice.

The crowds had dispersed and Basma came bounding over. She gave Mae an over-the-top hug.

'Ari's just signing some books, but he told me to tell you none of you lot are to even think about leaving without him.'

V sat back down, and Luke danced with excitement.

They waited in silence for a few tense minutes until Ari sashayed along the aisle between the banks of chairs. He threw his hands in the air and shouted, 'Lovers! I've missed you.'

Mae ran towards him and he locked his arms around her. She whispered something in his ear, and they unfurled their grip on each other but continued to stare into one another's eyes.

It was Luke who unfroze the moment.

'Oh. My. Gawd. Ari Hines. I'm literally not even joking, I'm like your biggest fan. I ... Would you mind just signing ... umm ...' He grabbed a random book from the shelf behind him.

Lewis, ever on hand with a practical solution to a problem,

fished a biro from his jacket pocket and handed it to his brother. 'Here, use this.'

The adults still hadn't moved. Luke edged forward with his arm outstretched as if passing an olive branch. Mae suddenly woke from her stupor.

'For God's sake, Luke,' she laughed, 'at least have him sign his own book!' She knocked the novel out of his hand playfully.

'So, you two beautiful humans must be Luke and Lewis. I wish I could say I've heard so much about you, but our friend Mae here is the Raymond Carver of emails – sparse on any detail.'

Luke gave an awkward curtsey and Lewis shook Ari's hand, saying, 'Mae doesn't shut up about you.'

V nudged him with her shoulder. 'Oi! Manners!' Then she walked elegantly up to Ari and kissed both his cheeks. 'It's good to see you, kid. But look, I've got to get the boys home, or their carers will give me an earful. And I'm not sure I'm in a party mood tonight. Ana will be there representing anyway; she's much better at having fun than me these days. You two go. It will be good for you to have time to catch up properly. Mae, I'll see you at home later. You can tell me all about it.'

Ari took the biro from Luke's hand and wrote *Minerva Fontaine 4 eva* on his inner forearm. Luke squealed, thrilled that Ari Hines knew that about him at least, and then V ushered the boys out of the store, calling to Mae in a flat voice, 'Bye, love you,' as she left.

'Just us then, handsome,' Ari said with a mischievous smile.

*

The party for Ari's UK book launch was in a gold-and-marble-bedecked basement bar on Greek Street. Staff topped up glasses so discreetly everyone lost track of what they'd been drinking, and a loose mood descended on the scene. Ana was there wearing a slip dress – she never missed a party. Mae tried and failed to not stare at her breasts as she reached across her in the crowd to swipe another drink from a passing waiter's tray. Ari was swept away by a current of somebodies thirsty for his company. Mae felt bad about V. She'd not been very nice to her recently; work stress and a lingering sense that it was on her to figure out how they were ever going to have a family had left her irritable and withdrawn.

She was feeling let down by Ari, too. It had been a year and a half since they'd last seen each other but he had barely looked at her since they'd arrived at the party and was flying back to New York early the next morning. Guests posed louchely on red velvet sofas. Mae was drinking too much, and emotions, all of them, were swirling just beneath the surface. She went to the bathroom, but before she closed the door, Ana slipped in behind her.

'I saw you looking at me, Mae. Do you like what you see?'

'Umm,' Mae laughed nervously, 'of course. You don't need me to tell you you're stunning.'

'Maybe I do.' Ana pushed her gently against the wall and pressed her petite body into her. 'You're a hot boi, baby, and I know your type. You have needs that I don't think are being met.' She grabbed Mae's crotch. 'Am I right?'

'I, er . . .'

'I can be that girl for you. I can give you what you need.' She turned around and placed Mae's arms around her waist, guiding her hands up to her breasts. Mae felt blank and passive; she was relinquishing herself, enjoying the moment. But as Ana lifted her dress, Mae mustered every last remaining millimetre of willpower to say, 'Can I meet you back here in like ten minutes. I just . . . I have to do something first.'

'Sure, give me the nod when you're ready, darling. I'm all yours.'

Mae hastily opened the bathroom door and snuck out. She pushed through the crowd and ran up the stairs to the street, scrolling through her phone contacts for 'Home'.

Janet answered, sounding surprised.

'Mum,' said Mae, 'I'm about to make a really, really big mistake and I think you're the only person who can stop me.'

'Take your time, darling,' said Janet calmly.

Mae was struggling to find the words to match her reeling thoughts. Finally she settled on the truth.

'I almost did something with a woman who isn't V. And I might still. She's just so *gorgeous* and she's into me. She *wants* me, in a way I don't know if V does any more.' She forgot it was her mother on the other end of the phone and just talked. 'I've felt so down about my body since I found out I couldn't conceive. I don't know if I can resist this.'

'What do you mean, you can't conceive? Even I know two women need a little something called spermatozoa to make a baby, dear.'

Mae hadn't told her mother much about the plan to have a child with Ari, let alone about the failed rounds of IVF and the toll they had taken on her. She'd said all was fine whenever they spoke on the phone. Nothing to report. And Janet, painfully tactful, didn't ask her daughter if children were on the cards, because she didn't know if that was something it was OK to say to lesbian people, even though the biological clock was ticking for them too.

A warm breeze kicked up the dust on the pavement. Mae acknowledged the chasm between her life and her mother's knowledge of it.

'I'm sorry I didn't tell you that I always wanted to be a parent.'

Janet let out an excited 'ooh' that turned into an 'oh' when Mae told her the short version of their failed plan. It didn't work out with Ari, she said, and it wouldn't work with anyone, because she was what Dr Granite had called 'potentially unable to conceive'.

'Apparently *you* were a fluke,' Janet said after the news had sunk in. 'Your father and I wanted so much to give you a sibling, and when it wasn't working for us, we saw a consultant, who told me it was highly unlikely I'd conceive again and that it was nothing short of a miracle that I ever had done. So miracles do happen, Mae, if you just kept trying.'

'It's not as easy as that, Mum.' Party guests were joining her outside now, for fresh air and to tell their assistants to cancel the next day's meetings. Mae moved to a quiet spot behind the recycling bins.

'V can afford it.'

'Yes, but I can't take it. My body can't take it. I need to move on.'

'I understand,' said Janet, surprising her. 'And now what I'm hearing is that you're sad and angry. It's no wonder you and V are drifting apart. The same happened with Michael and me.'

It was the first time Janet had used Mae's father's name when she spoke to her.

'You're processing the loss of something you thought you would share, and that can make you both feel very alone.'

Mae felt childish tears brewing and her voice cracked.

'Oh Mae, darling, why didn't you ever talk to me about this before? I could have helped you.'

'I didn't think you'd understand.'

'You never gave me the chance to! These things are universal. Being gay doesn't change your feelings; the stuff of life is what unites us. Boring straight people like your father and me, fantastic homosexual people like you and V. Pain is pain. OK, your experience of being in the world is different to mine. But I've always done my best to walk in your shoes. It's called empathy, for goodness' sake. It's just that you've never trusted me enough to come to me with your problems.'

'Well I'm coming to you now, aren't I?' Mae didn't mean to sound annoyed, but there was an urgency to this phone call her mother seemed to be missing.

Janet sighed. 'I'm pleased you did. Because you are about to jeopardise the best thing that's ever happened to you. You're tempted, and you phoned me because you wanted me to stop you. You assumed your judgemental mother would tell you that if you blow this with V, "Mum and Dad will be very disappointed". I'm sorry but I'm not going to do that. If you need to sleep with a beautiful woman to regain a semblance of respect for yourself, do it. If you're prepared to betray the trust of the person who has brought so much happiness and stability into your life, and helped you grow into the impressive woman you are today, then I imagine the experience will be worth it. You will make a choice as an adult and shoulder the burden of consequences. All I can tell you is that whatever happens, I will be here for you, darling.'

It was good to hear her say it, but it didn't solve the problem of Ana. Mae had wanted Janet to give her a compelling reason not to go back into the bar, find her and have bleary, illicit sex with her. She'd wanted the scenario filtered into a simple right and wrong. She'd wanted her mother to be morally outraged.

'Let me leave you with a question,' said Janet. 'When you close your eyes and picture your future without V – because she *will* find out, and once you break trust there is no going back – can you truly live with that feeling? Tell me how you get on, dear.'

After saying a meek goodbye, Mae did as her mother had asked and closed her eyes. The feeling she located was darkness, empty and uncertain. She sat on the pavement and burst into tears.

'There you are, handsome. I've been looking for you.' Ari crouched down next to her, not wanting to sully his expensive silk trousers. 'What's wrong? Things are tricky with the wife, right? I noticed a vibe at the bookshop.'

Mae gathered herself and stood up. Ari reached out his hand and she pulled him up too. She wiped her eyes with the handkerchief in her back pocket and he watched her carefully.

'V is not my wife.' She said the word again to herself. *Wife.* Marriage had always been for other people, not people like her. Weddings were about blushing brides and dashing grooms – a woman giving herself up for a man, being passed from father to husband like property. Gay marriage was legal, yes, but it was still dripping in straightness. She'd always felt embarrassed and uncomfortable at the thought of doing something so *basic*. She was better than that. But the word lingered like an aftertaste as Ari brushed the dirt from the back of her light blue jeans.

'I'm longing to talk to you, but it seems to me that the person you really need to talk to tonight is V. Go home, Mae. Nothing good ever happens after one a.m., remember?' He wrapped her in a tight hug. Nothing Ana could give her would feel as good as this, she reasoned.

Ari waited with her until her taxi arrived.

'Come see me in New York. I'll call you, OK?'

She watched through the car window as he stepped back into the sweaty throng without her.

'Ana wanted me to fuck her.' Mae called V from the cab. She stared out of the window as they crossed Lambeth Bridge.

'She acts like that with everyone when she's high. She's an attention-seeker.'

'No, V, she followed me into the bathroom and jumped on me. And I . . . I didn't tell her to stop.'

'Right,' V said coldly.

'Nothing happened.'

'But it might have done?'

'Honestly, yes. And that's why I had to tell you straight away. In all these years, I've never been tempted. I want to understand why now, and I want to fix it.'

'Oh. How noble of you.'

'Please don't be like that. I thought you'd appreciate my honesty.'

'Please don't tell me how to *be*.'

Back home, Mae made up the bed in her favourite of the spare rooms and V stretched out in the queen on her own. They switched off the upstairs lights and the whirr of the air conditioning sounded deafening. Mae felt shivery and alone. After some time staring at the red light pulsating from the smoke alarm on the ceiling above her, she got up and tiptoed into the master bedroom.

'Are you awake?' she whispered.

V rustled under the sheets, and when she spoke, her voice was disarmingly clear.

'Let's not be these people.'

Mae felt her way through the thick darkness to the edge of the bed. V wrapped her arms fiercely around her waist and pressed her face into her lower back. They stayed like that until their breathing slowed and mirrored each other's. When V finally untethered herself, Mae felt the patch of tears her girlfriend had left on her skin.

'Since we stopped trying, and Ari left, you've been drifting further and further from me. It's like I'm not enough for you without him here.'

Mae didn't rush to respond, because deep down she knew V was right.

'I'm not sure it's just Ari I'm missing. It's the family and the future we could have had.'

'Are you upset that *I'm* not giving you the child you want?'

'No, of course not. I would never want you to feel I was pressuring you to carry our child when I know that's not something you've ever wanted for yourself. Are you upset that *I'm* not giving you the child *you* want?'

'I'm upset that since we found out pregnancy is unlikely, you've shut down the whole conversation about parenting. I know you hate it when things don't go as you'd planned. And it's taken a long time to come to terms with Ari not being the father of your child. But we always said we'd talk about other options, and you haven't wanted to. You feel entitled to your original plan simply because you chose it and therefore you think it's owed to you.'

V sat up next to Mae. As their eyes adjusted to the darkness, they could just about make out each other's shape.

'Babe, you have no idea of your privilege,' she continued. 'You expect life to work out how you want it to because you've never had to fight for it, you've never known what it's like to be told you can't.'

Mae let V's words access the deepest part of herself to see what reactions the crystalline truth might set in motion there. Clarity came in streaks like a cloth wiping layers of dust from a mirror.

'I spoke to my mother tonight,' said Mae. 'She told me you were the best thing that had ever happened to me. And I realised something. I realised I've never wanted to accept my parents' love. It's absolutely a privilege to have two people devoted to me, trying so hard to understand me. They are there as my safety net, always, and I've rejected it because I know I can, I know that I can be awful, I can be awful to them and they will still be there loving me. Maybe something about that unconditional love scares me because I don't really believe I deserve it. I pushed it away, tried to control it.'

V reached behind Mae to turn on the bedside lamp. She never liked talking about important things in the dark.

'I think it's time for us to be parents,' she said with an absolute certainty that Mae adored. 'I've let you drive this because it was always your plan with Ari. I just said yes to it. But this is *our* future now, only ours, and I want to make it happen for us.'

'I do too. V, I'm sorry about Ana. I've been feeling so angry lately and that anger was all muddled up with desire.'

'Thank you for telling me. I'm glad nothing happened.'

'I touched her breasts.'

'Who hasn't?' laughed V, defusing the intensity in an elegant flash. 'I will be seeing to Ana,' she said firmly. 'I've been thinking about selling my share in the company anyway. If I'm honest with myself, I don't enjoy being in business with her. I do all the work and she ... Well, she's *Ana*. I'm done feeling forced into playing the palatable, sensible one so she can be wild and whimsical. I wanted to believe it was the industry that needed to change to make space for a woman like her. But I'm tired of it. And the fact is, she's not a good person. As evidenced tonight. This is it. I'm ending it tomorrow; my lawyer can get me out of pretty much everything we had set up, I'm sure. You belong to me, Mae.' And she kissed the back of Mae's neck like she was placing a wax seal on a precious letter.

The next day, Mae felt invigorated. Her long talk with V had brought so much she'd been shouldering silently out into the open, and now there was a lightness. She slid into her small desk space at FAM head office, turned on her computer and arranged her highlighter pens in an orderly line above her mouse mat.

'Someone's double-dropped the happy pills this morning.' Nigel grinned at her in between slurping his cereal.

Mae couldn't admit to him that she was excited to see Lewis and Luke when they came in for their tutoring session later that day, but they'd been on her mind a lot and V now seemed equally invested in their well-being. She had given Mae a copy of *Paris Is Burning* on DVD for her to pass on to Luke, with a postcard attached that read: *To Minerva Fontaine. Your drag herstory starts here. Come back to our House of Extravaganza soon. We miss you.* Mae read the message over and over again as she waited for the boys to find her in the computer room.

'There's been draaaaaama,' said Luke, pushing open the door with a flourish. Lewis sulked behind him, evidently more affected by the situation than his brother, who was gagging to spill the goss.

'Hello, Luke, hello, Lewis. I take it you'd like to tell me what's going on.'

'I don't know why *he's* so happy about it,' said Lewis glumly.

'Well, Mae, it turns out our foster carers extraordinaire are moving to the bright lights of Welwyn Garden City, and due to our studies, we will not be going with them.'

'Yikes, guys, that's a lot. Are you OK? What's happening?'

'Back to the children's home for a few more years,' said Lewis. 'Then we'll be early care leavers and get some shithole of a flat and can finally look after ourselves.'

'Let's get on with today's tutoring, then we'll talk more about this, OK? I'm not going to let anything bad happen to you. Trust me.'

At home later that night, once Reeva had left with instructions to engage lawyers and begin the business negotiations with Ana Palomo, Mae poured her girlfriend a glass of red wine and told her about the boys' predicament.

'It's so unfair,' said V as she started chopping carrots for dinner. 'The cards they were handed in life. Reeva too. I think about that a lot. She lost her mum just before she became a teenager and would have needed her most. And poor Luke and Lewis knowing that their whole family couldn't take care of them. Those boys are full of joy. They're great kids.'

The conversation was going exactly as Mae had planned. She'd planted the seed and now needed the idea to grow in V's mind so she would think she'd come up with it.

V put down her glass and looked at her.

'What if you and I took them in?'

Chapter 33

New York, March 2025

The muffled oomf of music from the warehouse on the floor above Ari's Williamsburg apartment was keeping him awake. He'd unconsciously started adhering to some of Mae's 'rules' since he'd been living alone. He made his bed every morning, planned his meals for the week, and tried to be asleep before 11.45 p.m. most nights. But tonight his neighbour's loud partying, coupled with his building's broken air con, was making that impossible. He got up and put on his kimono, then tied his hair, which was now as long as it had been when he first met Mae, into a high ponytail.

He walked up the industrial staircase and knocked assertively on his neighbour's door. A girl answered, looking flustered. She was naked except for a sarong she'd evidently grabbed in a hurry to cover up. Behind her, the vast space, which was identical to Ari's if somewhat more homely, was empty of people. Weird, thought Ari, who was expecting to have to be his most tactful to negotiate the music being turned down without killing the party's vibe.

'Oh hey,' he said over the noise.

'Hey, one sec.' She propped the door open and went to fumble with her stereo. 'Sorry about that,' she said, returning to where Ari stood at the open door, wondering if he should venture further in. 'I was having a little dance party for one. How can I help you? Ari, is it? I've signed for some packages for you, before you think I'm a stalker.'

'It was actually just that. The music. I couldn't sleep. I thought you were having a big do.'

'Do?'

'Sorry, I spent a long time in the UK. A party.'

'Ah. I see. Won't happen again, neighbour. Duly noted. It's just I had a kinda shitty day and I find dancing naked to disco music makes me feel a lot better.'

'Oh my gosh. Me too! I do the *exact* same thing.'

'Do you want to come in? Seeing as you're awake now anyway. I just opened a bottle of wine that I probably shouldn't drink alone.'

It was a novelty to realise, standing in his neighbour's doorway, that he had no one else to answer to or think about, and so he said nonchalantly, 'Sure.'

'I'm Kate. Come on in, then. Of course, I know who you are. Those are your books on the shelf over there. Busted. I'm a fan.' She retied her sarong as a dress, twisting the two top corners and knotting them behind her neck. Ari was suddenly very conscious that he wasn't wearing underwear. He perched on her big cosy sofa with his legs tightly crossed.

'Nice to meet you. Cheers,' he said, taking a glass of wine.

They talked until the sun glowed bright behind the roller blinds. He found her naturally easy to be with yet so unlike Mae, who he couldn't help but compare everyone to. Kate was subtler, less opinionated, and wafted through her space with a hazy vagueness that Ari found had a similar effect on him to the wine.

The next morning, back in his own bed, he awoke to find his silk robe was stuck to his sweaty back and he had an oblique fear that he'd crossed some kind of line with Kate. It was certainly the most fun he'd had in a while.

He made coffee and sat at the glass kitchen table where his laptop lived. He checked his email and found Mae's name at the top of his inbox; the subject was 'News'.

Hey, wanted to let you know we are fostering Luke and Lewis. All happening quickly, we're v happy. More soon!
   Mae x

The coffee was too weak. He pushed the cup to one side and stared at the words on his screen. Mae was building her family without him. He stood up quickly, without knowing why, pulled the belt of his robe tighter and wandered aimlessly into his huge living room, which Mae would think looked like the set of a millennial reality TV show, with its exposed bricks and leather beanbags. She would scoff at the incongruous snooker table that his interior designer had insisted on and Ari only ever used as a surface on which to empty the fan mail he received via Basma on a weekly basis; heartfelt letters, anguished drawings, small gifts that mostly went to charity.

He felt listless and like Mae had just told him he'd lost something for ever. He wondered if it would read as needy to invite Kate for breakfast. He'd told her last night all about

Mae and their failed plan; she'd be interested in this development. Or would she? Had he just spoken entirely about himself and come across as pathetic? As a familiar self-doubt began to tingle beneath his skin, his phone rang.

'How's the writing going?' Basma had an unmistakably throaty south London drawl.

'I just need time to figure out what it is I have to say now. Can you buy me six months?'

'You won't get paid.'

'I didn't realise I did get paid.'

'God, you really are rich. OK, leave it with me.'

'Thanks, Basma. You're the best.'

'Don't you know it.'

She hung up, and Ari found himself drawn back towards his dark, musty-smelling bedroom. He shook the knots from his bedsheets, then flopped onto the mattress and slept until noon.

Over the next months, as spring emptied out into a steamy East Coast summer, Ari knocked at Kate's door almost every day. It didn't take him long to discover that she too was 'from money'. Their financial parity made a specific difference to their growing friendship that neither of them would ever acknowledge, but that hovered discreet and attentive in the background like a good butler.

Ari introduced her to Spanish soap operas, and they could happily pass an afternoon watching TV, trying to guess at what was going on without subtitles. Mae would have called it wasting time. But Kate made popcorn and offered to open another bottle.

'I won't,' said Ari one afternoon. So much of his story was public now, he forgot that he still needed to talk about himself like a normal human rather than a facsimile, and was tempted to say 'google it' when Kate asked him questions. But he had made his name on honesty, so he laid his complicated relationship with alcohol out for her. It transpired that she had grown up with two functioning alcoholics for parents.

'Say no more,' was her simple response, and from then on, the bottle always disappeared after their second small glass.

It meant that when Kate leaned over to kiss him for the first time, and he kissed her back, neither of them could claim to be drunk. 'Take it you know I'm queer,' said Ari when they broke apart.

'Aren't we all?'

Kate was cool with the grey areas. The gay areas. And a month after that first kiss, Ari felt that he could open up the queerest parts of himself with her as his partner, in a way Oliver never would have allowed. She encouraged him to dress up when they went out. He walked better in heels than she did, she said. She loved his long hair and in bed would comb her hands through it, so it was Medusa-like against the white sheets.

He was sitting at Kate's breakfast bar – she was fixing them coffee but drew the line at cooking anything to go with it – when Mae phoned bursting with exciting news.

'We've been approved as adopters!' she yelled. He heard V in the background add an enthusiastic whoop.

'Hey, that's amazing. I mean, I never had any doubt you

would be.' He mouthed to Kate, 'It's Mae,' and took his coffee into her bedroom, shutting the door behind him. 'Tell me everything.'

'Well, we've had all these meetings with the social worker, where she's been grilling us about our relationship, our values . . . honestly, she knows just about *everything* about us. And then the forms! You wouldn't believe the paperwork and the emails, but V and I are like an efficiency machine together.'

'I can so imagine,' laughed Ari, picturing his friends in peak organisational mode and loving it.

'And it's been like couple's counselling. We've got all our issues out in the open, we've talked them through, and I just feel like we're in the most amazing place. It's got me thinking about how you always call V my wife.' She took a breath, then whispered, 'I'm thinking of making that a reality.'

Now it was Ari's turn to whoop. 'Shh!' said Mae, laughing.

Kate poked her head around the door to see what all the excitement was about, but Ari shooed her, kindly, away.

'Anyway, sorry, droning on about me as usual. How are *you*? Met anyone yet?' It felt like the first time in a long time she had asked him anything about himself.

'Oh no . . . you know me. Footloose and fancy-free for ever.' He had meant to tell Mae about Kate, but every time they spoke, there was a reason not to. 'I'm good, though. I'm happy.'

'Hey, get us, being all *happy*. I mean, V and I still have to apply to adopt the boys, but it's the first step.' Mae let out a satisfied sigh. 'Right, I need to get on. Call me soon? V sends lots of love.'

Ari needed to take a moment before going back out to Kate. He flopped backwards on to the Indian blanket that covered her bed.

Kate taught hot yoga. Ari took her Saturday morning class and had fallen in with her bougie Bikram crowd. He liked how much they liked him. They always went for matcha lattes after, and would laugh encouragingly at his jokes and listen wide-eyed and engrossed as he told them about his writer's block or how he felt he'd made a mistake with the colour palette in his living room.

'It's so refreshing to talk to such an emotionally intelligent man,' Kate's friend Teri said that morning. Teri claimed that cupping had cured her depression, and she had a nose ring Ari found unconvincing. 'I'd love you to meet my husband. He could really learn a lot from your energy.'

Later, when Kate and Ari were walking home, carrying their rolled-up purple yoga mats under their arms, she apologised for her friends treating him as such a curiosity.

'They've just not met anyone like you before,' she said. 'They ended up in such an expected world of men and women, the fact that you're so different is getting their mula bandhas in a twist.'

'I don't mind at all,' said Ari, slipping his hand into hers. 'It's sweet. They're nice people. Do they think I'm your boyfriend?'

'Do *you* think you're my boyfriend?'

'I've never had a girlfriend.'

'Would you like one?'

'I like you.'

'But would you like me to be your girlfriend?'

'Honestly,' said Ari after a long pause, 'I don't know right now.'

Mae had always said it was the thing that was the same that was the sexiest. Soft lips against soft lips. But Ari was attracted to the danger in difference. Oliver was everything as a man that he was not, and for all that was toxic about that relationship, feeling his boyfriend's oppressive weight straddling his back had never failed to turn Ari on and transform the hate they had for each other into a feral kind of love. Kate was closer to him as a person, but her body was something else. She held space for him.

Chapter 34

Connie said she was never going back to New York, and she meant it, so she stayed in Yorkshire, 'minding the house', when Alice and Letty visited in July. Alice insisted on taking the subway from the airport, so when they arrived at the unmarked steel door of Ari's warehouse complex, a grey brick building with black fire escapes zigzagging down the middle and graffiti adding a fluorescent splash at street level, they were perspiring.

'A nice dyke in a leather jacket who looked like she was headed straight back to 1989 carried our cases up the stairs at the train station,' said Alice, still breathless and flustered from the journey.

'Mum, you can't say "dyke" any more.'

'Letty, love, I appreciate that, but if you're a dyke, you can call a dyke a dyke.'

Letty covered her ears and Ari tried to scoop her up and twirl her around like he used to, but struggled.

'Look at you! When did you get so big? You're an actual teenager!'

'When did she get so clever, don't you mean,' said Alice, holding out her arms for a hug.

Ari took them up in the service elevator, and when they stepped into his apartment, he noted their reactions.

'It's open-plan living,' he explained.

'It's not very cosy, is it,' said Alice, running her hand along the concrete work surfaces. 'Bit brutalist for me, but as long as you're happy, Ari, that's the important thing.'

'I think I am. Actually, I know I am. I'm just scared that if I say it out loud too often, the rug might be pulled out from under me again.'

'A rug! That's what you need in here, a nice big rug or two. We could go and do the shops together if you want. I'll help you pick one out.'

'Mum has the worst taste.' Letty rolled her eyes like she'd just watched a 'how to be a teenager' tutorial.

'I'd love that.' Ari winked at her.

'Made many new friends?' asked Alice, opening cupboards and drawers in the kitchen for a snoop.

'A few, actually. Kate – you'll meet her. We're kind of dating.'

'But Kate's a girl's name!' Letty looked confused.

'Kate *is* a girl.'

'You're dating a girl? That's sooooo weird.'

'Letty!' snapped Alice. 'She's not got to the chapter on the fluidity of sexuality yet. Thinks you're either gay or not gay, nothing in between. She'll figure it out eventually.'

'I blame Mae's early influence. And Alice, on that. I've not actually told Mae about Kate yet. I just don't know that she'll get it.'

Alice said, 'I think she'll *get it*, Ari. She will just be jealous that you might love another woman more intensely than you love her, that's all. She didn't even like you having boyfriends, did she? Not that any of us liked that Oliver.'

'I remember thinking he looked like Mr Potato Head,' said Letty.

Ari laughed. 'Right, we're getting too deep too quickly. Who wants a cup of tea?'

Ari had briefed Kate on his family. She knew the big stuff already, as he'd covered most plot points in his 384 confessional vlogs and she admitted, somewhat shamefaced, that she'd watched them all.

'Alice feels like home for me,' was how he explained it. 'When Mum and I turned up at her door, after we'd escaped Dad and New York, she didn't ask any questions, just welcomed us in. She's completely unflappable and lives to make people feel comfortable. But she's funny and totally no-nonsense too. Mae always used to say she was her hero.'

Kate was used to Ari's best friend's name being dropped into conversations. At first, he'd apologised for talking about her too much. But once he'd told Kate all about their plan and then Mae's infertility – the one thing he had vowed never to share publicly – Kate said she got it.

Of course, she hit it off instantly with Alice, and Ari felt a flicker of the satisfying completeness he'd had when Mae had first slotted so effortlessly into his world. He liked the way they both gently poked fun at him one minute and then made him feel like a superstar the next. Kate asked Alice lots of questions about dating in the British countryside and fell about laughing at her stories. She smiled as easily as she breathed. Mae would seem edgier than a dodecahedron compared to her. But Letty was forgotten about as the adults talked raucously, sitting on sofas opposite each other and only stopping to take a breath when reaching down to the coffee table for their drinks or a handful of chips. She lay on the floor under the towering bookshelves and stroked Ari's whippet, Willow, who lay companionly beside her and growled every now and then. She looked sad. Kate noticed and excused herself from the conversation to crouch down at her level.

'What's up?'

'I just miss Mae,' Letty said. 'She was Ari's best friend and ... well, she was a bit like a big sister to me and now I never see her. It feels weird she's not here.'

Ari and Alice stopped talking and watched as Kate sat down and crossed her legs. 'Mae sounds awesome. Ari has told me all about her and I'd love to meet her myself one day soon. How about this. I promise I'll do my best to get your cousin to call her more and come and visit you in England – which he will, soon.' Here she stopped and threw a determined look over to Ari, who was listening intently. He smiled awkwardly but nodded.

'OK,' said Letty quietly, pleased but a little embarrassed that she'd called her cousin out. 'I didn't want you to feel bad that I like Mae more than you.'

'Letty!' interjected Alice. 'You can't say things like that to people, especially when they're being so nice. You'll hurt Kate's feelings. It's true what they say about teenagers having the emotional intelligence of a psychopath.'

Letty blushed and stood up. 'Oh, sorry, I didn't mean ...' She didn't know what to do with herself.

'Not at all!' laughed Kate, hopping up and gently guiding Letty to the pool table. She cleared it of books and papers and took the balls from each hole. 'You were being honest, and I would always rather people said what they felt. It makes life much easier. It stands to reason you like Mae more than me. Ari does too, I think, but that's OK. You folk have history; you're only just getting to know me. It's all good.'

She racked up and broke, sending a clatter of balls into a swirl of chaos. She handed the cue to Letty in the quiet that followed as the balls rolled into place and she pocketed a red. 'You're stripes, buddy.'

On their last night before flying home to the UK, after Letty had gone to sleep on the air mattress in the spare room and Alice had made her famous casserole for dinner, which was a delicious change from all the takeout sushi he'd been eating, Ari asked his aunt what she thought of Kate.

'I like her, Ari. She's smart and funny, and not dissimilar to your mother, if Connie had gone to India to find herself rather than become a supermodel and marry a plastic surgeon.'

'Oh my God, eww,' Ari laughed. 'Kate is nothing like Mom.'

'You asked me for my opinion!'

'OK. Fine. Go on.'

'I can see how you fit together, and I think she's a wonderful person. I'm not worried for you like I was with Oliver. But I'm not, you know, *excited* for it. Because I don't think you are either.'

Ari should've known better than to ask his aunt for her opinion. She'd happily get along well with anyone. But if you gave her permission to be honest, she'd lay out her opinions like dishes at a potluck. It was no wonder she and Mae had always got on roaringly.

Once his family had left, Ari suddenly had so many creative ideas he couldn't get them down fast enough. He was writing poetry, short stories and scripts and taking meetings. It meant he knocked on Kate's door less often and instead made new vlogs almost daily.

Kate said, with less sarcasm than she was entitled to, that at least she could keep up to date with what her 'boyfriend/ fuck buddy/whatever' was doing from the videos he posted to social media. She didn't mind seeing less of him. She kept her depths from Ari too. He knew that her family life had been fraught, but selfishly he was fine with not finding out more; he felt he was at capacity, emotionally; there was no room for another full and complex person in his life. Kate's default of 'it's all good' suited him.

But one scorching afternoon, when it was too hot to write or to leave the house, he knocked for her unannounced. She was naked, which wasn't surprising. What took him aback was the hirsute naked blond man standing by the air-conditioning unit in the living room, his lengthy beard fluttering in the breeze.

'Ari, this is Frank. He goes to my yoga school,' said Kate, completely unfazed by the potential awkwardness of the encounter.

'Hello, Frank.' Ari sounded suspicious, but was more intrigued. 'I suppose I should leave you to it?'

Kate looked at Frank, who flashed back an unmistakably

suggestive smile, then she said, 'Come over tonight instead, Ari? Bring ice cream.'

Ari spent the day lying in a bath of cool water. After dunking his head again, he took his phone from the bathroom shelf and called Mae. 'OK, I *have* met someone,' he said without giving her room to hijack the conversation with anecdotes about Luke and Lewis.

'Ooh, tell me more. Who is he?'

'He is a *she*. Cis. I mean, a girl. Kate.' Ari sounded in more of a muddle about it than he was.

Mae was silent for a second. Processing.

'What's this *Kate* like then?' she said, evidently struggling.

'I knew you'd be weird about this. It's why I haven't told you about her for so long.'

'How long?' Mae asked angrily.

'Um, like, three months. Alice and Letty met her when they visited.' He put her on speaker and placed the phone back on the shelf so he could submerge his head underwater again.

'Oh.'

She was wounded and he felt terrible. He stepped out of the bath and, without drying himself, took the phone and walked into his bedroom to lie like a starfish on the bed.

'I should've have told you. But you had so much going on with the kids.'

Mae exhaled a judgemental 'hmm' that reminded him of Janet. 'You should have ... But look. I'm happy if you're happy. Seriously, tell me about her.'

'Well, I think she's a swinger. I mean, we never exchanged

"going steady" rings or anything, but *I've* not been seeing anyone else and today I discovered she is.'

'Good for Kate! I like the sound of her. Free love. Why not? Since when did you become such a prude, Ari? You should do the same if she's open to it. Explore!'

'Meanwhile, over in heteronormative land . . . ' he said, changing the subject. 'You proposed yet?'

'Maybe I have. Maybe I'm just going to wait three months before telling you.'

Ari laughed, but the comment stung. He said goodbye and threw on a pink sleeveless T-shirt dress. It was time to get some answers from Kate.

He was sweating when he rang the buzzer to her apartment. The walk to the deli on the corner had felt like wading through treacle. He held the ice cream at his chest and the tub left a wet mark on his dress. 'I'm a hot mess,' he said when Kate opened the door, looking perfectly reassembled after her time with Frank. She recoiled a little as he leant in to kiss her.

'Sorry, it's not you. I have an insane sense of smell at the moment.'

He followed her into her dark living room. Purple candles burned on the teak coffee table along with a row of hemp incense sticks in jam jars. Two expensive turbo-powered fans blew out gusts of icy air – much to the annoyance of the well-heeled residents, the building's air conditioning had stopped working earlier in the year. Kate disappeared to get spoons, and Ari twisted the ponytail that hung at his neck into a bun. He sat on the sofa; the embroidered velvet throw felt illicit against his bare legs.

They were halfway through the ice cream when Ari licked his spoon and said, 'So . . . Frank seems fun.'

Kate leant back against her bank of Indian cushions. 'I guess you could call me polyamorous,' she said. Her voice went up a note at the end, making it sound like a question, but Ari knew she was certain.

She continued, 'Baby, what we have is great, but it's not enough for me and I know it's not enough for you. We have parts of ourselves we need to honour separately.'

Ari nodded and stared into the flame of a candle until his eyes crossed. It was strange to hear his deepest, most complex desires voiced so simply.

'Frank and I aren't fucking yet,' she continued, placing a cool hand on his thigh. 'I wanted to check you were OK about it first. I like to be open in every sense.'

Ari said, 'I'm fine with it.' He slipped his fingers in between hers. 'I'll tell you about anyone else I meet too. Is that how it works?'

'I knew you'd learn fast,' said Kate, then planted a soft kiss on his lips.

That night Ari went out clubbing on his own, to one of his favourite old haunts in Chelsea.

'Miss Ari, it's been a minute,' said the door queen.

'Tiara Monsoon, I'm afraid I've been otherwise engaged.'

'Sweetie, we all watch your sad little videos, and you know there's a line from one of your poems scratched into the cubicle door in the ladies. "Lay out your gold for me." Ooh, I wish you would, sis. You making it rain.' Tiara's laugh was deep and throaty. 'You're slaying,' she added.

'We're proud of you, Ari.' She fanned herself and pretended to faint.

Ari was wearing his shortest shorts and a sleeveless silk shirt. On the dance floor, his eyes clashed with strangers, held there for a moment as a silent yes or no passed between them, and then moved on, scanning and assessing and occasionally acquiescing. Once you understood the rules, cruising for guys was deliciously transactional. It was dark and the lights spun from blue to red, while a disco ball cast white sequins onto the surrounding mirrors. Then, a flash of recognition.

He shimmied closer, circled him like prey, and when the song was right, he shifted so their hips brushed against each other. He silently pressed his chest into Sam's, still responding to the beat of the music. The denim of his old friend's shirt felt sturdy against his own whisper of clothing. He wrapped his arms around Sam's neck and Sam took his waist like it was the last dance at prom. Ari kissed him then with a passion he worried was too violent. But Sam moved with it, taking his lips softly when Ari pressed hard, pushing more when Ari melted. It was a give and take of equal power. Sam's baseball cap fell to the floor, and it broke the spell.

'Well, hello again, mister,' he shouted over the music.

'I wish all school reunions were like this,' said Ari, taking his hand and leading him to the outdoor space so they could talk.

'Finally, after all these years, I get my answer. You do like me *like that*.' Sam stood directly in front of Ari with his arms crossed, smiling playfully. Ari blushed and fiddled with the pearl hanging from his ear.

'I've always found you incredibly attractive.'

'You could have fooled me!' Sam laughed and placed a hand on Ari's lower back. Ari imagined how the fabric must feel against his palm. He hoped the way he softened signalled something to his friend that he wouldn't have to say.

'I'm so sorry I didn't reach out, Sam. That I didn't come to see you in London that time, before you moved. I was in a weird place.'

'I still speak to Mae sometimes. She keeps me up to date with your movements. Did a lot of explaining on your behalf back then, put it that way. I was pissed off you didn't even message me, Ari. Anyway, I'm only in town for two nights. Job interview. I would have got in touch if I was here longer. You know I'm not the type to hold a grudge.'

'I don't want tonight to end if you have to leave so soon,' said Ari.

'It doesn't have to,' Sam replied, brushing off his baseball cap and placing it back on his head. 'Do you fancy getting out of here?'

It was as hot at night as it had been all day. Ari's shirt clung to him. He was drenched in sweat.

'I didn't think this through.' He undid the top button.

'Here, take it off and you can wear my jacket.'

They were standing outside an old-school lesbian joint. Ari carefully undid the remaining buttons and peeled the shirt from his wet skin. Sam draped his white denim jacket over Ari's bare shoulders. A woman smoking a cigarette while her girlfriend held her beer shouted out to them.

'You boys look like you could do with a drink. Why don't

you come in? We don't bite. And heck, you're prettier than half the women in here tonight.'

Sam and Ari sat up at the bar. A stud with spiky black hair passed them two cold ones, and Ari said, 'Gay women always want to take care of me. It's funny.'

'Or they can still sniff Mae on you,' countered Sam. 'I've never known anyone to pull as much as she did. It seemed a shame she dumped girls before it ever got serious. Makes total sense she's dating Virginia Bates. Mae was destined to be with someone special.'

'V *is* that. You know, I really adore her. They are so well matched as a couple. I was kind of jealous that Mae found someone so good and easy to be with. They bring out the best in each other and there is a lot of love in their house. It's such a happy place, full of light and fresh flowers and great snacks, and sofas you could sink into and cashmere blankets to wrap yourself up in. I miss hanging out with them so much.'

'What happened between you two? Why did you come back to New York? I thought you might post about it or write something, but you never did.'

'We were going to have a kid together, but it didn't work.'
'Whoa.'

'Do you mind if we don't go there tonight? Mae has a way of taking over once I get talking about her, and I'd like it to just be us tonight.'

They stayed in the girl bar until closing. They'd befriended everyone there, and Ari started a conga line that snaked through the bar and back out onto the street.

'You're like the Pied Piper of lesbians,' Sam laughed. It

wasn't far off five a.m., so they walked West 4th looking for a place to get breakfast.

On Perry Street, Ari pointed out Carrie Bradshaw's apartment and Sam wanted a photo on the iconic stoop. 'I'm more of a Miranda,' he said. 'And you, *Miss Thing*, you are all Carrie.'

'I am sooo not Carrie! I'm Samantha, surely?'

'We'll have to see about that,' said Sam suggestively, and Ari's heart soared.

They found a deli that was almost open and waited outside talking about nothing important but enjoying the cadence of each other's whimsical thoughts. When the owner switched the sign on the door, they ordered coffee and bagels to go. Their kiss in the club remained unspoken of, but excitement fizzed between them.

Ari took Sam's bagel wrapper and chucked it in a trash can along with his own.

'Would you want to stay at mine tonight, Sam?'

'There's no tonight left. It's tomorrow already. I have meetings, I have to work. But how about we meet later?'

'Shall I walk you back to your hotel?'

Sam kissed him. 'It's OK. Go home and sleep, but call me.'

Back in his bedroom, Ari hung Sam's jacket in his wardrobe and appreciated the way it looked among his things. He showered and was ready to crawl into bed, grateful that his freelance career allowed him to sleep an entire day if he needed to, when there was a knock at his front door.

Kate, he thought; she must want all the details of his conquest already. He sleepily opened the door, ready to tell her that he'd be over in a few hours for the full debrief. But he was struck by how small and delicate and sad she looked standing on his doormat.

'Hey,' he said, kindly. 'Kate, what's the matter?'

'Soooo, it turns out I'm pregnant.'

Chapter 35

Janet was in the kitchen, fussing. Mae had told her mother to relax, but she didn't know how, so was buzzing unhelpfully between V and Mae, offering to help over and over again. Instead of snapping at her, Mae took her arm and led her out into the living room, gently forcing her down on the sofa between Michael and Leah, who were deep in conversation about a new crime drama. 'Keep an eye on her for me, will you?' She winked at them and rushed back to her gravy, which needed more stock.

Since recognising that she'd never given her parents the chance to be involved in her adult life, and had thus denied them the opportunity to reap the benefits of her partner's generosity, comfortable lifestyle, and catering abilities, Mae was making more of an effort to include them.

She felt guilty for deciding her mum was a certain type of person, and never giving her space to grow. But the ulterior motive for the monthly Sunday dinners Mae and V now hosted for their parents was that their social worker had said they would be more likely to be approved for adoption if there was a strong and healthy connection with their wider families, and they'd kept it up even after their approval. The next step was a court date, and then they could formally become Luke and Lewis's parents.

'Can I go to my room now? I'm in the middle of *Call of Duty*.' Lewis came back from handing round a plate of mini bruschetta looking like he'd just returned from battle. The 'Olds', as he almost affectionately referred to Mae and V's parents, smothered the twins with all the love they'd stored up for grandchildren.

Lewis found it overwhelming. He'd been barely used to one person taking an interest in his well-being; now he had five people tousling his hair and kissing him on the cheek and asking him about girlfriends. Mae felt his acute discomfort in these moments as if it were her own. He was navigating the awkward hinterland between boy and man and he wanted to be locked away in the chrysalis of his bedroom for the metamorphosis, not paraded in front of their families' eager, needy affection.

'Ask V,' said Mae. 'She's the boss.'

He skulked over to where V stood by the oven, watching her nut roast crisp to perfection, and repeated his question.

Lewis was an agile, graceful dancer – Mae hoped he'd go to performing arts college with his brother – but offstage he lolloped through the house in his size 11 high tops, jeans halfway down his bum, baseball cap pulled so low his face was permanently in shadow. Mae watched V nod and give him a hug, and Lewis disappeared in a flash.

The twins had moved in once Mae and V had been fast-tracked as emergency foster carers and subsequently approved as adopters. Mae was keen to reassure them that this could be their forever home if they wanted it to be, and the boys seemed as keen on the idea as their new mums were, so V spoke to their social worker and began the process of adoption. She had pressed pause on work to focus on the boys. She cleared out her exercise gear from the two spare rooms, and Mae painted the sage-green walls white. They bought two double beds, and wardrobes. Mae drew the line at V's suggestion of beanbags, which she claimed promoted laziness and bad posture. V raised an eyebrow and said, 'Weird, pointless opinion. But fine.'

Anyway, they wanted to let the boys put their own personality on their rooms, so one of their first outings as a formative family was to IKEA, where Luke filled a trolley with cushions, picture frames, tea lights and blankets. Lewis just wanted to make sure his desk could accommodate his PlayStation.

'At least choose some sheets you like,' encouraged Mae in the bedding aisle, when her and V's low patience was dropping to 'critical'.

'Whatever, I don't mind,' said Lewis, shrugging.

'You must have an opinion?'

'I honestly don't.'

'OK, so if you don't have an opinion, it's always good to pretend that you do, or people will think you're a pushover.'

'Fine, those striped ones then.'

'I think the plain blue might look nicer?'

'Mae! He chose the striped ones, for God's sake,' reprimanded V.

They were learning to be parents together, playing to their strengths and reminding each other all the time that the most important thing was for the boys to feel safe and loved. The rest they'd muddle through.

Lewis stomped back downstairs once lunch was ready. Luke had laid the table. They all took the exact same places they had done on the day three months ago when they'd met for the first time. The seven of them had stuck to the configuration ever since, each perhaps looking for something fixed amid this haphazard new family arrangement.

After the kind of polite, meaningless chit-chat Janet revelled in and Mae had learnt to just about tolerate, Mae's father asked Luke if he was seeing anyone. Which was a question that made any teenager cringe.

'You do know I'm gay?'

'I do,' said Michael, not rising to the provocative tone. 'What I mean to ask is if you've met any nice boys?'

Mae recognised that her dad had always been uncomplicated and open-minded. He used to ask her about girls, but she'd shut him down. She would have preferred it if he'd been her antagonist, someone she could define herself, and her sexuality, in opposition to. Now she looked at his sprightly, handsome face that was a permanently deep terracotta colour on account of the time he spent outside, pottering in his allotment, and felt nothing but tenderness.

'I don't really have time for boys at the moment. I'm too busy working on my performance,' said Luke.

'He's getting really good, you know,' said Lewis, who always had his brother's back, no matter what mood he was in himself.

'I've been lucky enough to meet her and I have to say I'm impressed,' said Leah from the other end of the table.

Janet visibly smarted. She was hurt that the other granny knew something about Luke that she didn't.

Mae had been pleasantly surprised by her parents' reaction when she told them they would be fostering to adopt two teenage boys. She understood that her mother would have reservations, but Janet was gracious enough to offload them, probably, on her husband rather than her daughter. Michael had been genuinely thrilled to expand their small family, and when they turned up at the house to meet the boys for the first time, he had handed them both an Aston Villa football kit and said he couldn't wait to take them to a match.

But it was V's Mum, Leah, who had been their greatest ally throughout the difficult process of arranging for the kids to officially move in and then for the few months after, when initial excitement shifted into a daunting realisation that this was it now. Mae knew Janet was a bit threatened by their closeness. But Leah lived nearby, for a start, and had raised V's brothers single-handedly so knew how to get teenage boys to do homework and pick towels off the bathroom floor.

'They need to appreciate you ain't messing around,' she told Mae when she had called Leah in a state a week after the boys moved in when she found, to her dismay, that a pile of damp and now smelly laundry had been left on the floor by the washing machine, and from that pile, one single T-shirt, belonging to Luke, had been placed on its own in the tumble dryer. 'But you got to show them how to do things, because these boys don't know. Be clear in what you expect. Set boundaries and you'll be fine. You'll be great, Mae. I've seen you with V's nieces and nephews. You're a natural.'

V, too, had picked up on Janet's jealousy at the lunch table that Leah had been part of something with Luke that she hadn't, so she jumped in, saying, 'He's been waiting to tell you about it in person, Janet. Isn't that right, Luke?'

'Oh yeah, sure, that was it. Here, you can look now.' Luke retrieved his phone from his jeans pocket and passed it across the table to Janet.

Mae forensically examined every twitch of her mother's lips and the aperture of her pupils as she squinted to make sense of the image of her foster grandson in drag. She was processing ... processing ... searching for the right reaction in her catalogue of options. Michael peered over her shoulder and saved her the bother.

'Wonderful!' he said. 'You look quite spectacular. And does this young lady have a name?'

'Minerva Fontaine.'

'Ah, perfect, the Roman goddess of wisdom. Proponent of defensive war. And Fontaine?'

'Just liked how it sounds.'

Janet had in that time arranged her face into something Mae would describe as curious. 'Well, I'm looking forward to meeting Minerva. He ... she sounds really quite something.'

The 'Olds' began getting ready to leave later than Mae and V would have liked. This meal was the highlight of their month and they eked it out as long as possible. Meanwhile, the new parents were exhausted and desperate to collapse on the sofa. The twins were far from being newborns, but they were just as demanding.

When Janet and Michael were finally at the door, flushed

with wine and holding a Tupperware full of leftover nut roast, Janet clung to Mae with an intensity that took her aback.

'You are doing a fantastic job with them, Mae. Your father and I are so proud of you. We love you. And we think V is just so solid. And good for you. We do hope you pop the question soon. That ring won't propose itself, you know. Plus I've seen the perfect hat in John Lewis.'

'Thanks, Mum, that really means a lot. And I'll keep you posted, OK? Don't buy the hat just yet.'

At midnight, Mae's phone vibrated on her bedside table, which could only signal an emergency. 'Ari, what is it?' she said groggily. 'What's happened?'

She was expecting the worst, so when Ari said chirpily, 'I'm so sorry to wake you, but I have the *best* news,' she sat up and pulled the duvet over her head so as not to disturb V. 'Kate's having a baby. My baby.'

Mae felt like she'd been punched in the gut. She gripped the phone and jumped out of bed. She turned on the overhead light and began pacing.

'Fuck, Mae what's happened?' V mumbled, rubbing her eyes.

Mae didn't answer. Instead she said to Ari, very slowly, 'Let me get this straight. You phone me in the middle of the night to tell me that your fuck buddy is pregnant, that you are going to be a father, and what? I'm supposed to be *happy* for you just like that?'

V stood by her side and put her arm around her. She tried to prise the phone from Mae's hand. 'Let's talk to Ari about this in the morning,' she said calmly.

'No!' Mae shouted at both of them. 'I have *feelings* about this, I am allowed to have feelings about this.'

'Mae, please . . . I'm sorry, I know this is complicated for us. But I was just so excited and you were the first person I wanted to tell. I figured that with Luke and Lewis . . . well, I guess I thought you'd be OK with it.' He sounded sad.

V finally wrenched the phone from Mae's grasp.

'We'll call you tomorrow, Ari, OK? Congratulations. Let's just give Mae some time to process this and you guys can talk again.'

V hung up and guided them back into bed. Mae curled her legs into her chest. V wrapped her arms around her while she sobbed quietly into a pillow.

Kate was dipping whole carrots into a tub of hummus and devouring them when Ari stormed into her kitchen, his sadness had now evolved into outrage. She held out a carrot to him and he shook his head in disgust. He had wanted Mae's approval, and without it his own joy felt tempered.

'It's selfish is what it is,' he said, taking a carton of orange juice from Kate's fridge and pouring himself a drink.

'Can I get one of those?' asked Kate as he put the bottle back.

'Oh, sure. Sorry, didn't think you'd want one.' He handed her a glass and sat at the table, resting his chin on his hands and pouting.

'Sweetheart, of course Mae is mad at you right now. It's curious you can't see why.'

Carefully, and without making Ari ashamed of how thoughtless he was being, Kate reminded him of what Mae had lost.

'She wanted a family with *you*, Ari. She loves her boys but there's a grief there still for what could have been. You've just called her out of the blue to tell her that the future you had planned, that you spent years perfecting, and that fell through your fingers like sand – that life with you and her girlfriend – is now something you're doing with me, a complete stranger as far as she's concerned. It's a lot for her to process. Don't make it about you.'

She gave Ari a friendly nudge and smiled. He was still cross. He clasped his hands behind his head and looked up. 'Are you saying I've been a dick?'

'Well, it's lucky I'm one of your female friends who actually likes a dick,' said Kate.

Ari laughed so hard he spat out his orange juice.

Chapter 36

Ari swished the diaper onto his plastic baby with a flourish and did up each sticky flap in a seamless move.

'*Voilà*,' he said theatrically, and the group clapped.

Kate rolled her eyes. As soon as the session ended, she tossed her plastic newborn at the tutor and left, giving Ari a kiss on the cheek before heading off to her pregnancy yoga class. Ari hung back to chat to the others. He'd been acing the Parents 2Be course, which was held in a vegan café on Bedford Avenue. Of all the expectant mothers and fathers, he was proving himself to be not only the most excited, but the most naturally competent.

While Kate had explained she was there to learn the basics and not to befriend what she called the 'clucking hens', Ari had gleefully joined the Pops2B WhatsApp group and was a leading contributor. Now he accompanied some of the men to a nearby sports bar. They sat in a booth under a giant TV screening a basketball game, and weepily offloaded their emotions.

'Man, I just worry I'm gonna love this baby so much *it hurts*, you know,' said the one Kate secretly referred to as Where's Waldo.

The soon-to-be dads had decided that Ari, with his long hair and floaty shirts, and his knowing all the answers to the questions about the female body, was their guru. They felt they could really open up with him. He'd never seen such neediness. When he didn't respond to a message on the group chat within an hour, they'd all be checking in and sending concerned-face emojis. He loved it.

He had a couple of light beers, but excused himself at a juncture between confessionals, claiming Kate needed some quiet time with him to connect.

'Totally get it, dude.'

They hugged him with extravagant intimacy.

Kate recognised the lengths to which Ari was going to be a good dad, but she didn't seem to feel the same pressure to prove herself. She'd also made it clear that becoming a mother would not change her desire for an open relationship, and repeatedly reminded him that 'I really don't need you to be this hyper-alpha dad. I want you to be yourself, and if that's somewhere between mother and father, that's fine by me.'

From the moment she had told him the news, standing outside his apartment with a look of weary acceptance, she had said that she expected nothing from him. But Ari was all in. Once he'd recovered from the shock of her announcement and established that it definitely wasn't Frank's, he'd carried her into his bedroom in a strange show of masculinity and gently laid her on his bed. The previous night with Sam had faded out like a dream. Kate's birdlike body was inconceivably home to a baby. He'd placed his hand on her stomach and told her everything was going to be OK. It was easier to pretend she needed him more than she did.

He hadn't called Sam. He'd felt paralysed by the thing he had wanted more than anything else for so long. Sam returned to Australia, no doubt feeling that he'd misread Ari's signals and that his old friend was flaky and selfish and frankly rude. He'd sent Ari a single question mark. Ari stared at it on his phone until it looked like half a heart or a pierced ear. He'd told himself that he made the right choice. It was grown up, unselfish. He owed it to his unborn child to commit unwaveringly to it *in utero*.

Kate had said she got too hot and needed to pee too many times during the night for sleeping together to be at all enjoyable. So Ari slept alone in his apartment, thinking of Sam and the white denim jacket that hung in his closet.

On a balmy morning in September, as he sat outside his favourite French café on the corner of 5th and Bedford, tapping his pen against the cover of his black Moleskine and hoping inspiration might strike, Ari noted that it was still early enough to call Mae if he wanted to. Despite Kate's gentle encouragement, he'd felt embarrassed about the way he'd told her and had been deep in avoidance. He hoped that in the weeks they hadn't been in touch, she'd made peace with the news. But Kate suggested *he* still needed to make peace with it himself. Beneath Ari's enthusiasm for the pregnancy, there was a tangled mass of feelings. Doing this with Kate, in such a heteronormative set-up, was nothing he could have predicted. He too was grieving for the future with Mae that never was.

His cell phone vibrated in the pocket of his shorts as he made space on the little table for the server to place his cup and cafetière. He answered and said her name as if it were the last word of a prayer.

'Mae. You must be psychic I was literally about to call you.'

'I'm sorry it's taken me a while. I just—'

'You don't have to explain. I know. I feel the same.'

'Like you were living our dream without me.'

'Yes. It's . . . complicated. It's not easy. I need to see you, Mae. Will you come to New York?'

'I'll think about it,' Mae answered sombrely. 'I'll let you know, OK?'

The conversation had left Ari flat. He arrived home feeling that he was hungry for something, but he couldn't decide what. Kate had refused to sublet her apartment and move in as he'd suggested. She wanted her own space. Ari was already thinking about turning the room he used for making his videos into a nursery, painting a light blue over the black walls that he scribbled lines on with chalk sometimes during live streams.

Kate said her mom would buy them all the complicated baby stuff they'd need, like strollers and cribs, so they had 'literally nothing to stress about'. She'd only introduced Ari to her parents once, in passing, and they seemed just as ambivalent as their daughter about the specifics of life. They liked him, apparently, and that was 'all good'.

His warehouse was beginning to look cosier with some of Kate's things haphazardly left in it. Aunt Alice would approve, now that Indian blankets were draped over sofas and a stone statue of Ganesh Kate had bought him as a birthday present stood in the hallway wearing colourful flower garlands. He liked the textures and the colours and the softness Kate came with. He kicked off his sandals and whistled for Willow, who skittered over the polished concrete floors hoping for treats. Ari tried cradling him in his arms, but Willow wasn't in the mood. He wriggled free and ran back to his basket. Ari sat at the kitchen table and picked at a spot on his neck until it bled.

When Kate arrived an hour or so later, she was chirpy, having spent the afternoon exploring chakras with Frank. She kissed Ari on the cheek and lay across his sofa digging into a bag of chips. She wanted to talk about life, but all Ari ever wanted to talk to her about now was the baby.

'I wonder if it will have my eyes?' he asked as he tidied up around her.

'You're obsessed,' she chuckled. 'Seriously! Do you think about anything else? If you're going to be all broody like this for the next four months, I'm not gonna be able to cope. Having a baby is one part of us. It's not all of me and it shouldn't be all of you.'

Ari looked dejected then. He flopped down onto a beanbag and hugged his knees. There was no one other than the members of the Pops2Be WhatsApp group who seemed to share his joyful fixation with becoming a parent. Mae and V would have definitely mood-boarded the nursery by now if the baby was theirs, and he imagined the long, indulgent conversations they would have had together about this growing foetus and the person it would eventually become.

'Have you been in touch with Sam? You should. I think a distraction from all this baby stuff would be good for you.'

'I think it's too late. We had a night out together, the one I told you about, and it was . . . well, I guess it was pretty great. But then I got back in the morning and was just about to sleep it off when you knocked, and then everything changed. I haven't spoken to him since.'

'You're saying that like you expect me to be impressed, Ari. Like I should *thank* you for treating someone you obviously really like so badly.'

'I did it for you. For us. So I could focus on our family.'

'Look, I want the father of my child to be his full fabulously queer self. I don't know much about kids, but I reckon having two fulfilled parents is a good start in life.'

He sighed. 'I've blown it with Sam now.'

'You don't know that. You don't need to sacrifice everything for me. Because I'm good, Ari. I'm more than good. I have you, Frank, this baby, friends, a vaguely functioning family. I have money. I'm fine. All I want is for you to have everything *you* need.'

'This baby is everything I need. I will never be an absent father. I don't want to fuck this kid up in any way.'

'I know that, and you won't. Ari, you're going to be the most wonderful parent. Our kid is going to adore you. And we'll muddle through together, in a family-shaped way that works for us.'

He smiled at her and relaxed into himself.

Kate said, 'I do have one request, which is absolutely non-negotiable. You have to be with me for the birth. I don't care what Basma says! No tour dates when we're getting close.' She stroked the top of his head.

'Oh my gosh, of course, I wouldn't miss it for the world.'

Ari leant into her and pressed his lips to hers, tears running down his face. 'You are a remarkable human, Kate. Thank you.'

'For what?'

'For seeing me.'

His phone murmured on the concrete work surface. It was a message from Mae.

Guess what? We're coming to New York.

Chapter 37

October 2025

'I can't believe we've ended up with *two* totally badass mums,' said Lewis.

V had just ripped open a brown envelope from the council and read aloud the contents of the letter, which confirmed the date for their adoption hearing as 16 November. The boys had started calling Mae 'Mum' and V 'Mother' as a joke, but it was slowly sounding less weird, and Mae hoped it would stick.

'We have a date! You're almost officially ours for ever and ever, mwah-ha-ha!'

Luke and Lewis cringed at her evil laugh.

'And you're almost officially an embarrassing parent, darling,' laughed V, opening a bottle of champagne from the drinks fridge, where it had been on ice in hopeful anticipation. Mae felt happiness swoop through the house like a blast of cool air on a hot day. She was excited about their trip to New York, which would be followed by six months' adoption leave.

*

The whole adoption process had been more laborious than either Mae or V had anticipated. They figured their wealth and social standing would have adoption agencies falling over themselves to sign them up. But they were put through the same rigorous examination as all potential adopters, and quickly became aware that their connections and their kudos were meaningless here. Instead, they had regular meetings with a social worker called Jackie, who came to their house and inspected their 'lifestyle'. Jackie had several questions about the photographs that hung on the walls – the black-and-white naked bodies mainly. How appropriate, she wondered, were these images for two teenage boys? After she'd left, V gave an impassioned monologue about the intellectual value of these pieces. Mae listened, nodding at all the right places. The next time Jackie visited, there were photos of Luke and Lewis with their soon-to-be grandparents up in the space where the images had been.

'Oh, we just felt that reinforcing the twins' place in the family was more important than art,' V explained valiantly.

Jackie interviewed their friends and their parents, and she asked Mae and V so many questions about their relationship and their values and where they might align or disagree on child-rearing it felt like couples therapy. They attended work-shops in church halls on therapeutic parenting and joined a WhatsApp group of other potential adopters. Despite the paperwork and the scrutiny, it was fun because it was so different to anything V had ever experienced. Mae, now seasoned in her role at FAM, was not unfamiliar with draughty church halls, lanyards and plates of biscuits. But it was all such a novelty to her glamorous girlfriend, who despite priding herself on being 'of the people' could not remember the last time she had taken public transport.

Even with Jackie sitting in between them – each meeting wearing one of a rotation of denim jumpsuits and clutching her trusty yellow file – Mae felt a new and different kind of closeness to V. They were being shaped, with some help, into what the social worker called a 'parental unit'. And now, finally, it was good news. The boys were allowed a tiny bit of Moët in the bottom of two crystal coupes. When they all clinked their glasses, V demanding eye contact from everyone, Mae felt a profound contentment. She enjoyed the lightness of having finally let go of what could have been with Ari. Now there was space for a new plan to take shape, but she'd need Luke and Lewis's help.

The following Wednesday, Luke had friends over to study. Mae heard nothing but laughter and power ballads coming from his room. He had a crew of queer friends, and the evident joy they felt at having found each other reminded her of the thrill she'd felt when she first discovered Kween. She knocked on the door at seven p.m. and found V sitting cross-legged on Luke's bed, the gaggle of gender non-conforming teenagers staring up at her in awe from where they sat on the floor. Sheets of paper covered in scribbles and diagrams were scattered across the bed, and V was frantically writing in her notebook.

'What's going on?' asked Mae.

'Kaz here has given me the most brilliant idea. Once Ana buys me out of the company and I'm free to pivot career again, I'm starting a new magazine, for queer kids. It'll give them a sense of belonging and community and be something they'll covet. There's nothing like it. It's all online, but I'm convinced these young people will discover the joy of something to have and to hold.'

'Sounds brilliant, darling. Oh, um, remember to keep Saturday night free for that charity awards thing I was telling you about.' Mae quietly closed the door and began plotting.

By Saturday, she had hired a beautiful but dilapidated music hall in east London. She sent Luke and Lewis ahead with detailed instructions on how to dress the space and when to light the candles. Luke was in charge of the engagement ring. Janet had slipped the box into her hand one Sunday after a family lunch and said, 'I do hope Granny's diamonds will get an airing soon.'

She told the boys to wait in the wings and come out when they saw her get down on one knee.

It had been a full-on week, packing for New York and tying up loose ends at work. Meanwhile, after settling on her next career move, V was putting together flat plans for her first issue and calling up old colleagues, assembling a dream team to work with her on the launch of *Queer*. She had a wild, manic look in her eyes and was running on adrenalin. She struggled to focus on anything else, and it seemed like a big effort to pull on a dress and heels and be ready to accompany Mae to the 'charity awards thing' on Saturday night.

In the cab on the way there, Mae worried she'd gone overboard. It was cheesy and bound to misfire. V used the journey to speak non-stop about her plans for the magazine, and Mae decided that no amount of romance could compete with the excitement her potential fiancée felt in the face of a new work challenge.

She could have proposed sooner. Jackie would have liked it, but whenever the subject came up in their adoption interviews, V would eloquently shut it down.

'We don't need a patriarchal, deeply heteronormative institution to validate our love for each other. Mae and I are confident enough in our commitment not to need to "put a ring on it".'

Jackie would hum the Beyoncé song as she wrote some notes in her yellow file.

When the cab pulled up outside the venue and there was no one to be seen, V was still in such a daze she didn't notice. Mae was wearing black jeans with a white T-shirt and black blazer. She pushed open the door and was astounded by what an impressive job the boys had done dressing the space. V clasped her hand.

'What is this?' she whispered as they walked through aisles shimmering with the flicker of candles. On the small stage, a spotlight shone on two white roses. Tangled trails of fairy lights that had been hung in a rush emitted a golden glow, and as V, speaking louder now, said, 'What the fuuu …', the opening bars of Bobby Bland's 'I'll Take Care of You' began to play.

Mae led V slowly to the steps up to the stage. Lewis, who was sitting in the lighting box, turned up the music and changed the spot to an ambient pink. Mae was nervous. Her hands were cold and clammy. She wiped them on the sides of her jeans. The music faded out. 'I love you, Virginia Bates,' she said, and as she sank to one knee, the old colorama at the back of the stage fell to the floor with an almighty crash, revealing Luke dressed in half drag – a slip dress and heels, but without his wig or make-up – shiftily holding the ring box.

'That wasn't meant to happen,' he said. But ever the true professional, he sashayed elegantly towards Mae and handed her the box. As she opened it, her grandmother's ring sparkled like a comic-book diamond. V clasped her hands to her face.

'Will you marry me?'

V didn't answer straight away. Instead, she pulled Mae up off the floor and stood looking at her for what felt like a very long time.

'I do,' she said. 'I mean, I will . . . whatever. Fuck yes, Mae, I will marry you. I thought you'd never ask!'

There was a loud whoop from the rafters, and Lewis came bounding down onto the stage. The four of them wrapped their arms around each other in a tight crush of love.

Chapter 38

After his talk with Kate, Ari was tempted to call Sam straight away, but he had one shot to get it right, and for all he knew, Sam might have met someone else since he'd last seen him, and would surely have forgotten all about the spark that had almost, almost become a flame.

Perhaps, he thought, it would be better not to try. He'd just add what could have been to the stack of alternative lives that ran in parallel to this one. He pictured them like light beams – in one, he was in Romania, raised by the man and woman who had conceived him; in another, he never met Oliver and he and Mae were co-parents; in yet another, someone different adopted him, and elsewhere, Lilly still lived. The possibilities were infinite and overwhelming. He believed each was real, but his consciousness, maybe his soul, had simply tethered itself to this light beam for now.

Mae, V and their sons were landing that evening. Ari felt desperate to talk, properly, to his best friend. He needed to unpick things like a poem. Light beams, love, rejection, fathers, children – Mae was the only one he could talk and talk to about this kind of nonsense. Deconstructing, highlighting, leaving notes in the margins, until there wasn't a word or an idea left untouched.

'I'll head to the store and get some bits for breakfast tomorrow. You need more snacks?'

Kate slowly uncurled from the child's position on Ari's carpet and said she'd come too.

They walked down Bedford Avenue. It was raining, but Kate didn't believe in umbrellas; she preferred to feel the water on her skin. Ari adjusted the collar of his trench coat and linked her arm.

A bell jangled as he pushed open the door of his favourite organic grocery store. He took a basket, but Kate told him they'd need a cart – she was eating for two, remember.

If Ari just did what Kate always advised and stayed in the moment, he was happy. He had helped create what would become a whole new person. And that was what he'd always wanted to achieve in life. They would be someone he could shape in many ways, but he was most looking forward to sitting back and watching as they spectacularly inhabited themselves and became as unknowable as everyone else.

He loved Kate just enough for it to feel easy. He looked at her. She was glowing; early pregnancy suited her. Her hair, henna red and still wet from the rain, stuck to her face, and Ari brushed it back. They were side by side, both pushing the cart as they slowly glided through the global food aisle. Then Ari stopped, abruptly, and felt his body take a hit like a shot. He gasped and gripped the cart. There, dead in front of him, was Mae, flanked by Luke and Lewis, who had grown into young men since he'd last seen them.

'Ari!'

'What are you doing here?'

'We took an earlier flight; V had an opportunity for a meeting this morning. We landed last night. We're staying in a hotel on this street, so we were just popping in to get some supplies.'

After the unnecessarily lengthy explanation, Mae instinctively threw herself at him in a rough embrace.

'We weren't supposed to meet like this,' said Ari, pulling away, still shocked by the encounter. 'I'm here buying our breakfast for tomorrow!'

He had wanted to curate Mae's first meeting with Kate; he still needed to talk to her about all the things she should and shouldn't say. The chaos of the coincidence was making him feel unreasonably nervous.

V turned into the aisle wielding two enormous bags of crisps. 'Which one?' she asked loudly. 'And you can't say both.'

She tossed both bags into their basket and darted over to the centre of the scene.

'Oh my goodness, Ari!' She gave him a tight hug. 'And you must be Kate,' she said seamlessly. 'We've been so looking forward to meeting you.'

Mae felt V's eyes on her and stopped looking for a subtle bump beneath Kate's sweater.

'Gosh, yes! We *so* have been. May I?' she asked, reaching her hand towards Kate's midriff.

'I'm not showing yet, but sure,' Kate said breezily. She took Mae's hand and placed it on her stomach.

Lewis and Luke could sense something important was happening, though they couldn't discern what exactly.

Ari laughed uneasily. 'I've been so jittery about you all coming over and meeting Kate and everything. I just froze. It's good to see you. To see *all* of you. I guess the pressure's off for tomorrow now at least.'

Mae removed her hand. 'Congratulations,' she said earnestly, emotion catching at the back of her throat.

Kate couldn't help herself; she reached out for Mae and hugged her. Mae smelt rain, patchouli, maybe weed.

'I am so, so sorry about your miscarriage, and how hard it was for you,' Kate whispered into her ear. 'I don't know how you ever get over that, but Mae, your family is beautiful.' She took a step back. 'I'm a stranger, I get it, but honestly, Ari does not stop talking about you. I know how you take your coffee, I know you will never sit on a beanbag, I know Ari adores you, and I feel like I could too.'

She looked at Mae and the three other people who flanked her despite much tutting from fellow shoppers. 'I'm worried I've overstepped, bringing up all that. It's the yogi in me – I speak my feelings. I'm sorry if—'

'No apology needed. It was nice of you to. People don't normally.'

Just as Mae was taking in Kate's full ethereal beauty, an elderly man with a basket pushed past them to reach for a can of chickpeas. They shuffled awkwardly together towards the end of the aisle. Mae looked at Ari, searching for her best friend. She'd always assumed he'd be there, her shadow when the sun was high. But it had been dark for so long. And now his face was unfamiliar. 'I suppose there's a lot for us to talk about,' she said with a smile, so it didn't sound too ominous.

'I'm not sure I can wait till tomorrow,' Ari replied, bouncing eagerly on the spot.

'Well, I'm taking the boys to the Empire State this afternoon,' V chipped in. 'Why don't you have the time to catch up. You can meet us back at the hotel later, Mae.' She looked encouragingly at Kate. 'Perhaps we could all meet for dinner this evening?' She waved goodbye and steered the boys towards more snacks.

'That sounds like a great plan. Ari, I'll finish the shopping,' said Kate. 'You get out of here. Go have fun with Mae.'

'No, no, let me help with the—'

'Ari, I'm fine! Please don't fuss.'

'OK, well if you're sure . . .' He gave Kate a casual kiss on her cheek and Mae tried hard not to wince.

'It was lovely to meet you, Mae, finally. I'll look forward to spending a heap more time with you,' said Kate. She pushed the cart down the aisle and out of sight, leaving Mae and Ari standing next to each other in front of a shelf stacked with pulses.

Neither dared be the first to move, until Mae said, 'Shall we go for a walk?'

Ari was wearing clothes she'd not seen before. She had once been so intimately acquainted with his wardrobe, if he bought something new without showing it to her, she felt he'd been unfaithful. His style now was more lived in. He had on a trench coat with a shocking red tartan lining. Under it he wore a light grey cotton T-shirt with a low neck, revealing a hairier chest than she remembered. Black skinny jeans made his long legs look Giacometti-like, and he had taken a pen to his white Converse, drawing hearts and stars and spirals on them in an act that struck Mae as sweet and childish.

It had been over a decade since they first met. Mae wondered how she looked to him. She liked to dress for the landscape of a city. Her New York look, inspired by Dennis Stock's photos of her hero, James Dean, suited the season. For her first day out in Williamsburg, she had that morning pulled from her suitcase an old fisherman's jumper that was in fact new and very expensive, loose wool trousers and brown leather lace-ups.

Her hair was less blonde now that all the peroxide of her youth had grown out. It was the colour of grass after a long dry summer. She kept it cropped and short at the back, but still left a bulk of thick locks at the front that she could sweep into a quiff or slick down depending on the occasion.

The air was warm and steamy after the rain, and fat drops of water fell from the silver maple trees as their leaves shuddered in the wind. Mae was walking purposefully but had no idea where she was going. At the end of Bedford, she saw Williamsburg Bridge looming large against the steel-grey sky. It felt right to cross water together, so they veered past a shuttered Chinese restaurant, up onto the ramp that led to the walkway over the East River to Manhattan.

New York had always felt to Mae like Ari's secret. It was the part of him she couldn't know. In the years since university, she had accompanied V on many work trips to the city. She understood its cadences and its latent aggressive energy, but the patchwork of avenues and numbered streets seemed impenetrable.

'So where do we start?' he asked softly.

The bridge now was more like a cage, with a fence to deter jumpers obscuring the view.

Mae answered slowly. 'What we had planned . . . ' She took a breath, and Ari interrupted.

'Water under the bridge?'

'Rather a convenient metaphor for a poet of your standing, no?' She smiled wryly and clocked him relax a notch.

A train clattered by on the tracks beneath them. The traffic roared. Ari thought about how they had started out tethered to each other on the same raft. It was as if they'd only survive the sea if they stayed that way for ever. And then, when the thing that held them broke apart and the waves took them, raising them up, sinking them deep below the surface, they had found their own ways to go on. And now they were back to explore the wreck. He searched the annals of his brain for the line from the Adrienne Rich poem: *The thing itself and not the myth* – that was it.

He said, 'Hey, you didn't tell me you'd proposed. I noticed the diamond.'

'I wanted to tell you in person. V and I have been through such a lot together the last few years and she's always made it OK. We were grilled for months to be approved as adopters. We were turned inside out. But really the adoption was all V. She took charge, and once we'd decided we wanted the boys to be part of our family, she made it happen for us. I was so grateful. I wanted to do something solid and for ever for her.'

A running team jogged past, stopping Mae's flow for a moment. 'She still surprises me, you know. Even doing the most mundane things with her takes on this frisson. I'd almost rather spend an evening at the twenty-four-hour Tesco together than at one of her parties. She somehow makes the experience feel just as important.'

'Sam told me he knew you were always meant to be with a *glittering somebody*.'

'Was that on your magical night together?'

'You've spoken to him? I suppose he hates me.' Ari's back tensed. He did up the buttons of his coat.

'Is that a question?'

'Yes.'

'Then yes, he likely does. But . . . I think it could be salvageable. If you want it to be.'

Mae had always known that Sam was Ari's person. It was jealousy, plainly, that stopped her from telling him; a fear that if *they* were together, she would be pushed to the margins, and Mae had wanted to be Ari's centre. She had wanted to hold onto his heart. How wrong she'd been. There was space, so much space for this love. She felt a terrible guilt that was too big to admit to now.

Ari said, 'Kate is so cool. Honestly. She's an incredible person but she knows she's not mine, and I'm not hers. Not entirely. She's really encouraging me to chase down Sam.'

'Wow, that's evolved of her.' Mae's shoulders curled inwards. 'I was never that generous with you, and we weren't even sleeping together. Let alone having a baby!'

The significance of those last words hung in the air.

On a whim, Ari said, 'We might as well have slept together, don't you think?'

Mae couldn't help but laugh. 'No. Eww. I loved you easily because it was platonic, Ari. And I could *not* have gone through with it. Can you imagine! That kind of love was not for us. We're soulmates, I suppose, that's always felt the nearest to it.'

They were walking faster now and standing closer. The rhythm of their conversation returning, like the memory of a song.

'So, the wedding! Tell me *everything*. How did you propose?'

'Roses, candles, one knee. All of that. And the boys helped. Luke – your biggest fan – he had the ring.'

'And when's the big day?'

'Next year sometime – probably September, once we've had the adoption approved and we've all settled into it. It'll be low key. Everyone expects us to have a big fancy do, but you know that's not us.'

'I wouldn't be surprised if you did it in the Talbot,' he joked. 'I'm sure it'll be perfect, Mae.'

'Kate's invited too,' she said, looping her arm in his, 'and the baby, of course.'

Ari stopped walking so he could look her in the eyes. 'Thank you.'

She bit her lip and gazed out over the Hudson. It looked like another rainstorm was coming. She knew that this was the time to apologise for having held Ari back from Sam for all those years. He had ended up here, on this wild trajectory, because of her. But she couldn't bear to open up a new chasm just as one was closing. Instead she said, 'Fuck, Ari. You're going to be a father. How does that feel?'

'Honestly? I'm ready for it. And *this*. Well, it isn't ever what I imagined, but it's happened.'

They walked without talking for a few minutes.

Then Ari said, 'Tell me what to do about Sam.'

'I think you already know. And Ari, in case it's not clear, I thoroughly endorse any future endeavours to win him back.'

Mae looked at her friend, noticing his tired eyes and the shadow of a beard. She felt at once that she understood him better than anyone else in the world and that she didn't understand him at all. Skyscrapers rose like the tips of icebergs in the distance. They were almost on the other side of the bridge.

Epilogue

London, May 2026

Ari looked in the full-length mirror on the wardrobe door and wondered if it was too much. It wasn't white, at least. But it *was* a custom-made chiffon cape dress. And with his hair down and freshly blow-dried, he felt very pretty. He didn't want to outshine the brides so decided he should do a pony-tail instead. White Doc Marten boots would add a dash of butch, but if he couldn't go full femme at a lesbian wedding, when the hell could he?

'Da,' said his daughter, August Mae, who he'd propped up in a nest of cushions on the hotel bed while he rushed to get ready. 'Daaaaaa!'

'Darling,' Ari called, pulling his hair off his face and magicking it into a knot. 'I think it's a nappy situation. Would you mind doing the honours? I'm all dressed up.'

'I did the last one, remember,' came a voice from the bathroom.

'I didn't know we were keeping a tally.' He wandered over to his daughter and lifted her off the bed, kissing her tiny nose.

*

Meanwhile, in the bridal suite down the corridor, Lewis stood in front of Mae and adjusted her tie. Luke flapped around her.

'It's a nightmare! I've left my shimmer brick at home. What am I going to do? I can't just *produce* that kind of sparkle. I'm going to have to dash home.'

'Luke, don't even think about it. I know Minerva is a diva, but she's beginning to get on Mi nerves.'

'Dad joke alert!' the twins said in unison.

'Be nice to me, it's my wedding day.'

There were four perky knocks at the door. 'Yoo-hoo, is there a blushing bride in there?'

'Ah, it's Mum. Can you boys deal with her for me? I can't cope right now. My anxiety is skyrocketing.'

'I thought Reeva was taking care of the Olds,' said Luke.

'No one can keep Janet in one place for long. Please. Tell her I'm not here.' Mae was dressed but for her suit jacket and shoes. She ran into the walk-in wardrobe to hide.

'I need a moment with my daughter, please, gentlemen.' Janet's schoolteacher voice came through loud and clear. Mae heard Luke say she was meditating and couldn't be disturbed. Her mother tutted, walked straight to where she was hiding and opened the door.

'It's not like you to be in the closet, dear.'

Luke and Lewis giggled.

'Give us five minutes, will you, chaps? People will be arriving soon. Perhaps go and see if that delightful Reeva creature needs a hand with anything. She seemed a little overburdened.'

Once Luke and Lewis had shuffled off downstairs to where

the ceremony would take place, in the Great Room overlooking the Thames, Janet pulled Mae into the daylight.

'Mae,' she said, sounding less like an Oscar Wilde grande dame and more like the woman Mae had come to know well and like over the past two years. 'How are you?'

'Nervous,' said Mae. 'And sad somehow. Like this is the end of a big part of my life, as much as it's the beginning of something new.'

'The thing about a marriage is, it never stays the same. It grows with you, changes, becomes something with its own rhythms and moods. And it's wonderful – you can let it meander because you know you've made this commitment to each other, to see it through regardless. It's very freeing in that way. The anchor lets you explore. Now … let me see you.'

Mae recognised the look in Janet's eyes as one she herself now cast on Luke and Lewis. Absolute pride, and devotion to their happiness. She felt moved.

'Thank you for everything you and Dad gave me so that I never even knew you were giving me anything at all,' said Mae. 'I understand what that took now.'

Janet could never accept a compliment.

'You look very dashing,' she said, expertly changing the subject. 'You wear that suit so well. Your father asked me to give you these – his lucky cufflinks. He said you probably had some fancy ones already, but I know it would mean a lot to him … here.'

Mae opened the box. The small silver sailboats wouldn't go with her look like the antique gold cufflinks she'd bought, but she would wear them, without a shadow of a doubt.

*

The Great Room was beginning to fill with fabulous outfits and their occupiers. It was an eclectic mix of people Mae had kept up with from Leeds, plus V's fantastically successful friends in film and fashion, as well as her large extended family. In the absence of her own siblings, aunts or uncles, Mae had permitted her parents to bring some of their social set, so there were a number of John Lewis hats with jostling circumferences.

Connie, Alice and Letty joined Mae's colleagues from the charity and some of the kids she had worked with over the years. Luke and Lewis had been allowed to invite two mates each, and their old foster carers. Reeva was a guest, once she'd finished the final arrangements, and was in charge of keeping a handful of the old *Edit* team out of trouble. In the end, there was nothing low-key or intimate about the wedding.

V wore an elegant asymmetrical ivory gown, made specially for her by a young designer she was championing. Her hair was blown out, and in four-inch Louboutins, she looked magnificent. The FAM gospel choir accompanied her down the aisle with Leah by her side. Mae was waiting at the altar, flanked by her best man, who she had to admit looked more like her maid of honour in an outfit he had promised would not steal her thunder. He squeezed her hand just as August gurgled loudly from the audience. Ari turned instinctively to check on his daughter and her mother, who had been on knee-bouncing duty.

When V arrived next to her wife-to-be, Ari kissed her on the cheek, then leant in close to Mae and whispered a fragment of a poem she knew by heart.

"'This is the place. And I am here.'" The words tripped out

lightly, but the meaning lingered. They looked each other in the eye, then he pressed his lips together and nodded, letting her go.

He took his seat on the front row next to Kate. She handed him the baby and he passed her on to his right. Sam balanced August over his broad shoulder. He'd pre-emptively placed a muslin on his cream linen blazer and proceeded to shush the baby into submission. Ari gave his boyfriend's thigh a grateful squeeze.

On cue, Luke and Lewis entered with the rings, and Ari stood up to cheer. The late-afternoon sun reappeared from behind a white cloud. Through the big window at the front of the room bent a bright beam of light, which by the accident of their positions caught only Mae and Ari in its glow.

Four years after the wedding

There is nothing exceptional about the night she dies. Ari puts August to bed in the top bedroom and leaves the door open a little so she can see the light from the hallway if she wakes. The new baby, Adrienne, is snuffling happily in the bouncy chair by the Aga in the kitchen. Willow keeps his distance; he is an old dog now and has little patience for these unpredictable children. Sam sits by his daughter, rocking her gently with his bare foot.

Ari walks into the kitchen and bends down to kiss Addie on the forehead, then he kisses Sam on the lips. He marvels once more that Kate suggested Sam be the biological father of their next child and that it worked out with no drama. Kate has a magic touch; it is some kind of sorcery the way issues dissolve in her presence. They bought the house together while she was pregnant for the second time, and the only disagreement was over the colour of the walls in the living room, because V and Mae wanted them white to offset the proportions, and Sam being a graphic designer wanted a colour, and Ari wanted to make Sam happy, and Kate quite honestly didn't care either way.

And because it was all so easy between them, Ari decided to give Mae and V a whimsical present for her birthday. He made a deposit at the sperm bank and paid for a single round of IUI. They went into it, really, as a bit of a joke. And now they are waiting – barely with any time to think about it with the children to look after – to find out if they are pregnant.

After the insemination in London, Mae and V, Luke and Lewis take the train to the south coast rather than drive.

They can work during the journey, and the boys can stare at their phones without getting carsick. It is a meaningless decision, made in a moment. That's what's so hard to accept – the *if only*.

Kate leaves the cottage at seven p.m. to pick them up from the station. She shouts a breezy goodbye to the daddies, as she's taken to calling Sam and Ari, and shuts the door quietly behind her so as not to wake their daughter. Fifteen minutes later, she collides with a truck on a narrow country road. She is pronounced dead at the scene.

Night

Summer 2030

The mahogany grandfather clock is a monstrosity, they all agree, and being neither contemporary British nor a nod to Morocco, it really has no place in the country house at all. But Aunt Alice gave it to Ari and Sam as a wedding gift, and it is at least more at home in the English countryside than it was in their New York loft. Kate said it could've been worse, it could've had a cuckoo.

Mae watches the second hand tick round a full minute. She leans back against the coat rack opposite it in the hallway, smelling the heady mix of their old jackets, bags and scarves, V's perfume, Ari's infrequent cigarettes, hints of Luke and Lewis's teenage sweat and a base note of Kate's yoga studio incense. She tries to push a rising nausea back down with a gulp, and her legs feel weak.

She thinks about how time passes in tiny increments like a string threaded with pearls. And how it also passes in huge swathes; days crash into a waterfall of days and days and days until you aren't young or hot or cool or new or now any more. She steadies herself on the long arm of an umbrella. She is going to give birth in eight months. Raising children means there is something to show for each slow-fast passing of the earth around the sun she reasons.

The others are talking loudly in the living room. She had to excuse herself because she felt spacey and overwhelmed with their presence (and the absence it revealed). Soaring pregnancy hormones make her sick but also aware that something is actually happening this time. It is a good sign, everyone says.

'It'll be an adventure for sure,' V replied when Mae broached the subject of living as one big family unit the previous afternoon, before the big fall-out. They were chopping onions; dark clouds gathered in the small canvas of sky through the kitchen window. Mae was whispering because Sam and Ari were putting the girls to bed, and she needed to talk her idea through with her wife and then make sure their kids were on board before she suggested it at dinner.

'It makes so much sense. We just need to shift that heteronormative rock off our backs, then we can totally reconfigure the dynamics of a nuclear family.'

'Sweetie, this isn't a Woman's Hour interview,' V said kindly. 'I don't need convincing – I just want to make sure there's enough space for us all. You know I love Sam and Ari, but do we want to be under each other's feet every single day? That's not the patriarchy talking, it's practicality.'

Luke and Lewis walked through the French doors swinging tennis rackets. They were home from university for the summer and seemed to have grown outwards as well as upwards in the time away from their parents.

'Cussing us heterosexual white men again?' asked Lewis, smiling to reveal the glinting silver grillz on his incisors.

'It's a cross you have to bear, I'm afraid, son,' said Mae. 'Seriously, though, how would you feel about us having this as our base and living here with Sam, Ari and the babies?'

'Like a drag house, you mean, but with screaming kids instead of screaming queens?' offered Luke, wiping his sweaty hands on his tennis skirt.

'Sure. That's one way of looking at it.'

'Mum, we grew up in foster care. That's what we know. We're only around for holidays these days anyway, and it's you that'll be stuck here holding the literal baby.'

'So we're cool with whatever,' interjected Luke, suggesting they were bored of the conversation.

Mae has been alone in the hallway for a while and is conscious she needs to re-enter the fray. But before she does, she unhooks Kate's small embroidered brown leather bag from its peg and presses it into her chest. She wasted too much time resenting the mother of Ari's children. But in the past few years, since they got the country house, the lightness and sense of wild freedom Kate brought to the group calmed Mae to her very core. She grew to love her like a sister. Ari's gift was Kate's idea. She'd always understood their connection. She would have approved of Mae's queer commune concept, no doubt. So why is Ari resisting it? she wonders.

She considers unzipping Kate's bag, rolling her lipstick through her fingers, eating a gum from the packet, counting her change. But it feels mawkish. The way to remember Kate is growing inside of her. This child will be August and Addie's sibling, connecting Mae to Ari and Kate, then across to Sam and to V and the twins like constellations of stars. This is her legacy, the *life she and Ari could never have imagined but were somehow destined for.*

The clock strikes eleven. She walks purposefully back into the living room and stands at the mantelpiece. The chatter dies down and Sam jumps to his feet. He registers the intensity of her expression and takes charge. 'Look, last night was weird, right? I'm just going to say it. We were all beastly, but we're grieving still, and so I for one want to say sorry, Mae, for not giving your big idea the space it deserved.'

V stretches for Mae's hand and pulls her onto her lap on the armchair. 'Sam and I have talked about it and we're up for a trial run, with some ground rules, and some rearranging of the interiors, of course.' She places her palm on Mae's stomach and addresses their sons, who are sharing the chaise longue opposite, starring at their phones. 'Luke and Lewis, you're entirely unbothered, right?' The boys nod.

'So, Ari, that leaves you,' says Mae as neutrally as she can muster. 'Will you stay here with us and try this way of living?'

He looks at his husband, then at the mother of his unborn child; at her wife and their twin boys. He pictures the soft faces of his daughters sleeping upstairs and remembers the unaffected ease with which Kate, their mother, moved through life. He cannot get used to the space she has left, the glaring lack of her. But the fear that sits in the very pit of his stomach maybe isn't fear at all. Because even without Kate, and united by loss, they are something new; a creature with a shared heartbeat and many limbs. A family.

Acknowledgements

Ettie, I hope one day when you're older you find this book and read it, or at the very least flick through to the good bits. Remember how I always tell you, 'finished' doesn't have to mean 'perfect', and how it's much more important to enjoy what you're doing while you're doing it? Well, I really, really loved writing this book.

To Jenny, thank you for being the most beautiful and supportive wife and friend. Mae would never have met V if I'd never met you. Thank you to my wonderful blended and extended family and to all the friends and colleagues who have helped me find the confidence to finish this book, particularly Stu Oakley. A special mention must also go to the gay boys who have been my passionately platonic people at different stages of my life. Will at Elliott School, Sam at Camberwell College of Art and Joe at Leeds University – what a joy it's been to navigate queer life with you. Finally a huge thanks to my agent Abigail Bergstrom and my editor at Dialogue Hannah Chukwu for helping me tell this story.

About the Author

Lotte Jeffs has spent her career writing columns, profiles and think pieces for the British press. She has worked as an editor for *ELLE* and *ES Magazine,* and is the author of *How to be a Gentlewoman: The Art of Soft Power in Hard Times,* co-author of *The Queer Parent* and the children's picture book *My Magic Family.* She co-hosts the podcast From Gay To Ze about LGBTQ parenting and pop culture. Lotte has won the PPA Writer of the Year Award and the Great British Podcast Award.

Bringing a book from manuscript to what you are reading is a team effort.

Dialogue Books would like to thank everyone who helped to publish *This Love* in the UK.

Editorial
Sharmaine Lovegrove
Hannah Chukwu

Contracts
Megan Phillips
Bryony Hall
Amy Patrick
Sasha Duszynska Lewis
Anne Goddard

Sales
Caitriona Row
Dominic Smith
Frances Doyle
Hannah Methuen
Lucy Hine
Toluwalope Ayo-Ajala

Design
Ellen Rockell

Production
Narges Nojoumi

Publicity
Millie Seaward

Marketing
Emily Moran

Operations
Kellie Barnfield
Millie Gibson
Sameera Patel
Sanjeev Braich

Finance
Andrew Smith
Ellie Barry

Copy-Editor
Jane Selley

Proofreader
Loma Halden